Malcolm slowly became aware that some kind of disturbance had just arisen ahead. He observed a horse harnessed to a driverless hansom cab hurtling crazily down the street and, directly in its path, a young woman struggling frantically to rise from where she had fallen on the cobblestones. At any moment she was going to be crushed beneath the horse and carriage, and killed!

Malcolm did not even stop to think of the danger to himself. He thought only of the helpless, terrified young woman. His heart pounding with fear for her, a rush of adrenaline abruptly surging through his entire body, he pelted into the street and, in one fell swoop, snatched her up…

For my step-daughter, Chrissy,
the daughter of my heart,
and
for bridge-captain Fraser,
for making Chrissy happy.

With much love and gratitude.

THE NINEFOLD KEY

Rebecca Brandewyne

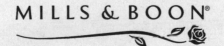

MILLS & BOON®

*First published in Great Britain 2006
by Harlequin Mills & Boon Limited,
Eton House, 18-24 Paradise Road, Richmond, Surrey TW9 1SR*

© Rebecca Brandewyne 2004

ISBN 0 263 84430 7

153-0206

*Printed and bound in Spain
by Litografia Rosés S.A., Barcelona*

CONTENTS

The Ninefold Key

FIRST SPIRIT

O thou, who plum'd with strong desire
Sweep low to pluck the stone, beware!
A Shadow tracks thy flight of fire—
Night is coming!
Bright the scarab, just like the air,
And among the beams and winds
The game's afoot; don't wander there—
Night is coming!

SECOND SPIRIT

The deathless stars are bright above;
If I would cross the shade of night,
Within my heart is the lamp of love,
And that is day!
And the moon will smile with gentle light
On my silvery plumes where'er they move;
The meteors will linger round my flight,
And make night day.

FIRST SPIRIT

But if the whirlwinds of darkness waken
Hail, and lightning, and stormy rain;
See, the bounds of air are shaken—
Night is coming!
The red swift clouds of the tempest's bane
Yon declining sun have overtaken,
The clash of the hail sweeps o'er the plain—
Night is coming!

SECOND SPIRIT

I see the light, and I hear the sound;
I'll sail on the flood of the tempest dark,
Ope' the locked past, so the light around
Will make night day:
And thou, when the gloom is deep and stark,
Look from thy dull earth, slumber-bound,
My moon-like flight thou then mayst mark
On high, far away.

FIRST SPIRIT

But the scarab's curse by the tempest borne
Hath left naught save ruin in its wake,
And the Ninefold Key is lost, forlorn—
Night is coming!
Leave that dragon's lair to eternal sleep
And the emerald stone it guards so fierce,
We, the Inheritors, shall not keep—
Night is coming!

THE TRAVELER

Some say there is a precipice
Where dragon's lair is frozen to ruin
O'er dusts of snow and chasms of ice
Amid Highland mountains;
And that the languid storm pursuing
That winged shape, for ever flies
Round those hoar towers, aye renewing
Its aerie fountains.
Some say when nights are dry and dear,
And the death-dews sleep on the morass,
Sweet whispers are heard by the traveler,
Which make night day:
And a silver shape like her bold lover doth pass
Upborne by his wild and ebony hair,
And when she awakes on the fragrant grass,
She finds night day.*

*Poem adapted from *The Two Spirits: An Allegory,* by Percy Bysshe Shelley

Prologue

The Scarab

Now fades the glimmering landscape on the sight,
And all the air a solemn stillness holds,
Save where the beetle wheels his droning flight,
And drowsy tinklings lull the distant folds.

—Thomas Gray
Elegy Written in a Country Churchyard [1750]

The sense of death is most in apprehension,
And the poor beetle, that we tread upon,
In corporal sufferance finds a pang as great
As when a giant dies.

—William Shakespeare
Measure for Measure [1604-1605]

    Ere the bat hath flown
His cloistered flight, ere, to black Hecate's summons
The shard-borne beetle with his drowsy hums
Hath rung night's yawning peal, there shall be done
A deed of dreadful note.

—William Shakespeare
Macbeth [1605-1606]

In the Shadow of the Horn

Now air is hushed, save where the weak-eyed bat,
With short shrill shriek flits by on leathern wing,
Or where the beetle winds
His small but sullen horn.

—William Collins
Ode to Evening [1747]

There are two gates of Sleep. One is of horn,
easy of passage for the shades of truth;
the other, of gleaming white ivory,
permits false dreams to ascend to the upper air.

—Virgil
Aeneid

And God stands winding His lonely horn,
And time and the world are ever in flight.

—William Butler Yeats
The Wind Among the Reeds [1899], Into the Twilight

1669
The Valley of the Kings, Luxor, Egypt

To speak the names of the dead was to make them live again—or so the ancient Egyptians had believed. At this moment, young Lord James Ramsay, Viscount Strathmór and heir to his father's earldom of Dúndragon, on the shores of Loch Ness, could almost believe it, too. Fervently he wished he had never come to Luxor and the Valley of the Kings, much less dared to invade the once-sacrosanct tomb of the High Priest Nephrekeptah, in which, presently unbeknown to him, he now stood. Somehow—although he could not fathom how—this sepulchre was different from all the rest that he and those who accompanied him had previously investigated.

It was bad luck to have come here. Jamie had known that almost from the very beginning. But it was even a worse misfortune to have breached this particular crypt, he sensed, highly disquieted. For although the graves of the pharaohs and other high-ranking dignitaries who had during their lifetimes reigned with supreme immunity and impunity over the Two Kingdoms of Egypt were concealed mile upon mile in this place, here, in the high priest's hushed mausoleum, there was not only Death, but also Power...power of a kind Jamie had never before experienced: rare, portentous and so absolute that it was almost tangible.

As a result, what had originally begun as a long-anticipated grand adventure and lark now seemed to him to have taken on a wholly sinister tone, punctuated by a weird, distant rumbling far aboveground, which made him fear that perhaps a rare rainstorm or even an earthquake was imminent.

His five companions appeared unaffected by his increasing sense of dread and doom, however. Or perhaps their excited talk and raucous laughter were merely a show of bravado, to hide their own faltering courage, Jamie speculated thoughtfully. For surely they could not be completely impervious to the eeriness of the tomb or to the peculiar grumbling of the earth beyond.

The small group of explorers, consisting of a close circle of young, rowdy males who had all gone to school together, had traveled to Egypt from Great Britain during their Grand Tour, spurred on by some of the more scholarly among them having read about "the place of the mummies" in a description of the fabled Valley of the Kings, written in an obscure book by Father Charles François, a Capuchin friar, and published the previous year. Whose idea it had originally been to journey to Egypt to dig up one or more of these ancient mummies, Jamie had now forgotten. But if he had been able to remember, he would have cursed his friend and fellow.

The trip to Egypt had been long and arduous. From Scotland he and his cohorts had traveled on horseback to Dover, where a boat had ferried them across the English Channel to the Continent. After touring France, Italy and Greece, they had sailed from the port of Piraeus, near Athens, across the Mediterranean Sea to Egypt. But locating the enigmatic Valley of the Kings had proved even more difficult, necessitating the hiring of a native Egyptian guide, for the valley itself was naturally hidden by the Theban Mountains. How he and his colleagues would ever find their way back to the ancient city of Luxor, across the River Nile, where they had taken rooms at a local inn, Jamie did not know. For despite how much they had paid him, when their native guide had finally learnt that their intent was to break in to and rob one of the many sepulchres in the valley, he had suddenly taken to his heels like a terrified fox fleeing a pack of hunting hounds, and the young men had seen neither hide nor hair of him since. That alone ought to have warned them, Jamie now reflected grimly.

But instead, he and the rest had resolutely persisted in their daring, challenging escapade, blithely undeterred by their guide's abrupt disappearance, shrugging it off by noting that the native Egyptians were notoriously lazy, superstitious and unreliable. After all, what possible harm could be done to crypts that had been opened up and looted since the time of the ancient Greeks and Romans? As for returning to Luxor, why, what need had the party of a guide for that? All they had to do was to trek east toward the River Nile, and that surely could not pose any difficulty for them, since the long winding waterway could be viewed from the mountainous plateau that rose like a behemoth from the desert plain on its west bank.

On the river's east bank, Luxor itself crouched like an Egyptian Mau cat, silently surveying all. Over the millennia of its existence, the ancient city had known many names. The Egyptians themselves had originally called it Wast, the Scepter, and it had once been the venerated capital of Upper Egypt. Some had referred to it simply as Nut, City, and then as South-Nut, to distinguish it from its counterpart, North-Nut or Menf, the capital of Lower Egypt. In later ages it had been called Thebes, perhaps after the ancient Greek city of the same name, for the Greeks had once ruled Egypt, founding the Ptolemy Dynasty, which had ended with Cleopatra, fated to die as exotically as she had lived. To the Arabs, the city had been El Qussour or Al-Oxor, the City of Palaces or Monuments, which foreign tongues had distorted into "Luxor."

And perhaps this last name, which had stuck, was the most fitting of all, for the city did indeed boast a multitude of magnificent palaces, temples and other monuments, although now only the ruins of all these remained. Still, somehow, against all odds, they had for millennia withstood the relentless desert heat; the harsh, scouring sands carried on the wings of the khamsins— the fierce desert winds that began in March to blow for fifty days across southern Egypt and the Red Sea; the infrequent but savage rainstorms that descended without warning upon the land; and the devoutly prayed-for annual River Nile floods that gave birth to the rich, fertile dark earth of sustenance. They had survived to tell their stories of the Egyptian people who had revered and worshiped the now-long-entombed pharaohs as the Children of the Gods, serving them even after death, interring them in great, mysterious pyramids or else in huge necropolises, in preparation for their perilous journeys to the Underworld.

Beneath the towering, pyramid-shaped peak known as Gebel el-Qurn, Mount Horn, which crowned the Theban Mountains of the jagged-edged plateau that hove up from the desert plain west of the River Nile and shadowed the valley below, lay the necropolis that Jamie and his friends had set about to explore. The valley, Biban el-Muluk, the Gateway of the Kings, consisted of two serpentine branches that were like the slithering, hooded black cobras sacred to the goddess Meretseger, She Who Loves Silence, by whose name the looming pinnacle Mount Horn was also sometimes called. And as though to honor the great goddess, there *was* naught save silence here…the silence of the long dead, who lived and breathed and spoke no more, enshrouded and entombed for millennia in the valley that, as it had since time immemorial, sweltered under the brightly burning yellow sun in the rare humidity outside, and—currently unbeknown to Jamie and the rest—beneath an inauspiciously gathering pewter cloud that was dark with portent.

Pitching camp, the gregarious group had immediately undertaken an examination of the Wadjein, the Two Valleys, discovering that it was the east branch, known as the Ta Set Aat, the Great Place, that was honeycombed with pipelike corridors and mausoleums. Outwardly at least, the larger, western branch of the valley had appeared not to have any tombs cut into the native marls that underlaid the rugged cliffs of the plateau. How the young men had eventually stumbled into the sepulchre they now occupied Jamie had not a single clue, for the labyrinthine tunnels with which the valley was riddled were like a maze, and he felt certain that, lacking a guide, he and the others would now be totally lost had they not been smart enough to unwind a big ball of twine behind them wherever they went, so that they could find their way back out into the valley again.

Outside, beyond the High Priest Nephrekeptah's crypt, high above in the pale blue sky that stretched out endlessly over the desert plain far below, the blistering summer sun continued to blaze as hotly and fiercely as though it were but a scant few miles, not light-years, from the earth. Yet, despite this, the ominous cast to the firmament grew ever stronger and more threatening, as well. At one edge of the stark horizon, the dark, soughing, seething cloud massed like a nest of hissing, writhing serpents, periodically unwinding coils of gray that slithered stealthily across the heavens, intermittently occluding the luminescent sun beating down upon the sprawling, aeons-old city of Luxor and the mountainous plateau that rose from the desert plain.

But deep within the bowels of the earth itself, inside the dark, musty ancient mausoleum of the high priest, which had long ago been deliberately concealed amid the steep, soaring cliffs that formed the twin branches of the valley, the atmosphere was wondrously cool, in sharp contrast to the stifling, muggy temperature beyond.

Under any other circumstances, Jamie would have relished the darkness and coolness of the tomb, welcoming the respite from the blinding sun and the sultry air, thick with omen, that hung like the suffocating cloud now spreading across the valley. But ever since he and his companions had entered the secret sepulchre, he had experienced a strange, unnerving chill that had nothing at all to do with the cool but stale atmosphere within. Now, as he lifted his flaming torch high, he felt the fine hairs on his nape stand on end and gooseflesh prickle his strong arms.

In some dim corner of his mind Jamie tried to reassure himself that his physical reaction to the crypt was nothing more than the result of his heavily sweating body being subjected at length to the merciless heat outside and then, abruptly, to the coolness inside the mausoleum. But still, his uneasiness and the icy grue that chased up his spine did not dissipate. Instead, as he and the others probed deeper into the dark, moldering tomb, his trepidation only heightened, and the inexplicable Power he sensed within wrapped its folds like a cerecloth around him, making him feel as though he had somehow been buried alive.

Unlike some of the other sepulchres he and his cohorts had earlier investigated, the one they were in now was smaller in size, so that it seemed doubtful that it had belonged to a pharaoh or any other members of the royal family. What had initially excited the party about it was the fact that the entire door to the crypt had apparently at one point been hidden by a huge pile of debris swept against it by the flash flooding that sometimes occurred in the valley during its unusual but torrential rains that came every half century or so. Later floods had evidently shifted some of this rubble, revealing a portion of the mud-packed barrier, whose impressive seal, bearing the authoritative stamp of one of the ancient necropolis's administrators, was still intact. The group had hoped this meant that the mausoleum's contents were as yet undisturbed, had not been plundered over the centuries, as the contents of so many of the other tombs in the valley had been.

After digging away all the detritus, the young men had boldly broken the seal, then pried open the heavy door that had hitherto been closed and perhaps concealed for millennia. Eagerly entering the sepulchre, they had quickly descended the stone steps that sloped down to the first corridor within. Only Jamie had lagged behind, discomposed of a sudden by the abrupt, unwelcome realization that he and the others were bent on desecrating a grave. It had been with some small measure of relief that as he had tentatively progressed down the first hall, he had spied both a fine film of golden desert dust layering the stone floor and silvery gossamer cobwebs festooning the rough-hewn stone ceiling. All this indicated that the crypt had previously been breached and entered, even if not through the main door.

Now, as Jamie continued down the passage illuminated by the torches he and the rest carried, he observed that the stone walls were bare, undecorated by the intricate murals he had seen in other, more elaborate mausoleums, which had belonged to Egyptian pharaohs and other members of the royal family. Even the graffiti left by the ancient Greeks and Romans who had long ago trespassed in the Valley of the Kings was missing here. So, rather than that of royalty, this must be the tomb of some high-ranking dignitary, a priest or some other noble courtier—important enough to have been buried in the Valley of the Kings, but still not the equal of any of the royal family.

Unbeknown to Jamie at the time, the sepulchre was, in fact, that in which the aforementioned High Priest Nephrekeptah, who had served the Egyptian god Kheperi, had been interred.

Kheperi, He Who Is Coming Into Existence, was the god of the rising sun and creation, of life, death and resurrection. In figure he was depicted as a scarab, a scarab-headed man, or a man wearing a scarab crown. In some funerary papyri he was portrayed as a scarab in a boat borne aloft by Nun, the primordial waters of Chaos, from which all had come into being. Because the scarab beetle lays its eggs in a ball of dung, which it then rolls to a safe hiding place until the hatching of life within, Kheperi, in the form of a great scarab, had been thought by the Egyptians to roll the sun like a huge ball of dung westward each day across the infinite vault of the sky, then down through the Underworld that belonged solely to the Gods and the dead, and then back up to the eastern horizon to begin his lengthy journey anew the following morning, endlessly regenerating the sun and bringing life to the earth.

In his lifetime of many years, Nephrekeptah had been the god Kheperi's devoted servant. But now, in death, the high priest was nothing more than a mummy, as meticulously preserved as so many others of his ilk had been over the ages.

Still, even Jamie gave little consideration to the aeons-old history, the advanced culture and the complex religion of the ancient Egyptian civilization as he trod along the first corridor of the crypt, his boots stirring up the fine dust that had, until now, lain unagitated for centuries. Instead, uppermost in his mind was the thought that he wished he had not come to Egypt to begin with, much less have agreed to break in to one of the mausoleums in the valley, in search of booty.

Now that he was actually inside a tomb that might still contain at least some portion of its original treasure, Jamie was struck even more forcibly by the fact that the desecration he and his colleagues intended was a sacrilege, and his conscience gnawed at him sorely as a result. Surely it was bad luck to rob a sepulchre, and this was why their native guide had fled! he thought again.

The loud swearing of some of his friends abruptly started Jamie from his uneasy reverie.

"What is it? What's wrong?" he asked sharply, lifting his torch even higher in an attempt to see what was happening ahead of him in the semidarkness of the long hall.

"There be a large hole in t' wall here," Lord Thomas MacGregor reported, "where ancient masons working on another nearby crypt higher up in the cliffs accidentally tunneled down through into this one. A great pile o' rocks an' loose shards art scattered about on t' floor."

"Well, we knew that despite t' fact that t' seal on t' main door was intact, this mausoleum had to have been entered at some time or another," Jamie pointed out logically. "Otherwise, there wouldna be so much dust an' so many cobwebs in here, an' t' atmosphere would be fresher. So, no doubt, whate'er riches this tomb may once have contained have already all been looted— in which case, we art wasting our time proceeding any farther!"

"I disagree," Lord Andrew Sinclair declared coolly. "Perhaps 'tis only this first passage that has been invaded, an' t' masons who did it lacked t' time necessary to penetrate t' second corridor, as well as t' actual burial chamber itself. After all, they would have been closely watched o'er by both a foreman an' guards, one presumes. So I say we go on to t' next door!"

"Aye…methinks that makes sense," Lord William Drummond put in slowly. "For 'twould be a real shame to have come so far, only to return home with naught to show for our endeavors!"

Despite further protestations and cautions from Jamie, the rest agreed, and after a moment, gingerly picking their way over the rubble that littered the floor where the masons had so long ago hacked through the stone wall from its other side, the party continued along the hall to the sepulchre's second door. Upon examination, this was found to be inviolate, just like the first. After destroying the seal, the group passed through the barrier, descending a second flight of stone stairs that sloped down even deeper into the dark bowels of the earth, to another corridor that led to the crypt's burial chamber.

Upon finally reaching this last, the young men paused before its door, their excitement mounting as they observed that its seal, too, was intact. Even Jamie, despite all his apprehension, could not suppress his own rising sense of anticipation as some of his companions broke the seal and slowly shoved open the weighty barrier.

Beyond, what met the party's eyes held them transfixed with awe and incredulity as they crowded into the burial chamber, for here was splendor beyond their wildest imaginings.

Heavenly stars in shades of gold and silver spangled the ceiling, and equally beautiful, ornate murals depicting a profusion of liturgical scenes adorned the skillfully plastered walls. Inside the room itself was arrayed a stunning cache of funerary finery. Among the furniture, statuettes and other items displayed were a light ceremonial chariot with spirals and rosettes of gilded plaster; a luxuriously carved bed with a hammock woven from palm leaves and, nearby, yards of fine linens to serve as mosquito netting and sheets; a thronelike chair made of veneered wood adorned with gilt vignettes and text, and sporting ram-headed hand rests; a huge wooden jewelry box that stood on lion-footed legs and was fashioned of inlaid ivory, ebony and a mosaic of faience tiles in a rainbow of colors; a big wooden clothing coffer, also on four legs and with its top and four sides brilliantly painted with a series of ankhs and other symbols sacred to the Egyptians; a great canopic chest and canopic jars, as well as other pottery vessels that, when uncorked, still held wine, olive oil, honey, grain and dried fruit; dozens of papyrus scrolls and papyrus sandals; an intricate headpiece, a black wig and its wig basket; a veritable horde of scarabs and other jeweled amulets; and a mirror and a kohl tube, their silver as yet untarnished, such had been the pristine atmosphere inside the burial chamber before the destruction of its seal.

In one corner reposed the most stupendous piece of all. This was a grand sarcophagus coated all over with glistening pitch to give it an ebony sheen, and embellished with relief pictures and inscriptions of gold-leafed plaster. Instead of legs, it sat upon curved runners, so that it resembled an ark or boat, an important religious icon to the Egyptians.

Closer inspection revealed that inside the large sarcophagus were three separate smaller and increasingly lavish caskets, one within another. The first of these, the outer coffin, was shaped like the mummy for whom it had been fabricated. Like the sarcophagus, it was completely enveloped with gleaming pitch and decorated with more relief pictures and a text design of gilded plaster. Inside this was a smaller casket totally covered with silver leaf, upon which were inscribed bands of more gold-leafed plaster. Contained within the second coffin was the third and final casket, which was wholly gilded and richly ornamented with hieroglyphs of colored glass inlaid in gold. When at last opened, this coffin was found to be entirely silver-leafed inside.

Within it, the mummy lay peacefully, created by means of a mysterious process that had taken fully seventy long days to complete and that had involved removing the organs, desiccating the entire body with natron, then coating it with oil, balsam and *mūm*—beeswax—so that although the corpse had been left weighing hardly anything at all, it had nevertheless been carefully preserved for all time. Like others of his ilk, the High Priest Nephrekeptah had been wrapped in hundreds of yards of linen strips daubed with resin for adherence and painstakingly inscribed with magic words to protect his spirit and speed it on its way to the Underworld. When the linen strips that bound the high priest's mummy were partially unraveled, they revealed that his highly detailed gold funerary mask was still in place and that over his heart rested an enormous emerald heart scarab that glittered like luminescent green ice in the wavering flames of the torchlight. Strangely enough, it was from this scarab, Jamie thought, that all the Power he felt within the place appeared to emanate.

"God's breath! 'Tis a king's ransom we have stumbled upon here, lads—an' no mistake!" Lord George Kilpatrick whistled long and low. "How we shall e'er be getting it all home, I'm quite sure I dinna know. Ned, you're a good fellow an' a true friend. That being so, will ye please be kind enough to go an' fetch those blasted, beastly camels for us? For I myself shall have nowt more to do with 'em since they spat upon me!"

"Aye, that I will." Grinning as he remembered the spitting incident, Lord Edward Lennox turned and slowly made his way from the burial chamber to retrieve the camels the group had hired for their excursion, while his colleagues began to discuss the best means of transporting all the treasure they had found.

"Well, obviously, we canna take everything here back with us—more's t' pity!" Tom sighed glumly at the realization. "For, with t' money garnered from selling all this, we would each o' us be able to pay off all our gambling debts an' set ourselves up for life!"

"I dinna think ye ha'e to worry about that, laddie buck!" Andy laughed heartily, clapping his friend on the back. "Why, that emerald alone must be worth a fortune! Look at it! 'Tis the size o' a goose egg!" He indicated the heart scarab carefully placed on the mummy's breast. "And so must be many o' these other things, too. Since we have brought no wagons with us, let us not bother about trying to haul away any o' t' furniture or other large furnishings, but concentrate on all t' smaller objects instead. Now that we know where this place is, we can always come back for t' rest later."

"Right," Will agreed, nodding. Then, motioning toward a heaping stack of chatoyant silks and damasks, beautiful linens and cottons, he directed, "Give me a hand with all these bolts o' cloth, lads. We can use them to bundle everything up in."

"How art we going to transport t' mummy?" Geordie inquired, with a glance at the now-open sarcophagus and three coffins. "Shall we just wrap him up, too, an' toss him o'er one o' t' camel's backs?"

"Mayhap 'twould be better if we left him in peace," Jamie suggested tentatively, also looking at the sarcophagus and caskets. "Even stealing t' mummy's possessions seems wrong somehow, let alone carting away his very corpse!"

"What? Art ye daft, laddie buck?" Tom exclaimed, clearly astonished. "He's long dead and buried, isn't he? An' he's got no need o' either his body or his belongings now—besides which, entombing a corpse in such a way as this is a heathen custom, not a proper Christian rite at all. So ye need have no worries on that account. 'Tisna robbing himself and his grave we be, but merely claiming ownership o' what is rightfully ours, since we be t' ones that found all this treasure."

"That's right," Andy stated calmly. "God's bluid, Jamie! Ye dinna come halfway around t' world to Egypt only to get cold feet at t' last minute, did ye? I thought ye came to make your fortune, seeing as how so much o' what ye ought to have inherited was lost under t' tyranny o' that Sassenach Cromwell an' his bluidy Roundheads before Charles was properly restored to t' throne!"

"Aye, that's true. I canna deny it," Jamie admitted slowly, duly chastened.

"Then cease your blathering, an' get o'er there an' help Geordie with that infernal mummy! T' Barber-Surgeons in Edinburgh will no doubt pay quite a pretty guinea for it, I'll wager!"

Knowing that this, too, was true, Jamie at last obediently, however reluctantly, did as instructed, uttering no further protestations, despite how his conscience continued to eat at him. Together he and Geordie unwrapped a long bolt of material, preparing to fold the mummy of the High Priest Nephrekeptah up in it.

"Take that scarab off him, Jamie, will ye? Whilst I get his mask. They might fall out o' t' cloth an' be lost, otherwise," Geordie said.

For a seemingly endless moment Jamie hesitated, some instinct warning him, so that his entire body was pervaded by a terrible sense of premonition and dread. He was dimly aware that beyond the mausoleum the sound of the distant rumbling he had heard earlier had now grown closer, stronger and more ominous, and this, too, increased his fear. Despite the coolness of the tomb, both his dark, handsome young visage and his palms were beaded with sweat. He did not know with certainty what was happening aboveground, and he surely did not like what was happening below.

The Egyptians had believed that it was not the brain, but the heart that was the fount from which all human intelligence and emotion sprang, that it was within the heart that one's personality and soul were contained. Because of this, the Egyptians had venerated the heart. So, unlike the body's other organs, it had never been removed during the mummification process, but left whole and in place, guarded by a heart scarab. In the Egyptian *Book of the Dead,* the heart of the deceased was portrayed as being weighed on a set of scales against the delicate feather of Ma'at, the goddess of universal truth, order and balance. So, in death, the heart bore witness either for or against the deceased, and to ensure that the testimony was favorable, the heart scarab was usually engraved with a verse from a chapter in the *Book of the Dead.*

> O my heart that I received from my mother,
> O my heart that I had upon earth,
> Do not rise up against me as a witness!
> Do not create opposition against me among the
> assessors!
> Do not tip the scales against me
> in the presence of the Goddess of the Balance!
> Do not tell lies about me
> in the presence of the Great Lord of the West!

Thus was the heart scarab of the High Priest Nephrekeptah inscribed. It was set in gleaming gold and suspended on a fine gold chain as well, by means of a hole that had been bored through one end of the talisman. But of this last Jamie was oblivious until he finally stretched out one hand to steal the heart scarab. Then he realized that it hung around the mummy's neck. Gingerly, trying hard not to touch the mummy itself, he carefully lifted the gold chain over its head and once more attempted to take the amulet.

But much to Jamie's consternation and confusion, it still would not budge from its resting place, and for an interminable instant he thought wildly, horrified, that the mummy had somehow seized hold of it to prevent him from taking it.

"For God's sake, Jamie!" Geordie hissed impatiently. "What're ye just standing there like a village idiot for? Get t' scarab! Or art ye turned coward on us, after all?"

"Nay, 'tisna that, I swear!" Jamie insisted stoutly, resolutely forcing himself to marshal both his courage and his wits. "'Tis that t' bluidy thing willna come loose…ah, ne'er ye mind, Geordie. Now I ken what t' trouble is. 'Tis sewn to t' damned bandages! Christ! Here, hold my torch whilst I cut t' accursed thing free!"

Reaching into his right boot, Jamie drew forth his *sgian dubh*. With the sharp, silver-bladed dagger he sliced through the many threads binding the heart scarab to the linen wrappings that enveloped the mummy. Then he returned the dirk to his boot and snatched up the talisman. When he did so, to his everlasting terror, the mummy suddenly and violently heaved up at him from its sarcophagus and coffins.

Crying out, aghast, Jamie leapt back from the bloodcurdling bandaged figure, staggering heavily as the very earth abruptly seemed to quake and shift beneath his feet. In his fist he still clutched the heart scarab, and as he strove to escape from the mummy's onslaught upon him, he at last wrenched the amulet from its dead owner, tearing away several long strips of linen in the process and causing his deceased assailant to topple heavily to one side, banging savagely into Geordie.

"My God, 'tis alive!" Geordie shrieked, flailing at the mummy wildly with the two torches he bore.

Years afterward, Jamie would tell himself that in the semi-darkness of the tomb he must have missed cutting through some of the strong threads holding the heart scarab fast to the mummy, so that when he had taken the talisman, he had inadvertently jerked up the light, desiccated, bandaged figure with it. But still, he would never quite manage to convince himself of the truth of this.

Now, however, he knew only that the mummy appeared to have somehow come back to life and to be attacking them all. By this time, Tom, Andy and Will had rushed to join the fray, and they shoved and pummeled the mummy furiously until at last it lay still, broken and battered upon the stone floor of the sepulchre.

"'Twas alive, I tell ye!" Geordie averred, his countenance ashen in the half-light.

"'Twasna!" Andy rejoined sharply. "'Tis been dead and mummified for millennia! Jamie must have caught its bandages somehow an' yanked it from t' coffin, so that it seemed alive, an' that impression was reinforced by our own selves pushing an' pulling it about in the shadows cast by t' torches, that's all. Now, get back to work, or we'll ne'er get finished here—an' from t' sound o' it, a bad storm must be blowing up outside!"

But before the others, muttering under their breath, could do as Andy had commanded, Ned came running back into the burial chamber, gasping for air and soaking wet.

"We've all got to get out o' here now!" he cried, his young face filled with fear. "T' camels have come untied somehow an' art gone, an' 'tis storming summat fierce outside! Rain be pouring down so hard that 'tis flooding t' entire valley! These tombs art a death trap now!"

As though to punctuate Ned's terrifying words, the ground beneath the young men's feet trembled and heaved once more, and somewhere above them there echoed a spine-chilling roaring sound, which they now knew must be floodwater increasingly gathering speed and force, streaming like a tidal wave down the mountains into the valley below. This was exceedingly dangerous, for the valley was composed principally of hard Theban limestone and brittle Esna shale, the latter of which was extremely frail and unstable. Whenever it came into contact with moisture, it rapidly expanded, the resulting impetus often ripping apart entire hillsides in the valley—or so the party's native guide had informed them before fleeing and leaving them to their own devices.

Now, as a result, the young men needed no further urging from Ned to make good their escape. Greedily snatching up the nearest plunder they could carry, they started to run, exiting the burial chamber and pelting down the corridor beyond.

Jamie was so intent on getting away from what he now viewed as a completely ill-omened and evil place that he hardly even realized he still bore the heart scarab in his hand. It was not only as large as a goose egg, but also even heavier, and colder than ice in his tight grip, so that it seemed as though it were frozen to his palm, had become a part of him somehow. But although his hand itself felt numb from clutching the amulet, the scarab seemed increasingly, eerily, to throb like a strengthening heartbeat in his grasp, radiating Power. But he did not dwell upon that now. He thought only of reaching the earth's surface and higher ground, where he stood a much greater chance of survival.

His heart hammering hideously, so that it felt as though it would burst in his chest, Jamie raced desperately after the others, his booted feet pounding up the first set of steps that led away from the burial chamber and into the passage beyond. Here, to his horror, he discovered that the stone floor was slick with rainwater that had already first trickled and now poured into the crypt. All the broken rock and loose shards from where ancient masons had inadvertently tunneled into this mausoleum from the one higher up next door proved a dangerous hindrance as well, so that as he trod through the puddles and wet debris, he lost his footing, slipping and then falling heavily to his knees.

"Wait!" Jamie called hoarsely after his cohorts as he struggled mightily to rise. "Wait!"

But no one heard him over the terrifying, thunderous crash of the deluge that now suddenly spewed into the tomb, cascading like a violent waterfall down the stairs ahead.

"We're too late—" Ned shouted, before he was savagely knocked from the stone steps by the fearsome flood that gushed in, swamping him, so that he went under, disappearing from sight, the torch he had carried abruptly extinguished.

Jamie did not wait to see or hear any more. Some atavistic instinct for survival propelling him to action, he heaved himself to his feet and, without even thinking, leapt through the jagged-edged hole in the sepulchre wall into the dark, higher crypt beyond—still unwittingly clenching the large, priceless emerald in his hand.

Book One

The Game's Afoot

I see you stand like greyhounds in the slips,
Straining upon the start. The game's afoot.
—William Shakespeare
King Henry V[1598-1600]

Come, Watson, come! The game is afoot.
—Sir Arthur Conan Doyle
*The Return of Sherlock Holmes [1904],
The Adventure of the Abbey Grange*

Chapter One

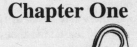

By Our Beginnings

Youth, what man's age is like to be doth show;
We may our ends by our beginnings know.
—Sir John Denham
Of Prudence

Soon fades the spell, soon comes the night;
Say will it not be then the same,
Whether we played the black or white,
Whether we lost or won the game?
—Thomas Babington, Lord Macaulay
Sermon in a Churchyard

To give the devil his due.
—Miguel de Cervantes
Don Quixote de la Mancha [1605-1615]

1754
Medmenham Abbey, near London, England

Situated between the Hambledon and Hurley Locks, near Marlow, Medmenham Abbey stood in a secluded grove on the west bank of the River Thames, just outside London and about six miles from West Wycombe, the ancestral home of Sir Francis Dashwood, Baronet. The twelfth-century abbey had begun life quietly and modestly enough as a Cistercian monastery. However, during the year of the Reformation it had fallen into the secular hands of the Duffield family and been transformed into a large Tudor manor house.

In 1751, Dashwood, the son of a rich merchant who had married into the aristocracy, had leased the abbey from the Duffields and had immediately set about to renovate it, converting it into a fitting headquarters for the Order of the Knights of St. Francis, which he had founded five years earlier. Previously, the order had convened its meetings at the George & Vulture public house in St. Michael's Alley in the Cornhill parish of London. But now Medmenham Abbey served as its base of operations.

Dashwood, who had traveled widely during his Grand Tour and, in Florence, Italy, had been initiated into the ranks of the Freemasons, had spent considerable time and money remodeling the ancient abbey. Builders and gardeners from his own nearby estate of West Wycombe had labored to construct a deliberately ruined square tower at the southeast corner of the abbey, along with a cloister of three arches, which fronted on the River Thames. The surrounding gardens had been redesigned and replanted by Maurice-Louis Jolivet, and boasted a number of statues, which included a wholly naked Venus, the Roman goddess of love, carefully positioned in a bent-over stance, so that unsuspecting visitors accidentally strode into her bare buttocks, and a well-endowed, equally naked Priapus, the Roman god of fertility. The abbey's austere stained-glass windows had been replaced with ones of a pseudo-ecclesiastical nature, while its interior had been decorated in part with ornate frescoes painted by Giuseppe Borgnis. Above the abbey's grand main entrance Dashwood had caused to be inscribed the words *Fay Ce Que Voudras*—"Do What Thou Wilt"—the infamous but celebrated motto of François Rabelais's fictional Abbey of Thélème, built by the giant Gargantua.

Inside Medmenham Abbey, a statue of Harpa-Khruti, the Egyptian god of silence, known to the Greeks and Romans as Harpocrates, stood at one end of the elaborate dining hall, one finger held to his lips. At the opposite end of the sumptuous room, in a pose identical to that of her male counterpart, was a statue of Angerona with her bandaged mouth, the obscure Roman goddess of the winter solstice, death, silence and secrecy. In ancient times it was she who had protected the secret name of Rome, so that no harm might befall the city and its inhabitants. To the Freemasons, these two deities were the guardians of secrecy, and it was said that their presence in the dining hall was to remind the abbey's patrons that nothing discussed or done within its ancient walls was to be spoken of beyond them.

Sir Francis Dashwood himself was the "abbot" of Medmenham Abbey, the head of an inner circle composed of twelve "apostles." These thirteen men were the only ones admitted to the abbey's inner sanctum. The remainder of those inducted into the Order of the Knights of St. Francis were either "monks" or "nuns," depending upon their gender, and comprised the rank and file of the order.

Lord Iain Ramsay, formerly Viscount Strathmór and newly Earl of Dúndragon, was one of these "Monks of Medmenham." Tonight, however, he wished fervently that he were not, that he had never allowed himself to be drawn into the raucous, lewd company who frequented the old abbey, which would later be known as the "Hellfire Club" to many, although no one at Medmenham Abbey ever actually referred to it by that name.

Such wild, pagan goings-on there were conducted upon this once-holy ground! The long-dead Cistercian monks who had founded the abbey no doubt turned in their graves at even the very thought, Iain reflected glumly in some hazy corner of his wine-muddled mind. Beyond the abbey's high walls it was rumored that Satan worship took place within, and although that was patently untrue, it *was* fact that the so-called Monks of Medmenham revered the Earth-Mother Goddess and honored her with all manner of drink, masked revels and licentiousness.

In the erotic gardens, cups of rich wine and other such offerings were yielded up to the Bona Dea, the Good Goddess, and in the labyrinthine underground caves a short distance from the abbey, the "monks" and "nuns" of the order copulated in small "cells" that had been designed for just this purpose. Amid the surrounding yew trees, an imposing entrance resembling a Gothic church had been constructed to front these caves, which lay beneath West Wycombe Hill and stretched almost half a mile to High Wycombe, crossing a stream known as the River Styx and culminating in a large, impressive banqueting hall with a high ceiling and housing more Roman statues. Atop the hill stood the Church of St. Lawrence, crowned by a huge golden ball and fittingly, however ironically, dedicated to the patron saint of prostitutes. Sometimes, when in his cups, Dashwood would climb up inside the golden ball, slurping what he called his "divine milk-punch" and, at the top of his lungs, singing ribald parodies of the Psalms.

Now, as Iain thought of all these dubious things, he involuntarily shuddered. What a fool he had been ever to get mixed up with such people—no matter if they *were* some of the highest-ranking peers of the realm! His hands, clutching his playing cards close to his chest, trembled ever so slightly, and his brow was beaded with sweat. Because of his own stupidity, he currently stood to lose everything that had belonged to his family for generations—their estates in both Scotland and England. The game was piquet, and Iain was many points behind his opponent, Lord Bruno, Count Foscarelli, a friend of Dashwood's from his days spent in Florence.

How he had come to be playing cards with Foscarelli, Iain could not remember. One minute, it seemed, he had been eating supper in the grand dining hall, and the next he had been seated across a table from the Italian count, preparing to embark upon what had soon proved the disastrous game of piquet. Iain neither liked nor trusted Foscarelli, believing that all Italians were deceitful and treacherous—in fact, a race of poisoners and back stabbers. As a result, he felt certain Foscarelli was cheating him somehow and had been all evening. Nobody was as lucky at cards as the Italian count had been tonight!

Still, none of the game's interested onlookers appeared to find anything out of the ordinary about Foscarelli's uncanny good fortune, and since Iain could not determine just how he was being swindled, he dared not accuse the Italian count and attempt to expose his trickery. Further, even had Iain known how he was being cheated, Foscarelli was both an expert swordsman and a crack shot, and regardless of all he might lose this evening, Iain did not plan for his life to come to an abrupt end during a duel at dawn. The Italian count had a reputation that, far from sterling, hinted obscurely at dark undercurrents. It was rumored that he had killed more than one adversary on the field of honor and had left his native Italy under a nebulous cloud of scandal and suspicion, although what this had involved, no one knew. So Foscarelli was clearly not the type of man to be satisfied with only drawing first blood.

Besides, unbeknown to the Italian count or anybody else in the world, Iain still held one ace up his sleeve, and with it, he would ultimately best his opponent—just as he had bested his own father.

Iain's father, Lord Somerled Ramsay, the old Earl of Dúndragon, had disapproved of him and thought him a fool and a profligate, so he had during his lifetime taken steps against Iain, to prevent him from acquiring the family legacy. But in the end, Iain had outwitted and outlasted his father.

Deep in debt from gambling and other unsavory vices, he had long been counting on his inheritance to repay all the money he owed, since he had intended to sell some of his family's land to acquire the necessary funds to discharge his IOUs. So he had been glad when his father had finally died. Within the fortnight, he would indeed have sold what land he needed to dispose of to cover all his considerable obligations, for immediately after his father's funeral, with every good intention of doing just that, he had journeyed posthaste to London. But unfortunately, upon his arrival in the city, Iain had fallen in with Dashwood and several of the other Monks of Medmenham, and now here he sat in the dining hall of the ancient abbey, all his best-laid plans in ruins.

He had lost track of the number of parties that he and Foscarelli had played, although he knew it must be several, for each partie consisted of six hands, and the two decks of cards he and the Italian count were using had been shuffled and dealt numerous times over the long course of the evening. And after each deal, it had seemed to Iain as though the gap between his accrued points and those of Foscarelli had widened immeasurably, and the stakes for which they gamed had risen until, in the end, Iain had wagered even the family legacy to keep on playing. Like many gamblers, he had felt as though he were in the grip of some strange, tantalizing fever, and he had believed that surely his luck must change for the better sooner or later. Only, it had not.

The Italian count *must* be cheating!

"A point of four," Iain declared now.

"Not good," Foscarelli replied coolly, as he had all night. "A point of five. I score five."

"A sequence of a quart."

"How high?" the Italian count inquired, arching one devilish black eyebrow.

"Knave."

"Not good. Queen. Also a tierce. I score seven."

"A trio of kings," Iain announced, biting his lower lip anxiously.

"Not good. A quatorze of aces. I score fourteen. I start with twenty-six."

"I start with one." Iain led to the first trick of the current hand, knowing, with despair, that he was already down twenty-five points before the actual play had even begun.

So things had gone all evening.

All around him the sultry summer night air was thick with salacious talk and boisterous laughter, the bawdy sounds of promiscuity and frivolity; with smoke from the burning candles in the crystal chandeliers and from the cigars being puffed by many of the men present; and with the perfume of the profusion of flowers that bloomed in the abbey's gardens, which heady scent wafted inside with each stir of the breeze. Beyond the abbey's walls the branches of the yew trees swayed and soughed, the River Thames lapped gently at its banks and the night birds called melodiously. But all these things Iain registered only dimly as he attempted to force his befuddled brain to concentrate on the game. A furtive glance at his gold pocket watch informed him that it was now well past two o'clock in the morning. In a few more minutes he would have nothing left to wager, would be cleaned out and virtually destitute, with all his creditors still dunning him. The thought of debtors' prison loomed large and unpleasantly in his mind.

"My partie, I believe," Foscarelli observed, his dark eyes hard, shrewd and calculating.

The sound of the Italian count's deceptively silky voice abruptly jolted Iain from his disturbing reverie.

"Aye, so it would seem," he uttered miserably at the recognition that he had, indeed, lost once more, lost everything now.

"Would you care to play again?"

"Nay, I've naught left. I'm done, finished."

"A pity." Foscarelli shrugged lightly. "'Twould seem that the rumors I have heard about your family are true, then. The curse of the Egyptian god Kheperi indeed lies upon your branch of the Clan Ramsay, because you have stolen his heart."

"That is only an old superstitious legend," Iain insisted, despite the fact that at this very moment he felt he must, in truth, be accursed, as the Italian count had averred.

"Is it? Then the story I have been told about one of your ancestors having robbed a priceless emerald heart scarab from the ancient tomb of an Egyptian high priest devoted to Kheperi is only a fable…?"

"If 'twere not, do you imagine that I would be in such dire straits as I am now?" Iain asked, more sharply than he had intended, flushing at the inadvertent admission of his own current state of affairs, his own gullibility in being taken in by such a depraved crowd as Dashwood's, and his own culpability in ever having consented to play the ruinous game of piquet. "If the emerald actually existed, gladly would I trade it for the estates I have now lost. But I myself have never seen it and know little more about it than what you yourself have spoken of just now. So I do not believe that the tale about it is anything more than that."

"I see. Then it appears that your ill fortune tonight at cards was merely the result of a run of bad luck."

"Och, 'twas more than just that!" Iain burst out before he thought.

"What do you mean?" Foscarelli's dark eyes narrowed dangerously of a sudden.

"N-n-nothing. I meant nothing."

"Oh, but I think you did. It sounded to me as though you were accusing me of cheating you at cards, Dúndragon!" Abruptly pushing his chair back from the table, the Italian count stood, his dark, hawkish visage filled with murderous rage. "By God, I'll not take that kind of an insult from any man—no matter the provocation! You will either withdraw that remark and apologize, my lord, or else my cartelbearer shall call upon you and yours, do you but give me your direction."

"I have nothing to apologize for. I have accused you of nothing, Count Foscarelli," Iain said grimly, after a long moment, in the deathly silence that had fallen in the dining hall as those present had grown aware of the brewing quarrel. He, too, rose, facing his opponent across the table. "'Tis you who have leapt to your own conclusions, however erroneous those may be. Still, if you cannot admit your mistake and must have satisfaction, then I am lodged at the George and Vulture, in Saint Michael's Alley."

With that, Iain pivoted on his heel and strode from the room, shaking all over. At the main entrance to Medmenham Abbey he called for his horse, and when it was brought, he galloped away, heading east toward London and cursing his wretched tongue. Why on earth had he ever spoken as he had to Foscarelli, insinuating that the Italian count was a cardsharp? He knew that Foscarelli was not a man to be trifled with. And why, when the Italian count had seemed so peculiarly intent on forcing an argument with him, had he not simply swallowed his pride and apologized? After all, he was ruined, anyway. So why quibble about being stripped of his dignity, too?

It must have been all the wine that had confused his wits and loosened his tongue, Iain thought, dismayed. Now, to save his life, he would have to flee from Scotland and England to the Continent, he realized, for he dared not risk facing Foscarelli in a duel at dawn. He would surely be killed! That was a prospect far worse than debtors' prison.

He had a few personal belongings left, which he could pawn. They would bring him enough money to buy passage one way or another across the English Channel. Yes, he could make good his escape if he hurried, Iain told himself, now wishing desperately that he had possessed the necessary foresight and presence of mind to give the Italian count a false direction, which would have bought him more time to get away. Well, there was no help for it now. He must do the best he could. Besides, many of the Monks of Medmenham lodged at their former headquarters, the George & Vulture, when in London. So it was entirely possible Foscarelli knew that, and certainly he could easily have learnt it from talking to anyone at the abbey.

So the wheels of Iain's brain churned furiously as he rode pell-mell toward London. Outside, beyond the confines of Medmenham Abbey, the summer night air was cool rather than muggy and helped to clear his head, so that he could order his previously muddled and chaotic thoughts. He had relatives on the Continent, in France, the de Ramezays, who were of the ancient Norman branch of his family. He could go to them, and they would not refuse to take him in, surely. The fact that he would come to them empty-handed and hard on the heels of a scandal gave him pause. But still, Iain saw no other way out for himself. Black sheep he might be, but he was still a Ramsay. So he did not believe that the de Ramezays would turn their backs on him.

Above, the silvery moon, nearly full, shone brightly to light his path, and soon he had reached London. Although it was relatively quiet on the city streets at this time of night, there were still the occasional hackney coaches, hansom cabs and revelers out and about, as well as the usual footpads, who would rob a man for a few shillings. So Iain kept a wary eye on his surroundings as he traversed the sprawling labyrinth of London's streets, the hooves of his horse clip-clopping on the unpaved roads and cobblestone streets, echoing loudly in the relative stillness of the city as he made his way along Cheapside and thence down Poultry. Just shortly, he came to the intersection of Threadneedle, Cornhill and Lombard Streets. Continuing along Cornhill, he rode past the Royal Exchange, which was shut up tight at this late hour, and on to St. Michael's Alley, which ran alongside the church and graveyard dedicated to the saint of the same name. Turning down the short narrow alleyway, he drew his horse to a halt before the George & Vulture public house, which had been in operation since the twelfth century, but which had been rebuilt during the seventeenth after the Great Fire of London in 1666, when the bakeshop of King Charles II's baker, Thomas Farynor, had caught fire in Pudding Lane and burnt most of London.

After handing the reins of his horse to the yawning stable boy who presently appeared, Iain stepped inside the tavern and hurried upstairs to his lodgings. There his valet, Westerfield, awaited his arrival, opening the door so that he need not fumble with his key in the semidarkness of the hall.

"You're back quite late, milord," the valet observed, taking Iain's hat, coat and gloves, then following him through the apartment to the bedchamber. "Did you have a good evening, then?"

"Nay, Westerfield, 'twas the worst night of my entire life— and we've not a moment to spare! We must pack up posthaste and get away from this place just as fast as we can!"

"Why, milord? What has happened?" The valet had never before seen his master in such a feverish state, opening the doors of the wardrobe and the drawers of the chest, yanking garments and smallclothes from their hooks, neckerchiefs and boots from their shelves, carelessly dumping the entire lot on the bed. "If 'tis the reckoning, milord, I've spoken to the landlord, and he has agreed that 'twon't be due until the end of the week."

"Nay, that is the least of my worries at the moment! I've lost everything, Westerfield, in a disastrous game of piquet with

Count Foscarelli. Perhaps you have heard of him? He has rather an unsavory reputation and is, I believe, a truly wicked man. I've no doubt at all that he cheated me somehow at cards. In my cups, I unwittingly intimated something of the sort to him, and he became enraged. The upshot is that when I refused to apologize, insisting that he had merely misconstrued my remark, he challenged me to a duel, and without thinking, I foolishly related my direction to him, so his cartelbearer could call upon me and mine. I dare not meet with Foscarelli. I've not his skill with either sword or pistol, and he surely would not be satisfied with merely wounding me. He will kill me!" Iain asserted grimly as he dragged forth his trunk, which stood in one corner, and flung open the lid.

"Well, why do you just stand there, Westerfield?" he continued wrathfully. "Have you not understood a single word I've said? Get a move on, man! Foscarelli's cartelbearer may be en route to the George and Vulture even as we speak! We must flee to the Continent, where we will be safe! Nay, I will pack us. You take this and this." Removing his gold pocket watch and signet ring, Iain handed them to the valet. "Run down to that Jewish pawnbroker's shop in Birchin Lane. Wake up the proprietor and see what you can get for those. Here, take this, as well." Reaching beneath his shirt, Iain drew forth a large, unusual, ornate silver cross that he wore on an intricate silver chain around his neck.

"Nay, milord!" Westerfield gasped out, shocked and horrified. "Not that—for I remember when the old laird first gave you that, before he took it back from you. He said you must never part with it, not even upon pain of death!"

"Well, my father's dead, so he'll never know I pawned the blasted cross, will he? 'Tis worth a pretty guinea, and I'm in dire need of funds for our journey, I tell you! Besides which, my brother, Neill, can easily pay the reckoning for it and retrieve it, should I prove unable to do so myself!" Determinedly Iain thrust the crucifix into the valet's hands. "Whilst you're at it, arrange for my horses and carriage to be brought around front, too. Hurry,

Westerfield! Every second that you delay may cost me my very life!"

"Aye, milord."

Turning, the valet exited the room, while Iain redirected his attention to the frantic packing of his trunk, glancing nervously at the ormolu clock that sat upon the mantel over the fireplace and that seemed to be ominously ticking away each passing minute. He would never get away in time, he feared.

By this time, his trunk was crammed full to overflowing— and everything he had brought with him to London still had not been put inside. It was because he had just thrown his belongings in, Iain knew, rather than folding them away neatly, as Westerfield always did. Swearing under his breath, he began to rearrange his possessions, trying to make more room. Finally he was finished. Sitting heavily upon the curved lid to force it shut, he buckled the trunk's leather straps securely. Then he started on the task of packing his valet's belongings, which, fortunately, were a great deal fewer than his own. He longed ardently for a drink to steady his frazzled nerves, but he knew his overindulgence in spirits was at least partially, if not wholly, responsible for his downfall, and that he must keep a clear head at all costs if he were to make good his escape.

So instead, once he had finished his tasks and there was nothing more for him to do, Iain paced the floor of the apartment restlessly, habitually reaching into the pocket of his waistcoat for his gold pocket watch to check the time—only to discover that the timepiece was missing from his fob and to remember that he had given it to Westerfield to pawn.

At one point it belatedly occurred to him to write his younger brother and heir, Neill, Viscount Strathmór, a letter, and he sat down before the desk in the sitting room, taking pen and paper in hand. However, he had hardly even begun the missive when, at long last, toward dawn, much to his relief, he heard the sound of his valet's measured footsteps treading along the corridor beyond the apartment. There was no time to write further. Breaking off in midsentence, Iain hastily signed the note, then dusted it with sand to dry the ink. Folding the letter, he sealed it with hot wax, scrawling his name on one corner so that the missive could be franked.

Then, cramming the note into his jacket pocket, he hurried to open the door for his valet. To Iain's abrupt and everlasting horror, however, it was not Westerfield who stood without, but a total stranger to him—a swarthy, brawny Italian, who, teeth flashing whitely, smiled at him broadly, but in a nevertheless thoroughly unpleasant and even frightening fashion.

"Signore Dúndragon, I presume," the man greeted him smoothly. "Permit me to introduce myself. I am Cesare Spinoza, Conte Foscarelli's cartelbearer. The conte has informed me of your insult to his honor last night and also of his demand for satisfaction. Naturally, such a besmirching of his reputation must not go unchallenged—or unpunished—you understand. He requests that you meet with him at Green Park, at dawn today, when the two of you are less likely to be disturbed. In the event that you have yet to choose your own second, I have been instructed to tell you that Sir Francis Dashwood has offered to assist you. And of course, arrangements have been made for a surgeon to be standing by, as well, should his services prove necessary. As 'tis nearly first light now and time is thus short, I suggest that I myself convey you to the park, *signore*. Conveniently, I have a carriage waiting for us downstairs. So if you will accompany me, please—"

"I...I thank you for the offer, sir," Iain managed to get out, swallowing hard. "However, I am awaiting the return of Westerfield, my valet, whom I dispatched earlier upon some important business for me, which I'm afraid I must conclude prior to my meeting with Count Foscarelli."

"Ah, yes. I chanced upon your man on my way here. He informed me to advise you that he has been...unavoidably detained."

As he heard this, Iain felt a terrible chill chase up his spine, prickling the fine hairs on his nape—for he believed that the implication contained in the words was that Cesare Spinoza had done something to Westerfield to prevent his return...had restrained him in some way, or perhaps had even murdered him! Had it been possible, Iain would have slammed shut the door, bolted it from the inside and attempted to egress the public house through one of its small upstairs windows. But unfortunately, Spinoza stood in the doorway, so that the portal could not be closed. Besides which, Iain suddenly felt certain that if he were to look out onto the maze of narrow streets and alleys below, he would discover that the Italian had not come alone, that there were other henchmen of Foscarelli's lurking about.

"I see," Iain responded slowly at last. "Then, in that case, allow me to fetch my coat."

"Since your valet has been detained on his errand, I will be happy to assist you, *signore*." Deliberately stepping without invitation into the apartment before Iain could protest, Spinoza followed him into the bedchamber. Noting the trunks that stood ready and waiting in the middle of the room, the Italian inquired, "You are leaving London, *signore?*"

"Aye." Iain saw no reason to lie, for he could scarcely deny his intentions when it was plain that he was packed for a journey. "Business calls me away. I must depart directly after my meeting with Count Foscarelli."

"Then, by all means, let us make haste in this affair, *signore*. The sooner it is ended, the sooner you can be on your way to wherever you may be going, no?"

"Aye," Iain answered, praying that he would not be embarking upon a trip to hell.

Spinoza played the part of the valet, helping him into his cloak. Then the two of them left the apartment, going downstairs. There, when the Italian's attention was momentarily distracted by a sudden loud noise from the tavern's barroom off the long narrow dark passage in which they stood, Iain managed to surreptitiously slip his letter onto the little pile that sat on a small table in the corridor, waiting to be picked up by the postboy.

Then, passing through the large arched front door of the public house, he and Spinoza stepped into the street beyond, where

Iain saw that his earlier conjecture had been right: There were several other disreputable-looking Italian hirelings milling about. Standing outside were also four black horses harnessed to a gleaming ebony coach, which sported no coat of arms and which, to Iain, in the gossamer white mist that drifted ghostily along the tangle of narrow streets and alleys, vaguely—and disturbingly—resembled a hearse. The men sprang to attention when he and Spinoza appeared, opening the carriage door and lowering the steps for them, then assuming their own posts upon the vehicle. With a command to the horses and a lash of his long, snaking whip, the driver set the equipage in motion, and with a sudden lurch they were off, the coach's high wheels clattering loudly over the rough dark bloodred cobblestones in the predawn stillness of the city.

From St. Michael's Alley and Castle Court, the carriage followed George Yard to Lombard Street, thence rumbled its way down to Grace Church Street and Fish Street Hill, whence it wended through the city's web of streets along the River Thames, eventually coming to Charing Cross.

During the length of their journey, Iain and Spinoza sat in what was to the former a tense, uneasy silence, although the latter did not appear to notice and occupied himself with staring with seeming interest out the vehicle's windows at the passing sights, although these were partially obscured by the diaphanous white mist that hung low over the River Thames and wafted like a will-o'-the-wisp through the city.

From Cockspur Street, the equipage turned onto the wide avenue of Pall Mall, and Iain felt his nerves, already strung taut, stretched even tighter as the coach drew ever nearer to its final destination of Green Park. He thought he must surely be on his way to his own death, and dimly he wondered if Westerfield, too, had met a like fate. He felt a lump in his throat, choking him, as the carriage rolled by all the gentlemen's clubs and gaming establishments that lined St. James's Street, many of which he had frequented when in London and that now he would almost certainly never step foot in again. The realization further disheartened him, causing his depressed spirits to sink even lower. Then the vehicle swept on to Piccadilly Road and at last to Green Park, which lay just beyond Buckingham House, the London residence of the Duke of Buckingham.

After the equipage had come to a halt, Foscarelli's henchmen alighted to open the door and lower the steps so that Iain and Spinoza could descend from the coach. Then, together, the two of them entered the park, which was a roughly triangular, sweeping expanse of slightly less than sixty acres of open grass punctuated by a few woods, rather than planted with formal flower beds. For this reason it was favored by duelists, and many an unfortunate gentleman had met his end here.

Not far from the park's reservoir and fountain, Count Foscarelli, Sir Francis Dashwood and several of the other so-called Monks of Medmenham awaited Iain and Spinoza's arrival. The Italian count, Iain was momentarily angered to see, had already brazenly removed both his coat and jacket, and stood in his crisp white linen shirt and breeches, deliberately making a target of himself.

"Lord Dúndragon, good morning," Foscarelli greeted him with feigned joviality, looking as fit and fresh as though he had not spent all night drinking and playing cards.

As he slowly removed his own cloak, Iain was morosely aware of the pathetic contrast he must present, with his black jacket buttoned up to his chin, his face unshaven and his eyes bleary and bloodshot. Further, on his way to Green Park he had felt a migraine coming on, and now his head pounded as badly as his heart, making him feel faint and ill.

"I really do not know why you have insisted upon our meeting, Count Foscarelli," he uttered weakly, blatantly ignoring the fact that all dialogue between combatants in connection with a duel was supposed to be exchanged only through the cartelbearers. "For as I informed you last night, I said naught that was intended to impugn your honor, and if any of my remarks caused you to believe otherwise, then I do most sincerely apologize."

"Indeed?" The Italian count raised one black eyebrow demonically. "But surely you know that 'tis far too late now for apologies, Lord Dúndragon. Not only is that against the rules, but also, there were, I fear, a great many people present at the abbey last evening who overheard your insinuation that I cheated you at cards, and as you yourself must be aware, gossip travels quickly in London. As a result, my reputation has already suffered. Because of you, in the minds of many, I am now labeled a cardsharp! For that, I must—and shall—have satisfaction! As the challenged party, the choice of weapons is yours. Will you have swords or pistols?"

"Francis—" Iain turned imploringly to Dashwood "—I understand from Mr. Spinoza that you have offered to act as my second. As such, can you not reason with the count?"

"Believe me, Iain, as your friend, I *have* tried," Dashwood rejoined carelessly. "But I must admit that even to my own ears, it *did* sound as though you were accusing Bruno of having cheated you last night, and that is a serious charge, Iain. Had you apologized immediately, perhaps I could indeed have put a stop to this affair. But I'm afraid that now, as Bruno has already pointed out to you, things have simply progressed too far for that. We all know the rules—including you, Iain. No apologies can be accepted on the field of honor until after first blood has been drawn. Truly, I'm surprised at you for even thinking you could act contrary to that. Tut, tut. Now, let us have no further delay, but get on with the business at hand before we are discovered by the Watch. I have examined both the swords and the pistols, and I recommend that you choose the latter. They are well made, and as I believe that you are perhaps more accustomed to a heavier blade than the foil, the pistol should serve you admirably."

Iain had grave doubts about that, but unfortunately, it now appeared that he had exhausted all possible avenues of escape from the forthcoming duel. Slowly he took up one of the two pistols from the open wooden box that was presented with a flourish first to him and then to Foscarelli by the physician in attendance. The rules of the ritual combat were duly proclaimed by the surgeon.

Then Iain and the Italian count assumed the traditional back-to-back stance upon the field of honor. After what seemed an interminable moment to Iain, the counting off of the requisite twelve paces commenced. With each faltering step forward he took, Iain felt sickly that his heart hammered louder and louder in his chest, until he thought that, surely, all the others present could hear it, that the sound must, in fact, be reverberating throughout the entire city in the early dawn quiet. It beat in his brain, and the blood roared so in his ears that he felt as though he was going to pass out at any instant.

As he took his final step and turned, he swayed a little on his feet briefly before he managed to steady himself, raise the pistol he held in his trembling hand and fire at his target. But as Iain had feared, his shot went wide of its mark, missing Foscarelli completely and burrowing into the stout trunk of a nearby oak tree. From among the ranks of the spectators Iain thought he detected a ripple of poorly smothered laughter, and his visage, looking pale and haggard in the early silver-white light that stole over the horizon, flushed slightly with shame before once more turning ashen. Devoutly he prayed that the Italian count would misfire, as well. But as his terrified eyes met Foscarelli's own dark, chillingly ruthless, narrowed gaze across the park, Iain knew in his heart that he stared into the face of evil, that all his hopes for pity were in vain. He was a dead man.

The thought had no sooner crossed his mind than he heard the Italian count's shot ring out. The bullet struck Iain hard in the chest, the impact violently knocking the wind from him. As he gasped for breath he was vaguely surprised to find himself still standing, and for a moment, astonished and even gleeful, he believed that, somehow—miraculously—his life had been spared, that he must have suffered only a flesh wound. But then, as though in slow motion, Iain felt his grasp on his own pistol suddenly slacken, the spent weapon falling heedlessly to the ground, and without warning, his knees gave way beneath him so that he crumpled to the green, green grass, wet with morning mist and dew that chilled him straight through, leaving him cold...so very cold. Strangely, from a very great distance, it seemed, he heard shouts and the sound of booted feet running toward him, felt his body half lifted and hands yanking savagely at his jacket, popping its buttons and sending them flying. In some obscure corner of his now nebulously clouding mind, he thought how angry Westerfield would be at having to sew them back on.

"I'm afraid there's nothing I can do," the physician announced gravely before rising from where he knelt over his prospective patient. "Lord Dúndragon's injury is mortal."

No, no! Iain wanted to protest. But when he parted his lips to speak, he tasted blood, salty and sickening, thick upon his tongue. Coughing and gurgling, he tried to spit the bubbling liquid from his mouth. A baleful shadow fell over his face, blotting out the pale dawn sunlight. Like that of the devil himself, Foscarelli's swarthy, hawkish visage swam before Iain's eyes as the Italian count bent near him, so that no one else could overhear their conversation.

"Tell me where the Heart of Kheperi is!" Foscarelli hissed, the sound like that of a sibilant snake in Iain's thundering ears. "Tell me what you have done with the ancient scarab that your ancestor stole from the tomb of the Egyptian high priest!"

"Don't...know.... Never...saw...it.... It...doesn't...exist," Iain somehow managed to gasp out.

"Filthy liar!" the Italian count spat softly. "I know that it does—and now that your estates belong to me, I shall search them high and low for the emerald, and I *shall* find it!"

At that, much to Foscarelli's puzzlement, a faint, peculiar smile of satisfaction curved Iain's bloodily frothing lips.

"Search high and low...all you want, Count. The joke's... on...you. I've won...and you've lost. You just don't...know it yet. Without the key...you'll never...unlock the mysteries...of my family's legacy...and in the end...your heirs will never... rule Castle Dúndragon, either. 'Tis the seat of...my branch of...the Clan Ramsay...and always will be...no matter what...."

With that triumphant pronouncement Iain felt his eyelashes

flutter feebly one last time, then close, so that all went dark. Then, mercifully, much to his vast relief, the pounding pain in his head and heart abruptly ceased.

Chapter Two

Chance Encounters

So weary with disasters, tugged with fortune,
That I would set my life on any chance,
To mend it or be rid on 't.

—William Shakespeare
Macbeth [1605-1606]

The hard, half-apathetic expression of one
who deems anything possible at the hands of
Time and Chance except, perhaps, fair play.

—Thomas Hardy
The Mayor of Casterbridge [1886]

There's no such thing as chance;
And what to us seems merest accident
Springs from the deepest source of destiny.

—Johann Christoph Friedrich von Schiller
Wallensteins Tod (The Death of Wallenstein) [1798]

1835
Oxford Street, London, England

Septimus Quimby had lived in London all his life. He had been born fifteen years before the turn of the century, to parents of comfortable, if not luxurious, means—his father having been a cartographer and map seller, and his mother having been an artist. Prior to the birth of their only child, Mr. and Mrs. Quimby together had had the astute foresight and good fortune to pro-

duce an ornately beautiful, elaborately detailed map of London
that had proved highly popular, thereby ensuring the success of
what had then been only their fledgling establishment, Quimby
& Company (Cartographers & Map Sellers), located at No. 7B
Oxford Street.

From his industrious parents, the younger Mr. Quimby had
learnt his profession at an early age, eventually following them
into their trade and, when they had died, stepping into their
shoes and taking over the family business, devoting himself to
its continued prosperity. His parents would have been inordinately proud of him, for he had done so well that, finally, requiring the space above his shop for his expanding enterprise,
Mr. Quimby had some time ago been compelled to move from
what had previously served as his private premises into separate
lodgings of his own, which he had acquired on Baker Street, not
far from Regent's Park, in the fashionable district of Marylebone.

Since his quarters were not a very great distance from his shop
on Oxford Street, it had, over the years, become Mr. Quimby's
practice each midday to return home for a good luncheon and a
short doze afterward—he being of the firm opinion that both the
brisk walk and the nap benefited his constitution. He had working under him two competent journeymen to whom his establishment could safely be entrusted for a few hours, as well as two
apprentices, the elder of whom was also a solid hard worker, but
the younger of whom, quite perturbingly, was truly a most unpromising, sly, bone-idle lad who, if Mr. Quimby were any
judge—and he most assuredly was—was never going to have the
slightest chance of developing into even a remotely decent map
seller, much less a qualified cartographer.

It was, in fact, his employees who preoccupied Mr. Quimby's
mind this day as, at noon, as was his usual habit, he departed
from his shop to begin his stroll homeward along Oxford Street,
in the direction of Hyde Park and the Tyburn Turnpike, where
the dire old gallows-tree had used to stand decades ago, and a
few blocks before which he would reach his turnoff at Orchard
Street, which, at Portman Square, became Baker Street.

His senior journeyman desired now to leave him to become his own master and to set up an establishment of his own, and while Mr. Quimby did not fear competition and wished the younger man he had trained for so many years nothing but the best, the outcome was that he himself would be left shorthanded. Although his junior journeyman and senior apprentice were experienced and old enough that they could be promoted, respectively, to the resulting higher ranks, his junior apprentice was not only too young, but was also, as has already been noted, a sad case and therefore could not be accordingly advanced. Worse, although he had as yet no proof, Mr. Quimby suspected the wretched boy of stealing from him, despite the fact that he paid him a fair day's wages for a fair day's work, along with room and board. When Mr. Quimby had, out of both pity and a kind heart, and much against his better judgment, taken him on, the financial situation of the lad's family had been precarious at best, and now all his relatives appeared to have vanished—gone either to a workhouse, to Fleet or Marshalsea debtors' prisons, or to their graves. So Mr. Quimby was at a complete loss as to what to do with the boy, since it was not in his good nature simply to turn him out on the streets to fend for himself.

So long accustomed was Mr. Quimby to the route he walked daily, and so engrossed was he in his contemplation of the current situation at his shop, that he paid little heed to his surroundings. He was thus rudely startled from his reverie when he suddenly, accidentally and roughly bumped into a young passerby on the street. After tendering his profoundest apologies, Mr. Quimby, had he not been born and reared in London, would have thought no more of the matter. As it was, however, after a moment in which he had time to recollect both his wits and environs, his pale blue eyes behind his silver-rimmed spectacles abruptly narrowed shrewdly with suspicion, and instantly he fumbled among the pockets of his jacket, in search of his purse. It was gone! What had initially seemed naught but a chance encounter had actually been deliberately brought about by a pickpocket with the sole aim of robbing him!

"Stop, thief!" Mr. Quimby cried, outraged, wildly brandishing his brass-knobbed cane in the air, in the hope of attracting a constable's attention, before he himself determinedly started after his assailant. "Stop, thief!"

Before that fateful year of 1835, if his family had ever lived anywhere other than the old stone house at Whitrose Grange, Malcolm did not remember it. As far back as his own memories would go, there was only the Grange, which lay some distance beyond a quiet village nestled upon a country hillside, far away from the hustle and bustle of all the big cities of the land. For that year of 1835, London was still just a place that Malcolm had only heard about, and never yet seen—although, quite unbeknown to him, that was soon to change.

His family were of that betwixt-and-between class of people who are neither rich nor poor. So although the Grange was a leasehold, rather than a freehold, and Malcolm's family, being tenants, must therefore toil for their daily bread, they still lived comfortably enough that they could afford a handful of servants, as well as farm laborers, and although they dwelled for the most part in relative seclusion and obscurity—Whitrose Grange being somewhat isolated—they were nevertheless happy.

For sixteen years Malcolm's days passed one after another almost as though in a dream, his life like a pond with scarcely a ripple, much less a splash, to disturb its tranquillity. He studied and learnt, receiving an education as befitted a young man of his station, and when he was not at his lessons he worked alongside his father on the Grange, turning his hands to any number of tasks that needed doing and thus acquiring practical skills in addition to his academic knowledge. He had few friends, other than his parents and the servants and the farmhands, yet he seldom felt the lack, for he was one of those solitary youngsters who live in richly detailed imaginary worlds created inside their own minds, to which they are able at any given moment to escape for hours on end, losing themselves in countless adventures and fantasies.

Books, which were to prove a lifelong passion with Malcolm, also carried him to both fictional and actual places he had otherwise never envisioned or seen, and maps showed him where they were located in the grand scheme of both fanciful worlds and the one he knew was real. His toy soldiers, lined up on his land charts laid upon the floor of his bedchamber, marched out from towered strongholds that had only ever existed in fables, or else advanced over ancient, worldly hills and battlefields whose names and the dates associated with them he could recite from memory. His toy boats, floating upon the still, marshy pools and gurgling silver streams of the countryside he tramped and explored, sailed the seven seas like the Arabian Sinbad the Sailor. From scraps of silk, wood and twine, he constructed kites and flew them in night skies proliferate with constellations whose stories were the shining threads from which myths and legends were woven, and he knew both the names of the stars and all their wondrous tales by heart.

But that momentous year of 1835, Malcolm learnt what, afterward, he was to deem one of the greatest lessons of all: He discovered that, whether for good or for ill, the course of one's own life could in a heartbeat be forever changed by another human being—even a stranger.

The event that was to so alter Malcolm's own life's journey began with the arrival at Whitrose Grange of his uncle Charles and his family. Prior to their coming to the Grange, Malcolm had been only vaguely aware of their existence and had never before met any of them, despite the fact that Uncle Charles's wife, Katherine, was his father's younger sister. To have visitors at the Grange was a new experience, and at first Malcolm was ambivalent about the intrusion, at one instant thrilled and exhilarated by the air of bustle and excitement that pervaded the Grange, and at another, disturbed by and resentful of the total disruption of his previously placid days. Although he was not spoiled, still, he was accustomed to being the center of attention at the Grange and to the lives of his parents revolving around his. Now he realized they, too, had lives of their own, which stretched back in time, beyond the moment of his existence, and this both intrigued and nettled him. It did not seem right, somehow, that he should not always have been a part of their world, especially when Uncle Charles and Aunt Katherine had been.

However, as time wore on, Malcolm grasped another lesson—that no matter how much it gives away, the heart never runs out of love, and reassured of his parents' own for him, he eventually came gladly to widen the circle of his being to include the visitors at the Grange. Now, tonight, most all in the household having long retired for the evening, as he slept peacefully in his bedchamber Malcolm's dreams were peopled not only with those long near and dear to his heart, but also with the newcomers who had found a niche therein. But then, as he slumbered, a troubling element gradually insinuated itself into his dream, and somewhere in his subconscious he became aware of the niggling sound of muffled voices raised in anger. At first, still asleep, Malcolm believed that it was a part of the equanimous but disjointed dream that unfolded in his incognoscible thoughts, and, as dreamers inevitably do, watching himself as though he were somehow removed from his own body, he sought the source of the disturbance in the mists of his mind. But when it was not discovered, he little by little recognized that it lay somewhere beyond the confines of his dream and subliminal reality, and from those dark and unfathomed depths he suddenly ascended in a rush to a momentarily confused wakefulness.

What had woken him? he wondered dimly, in the darkness of his room illuminated only by the silvery moonlight that filtered in through the cracks of the wooden shutters at the windows.

Then he realized that it was the hushed sound of heated voices, which he had thought he had only dreamt. They were coming from below, in his father's study, which lay directly beneath Malcolm's bedchamber, and in which, following supper, his father and Uncle Charles had firmly closeted themselves, lingering over their port and never joining the rest of the two families in the sitting room.

Pushing back the bedclothes, Malcolm sat up anxiously in

bed, wondering what was amiss and straining his ears in an effort to eavesdrop upon his father and Uncle Charles's conversation. When he could make out nothing of what was being said,
however, he slipped from bed, taking care not to step upon floorboards he knew from experience creaked and groaned when trod
upon, and, shivering in his nightshirt in the chilly air—for the
fire in the stone hearth had died down to embers that smoldered
in the iron grate—he knelt and gingerly pressed his ear to the
floor. To his vexation, he still caught only muted snatches of the
dialogue, and at last he stealthily shifted to a place where there
was a small knothole in the floor and he could see through it into
his father's study below, although all in the room was dusky and
indistinct, the candles in the single lamp lit upon his father's desk
flickering and casting long, dancing shadows on the roughly
plastered white walls. Even so, from this bird's-eye vantage
point, Malcolm could spy his father, Uncle Charles and, much
to his surprise, a third— unfamiliar—man garbed in a black,
many-caped greatcoat and whose back was turned to him, so that
he could not discern the stranger's face. The three men stood in
close proximity together in the confines of the study, conducting a soft but clearly hostile discussion.

Long after most all in the household had gone to bed, the unknown man must have come like a furtive thief in the night to
Whitrose Grange, Malcolm speculated, and been admitted by either his father or Uncle Charles by means of the French doors
in the study. But who was the dark, cloaked stranger—and why
on earth was he here, especially at this late hour? Malcolm wondered uneasily. For from their watchful countenances and ready
stances, he correctly deduced that neither his father nor Uncle
Charles liked or trusted the third man.

Without warning, even as the worrisome thought occurred to
Malcolm, to his consummate shock and everlasting horror, the
stranger suddenly yanked a gleaming silver dagger from beneath his long greatcoat and plunged it into Uncle Charles's
chest, then, with a savage twist of the wrist, jerked the blade free.
For what seemed an interminable moment, Malcolm was so

stunned that he was incredulous and mistakenly believed that in the gloom of the room below he must not have seen properly what had actually happened. But then, his face abruptly ashen and grimacing with pain, Uncle Charles staggered back, groaning and clutching his breast tightly, a dark crimson liquid seeping between his fingers and spreading in a stain across his fine white cambric shirt.

"Oh, my God!" Malcolm gasped out—causing the cloaked man to glance around sharply, so that for an instant his dark visage was clearly illuminated in the wavering candlelight.

In the next moment Malcolm's father and the stranger were locked in mortal combat, and the lamp was knocked from its perch, its molten wax spewing and running in hot rivulets on the desk and the floor, its candles rolling from their sockets and scattering, igniting stacks of papers on the desktop and then, as the burning sheets were lifted and blown by the draft within the study, the long curtains hanging at the French doors. Heedless of the burgeoning fire, the two men battled on savagely, briefly riveting Malcolm to the brutal scene. But then, finally, he managed to collect his wits.

Viciously scraping his knees as he scrambled desperately to his feet, he flung open the door to his bedchamber and raced outside, shouting an alarm and pounding on the other bedroom doors along the corridor before sprinting pell-mell down the long hall toward the staircase that led to the ground floor. Behind him, he could hear the anxious cries of his mother and Aunt Katherine as they were roused from their beds and hurried out into the passage. But as he grasped the balustrade and swung around it to pelt down the stairs, the only clear thought in the unbridled turmoil of his mind was of reaching his father to try to help him however he could. But to Malcolm's eternal guilt and despair, the uncontrolled blaze had spread with a frightening swiftness, and the study, when he got there, was already an inferno, the flames crackling and leaping with a frenzy and thick black smoke billowing from the room, borne on the wings of the wind that swept inside through the now-open French doors to breathe even more life into the conflagration.

"No!" Malcolm cried in anguished protest—and would have dashed inside anyway, had his mother and Aunt Katherine not arrived on the scene and, together, forcibly dragged him back. "No, let me go! Let me go! You don't understand! Father and Uncle Charles are in there!"

But even as the two women, utterly stricken, heard these words, there was nothing to be done. With loud, furious snaps and pops, the wooden beams in the ceiling were breaking and plummeting to the floor; the plaster was cracking and falling from the stone walls; and as it greedily consumed this new fuel, the rampaging fire grew even hotter and wilder, tongues of yellow-orange flame licking from the study into the adjoining rooms and shooting up into the story above. From their own small bedchambers in the dormered attic the servants had come running, and now, while Aunt Katherine, sobbing, and some of the staff stumbled upstairs to save her two young children and whatever else they could salvage, the rest of the household rushed outside into the yard to form a bucket brigade from the old stone well.

How long they worked, Malcolm did not know. He knew only that his eyes and throat burnt from the acrid, suffocating clouds of smoke, that his eyebrows were singed and that even his face felt scorched from the heat of the blaze, that the muscles in his leaden arms ached in every fiber of their being and that his hands were chafed raw from the number of pails of water he had cast onto the flames, and that his nightshirt was gray and grimy with smeared soot and charred with tiny holes born of flying embers. Still, as though a man possessed, he labored on frantically, tears of anguish streaming down his cheeks as he worked—until at last his mother put her loving arms around him and just held him until he ceased to struggle and, instead, wept bitterly upon her shoulder. He felt sick and ashamed of his failure to rescue his father, or even to save their home, which, despite all his and the servants' valiant efforts, still burnt with a terrible, disheartening vengeance. They simply lacked both the necessary manpower and resources to extinguish the conflagration.

"Come away now, Malcolm, my dearest son," his mother insisted gently. "Your father…your father would be so very proud of you. You did your best. You did *more* than your best. But there's nothing more you can do now. There's nothing more that any of us can do."

"I should have saved him! I should have saved him and Uncle Charles!"

"You tried, Malcolm, and that's all that matters. The fire was an accident…a terrible, tragic accident—"

"No, 'twasn't! 'Twasn't! I saw what happened, and *'twasn't* an accident!"

"Hush, Malcolm! Hush! You're utterly exhausted and distraught with sorrow, and you don't know what you're saying!" His mother spoke sharply, and when he would have protested again, she deliberately pressed her hand over his mouth, giving him a small, imperceptible, warning shake of her head, her eyes anxious. "I said hush! Do you understand me? Now, come away. You'll make yourself ill standing in this chilly night air, in naught but your nightshirt. Aunt Katherine and some of the servants managed to save a few of our clothes and possessions. You need to get dressed, so you'll be warm. We'll have to spend the remainder of the night in the barn and decide in the morning what must be done."

Puzzled by his mother's strange behavior in silencing him, but too grief stricken and weary to the bone to try to question it now, Malcolm spoke no further, but numbly did as she had bidden him, following her to the old stone barn. In light of the still-burning house, it was the bitterest of ironies that because of the coldness inside the outbuilding, the two families and the staff were compelled to build a fire in the center of the floor. After that, they made beds out of heaps of the sweet-smelling hay within, covering it with blankets salvaged from the house, beneath which they huddled together for comfort and warmth. They said little among themselves, still shocked and disbelieving, and worn out from battling the blaze that had claimed the lives of two of their number and rendered the rest of them homeless.

Sleeping in fits and starts, they spent an uneasy, woebegone night in the barn and arose before dawn, still unrested and, now that their meager fire had died down to embers and ashes on the floor, cold and hungry, too. By this time, the flames that had ravaged the Grange so hotly and wildly the night before had finally been extinguished by the gray drizzle that had begun to fall earlier, leaving only a badly blackened stone shell smoldering in the grass where the house had once stood. The first task of the solemn little group was to investigate the study. Even though Malcolm knew that it was highly improbable, still, deep down inside, he dared to believe that perhaps his father had somehow managed to escape the previous evening, carrying Uncle Charles away with him. Unfortunately, however, it was soon discovered that the room was so badly burnt that there was no way to tell what had actually become of the two men, so that in the end, Malcolm was left to cling to his desperate hope, in an agony of doubt and despair about the fate of both his father and Uncle Charles. However joyous or grievous, it would have been far easier and kinder, he thought, to have known for certain one way or the other.

"Maybe Father and Uncle Charles *did* have enough time to get out," he remarked hesitantly to his mother, unsure, after her peculiar silencing of him the previous evening, how she would receive the suggestion.

"If so, they would certainly have made their escape known to us last night, Malcolm," she pointed out gently, "and not left us to believe they lost their lives in the fire."

"Perhaps they are lying injured or unconscious somewhere and cannot call for help, Mother. Ought we not to at least search the grounds for them, just in case...?"

"Aye, that much we *will* do, Son, to set our minds at rest."

So a diligent search was undertaken, but when no trace of the missing two men was found, it was presumed they had indeed perished in the blaze, and as a result, it was a sober, mournful assembly that gathered near the charred silhouette of the house to hear Malcolm's mother address them in the mizzle that continued to sprinkle from the leaden sky.

"The first thing we need to do now is find something to eat," she averred quietly. "After that, we must see if there is anything further than can be salvaged from the house."

Incredibly, once they started to sift through the smoking ruins that still steamed and hissed in the wet, they did discover that some odds and ends in the house itself and all the food stored in the cellar beneath it had been spared. Returning to the barn and stoking the fire, both for warmth against the chill of the misty morning air and for cooking, Malcolm and the others broke their fast on apples, walnuts and potatoes from the cellar, and eggs they had gathered from the chicken coop. While they ate, Malcolm's mother told the grave-faced servants that with their master dead and the house destroyed, they would be unable to continue on at the Grange, that she did not know what steps the owner would take when he learnt of his loss, but that even if he rebuilt the place, she could not manage it by herself, without her husband.

"You have all served us well, and for that and your many kindnesses to us over the years, I thank you," she stated simply, fighting back the tears that brimmed in her eyes. "I shall write each of you a testimonial so you will be able to find good positions in other households."

Several of the staff had been with Malcolm's family for years, and they, too, had tears in their own eyes at learning this sad news, although, in truth, they had expected no less.

"God bless ye, missus!" one of the servants said, her voice choked with emotion. "God bless ye an' t' young master!"

The others took up the cry, and Malcolm sat with a lump in his throat, visibly moved by the staff's affection and devotion, and at hearing himself referred to as the "young master," as well.

After breakfast, his mother directed him to harness their team of sturdy horses to the wagon, and once he had done so, what belongings and food that had been scavenged from the burnt house were loaded into the vehicle, along with wooden crates carrying the chickens from the coop. The family's two milk cows were tied behind, but the flock of sheep and goats must be left in the pasture, for Malcolm and his mother had no means of herding them to market.

"I shall write to Mr. Cameron, the owner of Whitrose Grange, informing him of what has occurred here and directing him to take possession of the flock, applying its worth to whatever may be owing on the remainder of the lease," his mother explained to Malcolm as he assisted first her and then Aunt Katherine and her children into the wagon.

Then, climbing up to sit beside his mother on the seat, he gathered up the long leather reins and clucked to the horses, and they started slowly down the long winding path that led away from the Grange. He glanced back once, lifting a hand to wave to the staff who still stood dolefully before the smoldering ruins of the house, whence they would later make their way on foot to the village. Then, determinedly, Malcolm turned his face forward and set the team on the road to the nearest town of any size, which lay to the north of Whitrose Grange. It was a journey of ten miles in the drizzle, so that by the time Malcolm and the others arrived, they were all soaked through and chilled to the bone, and longed to warm themselves before a fire. But still, his mother announced that they must go first to the marketplace, and once there, she sold the team and wagon, the two milk cows, the chickens and most all of the possessions and food that had survived the disastrous blaze at the Grange. After that, carrying what little now remained to them, Malcolm and the rest made their way on foot through the stalls that lined the marketplace. At a stand that dealt in secondhand clothes, his mother bought him and the others a change of garments, for they had lost most all of their own when the house had burnt, and at another booth she purchased two small traveling trunks that had seen better days, packing their belongings in them.

"Now we must find a hackney coach, Malcolm, to take us to an inn," she said.

One of these vehicles was duly located and its driver instructed to convey them to the nearest coaching inn. Presently they and their two trunks were set down in the yard of the Grouse

& Trout public house, where Malcolm's mother inquired within for lodgings. After paying in advance for the night, she and the rest were shown upstairs to a small but comfortable apartment and, there, able at last to warm themselves before the fire the chambermaid built in the hearth in the sitting room.

"Will you see that we are brought up some hot tea and luncheon, as well?" Malcolm's mother directed to the comely lass. "Some soup or stew and bread and cheese will serve us nicely."

"Aye, mum." The chambermaid bobbed a small curtsy, then exited from the room.

A short while later, she returned with a second chambermaid, both of them bearing wooden trays laden with the tea and meal that Malcolm's mother had ordered. Once the two girls had gone, he and the others fell ravenously upon the food, while his mother poured the tea into the cups and handed them around. When, finally, the luncheon was eaten and their appetites were sated, Aunt Katherine's children fell asleep curled up on the braided rug before the fire, worn out by the previous evening's and the day's events. It was then that Malcolm's mother turned to him.

"Son," she began, setting her empty teacup on a nearby table, "because of the presence of the servants and also for other reasons of which you are not yet aware, I could not previously let you tell me your story about what you saw in your father's study last night. However, now that we are alone, your aunt Katherine and I would like very much to hear it."

So, startled by his mother's explanation, but nevertheless glad of the chance to relate what he had seen, Malcolm told the two women about the dark, mysterious, cloaked stranger who had come to the Grange, how he had argued with his father and Uncle Charles, stabbing the latter.

"Then the stranger and Father fought, and during their struggle they accidentally knocked the lamp off Father's desk. That's how the fire started."

"I see." His mother's brow was knitted in a thoughtful, anxious frown.

"What do you think, Elizabeth?" Aunt Katherine queried worriedly. "Do you truly believe that both Charles and Alexander are dead? That one of our enemies has killed them?"

"What enemies?" Malcolm asked sharply. "Mother? What is Aunt Katherine talking about? What enemies? Who would want to murder Father and Uncle Charles?"

"That is a very long tale, Son," his mother declared soberly, after a long moment in which he had thought she was not going to answer him. "Someday I will tell it to you. But right now your aunt Katherine and I need to determine what is best to do, what course of action we must take in light of all this information. After what you said last night, I feared that it was something like this that had befallen your father and your uncle Charles. Further, if our adversaries have learnt that we ourselves did not also perish in the fire at the Grange, as was undoubtedly intended— for the cloaked stranger you saw could not know that you were watching what happened in the study and thus awake to sound an alarm and rouse the household—then we won't be safe, either. 'Tis a good thing I thought to use my maiden name here, but even that may not protect us."

Malcolm was stunned by her revelations.

"But...but why would anyone want to kill us?"

"Because they believe that as long as we live, we are a threat to them, that's why—and that's all you need know at the moment," his mother reiterated. "So please don't ask me again, Malcolm. Now, be a good lad and run downstairs to the tavern. Inquire of the innkeeper when the next coach leaves and where it goes, for we dare not linger here, so close to the Grange. Find out how much the fare is, also—for inside the coach, mind. We shall not wish to sit up top."

His brain in a chaotic whirl of curiosity and apprehension, Malcolm did as she had bidden him. Until last night, his family had been simple tenants at the Grange, and in his blissful ignorance, as far as he himself had been aware, they had not had an enemy in the world. Now it appeared that they had several! Shadowy, faceless, unknown adversaries who had already murdered his father and Uncle Charles, and who would kill him and his mother, and his aunt Katherine and her two young children, too, if they could. Malcolm was shocked, horrified and incredulous. How could he and his family be a threat to anyone? he wondered. He did not know, but he determined that one way or another, he would find out and avenge his father's and Uncle Charles's murders!

After speaking with the innkeeper, he went back upstairs to report what he had learnt to his mother, who then took several pound notes from her reticule and handed them to him, instructing him to return to the public house below and to purchase the necessary coach tickets for all of them. It occurred to Malcolm that she was perhaps keeping him out of the way so that she could converse with Aunt Katherine alone. Such was his pride in the responsibilities she was entrusting to him, however, that he could not be wholly upset at not being privy to their dialogue. Still, he wondered what thoughts and secrets the two women were exchanging that did not include him.

This time, when Malcolm got back to the apartment upstairs, it was to discover his mother seated before the desk in the sitting room, composing a letter, Aunt Katherine having retired for a nap to the adjoining bedchamber, to which she had also carried her younger child, although the older still slept upon the braided rug before the hearth

"Who are you writing to, Mother?" Malcolm asked, giving her the coach tickets.

"My London solicitor, Mr. Nigel Gilchrist."

"I didn't know you had an attorney in London."

"There is a great deal you don't yet know, Son. But sit down, and I will tell you a few things now. As you are aware, your aunt Katherine and I have been talking, and after much discussion, we have finally decided upon our next steps. She and her children will accompany us on our journey as far south as Newcastle-upon-Tyne, whence they will make their own way home, whilst you and I continue on to London. You probably don't remember my parents—your grandparents—because they died when you were still a child. But they loved both you and me very much, and they wished us to be provided for in the event that anything untoward should ever happen to your father. They lived prudently and so were able to put aside some money every year, which they invested wisely and with which proceeds they established a trust fund for me. 'Tis not large, but 'tis enough to keep us comfortably if we, too, are careful with our income, particularly since my parents also willed me a piece of property, a small cottage in St. John's Wood, which is an outlying district northwest of London. I have informed Mr. Gilchrist—who has advised me on business matters in the past—that I earnestly desire to take possession of Hawthorn Cottage, as the place is called, at once, and I have instructed him to notify the tenants that they must therefore seek other lodgings. You will need to take this downstairs and post it for me."

Pausing, Malcolm's mother signed her name to the missive, then lightly sanded the ink to dry it. After dusting away the sand and folding the note, she sealed it and handed it to him, along with a groat, the cost of posting a single letter to London being exactly four pence. Then she continued.

"I have imparted all this to you, Son, so you will not worry about what is to become of us now that…now that—" Her voice broke, choked with emotion, and her eyes filled with sudden tears. One delicate hand flew to her tremulous mouth, and she was silent for a long moment before she determinedly mastered herself. "Now that your father is no longer with us."

"He may still be alive, Mother," Malcolm pointed out quietly, resolutely blinking back his own hot tears.

"I cannot think he is—nor your uncle Charles, either. For surely they would have let us know they were still alive, and we have heard nothing, neither last night nor this morning. And had they managed to escape but been hurt and unable to call for help, we would almost certainly have found them during our search of the grounds. No, we cannot allow ourselves to believe they are still alive, Son. 'Twould be too cruel to hope, only to learn that they did indeed lose their lives in the fire. We must try to be brave and to go on without them, as they would have wished."

Although Malcolm could perceive the wisdom of his mother's words, still, he inwardly chafed against it, not wanting to think that his father was truly dead and gone, that he would never see him again. Taking the letter for Mr. Gilchrist, Malcolm went downstairs to post it, his mind still in a tumult that did not leave him even after his supper had been long eaten and he had awkwardly settled himself on the sofa in the sitting room for the night. From beyond the closed door of the adjoining bedchamber, he could hear the low sounds of his mother and Aunt Katherine talking and of one or perhaps both of them weeping. But such was his own inner turmoil and grief that he had no solace to offer either of them. Eventually he slept, but like that of the previous evening, it was an uneasy slumber, and he awoke before dawn, his muscles cramped and aching from his having bedded down on the couch, although he thought that Aunt Katherine's oldest child, who had made do with a chair and footstool, and who was still asleep, must be even more uncomfortable.

Stiffly rising from where he lay, Malcolm first stoked the fire in the grate to take the chill from the room. Then he washed himself with the frigid water in the porcelain basin his mother had prepared for him before retiring last night. Once he had dressed, he sat staring out the windows overlooking the town, which was gloomy and gray in the morning mist, until his mother and the others were ready to depart from the Grouse & Trout inn. Their meager belongings were quickly packed in their two small trunks, except for his father's engraved silver strongbox, which Aunt Katherine had saved from his parents' bedchamber the night of the fire and in which his mother had, last evening, locked away most of what money she now had remaining from the sale of their wagon and animals. Breakfast was eaten below in the main room of the tavern, after which Malcolm and the rest boarded the first of a series of coaches that would carry them to their destinations.

Traveling by public coach was a new experience for Malcolm, so that were he not still beset by emotional upset, not only over the loss of his father and the burning of the only home he had ever known, but also at watching all that was dear and familiar to him seem to evanesce into the morning mist with each passing mile, he would have been filled with excitement and awe. But his inner conflict proved such that, instead, when he did not doze fitfully in his seat, he saw most of the sights along the way through eyes blurred with unshed tears, which he fought determinedly to hold at bay so as not to distress his mother and Aunt Katherine, for he could tell that despite their brave front, they, too, were woeful and frightened by the journey they had undertaken without either his father or Uncle Charles to protect them. It occurred to Malcolm then that he was now the man of the house, and that this was why, despite all her decision making, his mother had instinctively entrusted him to make the inquiries regarding their travel arrangements and to purchase their coach tickets. At the realization, he sat up a little straighter in his seat. His family had enemies. He might not know who they were yet, but even so, it was now his responsibility to guard against them and to protect his mother and Aunt Katherine and her children.

Of them all, only the younger of these two last—still too little to fully comprehend all that had befallen them—appeared unaffected by grief, fretful and whining instead until Aunt Katherine finally produced a handful of the apples and walnuts taken from the cellar at the Grange and a sack of which she had prudently brought with her in case the children should grow hungry during the long trip. Munching the walnuts, the younger child soon quieted like the older, who had gazed morosely out the coach windows all day, saying little.

Eventually, after changing coaches en route at the White Hart inn, Malcolm and the others reached Newcastle-upon-Tyne, where he and his mother underwent a wrenching, tearful parting from Aunt Katherine and her children, leaving the three of them standing forlornly in the yard of the George public house to make their own way home. Alone, then, Malcolm and his mother continued their journey along the Great North Road to London. When the coach in which they traveled stopped again at a wayside inn to change horses and, this time, to allow its passengers to dine, as well, she told him over their supper that she felt that it would be in their best interests for the two of them to assume a different surname once they reached their destination.

"But…why, Mother?" Malcolm queried, disturbed by her suggestion as he hungrily ate his bowlful of thick, hearty stew and generous crusty slice of brown bread and butter. "Surely, so far from home, 'twill not matter what we call ourselves, will it? For how would our enemies ever be able to trace us to London— and even if they somehow managed to do so, how would they ever find us there, in such a big city?"

"I don't know. But I *do* know that we must never make the mistake of underestimating them, Son," his mother insisted, her pale face solemn and anxious, her eyes watchful and distrusting as she glanced around the main room of the public house. "Your father…your father and your uncle Charles were perhaps too bold and daring, and inadvertently showed their hand…. No, please don't ask me any questions, Malcolm, for now is neither the time nor the place to discuss this matter further. Our adversaries are long established, so they could have eyes and ears anywhere. You must always remember that. For the moment, 'tis enough that you understand the very grave dangers we face. Now, what shall we call ourselves, I wonder?"

The elaborately carved and painted sign that swung outside above the door of the old tavern at which they had halted proclaimed the place as the Blackfriars inn.

That was how he became Malcolm Blackfriars.

Resuming its journey, their coach reached the sprawling city of London at last, where he was initially overwhelmed and even a little frightened by the sights and sounds and smells that crowded in upon his senses. All his life, Malcolm had been accustomed to the quiet green solitude of the countryside, and there was precious little of that to be found here—although he did discover at least one such oasis once he and his mother were comfortably if still despondently installed in their new home, Hawthorn Cottage, on Cochrane Street in St. John's Wood, which was a relatively remote and secluded district of London's northwest suburbs, and lay at the southwestern foot of Primrose Hill and on the edge of the vast Regent's Park.

St. John's Wood had once belonged to William the Conqueror, but had eventually been bestowed upon the Knights of St. John of Jerusalem, whence its name had derived. Following the Reformation, however, it had changed hands several times before finally being divided into two principal estates, one of which was the Eyre Estate, which had been bought in 1732 by Sir Henry Samuel Eyre from the Earl of Chesterfield. During the Middle Ages a large forest had stood upon the land, but this had been cut down during the Commonwealth to make way for market gardens. Later, the Regent Canal had been extended into St. John's Wood, cutting a swath around the western boundary of Regent's Park and through the center of the suburb. But despite this, St. John's Wood still retained its original atmosphere of country tranquillity, and as a result, it was a haven for artists, authors, philosophers and scientists—although several of its richer, grander villas, Malcolm soon gleaned from local gossip, belonged to the mistresses and their illegitimate children of aristocratic lords. There was also a small Jewish section farther north.

Although Malcolm still grieved sorely for his father and missed Whitrose Grange immensely, he was glad that Hawthorn Cottage was situated in St. John's Wood and not one of the more densely populated outlying districts that formed the suburbs of London, for several of these, he quickly learnt, were filthy, labyrinthine slums that housed not only the poor and downtrodden, but also criminals of all sorts, from light-fingered cutpurses to ruthless cutthroats. Not that St. John's Wood did not have its own share of paupers and thieves, but at least these did not constitute the bulk of its populace.

Hawthorn Cottage was not nearly as large as Whitrose Grange had been. But still, it was a pleasant enough place, Malcolm thought, set on its own modest, rectangular plot of land and thus boasting unassuming but nevertheless attractive front and back gardens. In these grew not only the small, spreading hawthorn trees that had given the cottage its picturesque name, but also flowering crab apples and dogwoods, tall elms and rowans, and graceful hazels and willows. Shrubs of bell heather and bramble, of deadly nightshade and field rose, and of petty whin and tutsan crowded beneath the old trees, while a profusion of flowers in a multitude of colors filled the air with their heady perfumes. Cat's-ear, creeping thistle and goatsbeard burgeoned alongside heath grass, lady fern and pennyroyal. A dozen varieties of buttercups and pimpernels soughed in the breeze, and honeysuckle and ivy trailed over the tiny lawn and crept up the brick-and-stucco walls of the cottage, emphasizing its quaintness and charm. An abundance of sweet clovers and flavorous mint added their own fragrant scents to all the rest.

At the rear of the back garden, in one corner, stood a tall statue of an ancient maiden pouring water into a small pond at her feet. Here, as the weeks passed, Malcolm whiled away many a long hour, daydreaming and dwelling on the new course his life had taken—and feeling keenly in contrast the loss of his old life, as well as wondering to what dark secrets his mother was privy that she would not yet share with him, despite how he continued now and then to question her. For since he had learnt of them, the thought of his family's unknown foes was never far from his mind.

Now, as he trailed in his mother's wake along Edgware Road, Malcolm resolved that once they returned home from the market, he would ask her anew about all she still concealed from him. Until then, he would do his best to enjoy the day, he told himself firmly, although this would not prove as difficult as one might imagine, since the everyday hustle and bustle of Edgware Road was still a new and exciting experience for him, as was shopping with his mother.

Although, upon reaching London, Mrs. Blackfriars had hired both a cook and a housemaid, she preferred to do the marketing herself to be certain she was not cheated by either servant or merchant, for she watched their finances carefully to ensure that she and Malcolm would not wind up destitute.

"We have only the income from the trust my parents established for me to live on now," she had reminded him, when, curious, he had asked her why she did not leave the marketing to the cook, "and although Hawthorn Cottage is a freehold, there are still the taxes to pay on it and the staff's wages, too. Whilst we are not poor, Malcolm, neither are we wealthy. So we must take care to mind our shillings so we don't wind up like so many of these pitiful creatures in London, who are but one step away from a workhouse or worse—for you've no idea how terrifyingly easy 'tis to slide from modest means to penury, to find yourself homeless and cast out on the streets. If not for my trust fund, I don't know what would have become of us after the fire at the Grange and your father's death, and that is the truth."

"We would have managed somehow, Mother," Malcolm had reassured her. "Even now, I could get a job to help out. After all, I worked at the Grange."

But she had only shaken her head and smiled gently, observing that he was very young yet and still had much to learn about the world.

"That was different," she had said. "Your father was the Grange's leaseholder."

"Well, as you've told me yourself, Father is dead, and the Grange has burnt down, so both of them are lost to us forever. So what am I to do with myself now? I can't just go on idling away my time in the gardens. I'm sixteen years old and must begin to learn a trade of some kind, Mother, if I'm to have any kind of a decent future," he had pointed out astutely, and although, in the end, his mother had reluctantly been compelled to admit the truth of this, she had declared that, even so, she did not know how to go about binding him as an apprentice.

"I know—you could write to Mr. Gilchrist and inquire," Malcolm had cleverly suggested.

At that, his mother had sighed heavily.

"The truth is, Son, that I really don't think I could bear to lose you right now, on top of your father," she had told him quietly, so that he had suddenly felt ashamed of himself for not considering this aspect of the matter. "I know that you're right, and that sooner or later, you must make your own way in the world. But you've a few years yet before that happens. Still, I will at least think about writing to Mr. Gilchrist, and then we'll see. It may be that I can afford to hire a tutor for you until we can determine a course of action."

So, although he had clearly upset her and received no satisfactory answer from her about his future, besides, Malcolm resolutely refused to be annoyed or downcast by the memory, for as though to make up for their disagreement, his mother had promised him that, today, before doing their marketing, they would explore some of the area beyond St. John's Wood. To avoid becoming lost or taken advantage of by hackney coaches and hansom cabs, they had upon their arrival in London bought a map from a shop on Oxford Street, and today, after consulting this, they had decided that they would walk down Edgware Road as far as the Tyburn Turnpike near the northeast corner of Hyde Park and the Cumberland Gate, thence down Oxford Street as far as Regent Street, returning to St. John's Wood by means of Park Road, which wound around the southwestern edge of Regent's Park.

Now, as they strolled along, Malcolm eagerly drank in the sights—the tall old brick buildings several stories high, topped by a profusion of chimney pots spewing smoke skyward, so that a thick dark cloud hung over the city, with the air smelling of coal and soot streaking the walls of the edifices; the ornate street lamps, the older ones of which burnt oil and were gradually being replaced by newer ones, which burnt gas; the crowds of people who thronged the sidewalks and the multitude of horses and vehicles that clattered over the unpaved roads and cobblestone streets. Everywhere he looked, there was something new and exciting to see. When they reached the Tyburn Turnpike, he and his mother paused for a moment to watch the tollgate keeper collecting his due from the passing coaches and wagons that rumbled through the wooden gate, which opened into north London, south of Islington, and the Great North Road. Here Edgware Road ended, and he and his mother walked on down Oxford Street, past the northeast corner of Hyde Park, where Malcolm could see a man speaking to a small group who had gathered there. Continuing along, he and his mother passed the Portman Barracks and Orchard Street, and were just approaching Duke Street when suddenly Malcolm heard a hoarse cry of "Stop, thief! Stop, thief!" and he spied a tattered young lad running pell-mell toward him down Oxford Street, followed at a much slower pace by a well-dressed, gray-haired, somewhat portly gentleman wearing a pair of silver-rimmed spectacles and wildly waving a brass-knobbed walking stick.

"Stop, thief!" the gentleman giving chase shouted again.

A robbery had occurred, Malcolm realized. From the distance, he heard the loud shrieks of policemen's whistles being blown, and he saw two constables hurrying to the scene. But it was clear to him that neither these nor the miscreant's pursuer were going to prove able to catch him. Without pausing to consider the consequences of his actions, Malcolm pelted after the fleeing boy, blithely ignoring his mother's abrupt cries of dismay behind him and her calling him to come back at once. The sidewalk was hard beneath his booted feet as he sprinted on heedlessly, dodging passersby. Ahead, he could see that the scruffy imp had now dashed up Duke Street toward Manchester Square, and he himself did likewise, darting into the clogged street and perilously weaving his way between all the horses and vehicles whose drivers yelled at him and cursed him mightily. With each passing step, he gained on the thieving lad, who was not nearly as fast as he was, and his face flushed with satisfaction at the recognition, his entire body filled with exhilaration at the chase, so that he nearly laughed aloud as he ran on.

"Got you!" Malcolm crowed triumphantly as he flung himself at last onto the young rascal, knocking him to the ground.

As the unkempt boy attempted to squirm away, a determined scuffle ensued, which was ended only when both policemen and, a few moments later, limping slightly and gasping for breath, the well-dressed gentleman who had been robbed finally arrived at the square. Knowing their duty, the constables immediately set about forcibly hauling the two combatants apart, each policeman firmly securing his victim by the collar and giving him a rough shake to hold him still.

"Now, sir—" one of the constables addressed the gray-haired man respectfully "—p'rhaps you'll be good enough t' tell us exactly what these two disreputable young tatterdemalions did an' why you was chasin' after 'em so."

"Oh, no, 'twas only the one boy there whom I was trying to catch, Officer." With his cane, the gentleman pointed at the raggedy knave who had stolen his wallet. "He picked my pocket just as bold as brass."

"Why, you thievin' li'l urchin!" the policeman growled, fumbling through the lad's poorly patched jacket and pulling forth the pilfered purse, which he shook victoriously in the boy's face. "Caught you bloody red-'anded, didn't I? Now, what do you 'ave t' say for yourself, you scrawny, light-fingered clapperdudgeon?"

"Nowt!" the lad spat sullenly, trying but failing to wriggle free of the beefy constable's tight grasp. "'Cept I ain't goin' in for a vamp alone—for 'twere not me own game t' pluck t' fat goose what were t' plant, guv'nor, I swear! Gor, 'twere Badger who tole me that 'im were a real swell what could stand t' lose a bit o' blunt—an' allowed as 'ow I could cotch 'im at noon on Oxford Street an' pick 'im clean! We was goin' t' split t' rum quids fair an' square."

"'Ere now, mind you keep a civil tongue in your 'ead, you filthy clip-nit, an' don't gimme no flapdoodle, neither—or 'twill go all t' worse for you down at t' station 'ouse! An' just who might this Badger be?" the policeman queried.

"Why, 'tis one of my very own apprentices, by heaven!" the victimized gentleman cried indignantly. "His true name is Dick

Badgerton, and he's a bone-idle scamp whom I have for some time suspected of stealing from my shop!"

"Well, then, we'll 'ave 'im up on charges, too," the constable announced sternly, "as this dirty diver's accomplice. Now, sir, what about this 'ere other canary-bird? What's 'e done?"

"Done? Why, nothing, Officer, except to chase down the pickpocket and apprehend him, when he would otherwise have surely got away, absconding with my wallet in the process! No, that other boy is not to be arrested, Officer, for if not for him, I would have been several pounds the lighter today," the gentleman declared firmly. "He's to be set free, and I myself will reward him for his bravery and quick wits! What's your name, lad?"

"Malcolm. Malcolm...Blackfriars."

"Well, young Master Blackfriars, if I am any judge of character—and I pride myself that I am, although my kindness and good nature unfortunately sometimes get the better of me, so I wind up sadly deceived—you've the look of an honest, enterprising and hardworking boy about you. So I'm most grateful both to make your acquaintance and for your courageous action in running after the thief."

By this time, Malcolm's mother had at last appeared in Manchester Square, her lovely face filled with anxiety and trepidation as her eyes took in the sight of her disheveled son, his black hair tousled, his jacket now grimy and torn, his nose bloody and he himself still in the fierce grip of the policeman who had seized hold of him.

"Oh, Son, what has happened? What have you done?" she asked, distressed.

"Naught that need cause you any worry whatsoever, madam, I do most heartily assure you," the gentleman explained, turning to her and, taking her measure, politely doffing his stovepipe hat and favoring her with a bow. "Please permit me to introduce myself. I am Septimus Quimby, a cartographer and map seller by trade." Reaching into his jacket, he drew forth his calling card and handed it to her. "Do I have the pleasure of addressing young Master Blackfriars's mother—or perhaps even his sister? For, indeed, madam, I can scarcely believe you are old enough to have a lad of his age."

Mrs. Blackfriars blushed shyly and nervously.

"You flatter me with your compliments, but are far too kind, sir, I fear," she replied after glancing at his card. "Yes, I am Mrs. Blackfriars, Malcolm's mother. Oh, I do hope he is not in any trouble!"

"No, not at all, madam," Mr. Quimby earnestly reassured her. "For contrary to all current appearances, he is not to be charged and was, in fact, on the brink of being released when you arrived on the scene—for he has most fortuitously for me succeeded in nabbing that young pickpocket there, who only moments ago slyly relieved me of my purse."

At this point, the constable who had thus far conducted the interview interrupted, stating that they must all proceed posthaste to Mr. Quimby's establishment, there to take the unpromising apprentice Dick "Badger" Badgerton into custody before he suspected that the plan he had so artfully and ungratefully hatched with his accomplice against his employer had gone afoul, and he ran away to escape from the justice that was most assuredly due him. With Malcolm now at liberty, but the other boy, Tobias "Toby" Snitch by name, still securely restrained and being roughly dragged along by the policeman who gripped him, the little group made their way amid the stares of onlookers back down Duke Street to Oxford Street, and thence to Mr. Quimby's shop at No. 7B. There, Dick "Badger" Badgerton was duly arrested, after which both he and Toby Snitch were summarily led away by the constables to be installed in cells at the station house until the following morning, when they would be called before the bar to have their case heard by one of the local magistrates. Malcolm, his mother and Mr. Quimby were all to be witnesses.

"Well, this is a most regrettable turn of events!" The latter sighed heavily as, through the front window of his shop, he watched his apprentice and his accomplice frog-marched away. "Not only have I yet to enjoy any luncheon, but I've also lost one of my apprentices and shall now be left even more shorthanded than I was to be before—for one of my journeymen is presently departing to open up his own establishment." Turning to address his sole remaining apprentice, Mr. Quimby directed, "Harry, be a good lad, and run up to my lodgings on Baker Street. Inform Mrs. Merritt of what has happened and that I shall not, after all, be returning home for luncheon today." Then, to Mrs. Blackfriars, he said, "Madam, although I am inordinately grateful to your son, I fear that the effect of his action has been to involve you in this unfortunate affair. If you've no other pressing business, please allow me to make amends by having the honor of escorting both you and your son to luncheon at Verrey's. I assure you that 'tis a perfectly respectable café just around the corner, at Regent and Hanover Streets, so you need not hesitate to accompany me there."

"Oh, please, Mother," Malcolm coaxed, when it seemed to him as though she would refuse the invitation. "I remember Mr. Quimby's shop! This is where we bought our map of London when we first came here, so there must be a great deal that he can tell us about it and the city."

"I intend no offense, sir, but although I thank you very kindly for your generous offer, I'm afraid I'm not in the habit of accepting invitations from strangers," Mrs. Blackfriars stated at last to Mr. Quimby, although not impolitely.

"No, nor did I presume you were, madam," he responded calmly, unaffronted. "However, I thought that perhaps under the circumstances, you might make an exception, and I was further emboldened, I must confess, by an idea that has occurred to me with regard to your son. How old are you, young Master Blackfriars?"

"Sixteen."

"Hmm…well, that is two years older than the usual apprentice. Nevertheless, my situation is such that I am now in dire need of two likely lads to assist me here in my establishment—and you certainly appear to fit the bill. If your good mother can be persuaded to agree, would you be interested in one of the positions?"

"Aye, sir, I would." Malcolm spoke quickly, before Mrs. Blackfriars could protest.

In the end, recalling her son's fascination with books and maps, as well as his desire to begin to carve out some kind of a decent future for himself rather than idling away his time in the gardens at Hawthorn Cottage, and impressed by both Mr. Quimby's manner and his shop, Mrs. Blackfriars consented to permit herself and Malcolm to be escorted to luncheon at Verrey's café, there to discuss the particulars of her son's apprenticeship. Over a steaming bowl of carrot soup, a nicely done roast chicken flavored with rosemary and served with rice and mushrooms, and a pot of tea, it was eventually arranged that Malcolm would begin work on Monday, for a period of seven years and starting at what seemed to him a princely weekly wage, for it was higher than usual, his mother being quite desirous that he should continue to reside with her at Hawthorn Cottage, and Mr. Quimby, agreeing, thus not being required to provide him with room and board. As Malcolm's reward for capturing the pickpocket, Mr. Quimby also waived the master's fee he would normally have received for taking Malcolm on as an apprentice.

When, finally, both their delectable luncheon and their friendly business were satisfactorily concluded, the three of them departed from Verrey's café, each feeling that, despite its seemingly inauspicious beginning, the day had turned out very fine, after all.

Chapter Three

Monsters in the Dark

El sueño de la razón produce monstruos.
(The sleep of reason produces monsters.)
—Francisco José de Goya y Lucientes
Los Caprichos [1799], Plate 43

The healthy stomach is nothing if not conservative.
Few radicals have good digestions.

—Samuel Butler
Notebooks
Selected and edited by H. Festing Jones [1912]

For secrets are edged tools,
And must be kept from children and from fools.

—John Dryden
Sir Martin Mar-all

1848
The Hôtel de Lévesque, Paris, France

*N*urse *was asleep at her post again. She frequently was. Really, she was much too old and deaf to be a proper nurse anymore— or so Ariana had gleaned from snatches of conversation she had overheard between Cook and Tessie, the scullery maid, in the warm, cozy kitchen of the large old farmhouse that lay beyond the village. But since Nurse had been with the family for many long years now, no one considered pensioning her off. Still, that was just as well, Ariana thought now, smiling with secret satis-*

*faction to herself, since if Nurse had been the kind to stay awake
and vigilant at her post, then Ariana could not now have slipped
quickly and furtively from the nursery into the cold, adjoining
schoolroom, illuminated only by the pale gray sunlight that filtered dimly through the cracks of the wooden shutters covering
the windows.*

Only moments ago she had heard the back door leading from
the kitchen to the vegetable and herb gardens beyond bang shut.
Now, after dragging a wooden stool on which to stand over to
the windows, Ariana unlatched one pair of shutters and drew
them back, then pushed open one of the casements a crack.

"Where you going, Collie?" she called out to the young man
she spied below.

"Fishing. I'd hardly be carrying my rod now otherwise,
would I?"

"Can I come?"

"I thought you were supposed to be taking a nap, Ana."

"I'm not sleepy—and 'sides, I'm five years old now, far too
old for naps, anyway," Ariana insisted primly. "I wanna come
with you. I'm tired of being cooped up inside this place all the
day long!"

"Where is Nurse? What does she say to all this?"

"Naught—for she's away with the faeries, as usual."

"All right, then," Collie replied after a long moment. "I guess
there's no real harm in your tagging along with me. But mind,
Ana, you're not to chatter away like a magpie if you do, for I'll
catch no fish that way, with such a noise as that going on above
the water, will I? Fetch your hat, cloak and gloves, and come
down. I'll wait for you at the far gate."

Ariana did not linger to hear any more, but pulled shut the
window, climbed down from the stool and scampered away to
her bedchamber, filled with excitement. Tugging on her hat, coat
and gloves, she crept down the back stairs to the kitchen, where
she waited breathlessly until Cook and Tessie had their backs
turned to her before she scuttled covertly out the back door.
Once outside in the gardens, she hurried across the yard and

down the narrow winding pebble path to the far gate. There, Ariana saw that Collie had kept his word and was indeed waiting for her.

"I certainly hope you know I don't intend to make a habit of this, Ana," he said by way of greeting her, although not unkindly, as he straightened up from the iron gate, against which he had been leaning. "For I'll have you know I've got much better things to do with my time than play nursemaid to you."

"Aye, I know. But I shan't be any twouble to you, Collie. Really, I shan't. You'll see. I'll be as good as gold, I pwomise."

"Bite your tongue, lass, and don't be making promises that you cannot keep," he chided, tsking at her. "You're a changeling child and as mischievous as the faery folk. Haven't you just now sneaked away from poor old Nurse and the farmhouse, with nary a word to anybody?"

"Aye," Ariana confessed, shamefaced.

"'Tis a good thing, then, is it not, that I saw to fit to make it known that you were going to accompany me fishing. Otherwise, once it was discovered that you were missing, there would have been such a hue and cry raised as scarcely to be believed, and half the countryside would have been out searching for you."

"I—I didn't think 'bout that."

"Nay, I don't suppose you did. But perhaps now, next time, you will consider the feelings of others and not just your own," Collie asserted quietly. "But, there, I shan't be too hard on you, Ana, for you're very young yet and still have much to learn. And I don't imagine 'tis much fun for you, either, being stuck here at the farmhouse, in the middle of nowhere. You're a lively lass, with a bright, inquiring mind, and you get bored out here, I expect. So pick up that bait bucket and come along now, then. I want to get back home before dark."

Elated at being allowed to accompany the young man, Ariana did as she had been instructed, gaily swinging the tin pail at her side as she and Collie made their way through the woods, down the tumbling hillside to the shore of the great ancient lake below. As it did so often in the Highlands, a fine silvery "Scotch mist"—which, despite its name, was not quite mist, yet not quite a drizzle, either—hung over the land, so that the autumn forest was damp and chilly, smelling of rich dark earth and of fertile decay. Here and there, wisps of gossamer white brume that never completely disappeared from the Highlands drifted like plaintive wraiths amid the trees. Birds perched in the branches aflame with autumn called sweetly to one another and sang a harmonious tune; red deer and wild goats leapt and gamboled through the thickets. Bushy-tailed red squirrels on the ground, busy gathering nuts and rowanberries in preparation for the coming winter, chittered and skittered through the underbrush; and once, Ariana spied a fox stealthily disappearing into its hidey-hole.

Above, only a pale, sickly sun shone in the late-afternoon sky and made little headway in dissipating the swirling mass of thick gray clouds that more than once occluded it, so that its rays barely penetrated the gloom of the woods.

Ariana was glad of Collie at her side, for despite her fascination with the animals, she would not have liked to be alone in the long-shadowed forest just now, and as he was several years older than she was, he was much bigger and stronger. He himself seemed unperturbed by the duskiness of the woods, and his protective presence gave her comfort.

Despite the fact that she would have liked to spend more time with him, she saw him so seldom that now that she was alone with him, she was eager to learn more about him. But even as her burning curiosity prompted her to speak, Ariana remembered her promise not to blather and, although it was with difficulty, held her tongue. She feared that if she insisted on talking with him, Collie would perhaps change his mind about taking her fishing with him, sending her back to the old farmhouse instead. That would never do, for it would mean the end of her afternoon adventure and a most unwelcome return to the nursery.

So Ariana tramped on in silence, swinging the bait bucket and, with a short stick she had picked up along the way, poking now and then at the deep layers of wet leaves in shades of gold and scarlet that had fallen from the trees to patch the loam. She had thought she would soon grow cold in the chilly moist autumn air. But the pace Collie set, while not too hard for her, still compelled her nearly to skip to keep up with him, so that, instead, she felt heated in her hat, cloak and gloves, and wished she could dispense with them. But when she dared to mention this to Collie, he forbade it, saying sternly that she would catch a chill in the cold and damp, and that he would not be held responsible for that.

Presently the two of them broke free of the forest to emerge onto the bare grassy sweep of the rocky hillside before it flattened into the shingled shore below. Beyond this, the lake—Loch Ness, by name—uncoiled before them like some gargantuan serpent twining its way through the Great Glen, a seemingly endless fissure formed by the cliffs, hills and mountains that hove up on either side to imprison the water and to cut the Highlands in half.

In the past, Ariana had seen the lake only from a distance, from the road above, which ran alongside it. But now, as she and Collie traversed the hillside to pick their way carefully over the shingled beach below, it seemed from her new vantage point to be a vast body of water—not in width, for from where she stood she could, when the veils of low-lying, drifting mist parted, catch glimpses of the opposite shore, but in length, for no matter how hard she tried, she could spy neither the lake's beginning nor its end. A terrible monster lived in the loch, she had heard tell, and now, remembering, she shivered.

"Are you cold, Ana?" Collie inquired, observing how her dainty, graceful form trembled of a sudden—as he noticed many things, however small, that others would have missed, for he belonged to that ilk who had for generations been born and bred in the Highlands, who were as one with its mountains and woods, its moors and lakes.

"Nay, only a li'l fwightened. There's a monster in the loch, people claim."

"Well, if there is, I have never seen it. But if you are afraid, you can always wait here for me."

"Nay, I want to come with you."

"There's a brave, bonnie lass," he said simply, but the words thrilled Ariana, even so.

His small wooden fishing boat, christened the Sea Witch, *was beached on the shingle, and after lifting Ariana and settling her safely inside it, along with his fishing rod and the bait bucket, Collie pushed it into the shallow waters off the shoreline, then clambered aboard. Picking up the oars, which lay in the bottom of the dinghy, he inserted them into the oarlocks, then began to row surely and strongly—long, sweeping strokes that propelled the* Sea Witch *away from the beach, out toward the lake's heart, three-quarters of a mile distant, which was his destination. After half an hour or so, reaching it, he drew in the oars, allowed the vessel to drift freely and cast his line over the side.*

"Whatcha hope to catch, Collie?" Ariana asked in a whisper, still mindful of his warning to her earlier not to natter, lest she scare away the fish.

Lightly he shrugged.

"Brown sea trout and salmon, mostly…those are quite the best fish in Loch Ness—not like the minnows and sticklebacks. Those are too small and bony to be of much use to anyone, but since they live in the shallower waters anyway, we're unlikely to hook one of them. Here in the deeper waters now, salmon, especially, are plentiful this time of year, because autumn is when they come to Loch Ness to spawn. So we might catch several of those if we're lucky. Pike are rare, but not unknown. They are the biggest fish in the loch, I think—except for that monster you were talking about earlier, of course, but which, as I told you, I have never seen myself. So perhaps the stories about it are only tales with which nurses scare naughty children here in the Highlands. Once in a great while, I've managed to snag an eel or two in Loch Ness, as well. It just all depends on what, if anything, is biting on any given day."

"You ever swim in the lake?"

"Nay, the water is always far too cold for all but the hardiest of fellows, and 'tis clotted with peat, too, which is why 'tis

so dark that you can't see more than a few feet below the surface."

"*I see.*"

After that, Ariana once more fell silent, huddling on the wooden seat in the bow of the craft, her gloved hands clasped around her knees. Now that she was no longer walking, but sitting still instead, she could feel the chill of the autumn air seeping through her long woolen coat. The wind she had scarcely noticed before was stronger out upon the loch, and the earlier fine Scotch mist had turned into a harder drizzle now, too, so that without the protective canopy formed by the trees in the woods, her hat, cloak and gloves were soon soaked through. Almost she wished she were back in the nursery, safely curled up on the old Turkish rug before the fire.

It was so quiet upon the lake that the very stillness itself was eerie, as though some unknown, but hideous disaster had somehow occurred while the Sea Witch floated on the water, and now she and Collie were the only two people left alive in all the world. All around them, the billowing mist hung low, swirling like a diaphanous cerecloth being woven around them by mysterious, unseen hands that were not of this world, but of the next. The mizzle spattered into the lake—pitter-pat, pitter-pat—and the sound was like the light tread of faery footsteps across the water. Half expecting to see one of the small, otherworldly creatures, Ariana glanced around anxiously, and as she did so, the shroud of brume suddenly parted to reveal a frightening scene.

Seen from this angle, like a sharp-taloned eagle perched upon an aerie, the great castle clung to a high promontory on the northwest shore of the loch, seeming to grow up and out of the huge cliff upon which it stood, as though it were a part of it—alive, even. Built of red sandstone that had aged over the centuries to the color of a pale bloodstain, the forbidding stronghold boasted a somehow sinister mélange of soaring towers and crenellated turrets, of looming battlements and flying buttresses. Its narrow, Gothic-arched windows appeared like dozens of slitted black eyes staring out menacingly over the lake, and its heavy *iron portcullis resembled the gaping, spike-toothed maw of some unnatural beast crouched and poised to spring upon Ariana from the rocky hilltop. At the fearsome sight and the equally dire thought, she unwittingly gasped.*

"Collie, what's that horrible place?" she breathed, involuntarily cringing in the boat.

For a long moment, he was so still and silent that she believed he had not heard her question, or else that he did not intend to answer. But then, finally, he spoke.

"Dúndragon," he said grimly.

"What's that mean?"

"The Fortress of the Dragon."

"Is it—is it because the monster in the loch is supposed to be some kind of a sea dwagon?"

"Aye, perhaps. I don't know. 'Tis a haunted place, people say."

Now, before Ariana could speak further, as she gazed at the hulking, foreboding keep, she suddenly spied a young man standing on one of the stone parapets, as though he had just somehow materialized there from out of the ethereal white mist. He was tall, dark and slender, with a sinuous grace that reminded her of a hissing snake—a ghastly impression that was further and hideously strengthened when, to her complete horror, like a silkie lord turning into a sleek seal, the young man slowly began to metamorphose into a gigantic black sea serpent, then, once the transformation was complete, deliberately slithered down from the castle wall and into the lake.

Utterly petrified, Ariana tried to tell Collie, who had his back to the macabre scene, what was happening, but such was her overwhelming fear that no sound issued from her throat. Rendered mute, she could only watch, frozen with sheer terror in the small boat where she sat, as a great, whitecapped wave abruptly formed on the vast loch, undulating ominously toward the dinghy.

This, then, must be the dreaded monster of the lake! she thought dimly in some dark chasm of her mind.

Amid the moving ridge of foaming water, its long, serpentine body showed like three arches of some ancient cloister against the grayish-white horizon, rippling ever nearer. Then suddenly, without warning, its slinky, horselike head broke the surface, looming terrifyingly over the Sea Witch, *dwarfing the vessel. As the monstrous sea snake towered threateningly over the craft, it opened its enormous mouth wide, revealing a series of fangs that were like the sharp, predatory teeth of a shark, a long, forked tongue that twisted and writhed as though it had a life of its own, and, from deep within a seemingly endless throat, a burst of flames that shot forth apocalyptically. The dark, yawning maw bent toward Ariana menacingly, then suddenly snatched her from the* Sea Witch *and swallowed her whole, plunging her into blackness and fire.*

She screamed—again and again.

It was, in fact, the sound of her own high shrieks of terror that wakened her from the dream—from the horrifying nightmare that had held her tight in its ruthless grip until this very moment. Shaking uncontrollably, Ariana Lévesque abruptly sat straight up in bed, clutching herself frantically for comfort and to reassure herself that she was actually still alive, that she had not truly been savagely seized and gulped down by the bloodcurdling sea monster of her dream.

For a moment, such was her distraught state of mind that she did not know where she was. In the semidarkness of her well-appointed bedchamber, all her furniture appeared to have assumed sinister, unfamiliar shapes, as though she had somehow been transported to some alien planet. Her heart pounded; her breath came in hard rasps as she tried desperately to orient herself. Both her bedsheets and her fine white muslin nightgown were soaked through with sweat, and all that remained of the earlier cheerful fire in the hearth was a handful of embers that smoldered faintly in the grate. So she quickly felt chilled to the bone in the room and shivered violently.

Even the grand Hôtel de Lévesque, her father's town house in a fashionable district of Paris, was not proof against the January cold, it seemed. Outside, the city streets were quiet, save for the wind that soughed along the wide straight avenues and the narrow twisting alleys, the pitter-patter of the light rain that fell steadily and the lapping of the River Seine against its shores.

But inside, from the long corridor beyond her bedchamber, Ariana could now hear the sound of raised voices and running footsteps. There then came an urgent knocking upon her door, which was abruptly flung open wide to admit both her mother and her governess—the latter of whom, these days, served more as the eighteen-year-old Ariana's companion than her teacher. Both women wore white nightdresses and wrappers, and carried candles to light their way in the darkness.

"Ma pauvre petite!" Hélène Lévesque, Comtesse de Valcoeur, cried, visibly distraught, as she rushed into the room, setting her candlestick down upon one of the night tables. "What is it? What is wrong, *chérie?* Is it the nightmare again? Oh, what a stupid question! Of course 'tis the nightmare again—for there is nothing else that upsets you so! Mademoiselle Thibault—" she turned to address the governess "—please send for one of the chambermaids to come make up the fire and also for a cup of hot chocolate to be brought for my daughter."

"Oui, madame, at once." Mademoiselle Thibault departed from the bedchamber to carry out her orders.

In the meanwhile, the comtesse, gathering up Ariana's own dressing gown from where it lay at the foot of the canopy bed, now assisted her into the wrapper, urging her from bed and into a light blue velvet wing chair that sat before the Parian hearth. Once she had seen her daughter comfortably settled, Madame Valcoeur, muttering agitatedly under her breath, picked up the long brass poker and stabbed at the embers in the grate herself, soon coaxing a small flame into being. "Ah, Berthe, thank goodness, you are come! My daughter has experienced a very bad dream and is chilled through. See what you can do with this fire."

"Oui, madame." Curtsying, the chambermaid who had entered the room now moved to the hearth, shoveling several lumps from the coal bucket onto the fire until it blazed cheerfully once

more. Then, scooping some of the hot coals into the warming pan, she began to heat the bedsheets and to straighten them, restoring them to their former order.

By this time, Mademoiselle Thibault had reappeared, bearing a silver tray from the kitchen, on which reposed a hot-chocolate pot, two fine, delicate Sèvres china cups and saucers, and other accoutrements, including a plate of crumpets. She placed her burden upon a low round table before the hearth.

"I thought that perhaps you would like some hot chocolate, as well, *madame,*" she announced. "Shall I do the honors?"

"*Oui,* Odette, if you please," the comtesse uttered gratefully, sinking into the matching velvet wing chair opposite the one occupied by her daughter. "Although even with the hot chocolate, I shall doubtless have a difficult time sleeping again this night!"

"I'm so sorry, Maman," Ariana said quietly. "I did not mean to wake you."

"I know that, *ma petite,* so do not trouble yourself about it. It cannot be helped. I only wish there were something I could do to put an end to this dreadful nightmare of yours, so you would not suffer it anymore. 'Tis *most* worrisome to me!"

Once the hot chocolate had been poured and the cups and saucers handed to both Madame Valcoeur and Ariana, the governess and the chambermaid exited the room, leaving mother and daughter alone together in the semidarkness. While, with hands that still trembled slightly, the latter slowly sipped from her cup, the former sighed heavily, one palm pressed languidly to her brow, as though she had a headache.

"Ariana, you know that monsters such as the titanic black sea serpent of your nightmare do not exist," the comtesse insisted firmly but kindly. "'Tis only a bad dream, *chérie*—nothing more."

"But it all seems so real, Maman," Ariana protested, her own fair brow knitted in a puzzled, thoughtful frown. "And the Scottish Highlands and Loch Ness *do* exist, for Mademoiselle Thibault has taught me about them during our lessons together on geography. Oh, how I wish I could make you understand,

Maman! Whenever I experience the dream, 'tis as though…as though I have actually *been* there, to Scotland…as though I have seen all these things for myself—the Highlands, the loch, the foreboding castle—that I lived in that old farmhouse as a child, that I knew the young man Collie once, in another lifetime long ago…." Her voice trailed away as she realized how she must sound to her mother, and then she laughed a little, self-consciously. "Oh, I know I must sound mad! But I'm not, Maman. Truly, I'm not!"

"I know you are not, *ma petite*. But only consider what others would think if they heard you talking this way! They would believe that you are indeed touched in the head! Or, perhaps worse, a witch—cursed with déjà vu! You must promise me, *chérie*, that you will not discuss this nightmare of yours with anyone else besides me."

"*Oui,* Maman, I promise."

"*Très bon.* Now, be a good girl and drink your hot chocolate, as I will drink mine, and whilst we do, let us talk of other things more pleasant than this terrible dream of yours—for it disturbs me greatly even to hear about it! I can't imagine why it should ever have come to you in the first place, much less why it should continue to recur. 'Tis *most* upsetting! At your age, your head should be filled with thoughts of parties, routs and balls…of finding *un jeune homme* to marry—or, at the very least, to call your sweetheart! Why, when I was your age, I myself thought of nothing else!"

In her heyday, Madame Valcoeur had been the toast of Paris, considered one of its greatest beauties. Even now, in her middle years, she was still a lovely, charming woman whose company and conversation were much sought after in the fashionable salons of the city, and she still attracted the attention of men, although it was only her husband who held her heart.

"We must give a party—a ball—and invite all the eligible young bachelors," she continued with determined brightness. "I will speak to your father about it tomorrow. What a pity that there is all this radicalism and talk of revolution brewing again in the city, stirred up by those two dreadful Germans Karl Marx and Friedrich Engels! I was so glad when Marx was expelled from Paris! I sincerely hope he never comes here again! He and Engels went away to Brussels, I heard. Good riddance to both of them, I say! Otherwise, the next thing you know, the bourgeoisie will all be up in arms once more, wanting to get rid of Louis-Philippe, who—even though he *is* increasingly unpopular—is still the king! Lopping off the head of poor King Louis the Sixteenth was bad enough. France does not need any more of such craziness!" the comtesse insisted stoutly.

"How is your hot chocolate, *ma petite?* Good? *Oui.* 'Tis very sweet and pleasant, is it not? So drink up, *chérie,* or we shall neither of us ever get back to sleep tonight! *Oui,* a ball filled with dozens of handsome young men will be just the thing to take your mind off this horrible nightmare of yours." She returned to her earlier topic. "What theme shall we have, I wonder? A masquerade ball? Those are always quite popular. Everyone likes to dress up and pretend to be someone they're not—and whom they actually wish they were! *Oui,* that sounds good. Still, we must have something more…something a little different with which to divert and surprise our guests…. Oh, I don't know what that might be right at this moment. But I will think of something when 'tis not so very late and my nerves are not so very frazzled! Oh, I'm so excited! We shall begin planning our ball tomorrow, *ma petite.* 'Twill be the event of the Little Season! *Mais, oui?*"

"I'm sure 'twill be, Maman," Ariana agreed warmly, smiling softly.

Madame Valcoeur was one of those kind, well-intentioned but highly imperceptive women who believe that all the world's ills can be solved by means of good food and drink, entertainment, and romance. If one were too distracted even to *think* about one's problems, then they would surely all disappear sooner or later—languishing away through lack of attention, if nothing else. Ariana, wise beyond her eighteen years, had for quite some while been aware of this sad fault in her mother's character and so had long ago abandoned any attempt to have any discussion of a wholly serious nature with her. The comtesse, if vague and even at times flighty, nevertheless had a good heart, and she could not bear to see anyone, particularly those she loved, suffer. If her efforts to cheer them consisted of stuffing them with crumpets and dancing a jig afterward, well, at least her endeavors were sincerely meant and unselfishly undertaken. So Ariana accepted her mother's offer to host a masquerade ball in the benign spirit in which it had been intended and said nothing further about her troublesome nightmare, knowing that to do so would only renew Madame Valcoeur's earlier agitation.

The hot-chocolate pot now empty, the comtesse saw her daughter tucked safely and snugly back into bed and bestowed upon her an affectionate hug and kiss before taking up the candlestick on the night table to light her path back to her own bedchamber.

"Only sweet dreams now, *ma petite*," she urged gently, smiling tenderly at Ariana. Then she gracefully departed from the room, leaving behind only the warm, solicitous glow of her former presence and the faint, fragrant scent of attar of roses.

Once she had closed the door to her daughter's room and started down the long hall beyond, however, Madame Valcoeur was anything but easy in her mind, and despite the two cups of hot chocolate she had drunk, she still feared that sleep would not return to her this night, such was the inner turmoil she experienced. It was with a frown of anxiety on her usually serene, exquisite face that she entered her own bedchamber, so that her husband, Jean-Paul Lévesque, Comte de Valcoeur, was well aware of her discomposure and worry the moment he spied her.

Wakened earlier by his daughter's screams, he had betaken himself from his own room to that of his wife, which adjoined his, there to await her return.

"Ariana has suffered the old nightmare again," he now accurately observed, as he saw the Comtesse's fretful countenance.

"*Oui.* Oh, Jean-Paul, 'tis all *most* distressing! What are we to do, I wonder?"

"She is not a child any longer, Hélène—" the comte sighed heavily, with a trace of sadness, at the realization "—but a young woman, and as much as we would like to do so, we cannot shelter and protect her forever. At some point, we must tell her the truth. What if something were to happen to us? What would become of her then, ignorant as she still is of so much that affects her?"

"I don't know...I don't know." Sinking down in the satin-striped bergère chair opposite the one occupied by her husband before the crackling fire, Madame Valcoeur momentarily buried her face in her elegant hands. "She is still very young, and the burden that must weigh upon her is so very great.... Surely, Jean-Paul, we need not disrupt her happiness and her trust in us any sooner than is absolutely necessary!"

"These are difficult times, Hélène," Monsieur Valcoeur reminded her. "France has not truly been politically stable since the execution of King Louis the Sixteenth and poor Marie Antoinette, his queen. The horrible Reign of Terror, the Napoléonic Wars, our so-called Citizen King Louis-Philippe...none of these things has been good for our country. Now the Royalists scheme to restore the senior Bourbon line to the throne, whilst revolutionaries and radicals plot yet another rebellion and overthrow of the monarchy and government!

"*Alors,* who can say what will or will not happen in the future—or even tomorrow, such are the troubled times in which we live. We may awaken in the morning to find the world as we know it has gone forever, for 'tis not just France into which men such as Marx and Engels have spewed their contumacious poison. *Non,* the seeds of discontent and rebellion they and their dissatisfied, downtrodden lot have planted have taken root everywhere, and discord is growing throughout the entire Continent. In Ireland and elsewhere the potatoes rot in the ground, and the masses are starving, as a result. Many are homeless or infirm—or both!

"Such men as these are desperate men indeed—and worse, they have nothing left to lose, except their lives, and these are now, by circumstance, rendered so utterly valueless that most would easily surrender them! I tell you, Hélène, a change is coming that will sweep across the whole of Europe and beyond, and in all truth, I do not know whether 'twill be for the better or the worse for all of us!"

"You frighten me terribly, Jean-Paul, with such dire talk as this! Surely you do not believe that the bourgeoisie will once more revolt and instigate another Reign of Terror...?"

"I think that in these uncertain times, all things are possible. But there, do not worry your lovely head about such matters as these, *ma chère,* for they are men's business, and men will take care of them. I have spoken of them only so you will know the dangers inherent in keeping Ariana in the dark about perilous affairs that concern her so intimately. To continue to leave her blissfully ignorant—however kindly intended—may be to jeopardize even her very life at some point in the future. We would unquestionably be remiss in our duty if we failed to consider that, Hélène!"

"*Oui,* perhaps you are right," the comtesse conceded, although, still, her face was doubtful. "But, equally, would not revealing the knowledge we have deliberately withheld from her for so long place an unbearable burden upon her young shoulders? How do we know she is now wise and strong enough to carry such a ponderous load? She can still be mischievous and willful. What if she were to take it into her head to meddle in these hazardous matters, to draw attention to herself in a way that stirred suspicion from deadly quarters? Her tongue can still be impulsive and unruly at times. One slip of it to the wrong person, and what would become of her?" She paused, sighing heavily, then went on.

"Oh, Jean-Paul, I would never forgive myself if something horrible happened to her because we did not make the correct decision in determining whether or not to tell her all that we have kept secret from her these many long years now! Oh, how I wish we knew for certain the right thing to do! We must take our time in deciding what course to take in these dangerous affairs—and pray to *le bon Dieu* for guidance."

"Very well, Hélène. As you wish." The comte could deny his wife nothing, as he himself was ruefully aware. He smiled at her tenderly. "We will wait a little while longer, then, at least, and see how things progress. There can be no harm in that, surely."

"*Non,* there can be no harm in that," Madame Valcoeur echoed his words—but now that, at least for the time being, she had got her own way in the matter, she was plagued with doubt, and of a sudden, a strange, unnerving chill chased up her spine, as though a goose had just walked over her grave.

Chapter Four

Mrs. Blackfriars Speaks

…let him now speak, or else hereafter for ever hold his peace.
—The Book of Common Prayer
Solemnization of Matrimony

We know how to speak many falsehoods which
resemble real things, but we know, when we will,
how to speak true things.

—Hesiod
The Theogony

Wherein I spake of most disastrous chances,
Of moving accidents by flood and field,
Of hair-breadth 'scapes i' the imminent
deadly breach.

—William Shakespeare
Othello [1604-1605]

1848
Oxford Street, London, England

According to a decree issued in 1847 by Mohamed Ali, the greatly esteemed Pasha of Egypt, all the modernization currently being diligently undertaken in Cairo and elsewhere, as necessary throughout the country, was being carried out in "the European way, for the general benefit of the kingdom." But, privately, Khalil al-Walid himself was not at all certain the projects that had been embarked upon, in imitation of the European continent, would ultimately prove in Egypt's best interests. For as far as he could see, physically, his hot arid desert homeland had little or nothing in common with Europe, and therefore, what was deemed suitable for London or Paris, for Rome or Madrid, or for Berlin or Vienna, was not necessarily at all fitting for Cairo, he reflected. But with the seemingly endless influx of thousands of foreigners from the European continent, the Egyptian capital city had already—inevitably—changed, absorbing a new manner of thinking, a new way of doing things, and now determinedly marching forward in the name of the Infidels' Progress. Streets like Al-Mouski, Al-Qalaa, Boulaq and Fum al-Khaleeg had been cut and transformed into wide avenues in the European style, then paved, as well, and for the first time in Cairo's history, every road had been given a name, and every house had been assigned a number.

Now, as Mr. al-Walid stared inscrutably up and down Oxford Street at all the London shops before which he currently stood, he thought that if Pasha Mohamed Ali continued to have his way, it would no doubt not be long before all of Egypt's native, colorful mazes of crowded, noisy, open-air bazaars smelling pungently of herbs and spices, fruits and vegetables, cottons and silks, carpets and tents, and jewels and metals gave way to impersonal, imposing facades of brick and glass, just like those that now surrounded him and his manservant, Hosni. Although inwardly Mr. al-Walid acknowledged how backward his own country appeared in comparison to all this, still, he knew that it had not always been thus, that, once, Egypt had boasted an epic and highly advanced civilization, and it galled him to realize that this was no longer the case, that the once-barbaric Infidels had now far outstripped the Egyptians. As a result, he must do his own part to help restore his homeland to its former greatness!

He and Hosni had endured a very long trip to London. In Cairo they had unfortunately been compelled to purchase tickets on a tiny, disgusting, bug-infested paddle steamer, which had ferried them down the River Nile to the ancient port of Alexandria. There, in sharp contrast to their previous mode of

transportation, however, they had boarded a pleasantly luxurious steamer packet belonging to the Peninsular and Oriental
Steam Navigation Company, which ship, after some weeks'
journey, had borne them hither. It was a trip Mr. al-Walid would
most assuredly rather not have made. But still, he had been given
his orders, and he would succeed in carrying them out, for to do
otherwise would force him to return empty-handed, and therefore in disgrace, to his homeland, as those before him had done,
and he could not bear even the thought of that.

From his many predecessors and their highly detailed records,
he had gathered information, although he trusted no one except
his manservant, Hosni, who had been with him for many years.
That was the reason Mr. al-Walid himself stood now in Oxford
Street, shivering imperceptibly in the unrelenting drizzle on this
chilly gray winter afternoon and, in some dim, detached corner
of his mind, wishing he were back in Egypt, warm and dry beneath its bright, burning sun. The sooner he accomplished his
assigned task and left this dreary, cold, ceaselessly wet country,
the better, he mused dispassionately, glancing up and down the
long street, in search of No. 7B, which was the establishment of
Quimby & Company (Cartographers & Map Sellers).

Finding it at last, Mr. al-Walid carefully straightened his white
turban and smoothed the long, flowing folds of his *galabiya,* then
slowly crossed the street to enter the prosperous shop, Hosni following wordlessly and watchfully behind, awkwardly holding a
black umbrella over his master to shield him from the trickling
rain.

When Malcolm awakened in the early-morning quiet at the
small, quaint cottage he shared with his widowed mother on Cochrane Street, in the placid, relatively secluded parish of St.
John's Wood, he had no inkling whatsoever that, later that day,
not just one, but two highly unusual—and, in hindsight, portentous—incidents were going to take place, for it is a universal
truth that epochal and frequently dreadful events invariably have
their roots in wholly innocuous beginnings. In fact, he had for

so long now grown accustomed to the unvarying, although most often pleasant, routine of his life that, at times, much to his own surprise, he quite forgot that he actually lived daily poised on the precarious edge of a steep, dangerous precipice and that he could at any moment stumble—or be shoved—into the deep dark abyss beyond.

Or so his mother would have him believe.

In truth, if they had ever really had any enemies, as she still claimed, these must surely have long ago either completely lost track of them or else forgotten even their very existence. For in the thirteen years since Malcolm and his mother had abandoned the burnt-out shell of Whitrose Grange for London and he had been apprenticed to Mr. Quimby at Quimby & Company (Cartographers & Map Sellers), nothing else untoward had ever befallen them, so that now Malcolm could almost convince himself that he had imagined or, much more likely, dreamt that dark, mysterious, cloaked stranger in his father's study that night of the fateful fire at the Grange, which had claimed the lives of both his father and Uncle Charles. For certainly they must both be dead, Malcolm knew in his heart, for he and his mother had neither seen nor heard from either of them since that terrible night. So, after an extended period of time, during which Malcolm had been loath to admit that his hopes for his father and Uncle Charles's escape were all in vain, followed by an onslaught of grief that had been rendered even more wrenching and acute because of all the expectations he had cherished for so long and had only with the greatest of reluctance gradually relinquished, he had at last been compelled to reconcile himself to their loss.

Now, strangely, whenever Malcolm thought of his father and Uncle Charles, as he sometimes did, it was somehow as though he had known and loved them in an entirely different lifetime long ago and far removed from his present one. Their cruel, untimely deaths and even the memory of their dark, handsome young faces had receded with the passing years to a sheltered niche deep within his heart, and time had lessened his sorrow and pain to a bearable dull ache, sharpened only by an undeniable sense of guilt and a deep regret that he had never addressed himself to avenging their murders. Given the opportunity, he would indeed have been thus inclined, but unfortunately, no such chance had ever presented itself. Nor had Malcolm ever succeeded in persuading his mother to reveal to him the secrets she harbored. So, in time, he had ceased to question her, and he had allowed all thoughts of revenge to lodge themselves in a seldom-investigated place deep in his mind.

Nor, over the years, had any of the letters that his mother had written—at first hopefully, then later desperately, and then, finally, sadly—to Aunt Katherine ever been answered. So she and her children had been lost track of, as well, and Mrs. Blackfriars feared that something untoward must have befallen them and that, even now, like his father and Uncle Charles, they lay dead in their graves.

So it was not musings such as these that occupied Malcolm as he rose from his bed that morning at Hawthorn Cottage and set about all his usual ablutions at that early hour. Nor was it curiosity about the aforementioned incidents that, as yet unknown to him, were later that day to disrupt the normal pattern of his serene existence. Rather, Malcolm dwelled on nothing in particular as he washed and dressed, then made his way to the kitchen, there to eat the breakfast prepared for him each morning by the cook.

The Blackfriarses' cook—Mrs. Peppercorn by name—was a jovial rotund woman who, like the kitchen under her charge, was the heart of Hawthorn Cottage. During the past thirteen years of his apprenticeship to Mr. Quimby, Malcolm had more than proved that his employer's faith in him had not been misplaced, and he had eventually been rewarded by advancement to the position of junior journeyman at the flourishing map shop. With the knowledge of his steady employment and the resulting increase in his wages, he had been able to add to Hawthorn Cottage's previously small household staff of housemaid and cook by hiring both a housekeeper and a scullery maid. This latter had earned him Mrs. Peppercorn's everlasting devotion, since, until then, she had been burdened with not only all the cooking, but also all the cleaning chores in the kitchen. A widow with no children of her own, she had, because of what she perceived as Malcolm's kindness to her, grown to dote so on him that he was always assured of a good meal at home, and although, as the master of the house, he might have been served in the dining room, because of Mrs. Peppercorn's affection for him, he much preferred in the mornings the warm coziness of the kitchen that she ruled with a floury hand, a generous heart and a cheerful disposition.

Now, as he made his way from his bedroom, along the hall to the gleaming wooden staircase that led to the ground floor of Hawthorn Cottage, Malcolm could already smell the familiar aromas of fresh eggs and rashers of bacon frying on the cast-iron griddle, of porridge simmering in its pot and of deviled kidneys broiling in their pan. There would be an array of fruit, as well, and hot toast spread with jam that Mrs. Peppercorn had carefully put up last summer, and the kettle boiling for tea; and indeed, when Malcolm stepped through the swinging oak door into the kitchen, he saw that all this was exactly so, just as it had been every morning that he could remember for the past thirteen years.

"Good morning, Mrs. Peppercorn," he greeted her before sitting down at the old wooden table where she habitually served him breakfast.

"Good morning, Mr. Blackfriars—although, in all honesty, 'tis hardly that now, is it? What with the chill wind coming in off the Thames the way 'tis and this dreary drizzle that shows no sign of letting up, I'm very much afraid you'll have a long cold ride again to work this morning, sir!" Mrs. Peppercorn bustled about the kitchen, her round, apple-cheeked face flushed from both the heat of the stove and her exertions as she prepared a plate for him, then set it on the table before him, along with a cup of hot tea. "You'll be wanting your heavy coat again today, Mr. Blackfriars, and your umbrella."

"Aye, so 'twould indeed appear," Malcolm replied, sighing

absently as he gazed out through the square lead-glass kitchen windows, trickling with raindrops, at the bleak back garden, where even the naked trees seemed to shiver in the gray winter morning air, and the dead brown leaves they had weeks ago shed whorled like strange, contorted faeries in the brumous wind. "I will be glad when spring is here."

"Let us hope it comes early this year," Mrs. Peppercorn said as she put the finishing touches on the breakfast tray she prepared every morning for Mrs. Blackfriars.

Once he had become a man and assumed more and more responsibility in the household, Malcolm had insisted on his mother enjoying a few luxuries. Breakfast in bed was one of these. He had worried that ever since his father had died, his mother had been placed under an unaccustomed amount of stress and had worked too hard, so he was glad to have been able to relieve some of her burdens, ensuring that she ate enough and got sufficient rest. While her constitution had never been exceedingly delicate, she was not particularly strong, either, and for a time it had seemed to him that her health had declined. But now, although there was always about her the faint air of softness and wistfulness that had come upon her at his father's death, she was well and content in her house and gardens, he thought.

As Malcolm picked up his fork and eagerly dug in to the good, hearty breakfast before him, Miss Woodbridge, the housekeeper, entered the kitchen to collect his mother's tray and carry it up to her. Before doing so, she placed a few sprigs of holly she had gathered from the front garden into a small crystal vase and arranged it just so upon the tray.

"Very nice, Miss Woodbridge," Mrs. Peppercorn observed, nodding approvingly.

"'Tis so dismal out. I hoped that 'twould help to brighten Mrs. Blackfriars's morning," the housekeeper explained. "She does so love plants and flowers, and there's so little that blooms this time of year. But earlier, when I went out, I thought the holly quite pretty."

"I'm certain Mother will find it so, too," Malcolm declared, in between bites of his breakfast, causing Miss Woodbridge to color faintly at his praise.

In sharp contrast to the plump, gregarious cook, the house-keeper, a spinster, was a thin, dried stick of a woman, somewhat shy and reticent, so that she moved almost like a wraith through the rooms of Hawthorn Cottage as she quietly oversaw their up-keep. Still, despite her outwardly frail appearance, Miss Wood-bridge had an inbred backbone of steel, so that although she was unfailingly courteous, considerate and soft-spoken, she was nev-ertheless firm, and as a result, the household ran smoothly under her aegis. Malcolm was glad he had chosen his additions to the staff so well, for Lucy, the scullery maid, busy scrubbing pots and pans at the kitchen sink, was as bright and sunny as a spring flower, and as hardworking as honest, earnest Nora, the house-maid. Thus secure in the knowledge that his mother was well cared for at Hawthorn Cottage, Malcolm could, with a clear conscience, devote himself entirely to his work during the day and not be distracted with worrying about how she was faring in his absence.

Now, having finished his breakfast, along with the morning edition of *The Times,* which Mrs. Peppercorn always left neatly folded for him beside his plate on the kitchen table, Malcolm rose and went back upstairs. After knocking gently upon his moth-er's bedroom door and gaining admittance, he bade her good morning, chatting with her briefly and pouring her another cup of steaming tea from the pot upon the tray Miss Woodbridge had brought up earlier, before he once more descended to the ground floor. In the hallway he donned his hat, coat and gloves, and col-lected his umbrella before leaving the house. After closing the front door behind him, he put up his umbrella to guard himself against the steady mizzle that fell from the lowering pewter sky, then began his journey toward the map shop on Oxford Street. As had become his usual habit over the past thirteen years, Mal-colm trekked his way briskly to the St. John's Wood omnibus stand, where he would catch the lumbering public vehicle that, after a roughly two-and-a-half-mile ride, would set him down in

Oxford Street, whence he would walk the remainder of the short distance to the map shop.

Today, quite by chance, he arrived at his final destination at the same time as Mr. Quimby was being deposited by a hansom cab at the curb out front.

"Quite a wretched morning, eh, Malcolm?" his portly, gray-haired employer greeted him.

"Aye, sir, 'tis indeed," Malcolm rejoined, slowing his long stride so that Mr. Quimby, who had to increasingly rely on his brass-knobbed walking stick, could keep pace. "I was saying to Mrs. Peppercorn only this morning that I shall be happy when spring has arrived."

"I'm afraid 'twill be a while before then—more's the pity." Mr. Quimby sighed heavily as Malcolm opened the front door to the map shop for him and held it while he passed through. "For I fear I feel winter's cold in my bones far more acutely now than I did in my youth!"

Inside the establishment, the now-senior journeyman, Harry Devenish, along with the two apprentices, Jem Oscroft and Peter "Tuck" Tucker, were already hard at work.

The premises of Quimby & Company (Cartographers & Map Sellers) were divided into two parts. On the ground floor were situated the main room open to the public, where all the maps for sale were displayed, cataloged and stored, and Mr. Quimby's private office. Upstairs were the storerooms and the workshop in which the maps themselves were actually created and printed, and so which contained drawing boards, stacks of paper, ink, intaglio plates, printing presses and other such paraphernalia involved in the intricate mapmaking process. During his time with Mr. Quimby, Malcolm had learnt every aspect of the trade, from the initial drawing of the maps to the final selling of them. As a result, he was as at home upstairs in the establishment as he was down, and he never failed to be grateful for this, as well as for that long-ago day that had brought him to Mr. Quimby's attention to begin with—for not all map shops were as comprehensive and efficient as Quimby & Company (Cartographers & Map

Sellers). Some only produced and printed maps; still others only sold them. Over the years, from the many land surveyors who brought their rough sketches and detailed measurements to Mr. Quimby to be fashioned into actual maps, Malcolm had even gleaned some knowledge of the process whereby the maps originated.

This morning, to warm himself after divesting himself of his hat, coat and gloves, and neatly folding up his umbrella, he partook of a mug of hot tea before the welcome fire that burnt brightly in the hearth—for unlike many masters, Mr. Quimby was neither miserly nor mean-spirited, so did not stint on coal, which was therefore always plentiful both in the bucket and on the grate. Then, once the chill engendered by the winter air had left him, Malcolm climbed the stairs to the upper rooms and sat down on the high stool before his drawing board. Picking up his pencil, he applied himself to the map that was slowly but surely taking shape beneath his now highly skilled, artistic hand. Thus did he employ himself until the early afternoon, at which time he joined Harry, Jem and Tuck below, for they three had already gathered around the blazing hearth on the ground floor. Despite the fact that he was now getting on in years, Mr. Quimby still continued his habitual practice of returning home for luncheon, although, these days, if the weather were inclement, he generally relied on a hansom cab for transport instead of walking. But his journeymen and apprentices all ate at the map shop, and because they all got on well together, they especially enjoyed this break in their otherwise long day. From the pocket of his coat hanging on the wooden pegs at the rear of the map shop, Malcolm withdrew the two sandwiches that Mrs. Peppercorn always prepared for his luncheon, for unlike the other apprentices' contracts, his own agreement with Mr. Quimby had never included room and board. Then, with the tin of tea that he kept on the premises and the kettle Jem had earlier set to boiling on the grate, Malcolm prepared himself a "cuppa." After that, drawing a short stool up to the crackling flames in the hearth, he unwrapped the brown paper in which his two sandwiches were tucked away. Today it was roast beef, he saw, delectably layered between thick slices of generously buttered brown bread.

He had not managed more than a few large, hungry bites, however, before the front door to the map shop unexpectedly opened, the brass bell mounted upon it clanging loudly in the wet wind. At the sound, the congenial talk and laughter that had only moments before filled Mr. Quimby's establishment abruptly ceased, and from where they sat before the hearth, all four young men glanced toward the entrance to see who was there.

"'Od's bodkins! 'tis a couple o' them 'eathen, thievin' 'In-doo blokes!" Tuck, the youngest among them, whispered, his corn-flower-blue eyes round with astonishment and even a little fear. "Gor, do you s'pose they mean to rob us?"

"No—now, hush, goose!" Harry hissed sharply, while, as the most senior among the four of them, giving Tuck a small, reprov-ing cuff about the ears. "They'll hear you—and perhaps lodge a complaint with Mr. Quimby! And you know he'd have a real fit if he ever learnt you'd insulted a customer! Whose turn is it to man the counter?"

"Tuck's," Jem reported, smothering a laugh, "but plainly, you daren't send *him!* He's so rattled that he's dropping his aitches again, despite all of Mr. Quimby's training!"

"I'll go, Harry." Rising from his stool, Malcolm laid aside his half-eaten sandwich, brushed the crumbs from his trousers, then straightened his striped waistcoat before heading to the front of the premises. There he greeted the two dark and unfamiliarly garbed foreigners politely. "Good afternoon, gentlemen. May I help you?"

"That remains yet to be seen," Khalil al-Walid announced im-passively, his jet-black eyes flicking measuringly over Malcolm, then around the map shop, missing nothing. The main room of Quimby & Company (Cartographers & Map Sellers), for all that it was crammed to bursting with shelves and drawers filled with maps of all kinds and sizes, was nevertheless clean and tidy, the long marble-topped wooden counters and the matching wooden floor highly polished and glistening in the light cast by the fluted-glass sconces affixed to the walls, without a trace of dust in sight. "I am seeking some maps."

"Then you've indeed come to the right place, sir," Malcolm asserted firmly, "for you'll find no finer map shop in all of England than Mr. Quimby's. What sort of maps are you in need of?"

"Maps of Scotland over the past centuries."

With difficulty, Malcolm concealed his surprise that the two foreigners should be interested in that chilly, remote—although breathtakingly beautiful—country north of England, for mostly it was a place where the English went only to hunt, fish and ride.

"Any particular region of Scotland, sir? The Highlands? The Lowlands? The Borderlands?"

"The Highlands. I am a herpetologist and interested in exploring the area around Loch Ness, for I have heard tell of a mysterious monster in the lake, a large sea dragon or sea serpent. Do you know of this creature?"

"I have heard some stories about it, aye," Malcolm answered slowly, "but I am afraid I can tell you nothing more about it than what I have learnt from the occasional tall tales I have listened to here in the local public houses, for I've never journeyed to Scotland myself nor seen Loch Ness or its purported monster. However, I do have several different maps that I can show you of that region, sir." Turning to the stacks of wide wooden shelves behind him, Malcolm searched carefully through their contents, eventually withdrawing a number of maps, which he laid on the long counter before him. "You do understand that because these were all created during various periods of history, the amount of detail will deviate from map to map, sir, depending upon what was known of surveying and geography at the time?"

"Yes, I am aware of that."

Charily, so as not to accidentally tear it, Malcolm unfolded the first map he had selected to display, spreading it upon the counter and knowledgeably pointing out its characteristics, both pro and con, to the two foreigners, who studied it with avid interest.

"What is that place?" Mr. al-Walid indicated a small, ornately detailed building rising from a headland that jutted into Loch Ness. "A coaching inn?"

Taking up a nearby magnifying glass kept at hand for just this purpose, Malcolm bent to examine the artistically depicted edifice in question more closely. He cleared his throat.

"No, sir. 'Tis a castle…Dúndragon by name."

"I see," Mr. al-Walid remarked indifferently. "A pity, for it appears to be most conveniently situated on the lake. Where is the nearest coaching inn, then?"

"Here, sir, at Inverness." Malcolm pointed out the spot.

Much to his delight, when he had finally finished showing all the maps he had chosen from the shelves, three were picked for purchase. These Malcolm neatly refolded, then wrapped in brown paper tied up with string, while the foreigner who had done all the talking during their transaction withdrew his purse from beneath the lavish folds of his *galabiya* and, opening it, brought forth the requisite number of pound notes for payment. As Mr. Quimby had taught him over the years to do, Malcolm swiftly but unobtrusively recounted the money, then, with the key he wore on a chain at his waistcoat, locked it away in the cash drawer.

"Thank you, gentlemen," he said. " It has been a pleasure doing business with you, and I hope you will remember Quimby and Company in the future, should you ever again be in need of our services."

The two foreigners merely nodded solemnly in response, their swarthy faces phlegmatic. Then the one who was the herpetologist's assistant gathered up their parcel, and they departed from the map shop, their robes softly fluttering like butterfly wings across the wooden floor. In sharp contrast to the whispering of their long cloaks, the brass bell fastened to the front door once more clanged loudly behind them as they made their exit. Of a sudden, as the chill damp wind outside swept into Mr. Quimby's establishment from Oxford Street, a peculiar icy grue tingled up the entire length of Malcolm's spine, making the fine hairs on his nape stand on end and gooseflesh prickle his strong, bare arms, where he had his shirtsleeves rolled up for working at the drawing board. Unwittingly, as, through the expansive front mullioned-glass windows of the premises, he watched the two foreigners until they disappeared from sight, he shivered, feeling suddenly strangely and inexplicably as though a goose had just walked over his grave.

For a number of reasons, after the two foreigners had departed from the map shop, Malcolm could not get them out of his mind. For the remainder of the afternoon they occupied his thoughts, no matter how hard he tried to concentrate on his work. More than once, as a result, he was compelled to apply his rubber eraser to the pencil drawing of the map on which he labored, and the mistakes, which these days he so seldom made, both frustrated and annoyed him.

"Do you want to tell me what is wrong, Malcolm?" Appearing in the workshop upstairs, Mr. Quimby laid a friendly hand upon the younger man's shoulder. "For I can see that you are distracted from your work today, and that is most unlike you. But perhaps you are only understandably elated at the sale of three such fine maps earlier this afternoon, eh? No doubt poor Tuck, had he been emboldened to go to the front counter instead of fearing that those two foreign gentleman meant to do some mischief in my establishment, would not have done nearly so well."

"Tuck's still young yet…only sixteen," Malcolm noted.

"Yes—the same age as you were when first you became one of my apprentices," Mr. Quimby agreed, nodding. "But somehow, for all that, you were older and wiser than your years. You have always served me faithfully and well, Malcolm. I'm glad my faith in you that day you gave chase after the pickpocket who had robbed me of my wallet was not misplaced. Why do you not go home a trifle early today?" Glancing at his gold pocket watch, which hung on a gold chain at his waistcoat, Mr. Quimby continued, "'Tis nearly closing time, anyway, and I fear that if you apply that eraser any further or more vigorously, you are going to rub a hole in the paper! For…only look how thin it has already grown in that one spot!"

"Aye, so I see. My apologies, sir. You're quite right in believing that my mind is not on my work at the moment. I'm afraid I keep thinking about those two foreigners—oh, not because they bought no less than three maps from me, although I am, of course, happy to have made such a good sale, but, well, I suppose because they both fascinated and repelled me, if that makes any sense to you, Mr. Quimby."

"It does, for we are always both frightened and yet perversely curious about that which is foreign to us and we do not therefore understand. I myself should have felt the same, had I been present when the two Hindus appeared here earlier this afternoon."

"Well, despite what Tuck claimed, I'm not at all sure they were, in fact, Hindus, sir. They were certainly blackamoors, but they might just as easily have been Africans or Arabs or the like. 'Twas difficult to tell, for many of the Orientals wear turbans and robes, do they not?"

"Yes, but that is neither here nor there, for whether they were Hindus, Persians, Turks, or some other, we shall probably never see them again. For they'll be off to the faraway Highlands of Scotland—chasing after some mysterious sea monster in Loch Ness!" Mr. Quimby laughed heartily, jovially clapping the younger man on the shoulder. "Why, what a notion, eh, Malcolm?"

"Aye, sir." He forced a smile to his lips.

But after cleaning up his work area and leaving early, as Mr. Quimby had bidden him, Malcolm remained inquisitive and uneasy in his mind. Deeply lost in thought, he turned his footsteps toward the omnibus stand in Oxford Street, hunched in his heavy coat against the bitter wind that blew in from the River Thames and with his umbrella upraised to protect him from the dispiriting drizzle that had continued to fall all day without surcease. Along the street he swiftly traversed, the lamplighters were already hard at work, igniting the street lamps to dispel the gloom of the dusk that had even now begun to spread its amorphous cloak over the city, enveloping it in long dark gray shadows. But Malcolm scarcely noticed the descending twilight as he boarded the ponderous public vehicle for the ride home. Upon finally being set down in St. John's Wood, he walked on to Cochrane Street and Hawthorn Cottage. With his house key he let himself in through the front door, hanging his hat and coat on the hall tree and placing his gloves on the shelf and his umbrella in the stand.

"Malcolm…? Malcolm, is that you?" One slender hand held to her throat, Mrs. Blackfriars appeared in the doorway of the drawing room, peeping tentatively into the foyer, her eyes wide and anxious.

"Aye, 'tis I, Mother, so have no fear."

"You're home early. Is something wrong? Are you ill? You've…you've not been discharged from Mr. Quimby's employment for some reason, have you?"

"No, although 'twas Mr. Quimby himself who sent me home before closing time today. Only let me come into the fire, Mother, where I can warm myself, for I am chilled to the bone, and then I will tell you all."

"Oh, but of course, Son. How utterly stupid and thoughtless of me to have kept you standing in this cold drafty hall! Miss Woodbridge! Miss Woodbridge…ah, there you are," Mrs. Blackfriars observed, as, hearing her name called, the housekeeper lightly descended the stairs into the foyer. "My son is home early from work and frozen clean through from this inclement weather—"

"I'll fetch some hot tea straightaway, ma'am," Miss Woodbridge declared, correctly deducing her mistress's wishes and vanishing down the hallway into the kitchen.

Meanwhile, Malcolm and his mother made their way into the small but pleasantly styled drawing room, where a coal fire burnt cheerily in the iron grate. Taking a seat upon one of the two rose-striped satin wing chairs arranged cozily before the Parian hearth, Malcolm gratefully stretched out his chilly, numb hands to the crepitant blaze to warm them. He chafed his fingers vigorously for a moment, then settled back into the chair, tiredly shutting his eyes and heaving a long sigh.

"I wish you didn't have to walk such a distance in the cold every day," Mrs. Blackfriars said as she gazed with concern at her son.

"'Tis not that far at all to and from the omnibus stand, Mother, and the cost of a hackney coach or a hansom cab into London on a daily basis would prove prohibitive, as well you know. And was it not you who long ago charged me that we must mind our shillings, lest we wind up destitute?"

"Yes." She smiled faintly and wryly at the memory. "But Mr. Gilchrist has handled my trust very well over the years, investing its funds wisely, and you are nicely employed, too."

"Aye. Still, there is no point in spending a shilling when tuppence will do."

By this time, Miss Woodbridge had appeared in the drawing room, along with the housemaid, Nora, each carrying trays laden with the teapot and its accoutrements, which they set down upon the marble top of the small satinwood table between the two wing chairs.

"Will there be anything else, ma'am?"

"No, thank you, Miss Woodbridge. That will be all."

Once the housekeeper and the housemaid had departed, Mrs. Blackfriars did the honors, pouring her son a cup of hot tea, then filling a plate for him, choosing generous helpings of what she knew he most favored from among the assortment of sandwiches, cakes, biscuits and sweetmeats that Mrs. Peppercorn had prepared. For a few minutes, Malcolm ate as though famished, for he was always hungry after his long day at the map shop, and the winter air had sharpened his appetite, as well. But then, after the edge of his hunger was dulled, in between bites of what remained on his plate, he told his mother about the two foreigners who had come to Mr. Quimby's establishment that afternoon. As he related his account of the unexpected event, he watched her carefully from beneath the thick black fringe of his eyelashes, to see what effect his report would have upon her. His surreptitious scrutiny of his mother did not go unrewarded. As Malcolm spoke at some length, Mrs. Blackfriars's lovely oval countenance gradually turned quite pale, and she became increasingly agitated, her graceful hands fluttering nervously in her lap, her plate going untouched and the tea in her cup growing stone cold.

When at last he mentioned the two foreigners' seemingly innocuous inquiries about Castle Dúndragon, she gasped aloud, as though he had suddenly struck her a stunning blow, and one hand flew to her now-tremulous mouth.

"Oh, Malcolm!" she cried, visibly distraught. "You did not say anything, did you? You did not tell them that you knew that awful place?"

"No, I didn't. I lied and said I'd never been to Scotland."

"Well, thank goodness for that, Son! For if anyone should ever connect us with that terrible castle—" Mrs. Blackfriars broke off abruptly, burying her face in her hands.

"What, Mother?" Malcolm prompted, his heart pounding. "What will happen? I know that you always loathed and feared Castle Dúndragon, but I never understood why. Has it something to do with these mysterious enemies you claim we have? If so, what?" When she did not respond to his questions, he went on a trifle exasperatedly, "Mother, for God's sake, I'm nearly thirty years old! Don't you think 'tis about time you told me the truth about these matters? What are all the dark secrets you have harbored all these long years—and what have they to do with us and with Father's and Uncle Charles's murders? If we are in danger, as you seem to think, how can I protect us if you stubbornly insist on continuing to leave me in the dark like this?"

"Oh, I know you are right, Malcolm." Mrs. Blackfriars sighed heavily. "'Tis only that I fear what you might take it in your head to try and do if I tell you all you wish to know. You could be killed—just like your father and Uncle Charles!"

"But…why?" he demanded.

"That is a very long story, Son. But, yes, as much as the potential consequences frighten me, 'tis indeed time you were told the truth—because, for all I know, those two foreigners who came to Quimby and Company this afternoon were but our adversaries in disguise!" Picking up the little crystal bell that sat on one of the tea trays, she rang it briefly, and when, in answer, the housekeeper returned to the drawing room, Mrs. Blackfriars directed, "Miss Woodbridge, would you please be so kind as to fetch the silver strongbox from my bedroom for me?"

"Yes, ma'am."

Once the housekeeper had gone upstairs, Malcolm spoke again.

"What would make you think those two foreigners were our foes in costume, Mother? They seemed genuine enough, and moreover, there was the look of true Orientals about them."

"Our enemies are Italians—a treacherous breed to begin with—and I therefore suppose that were they to clothe themselves in such exotic turbans and robes as you have described to me, they would, with their black hair and eyes, easily be able to pass as Orientals, Son. Further, I feel quite certain 'tis the old one, Vittore, you saw that night in the study at Whitrose Grange and who thus murdered your father and Uncle Charles!"

"Vittore… Vittore who? I know no one by that name."

"No, you wouldn't. But *I* know." Involuntarily, Mrs. Blackfriars shuddered visibly. "He is Lord Vittore, Count Foscarelli—and a more evil man I never hope to meet! 'Tis *he* who possesses Castle Dúndragon!"

"But… I still don't see what any of that has to do with us, or why this Count Foscarelli would want to kill both Father and Uncles Charles." Malcolm's brow was creased in a puzzled frown.

"To understand that, 'tis necessary to go back to the very beginning of our tale, to a time and land long distant from present-day England. Ah, thank you so much, Miss Woodbridge." Taking the silver strongbox from the housekeeper, who, her errand now discharged, once more disappeared from the drawing room, Mrs. Blackfriars carefully placed the small chest on her lap. Then, with a tiny silver key she wore on a slender chain around her neck, she slowly unlocked and opened the casket. "Our story…the story of our branch of the Clan Ramsay—for that is our true last name," she began, much startling Malcolm, who had never before known this, but prior to becoming Malcolm Blackfriars had thought himself Malcolm MacLeod, "has its origins in ancient Egypt, just outside of Luxor, in a place called the Valley of the Kings, for 'twas to there that one of your ancestors, Lord James Ramsay, Viscount Strathmór and, after his father's death, Earl of Dúndragon, traveled on his Grand Tour in the seventeenth century, thus unwittingly changing the lives of all his descendants forever.

"As you are no doubt aware from your youthful studies, Son, 'twas the practice of the ancient Egyptians to mummify their dead, in order to preserve them for all eternity, and then to inter them in great pyramids and vast necropolises for safekeeping. But of course, over the millennia, because they so often contained extensive stores of riches in the form of magnificent grave goods, the burial chambers in these pyramids and necropolises were frequently broken in to and robbed—and not only of their wealth, but also of their mummies. Nearly a hundred years before Lord Dúndragon's journey to Luxor and the Valley of the Kings, apothecaries on the European continent were peddling what was, in fact, known as 'mummy'—a fine powder that was reputedly made from pulverized mummies and that was believed, when swallowed, to bestow upon its recipient various healthful benefits leading to longevity."

"Good God," Malcolm intoned, repulsed.

"Yes, well, naturally—however unfortunately for those subjected to them—the medical knowledge and practices of Europe's earlier centuries were not nearly as advanced as they are now," Mrs. Blackfriars observed wryly. "To continue, Lord Dúndragon and some of his school chums had heard about these mummies and, in an obscure book written by a Capuchin friar, had also learnt about the Valley of the Kings, to which they had subsequently determined to travel, their aim being to break in to one of the tombs secreted there and to carry off its mummy, which they intended to sell to the Barber-Surgeons in Edinburgh. But for whatever unknown reasons, their scheme went awry almost from the very start, as Lord Dúndragon himself explains in this journal, in which, following his return to Scotland, he recorded all his adventures." From the silver strongbox in her lap Mrs. Blackfriars now gingerly drew forth a small, incredibly old, bound diary, yellowed and crumbling with age. "Presently I shall allow you to read this, Malcolm. In the meanwhile, suffice to say that the burial chamber Lord Dúndragon and his cohorts robbed was apparently that of an exalted high priest who had in life served the Egyptian god Kheperi, to whom the scarab beetle is deeply sacred. This last part is important, because during the desecration of the tomb by Lord Dúndragon and his cronies, a rare thunderstorm blew up over the desert plain, and the Valley of the Kings started to flood, causing the burial chamber to become a death trap, so that Lord Dúndragon and his friends were compelled to flee for their very lives. However, in the end, 'twas only Lord Dúndragon alone who survived to tell the tale—and because of the storm and the deluge, the only thing he managed to plunder from the tomb was a priceless emerald heart scarab, which he unwittingly bore away with him when he made good his escape."

"Where is this emerald now?" Malcolm asked, utterly fascinated, even as he wondered where all this was leading and what it had to do with him.

"I do not know," Mrs. Blackfriars told him. "No one does. So all I can tell you is that 'twas purportedly a legendary Egyptian talisman called the Heart of Kheperi, as Lord Dúndragon himself later learnt from a blind old priest in Cairo before leaving Egypt. 'Twas believed by the Egyptians to have been created by the god Kheperi himself and therefore to possess many magical properties that could be employed by those who knew how to use them, including the ability to bestow eternal life upon whoever owned the amulet. 'Twas reputed to have been even larger than a goose egg and to have mysteriously vanished some millennia before Lord Dúndragon journeyed to the Valley of the Kings, and thus had been long lost until he discovered it in the high priest's tomb. 'Twas also said to be bad luck for all but a priest devoted to Kheperi to hold and wield it, such was its great power, and this Lord Dúndragon himself came to believe, as well, for from the time he stole it from the breast of the high priest's mummy, he felt himself accursed. And indeed, naught ever went right for him after that, for his father had died during his absence, and the young bride he married shortly after returning to Scotland herself died in childbed scarcely a year after they were wed, and he himself was later tragically killed in a dreadful hunting accident, at the hands of that same son—his only child and heir—to whom she had given birth. Although there is no record of it, one presumes that the son inherited the emerald, but what happened to it after that remains a complete enigma, I'm afraid." Mrs. Blackfriars paused for a moment, then she continued the story.

"But unfortunately, despite its disappearance, the emerald's wretched curse lingered on. For almost a hundred years later, 'twas the cause of the death of yet another Lord Dúndragon, a direct descendant—as you yourself are, Malcolm—of the one who had traveled from Scotland to Egypt. The name of this later Lord Dúndragon was Iain Ramsay, and as his was a foolish, wastrel nature, he had had the poor judgment to become mixed up with Sir Francis Dashwood and his so-called Monks of Medmenham Abbey—what people often refer to nowadays as the Hellfire Club, although the real Order of the Knights of St. Francis, as Sir Francis had named his foundation, no longer exists and has not for quite some time. Even before his death it had disbanded, I think, although I know of it only by rumor, of course. But I digress. So let us return to our tale. The Lord Dúndragon about whom I now tell you chanced one night at Medmenham Abbey to be coaxed, whilst in his cups, into an utterly disastrous game of piquet by an Italian…one Lord Bruno, Count Foscarelli—an ancestor of that same Lord Vittore, Count Foscarelli, whom I believe to have murdered both your father and Uncle Charles. After the card play had ended, Lord Dúndragon was ruined, for he had stupidly wagered and lost virtually everything he owned, including all the Ramsay estates in both Scotland and England. Frantic at the realization, he impulsively accused Count Foscarelli of having cheated him at cards, and for his pains, Lord Dúndragon was challenged to a duel at dawn, at which he was shot and killed by the Italian—and which had apparently been Count Foscarelli's evil scheme all along. For after he took possession of the property he had so nefariously obtained, he went totally mad—or so the servants and villagers claimed—and he began wildly tearing the interior of Castle Dúndragon apart piece by piece and also digging up the grounds."

"In search of the missing emerald?"

"Yes, so 'twould seem.

"But…I'm afraid I still don't understand…why should the Foscarellis consider us a threat to them, Mother?" Malcolm inquired, perplexed. "I mean, if they have our lands—"

"I think they mistakenly believe we know where the emerald—the Heart of Kheperi—is," Mrs. Blackfriars stated quietly, "and that we would retrieve it ourselves, if we could ever again somehow gain access to the Ramsay estates. And of course, that is exactly what your father had in mind when he became the tenant at Whitrose Grange. After nightfall, whenever he got the opportunity, he was taking that old fishing boat of yours and covertly slipping across Loch Ness, to Castle Dúndragon—to search for the emerald."

This last revelation stunned Malcolm even more than all the rest.

"But…what made Father believe that it even still exists, that it was not irretrievably lost forever ages ago?" he queried, more sharply than he had intended, but his mother did not appear to notice.

"On his deathbed, your paternal grandfather gave your father this." From beneath the bodice of her silk gown Mrs. Blackfriars slowly drew forth an ornate silver crucifix suspended on a long slender silver chain, which hung around her neck. After taking off the cross, she handed it to her son. "Your grandfather told your father that he must never part with this for any reason, even upon pain of death, but hold on to it always, because it was the one key to unlock the mysteries of our family's legacy. But when your father began his furtive forays to Castle Dúndragon, he feared to be discovered and captured, and to have the crucifix wrested from him. So he gave it to me for safekeeping. Since then, I have worn it always until now."

"But…how can this cross be the key to the vanished emerald—and how came my grandfather by it?"

"I don't know." Mrs. Blackfriars shook her head. "I know only that Uncle Charles, who was of the de Ramezay branch of our family, also had a crucifix just like your father's, which had been given to him by his own father, along with the same dire stricture. But who made them or what, if anything, they have to do with locating the Heart of Kheperi, we never managed to learn."

Malcolm's head spun ceaselessly all evening long, the wheels in his mind churning furiously as he attempted to assimilate all his mother had told him. *Malcolm Ramsay.* That was his true name—yet it seemed as cryptic and alien to him as the two mysterious foreigners who had come to the map shop that afternoon, thereby precipitating the enlightening conversation with his mother.

Before supper, Malcolm had carefully read the small old bound journal in which Lord James Ramsay, Viscount Strathmór and later the Earl of Dúndragon, who had traveled to Egypt and, there, stolen the Heart of Kheperi, had recorded the account of his adventures. In his diary, Lord Dúndragon had explained that after robbing the tomb of its invaluable emerald in the Valley of the Kings, he had journeyed to Cairo, where, posing as a historian, he had struck up an acquaintance with a blind old priest at a temple. Seemingly casual inquiries of this priest about heart scarabs had eventually elicited a description of the Heart of Kheperi, along with the tale of its legendary history and purported enigmatic magical properties. Afterward, instead of returning the pilfered jewel to the Egyptians, Lord Dúndragon had kept it, not only because his family's fortunes had suffered debilitating reversals during the reign of Oliver Cromwell and the Roundheads, but also because he had not wanted his disastrous trip to Luxor and the sacrifice of all his companions' lives to have been in vain. But it had not answered, for in the end, the ancient talisman had brought him nothing but misfortune, too, instead of the good luck he had hoped. As a result, he had come to believe that the amulet was accursed, just as the blind old priest had told him. Here the narrative had broken off abruptly and never been resumed, so that Malcolm had known that this must be the point at which Lord Dúndragon had been accidentally and tragically killed by his own son while hunting.

Now, the diary finished and returned to the small silver strongbox that had belonged to his father, Malcolm paced his bedchamber restlessly, his mind dwelling on, among other things, the two foreigners who had come to Mr. Quimby's establishment that afternoon. Could they actually have been Egyptians, Malcolm wondered now, in search of the priceless emerald? Oh, if only he had known earlier today all his mother had imparted to him this evening! He would have been on his guard and perhaps been able to make discreet inquiries of the two foreigners to discover whether or not they had any inkling about the Heart of Kheperi. Perhaps their foray into the map shop had even been due to their somehow having learnt his own true identity, he conjectured, and therefore his nebulous connection with the missing emerald! For under the circumstances, that the appearance of the two foreigners at Mr. Quimby's establishment had been nothing more than the result of mere coincidence was surely too fantastic to be credited!

At that unsettling thought, Malcolm felt an icy frisson tingle up his spine, prickling the fine hairs on his nape, for if the two Egyptians knew who he and his mother were, might not the Italians—the Foscarellis—know also? If so, then he and his mother were undoubtedly in grave danger, for she had warned him repeatedly that their enemies were utterly ruthless, that they would balk at nothing in their quest to locate the Heart of Kheperi, and that the one she had referred to as "the old one, Vittore" had surely murdered his father and Uncle Charles.

As he strode like a caged tiger around his bedroom, Malcolm played unconsciously with the silver crucifix and long chain his mother had given him earlier that evening. As though they were worry beads, he drew the cross and chain through his fingers, wrapped them around his palms and passed them from hand to hand. At last, growing aware of his actions, he stopped and once more took up the magnifying glass from his desk to study the crucifix. Although its design was intricate and beautifully wrought, still, there seemed nothing particularly significant about it, so Malcolm could not understand how it could be the one key that would unlock the mysteries of his family's legacy, enabling him to discover the emerald. As he had already done several times before, he turned the cross over. Engraved upon its back were the word and numerals "Revelation 22:13." Malcolm had already looked up the chapter and verse in his Bible. It read, "I am Alpha and Omega, the beginning and the end, the first and the last." But how this was of any assistance to him, he could not fathom.

Sighing heavily, he finally abandoned the attempt to decipher whatever clues the crucifix might hold and hung it around his neck, secreting it beneath his shirt. It felt heavy and strange against his chest, although it was warm from the heat of his hands.

Despite the fact that, with evening's onslaught, the winter air outside had grown even colder, and the unrelenting drizzle continued to fall, he abruptly decided to go for a walk. He hoped that perhaps the chill and trickling rain would help to clear his head, which had begun to ache from all the chaotic thoughts chasing through it. Going downstairs to the small drawing room, Malcolm informed his mother, who sat at a table before the cozily burning hearth, playing cards with Miss Woodbridge, of his intention to go out.

"I don't know how long I'll be gone, so you needn't wait up for me, Mother," he said.

"As you wish, Son." Mrs. Blackfriars's pale countenance was momentarily etched with anxiety, and she bit her lower lip gently. "Bundle up, and take care. You know there are footpads and…and other dangers abroad in the city after dusk." Her veiled reference to their foes did not escape his notice.

"Aye. Don't worry, Mother. I'll be fine."

Donning his heavy coat, hat and gloves, and collecting his umbrella, Malcolm let himself out the front door into the night. No bright moon or stars shone in the dark, dreary sky, but the soft lamplight that glowed in the windows of the cottages lining Cochrane Street illuminated his path as he raised his umbrella to shield himself from the mizzle and started to walk toward Regent's Park in the distance. He had some vague notion of calling on Mr. Quimby, to relate the whole of what he had learnt from his mother to the older, wiser gentleman and to seek his counsel. Despite his mother's parting caveat to him, Malcolm saw no one as he traversed the streets, and in some dim corner of his mind he thought that it must be too cold and wet out for even the cutpurses and cutthroats who preyed upon the city. Thus, lost in his musings, he wended his way unmolested around the southwestern edge of Regent's Park and thence down Upper Baker Street, toward Mr. Quimby's brick town house.

But when at last Malcolm arrived there, it was to discover that no light spilled from the windows, by which he correctly deduced that his employer must already have retired for the evening. For a long moment, Malcolm simply stood beneath his umbrella in the ceaseless drizzle, gazing at the dark town house, hoping to see some spark of light or other sign of life indicating that Mr. Quimby was still up and about. But then, finally, when there was none, he knew with an acute sense of disappointment that to ring the bell would only waken the household and needlessly disturb Mr. Quimby, so at last, reluctantly, he turned away to begin his long walk home.

He had not gone more than a few steps, however, when without warning he was savagely set upon from behind. It all happened so fast that Malcolm was initially slow to react, so that before he could collect his wits and marshal his defenses, he felt his hat violently knocked from his head. Then a silken hood of some sort was roughly yanked down over his face, so that he could not see and could hardly breathe. This frightening circumstance proving an impetus, he began to claw at the sleek cowl blinding his visage, dropping his umbrella as he did so, instead of using it as a weapon, as he ought. But then, recovering his composure, Malcolm started to struggle mightily against the fists that pummeled him furiously, tore at his heavy coat and pounded him to his knees. He knew from his attackers' grunts of pain and muttered curses that he had got in several good punches himself, but still, as he fought desperately with his assailants, he feared he was losing the battle. So it was much to his relief that Malcolm suddenly heard shouting in the distance, followed by the shrilling of a constable's whistle and running footsteps. Then, just as abruptly as the attack upon him had begun, it ceased, and Malcolm was finally able to snatch the suffocating hood from his head. As, gasping for breath and still stunned by the brutal blows he had received, he staggered to his feet, he spied a young man hurrying toward him from across the street, as well as a policeman hastening to the scene from the corner of Dorset and Baker Streets.

"I say, sir, are you all right?" the young man inquired anxiously, solicitously bending to retrieve Malcolm's hat and umbrella, both of which had been trampled upon in the scuffle, the hat staved in and flattened, and the black folds of the umbrella now broken and fluttering forlornly in the mizzle.

"Aye, I think so."

"I don't believe these will be much use to you now, unfortunately." The young man handed him the hat and umbrella.

"No, I don't suppose so."

By this time, the constable had arrived, along with Mr. Quimby, who, roused from his bed by the noises of the fierce fray below and by the shrieking of the policeman's whistle, had poked his head out of an upper-story window of his town house to try to determine the cause of the disturbance.

"I suggest we all retire to my drawing room," Mr. Quimby said now, "so we can not only get out of the rain, but also determine that Malcolm is really uninjured from this monstrous assault upon him!" The elder gentleman was obviously highly indignant that one of his most valued employees had been set upon in such a brutal fashion.

The others needed no further urging, but gratefully followed Mr. Quimby inside his town house. There, the tugging of a bell rope summoned Mrs. Merritt, his housekeeper, along with other servants, and in moments, hot tea was being served, and a welcome fire blazed in the hearth beneath its ebonized wood mantel. In a dark green velvet wing chair before the fire sat Mr. Quimby, wrapped up in his silk dressing gown, a long, tasseled nightcap askew on his head, and his feet propped up on a gout stool. Across from him, perched precariously on the edge of his seat, as though awkward and ill at ease in the drawing room, was the constable, making inquiries and taking notes. Malcolm and the dark, handsome young man who had so fortuitously come to his aid, and whose name he had subsequently learnt was Nicolas Ravener, occupied the sofa. Although Malcolm had previously thought himself largely unhurt, now that the rush of adrenaline that had sustained his body earlier had left him, he was painfully aware that he was, in fact, badly bruised, although nothing appeared to be broken.

"An' you've no idea, sir, who t' rum curs was what attacked you?" the policeman asked.

"No." Malcolm shook his head. "For as I've told you, they jerked a hood down over my head, so I never got a look at their faces. Still, I'm certain there was more than one."

"That's right," Mr. Ravener put in, "for I saw at least two men and possibly even three fleeing from the scene, Officer. 'Twas difficult to tell because 'twas dark, of course, and raining, so I'm afraid the street lamps weren't of much use. The men who assaulted Mr. Blackfriars ran down Baker Street toward Oxford Street. But I believe they may have had some sort of transport waiting for them, for I observed a delivery wagon of some kind leaving the curb rather rapidly shortly thereafter, and I didn't see the men again after that."

"Well, if'n I may say so, gentlemen, it don't sound like no ordinary footpad robbery t' me!" the constable declared stoutly. "It might 'ave been t' work o' one o' these vicious gangs o' thieves an' cutthroats we got roamin' t' city streets, but if so, I fear they must 'ave 'ad somethin' much more sinister than just pickin' 'is pocket planned for poor Mr. Blackfriars. You were lucky, sir, that Mr. Ravener 'appened along when 'e done!"

"Indeed I was!" Malcolm agreed fervently. "And I cannot thank you enough, Mr. Ravener," he said gratefully, turning to the young man.

"I'm only sorry I didn't arrive on the scene sooner, when I might have been of real assistance to you, Mr. Blackfriars," Mr. Ravener stated modestly. "As 'twas, I'm afraid all I did was shout at the scoundrels, which succeeded in alerting the policeman, thereby frightening the blackguards off. However, you yourself were putting up such an admirable fight, sir, that I feel quite certain the ruffians would not, in the end, have triumphed in their wicked scheme, whatever that may have been."

His inquiries finally concluded, the constable departed from the town house, followed by Mr. Ravener, leaving Malcolm alone in the drawing room with his employer.

"Malcolm, are you sure you're truly all right?" Mr. Quimby queried, clearly distressed by what had befallen his employee.

"Aye, sir, quite sure. I'll admit I'm badly bruised, but 'tis nothing that won't mend in time. I sincerely apologize for your having been wakened and dragged into this unpleasant affair, sir. I'm certain you must be wondering what I was doing outside your town house at such a relatively late hour and in the rain, and the truth is that I had hoped to speak with you. But when I saw no light at your windows, I realized you were already abed. I had, in fact, just turned away to retrace my footsteps homeward when I was attacked."

"I see. Do you want to tell me now, then, what is troubling you, Malcolm? What brought you here this evening?"

"No, sir, the hour grows late, and you've already been bothered enough tonight as 'tis, I fear. I simply wanted to relate to you a story my mother told me earlier this evening and to ask your advice about it, that's all. So 'tis nothing that won't keep until later."

"Very well, then. Let us plan on having luncheon together here tomorrow. You can tell me your tale then, over whatever savory fare Mrs. Merritt has planned for my dinner. In the meantime, however, in light of what has happened tonight...this scurrilous assault upon you...I absolutely refuse to permit you to walk home in the dark, especially alone. No, don't try to protest, Malcolm, for I assure you, I won't hear of it! You *are* injured and thus in no shape for a two-and-a-half-mile trek in the cold and wet. I'll send my houseboy for a hansom cab—no, a growler! 'Twill be slower but far more comfortable for you. Meanwhile, I suggest you retire to the washroom and tidy your appearance—for I feel quite certain you do not want to cause your good mother any worry, and she would be highly alarmed were she to see you looking as you do now."

"Aye, sir."

Presently, after repairing his dishevelment, Malcolm was ushered by Mr. Quimby, who held an umbrella over them both, outside into the hackney coach waiting for him alongside the curb in front of the town house. After seeing him settled comfortably amid the squabs of the "growler's" interior, his employer informed him that the fare to St. John's Wood had already been paid and to take his time getting to work in the morning. Then, affably brushing aside Malcolm's profusion of thanks, Mr. Quimby shut the carriage door and instructed the coachman perched on the box above to drive on. Its hooves seeming to clip-clop rhythmically in concert with the drizzle, the lone horse harnessed to the ponderous vehicle started forward obediently at its master's command, and the high wheels on either side of the equipage began to whirl like the cogs in Malcolm unquiet mind as he leaned tiredly against the cushioned bench within, wearily closing his eyes and inordinately grateful that he did not, after all, have to walk home alone in the winter's dark and rain.

Chapter Five

The Fortune-Teller's Prediction

Experience has shown that to be true which Appius
says in his verses, that every man is the architect of
his own fortune.

> —Sallust [Gaius Sallustius Crispus]
> *Speech to Caesar on the State, sec. I*

There is a tide in the affairs of men,
Which, taken at the flood, leads on to fortune;
Omitted, all the voyage of their live
Is bound in shallows and miseries.

> —William Shakespeare
> *Julius Caesar [1598—1600]*

Fortune favors the brave.

> Virgil [Publicus Vergilius Maro]
> *Aeneid*

1848
The Hôtel de Lévesque, Paris, France

The Hôtel de Lévesque was currently in an uproar—at the heart
of which was Madame Valcoeur, in unwitting concert with the
revolutionaries and radicals of Paris.

In all truth, the city had never really recovered from the brutal decapitation of King Louis XVI and his queen, Marie Antoinette, in the eighteenth century. Instead, ever since the violent
downfall of the monarchy, Paris had proved a place of dissen-

sion, defiance and unrest, home to one power struggle after another, and although the monarchy had eventually been restored, Louis-Philippe, the so-called Citizen King of France, had grown steadily more unpopular. During the previous month of January, the authorities had prohibited a banquet scheduled for the fourteenth, one of a series of such banquets that had been arranged in a determined campaign by protesters against the king's regime, his increasingly reactionary policies and the limitations that had been placed on the rights of assembly. Resolutely undeterred by its banning, however, the banquet's organizers had simply postponed, rather than canceled, their event, brazenly rescheduling it for February 22.

Most unfortunately, it was now deemed by the entire greatly discomposed Lévesque household—save for the comtesse herself—ignorant of the contumacious scheme of the banquet's organizers, she had, in January, decided to host her promised masquerade ball on February 22, as well, and she had dispatched her expensive, gilt-edged invitations accordingly. When the new date of the banquet had become generally known throughout Paris, her husband had wisely suggested that Madame Valcoeur change the night of her own grand affair, to ensure that it was not disagreeably disrupted by the brewing trouble. But the comtesse had adamantly refused to be persuaded by her husband's sage counsel.

"I really don't see how I can alter the date now, Jean-Paul," she had declared pleasantly but firmly, "for as you know, all the invitations were sent out last month, and everybody who is anybody in Paris has already made plans to attend. How could I disappoint them all—especially when 'tis quite likely that the authorities will forbid the protesters' banquet yet again, forcing it to be called off once more? *Non.* I shall not rearrange our own schedule and inconvenience all our expected guests simply because a handful of discontented rabble chooses to be most provoking—particularly when their banquet will all come to nothing in the end, anyway, as you will see, Jean-Paul."

But Ariana, now elaborately garbed in her costume for the

masquerade ball and standing before the ornate cheval mirror in her bedchamber, surveying herself in all her finery, was not nearly as certain about the outcome of all these events as her mother was.

It was true that, as had been dictated previously by the authorities and as Madame Valcoeur herself had correctly predicted, the protesters' banquet had been canceled yet again. But still, that had not quelled either the revolutionaries like Alphonse de Lamartine and A. T. Marie or the radicals led by Louis Blanc. Instead, both factions of the protesters had continued to foment rebellion.

Although morning had dawned with a lowering leaden sky filled with massing thunderclouds that had unleashed cold gray rain upon the city, Paris had nevertheless proved a beehive of activity. The night before, as a precaution against possible mob violence, squadrons of heavily armed cavalry had covertly infiltrated the city, some being secreted in the Hippodrome and others being bivouacked around Paris's fortifications; and in the dreary, miasmal predawn light, detachments of the municipal guard—troops of the line and of the cavalry—had begun making their way toward the city's central boulevards and the Palais Bourbon, where the legislature, the Chamber of Deputies, sat in assembly. For although the extremist journals published early that morning had carried prominent notices that the banquet had been called off, many in Paris still had not heard the news, and as the gloomy dawn had stolen over the horizon they had started toward the Church of Ste. Marie Madeleine, where the protesters had intended to congregate before willfully and disobediently parading through the city streets to their mutinous banquet.

From the French doors of her balcony overlooking the Rue St. Honoré, Ariana had watched uneasily as Paris's artisans, laborers and merchants had trekked along the maze of the city's narrow, tangled, twisting streets and alleys, heading for the Champs Élysées, the Place de la Madeleine and the Place de la Concorde. Her disquiet had only grown stronger when she had observed that the faces of many of those swelling the ranks of the procession were filled with grim determination and that beneath their cloaks a number of the marchers bore pistols, swords and daggers. To guard against the burgeoning throng, the authorities had ordered the military to be stationed along all the approaches to the Chamber of Deputies, with two regiments of the line and six pieces of artillery being positioned between the Quai d'Orsay and the Invalides to protect the legislature from the west, and a strong force being located upon the Pont de la Concorde, which bridge spanned the River Seine between the Place de la Concorde and the Palais Bourbon. Nobody except persons bearing tickets or deputies carrying their medals of office had been allowed to cross the bridge. The military had also occupied the area immediately surrounding the Chamber of Deputies itself. Fortunately, the Palais du Luxembourg, much farther toward the southeast, where the senate sat in assembly, had not appeared to be a target of the protesters, even though around ten o'clock a large group of fervent workers and equally fervent young men from the various schools of Paris had gathered at the Place du Pantheon, just east of the Palais's gardens.

However, from there, instead of marching toward the Palais du Luxembourg, the crowd had set out for the Place de la Madeleine via the Rue St. Jacques, the Pont Neuf and the Rue St. Honoré. Anxiously returning once more to the French doors leading to her balcony overlooking the latter street, Ariana, peeking through the curtains, had felt a violent shiver tingle up her spine as she had viewed the protesters below and heard them shouting, *"Vive la Réforme!"* and singing the "Marseillaise" and the chant of the Girondins. Until now, the front gate and front door to the Ministry of Foreign Affairs had remained open, and the soldiers who had stood guard before the place had been unarmed. But around noon, both the gate and the door had been tightly closed, and a detachment of heavily armed dragoons had been dispatched to protect the ministry, which had been attacked by a separate horde of rabble. Wielding sticks and iron bars, the substantial mob had attempted to break through the gate, stoning a sentry who had tried to pass through it to fetch reinforcements. Driven back, he had been compelled to seek shelter inside the ministry, whose windows were being smashed with rocks. Yelling, *"Vive la Réforme!"* the rioters had called for François Guizot, the powerful prime minister of the government, to show himself, but fortunately, by that time, the military had arrived at the ministry to disperse the protesters, and Guizot had been able to make his way to the Palais Bourbon unmolested.

Later that afternoon, Ariana had learnt that all over Paris, angry multitudes of people had attacked and looted shops and vehicles, and constructed barricades; and although, tonight, all the city streets seemed relatively quiet and undisturbed, still she remained tense and unsettled, all her anticipation of and pleasure in the forthcoming masquerade ball quite spoiled.

Even the Egyptian costume in which, as the ill-fated Cleopatra, she was dressed, and which would under any other circumstances have delighted her no end, this evening only heightened her sense of upset. Surely it was far too revealing! She could not believe her mother had approved of it, saying that it was no more risqué than the fashions that had been *au courant* during the days of Napoléon Bonaparte and Empress Marie Louise, when ladies had donned fine, clinging gowns instead of crinolines and masses of petticoats. Although Ariana was modestly covered, the graceful, pure white linen folds of her costume, trimmed with gold braid, nevertheless emphasized her full round breasts and molded themselves to her curvaceous hips. Atop her head she wore a smooth, chin-length black wig in the style of the ancient Egyptians, as well as an intricate gold coronet from whose center rose a cobra displaying its hood. Upon her dainty feet were sandals of braided papyrus. Her lovely face was heavily painted; her amethyst eyes were elaborately outlined with black kohl, giving them a slanted and deeply mysterious appearance. Staring at her reflection in the looking glass, she thought she looked exceedingly strange and most unlike herself—as though she had somehow just stepped from an Egyptian mural painted on the walls of a temple or tomb.

"Oh, *mademoiselle,* you look splendid!" cried Sophie, Ariana's romantically inclined maid, clasping her hands together and sighing deeply. "All the young men will be vying for your favor and longing to dance with you tonight! You shall be the envy of every other young woman present at the ball!"

"Perhaps," Ariana agreed slowly, loath to dampen her maid's well-intentioned flattery and enthusiasm. "But still, that thought does not lessen my fears for the future, Sophie! What news is there? Has there been any more rioting in the city streets?"

"*Non*—at least, not that I have heard about, *mademoiselle*. 'Tis as Madame Valcoeur said 'twould be—all the opposition's plans have come to naught. So you need not fret."

But still, Ariana could not help but worry. What if the guests attending the masquerade ball were assaulted en route to the Hôtel de Lévesque, snatched from their carriages by the protesters and beaten—or even killed? She wished devoutly that her mother had listened to reason and postponed or even canceled the masquerade ball. But it was too late now for that. Outside, from beyond the French doors leading to her balcony, Ariana could hear the rumble and clatter of coach wheels over cobblestones as the first of the guests began to arrive.

"'Tis time for you to go downstairs now, *mademoiselle*," Sophie pointed out.

"*Oui*, you are right." Ariana nodded.

Taking a deep breath to steady her frazzled nerves, she collected her ornately feathered-and-beaded mask on its long gold wand, then exited her bedchamber to make her way downstairs to the ballroom, where she joined her parents to receive those invited to the masquerade ball.

"How wonderful you look, *chérie!*" the comtesse exclaimed as she spied her daughter. "That costume was the perfect choice for you, as I knew it would be—for what man was not attracted to the beguiling and enigmatic Cleopatra of the Nile? Did not even all of Rome kneel at her feet? So will all the young men kneel at your own tonight, Ariana! Before morning, you shall be the toast of all Paris!"

"Maman!" Ariana blushed at her mother's boasting. "Our guests will hear you!"

Madame Valcoeur only shrugged her slender shoulders nonchalantly.

"And what if they do? What can they do but agree with me that I have the most beautiful daughter in all the city?"

"Indeed, you do, Hélène. We both do." His face beaming with pride, Monsieur Valcoeur bestowed upon both his wife and daughter an affectionate hug and kiss.

Then the French doors to the ballroom were opened wide, and the first of their guests were announced by the butler.

Ariana did not know how long she stood in the reception line, greeting those invited to the masquerade ball. But it seemed to her as though all her mother's claims about everybody who was anybody in Paris being in attendance must be true, for the butler's announcements appeared to go on endlessly. But finally she was released from her duties and able to mingle with the guests. At once her hand was sought by one young man after another for all the dances, and within minutes, her program was filled. The orchestra hired by her father for the evening and ensconced in the minstrel gallery struck up the melodious strains of the opening dance, and Ariana was whirled away by her first partner.

At any other time, she would have been thrilled by all the attention being paid to her by all the young men. But tonight it seemed that even this could not lift her depressed spirits, for whenever she ceased dancing to partake of the vast assortment of refreshments arrayed upon the long banquet tables at one end of the ballroom, she was privy to heated dialogue that further discomposed her—arguments over whether or not King Louis-Philippe would summarily dismiss the prime minister of France, François Guizot, from his post on the morrow in an attempt to pacify both the revolutionaries and the radicals, although it was thought by many of those invited to the masquerade ball that, ultimately, even this action would not mollify either faction of the protesters, that only the abdication of the king himself would serve. It seemed to Ariana as though the vast winds of change blowing across her homeland were very ill indeed, and she wondered anxiously what they would mean to her and her family, before she was abruptly startled from her troublesome reverie by her circle of friends.

"Oh, I'm so deathly tired of all this dire talk about the revolutionaries and the radicals!" Mademoiselle Gabrielle Fournier declared to the clique of young people gathered at one of the long banquet tables, tossing her head, forming her rosebud mouth into an impatient pout and stamping one petite foot with exasperation. "I thought we were here to have fun—not to debate the future of France! Besides, why should we care if Guizot is got rid of or not? Even if he is, he will be quickly replaced—and the king himself will hardly surrender his own position, I shouldn't think. Ariana, have you had your fortune told yet?"

"Non." She shook her head. "I have been dancing all evening and would be doing so still had I not informed Monsieur St. Quentin that some food and drink would please me more at the moment than yet another waltz. He was kind enough to oblige me."

"Well, you've partaken of the refreshments now, so you must go at once to the pavilion to inquire of Madame Polgár about your future!" Mademoiselle Joséphine de Hautmesny insisted firmly. "Oh, Ariana, she has told us all the most mysterious things that we scarcely know what to think!"

"Oui, that is true," Mademoiselle Véronique Richeville chimed in. "She is very cryptic—but also utterly fascinating...and, I don't mind admitting, even a little frightening! At first I thought she was probably just an actress whom your mother had hired to play the part of a fortune-teller for the evening to divert us. But I tell you, Ariana, after seeing her and hearing her predictions, I now feel certain that Madame Polgár is instead truly gifted, a genuine clairvoyant! I cannot imagine where Madame Valcoeur found her."

"I don't know," Ariana reported truthfully, intrigued by her friends' assessment of the fortune-teller whom her mother had arranged to be present at the masquerade ball.

In search of something to give her dazzling affair even more cachet while at the same time providing a novel amusement for her invariably jaded guests, the comtesse had finally hit upon the notion of having a fortune-teller available and had somehow conjured the evidently unfathomable Madame Polgár. To make even more of a production of the fortune-teller, at the far end of the ballroom, opposite the refreshments, upon a dais covered with thick Persian carpets in varying shades of ivory and gold, Madame Valcoeur had caused to be erected a huge bright multicolored striped satin marquee adorned with thick gold braid and heavily fringed tassels, which tent was normally used outdoors at the comtesse's garden parties. It was inside this elaborate pavilion that Madame Polgár had held sway all night, predicting the future for one and all either brave or foolish enough to seek her counsel. Ariana had no idea how many of those at the masquerade ball had actually done so, although, over the course of the evening, whenever she had chanced to glance at the marquee, there had always been a long queue waiting to gain admittance. So she supposed the fortune-teller to have proved quite popular. Now, however, as the hour had grown relatively late, the line had at last dissipated, so that when her friends had finally gaily finished escorting her over to the tent, Ariana was able to go inside right away.

In trenchant contrast to the brightness of the ballroom lit with an array of ornate chandeliers dripping with crystal ropes and prisms, and holding hundreds of candles, the interior of the pavilion was relatively dark, so that it took her eyes a long moment to adjust to the dimness within. Ariana did not know what she had expected, but certainly it was not the eerie, enthralling sight that met her gaze once she had grown accustomed to the gloominess inside. What she saw made her feel as though, by pushing aside the tent flaps and entering the grand marquee, she had suddenly somehow stepped into another time, another place—atavistic and arcane. Gone were the images, the music and the laughter of the ballroom beyond, now hidden and muffled by the heavily draped folds of the tent, wherein long shadows reigned all around, and the only sound was a strange, oddly discordant yet beautifully haunting melody that seemed to drift like mist through the pavilion, playing will-o'-the-wisp on the slight draft that filtered inside through the crack in the tent flaps. Except for the plush carpets piled extravagantly beneath Ariana's feet, the marquee was virtually empty save for one corner and at its very heart.

On the floor, in the obscure corner, was placed a large square gold satin pillow trimmed with gold braid and thickly fringed tassels. Upon this, his figure only barely discernible in the darkness, sat a dark-skinned, misshapen dwarf, plucking the strings of a harp. At the center of the tent were arranged the furnishings necessary for Madame Polgár's impenetrable trade. These included a massive, heavily gilded, thronelike chair intricately carved with goat and ram heads, snakes and dragons, and ravens and scarab beetles, and upholstered in a rich ruby-red velvet. Flanking the great chair were a matching pair of tall, lavishly embellished gold candelabra with twelve arms each, in each socket of which long beeswax tapers flickered. Other than that, the pavilion was devoid of light. From the branches of the candelabra, suspended on labyrinthine chains, hung gold, burning censers, from which curled tendrils of pungently scented smoke that smelled of a wholly unfamiliar fragrance, foreign and exotic. Before the thronelike chair stood a small round wooden table, also floridly carved and gilded. Upon it was draped a heavily fringed black silk shawl spangled with gold suns, moons and stars. Atop the shawl sat a baroquely carved gilded box and a large crystal ball cradled by a highly detailed gold stand. Across the table, opposite the ponderous chair and in sharp contrast to it, was a delicate four-legged stool, whose hammock seat was fashioned of sturdy gold brocade.

Regally ensconced upon the thronelike chair was the fortune-teller, Madame Polgár herself. In age, she might have been anywhere from forty to a hundred. It was extremely difficult to tell, for her dark, inscrutable face, with its high cheekbones and prominent hooked nose, was devoid of all but the faintest of wrinkles, so that it was only her hoary, brown-spotted, clawlike hands, with their long, talonlike bloodred nails, that bore witness to the fact that she was not a young woman, but a beldam of some advanced years. Her deep-set, slanted eyes, heavily outlined with kohl, were like those of a hawk and equally penetrating and golden in color. Her mouth was full and scarlet. Upon her head she wore a plumed crimson turban that concealed her hair; set into its front center was a large paste ruby surrounded by paste diamonds. Shapeless, flowing silk robes in shades of crimson and gold covered her body. Big gold hoop earrings hung from her earlobes, and a multitude of matching gold bracelets adorned her wrists. An assortment of gold rings set with a number of paste gems bedecked her fingers. When she spoke, her voice was like the croaking of a raven, low and smoky, and her French was heavily accented by the nuances of her own native Gypsy language.

"Come in, Daughter of Isis," she intoned throatily. "Long have I been expecting you."

"I'm supposed to be Cleopatra," Ariana announced, slowly advancing into the tent.

"Yes, I know…she who, whilst she lived upon this earth, was the goddess Isis personified, and who chose as the instrument of her death not the asp, as is popularly, however mistakenly, believed, but the cobra sacred to the goddess Meretseger—She Who Loves Silence—which goddess is but another face of Isis, also. For all the goddesses are actually but one goddess…each different face but the various guises in which the great Earth Goddess, who is the Divine Mother of us all, appears to us. So, I say again, come in, Daughter of Isis. Come in and be seated, and I will tell your fortune—and tell it truly, be it good or ill."

Hesitantly approaching the table, Ariana gingerly sat down upon the brocade stool before it. She was not exactly frightened, for she knew that her mother would scarcely have hired Madame Polgár if the crone had been likely to prove dangerous. But still, there was something inexplicably uncanny about the fortune-teller that caused a strange grue to shudder up Ariana's spine. All at once, weirdly, in the darkness of the marquee, it seemed to her as though Madame Polgár were incredibly ancient, had herself walked along the banks of the River Nile when Cleopatra had lived and reigned, although Ariana knew that, surely, that was not possible. Still, she began to understand why all her friends had been so excited and enthusiastic about the fortune-teller. If Madame Polgár were a fraud, she was a very good one, indeed.

"Do you believe in Fate, in Destiny, Daughter of Isis?" the fortune-teller now asked, abruptly jolting Ariana from her suspenseful musings.

"*Oui,* I suppose so. Doesn't everyone?"

"*Non...*some believe there is no such power, that, instead, our lives are what we ourselves make of them, because we have been gifted with Free Will. But of course, that is not entirely true, else what would be the point in praying to the gods and goddesses, who are the One God and the One Goddess, to intervene in the affairs of men, eh?"

"Why...I don't know. I guess I never thought of it that way before."

"You should. Now, let me see your hands," Madame Polgár commanded.

Obediently Ariana did as directed, stretching her hands out over the table, surprised to see that they trembled a little—but whether from excitement or fear, she did not know. Taking hold of them, the fortune-teller grasped them so fiercely for a moment that Ariana nearly winced, for she would not have believed that the beldam possessed such strength, and the many bejeweled gold rings she wore pressed into Ariana's tender flesh painfully, as well. But then, as though sensing the younger woman's pain, Madame Polgár slackened her grip slightly. Then she carefully turned Ariana's hands over to expose their palms.

"The right hand...that is the hand of Fate," the fortune-teller explained as she studied Ariana's palms intently. "The lines you see upon it were written also in the stars at the time of your birth, and had you no mind or will of your own, what is drawn there would indeed be the map of your future. But the left hand...that is the hand of Free Will, and as you can see for yourself, the lines upon it are different from those of your right hand. They are the map of the choices you have made in the past and that you will make in the future, also, which—whether for good or ill—will shape and change what Fate originally decreed for you in this lifetime."

"This lifetime?" Ariana inquired, her brow knitting into a thoughtful frown.

"*Oui*...for as you know, the soul is immortal and so does not die with the body, but merely continues its long journey to the One God and One Goddess—for the path to the Father and Mother of us all is neither straight nor easy, but a labyrinthine way fraught with many trials to test both our knowledge and our worthiness. It cannot be traveled in a single lifetime. So 'tis that the soul journeys through many lifetimes—until it has learnt all it must to become One with the One God and the One Goddess." Madame Polgár now clasped the younger woman's hands together tightly. "And during each lifetime, as your hands enfold thus, one with the other, so do Fate and Free Will entwine, and of them both is born your future."

"And what does mine hold in store for me?"

"Are you quite certain you wish to know the answer to that question, Daughter of Isis?"

"*Oui, madame.*"

"Then...let us see what we may see."

Releasing Ariana's hands at last, the fortune-teller turned her attention to the large crystal ball that sat to one side. Shifting it to the center of the table, she enwrapped it with one long corner of the black silk shawl and began to polish it, employing a slow circular motion that made Ariana feel as though she were somehow being mesmerized as she watched. The silent dwarf in the dark-shadowed corner continued to pluck the strings of his harp quietly, but now the music had grown repetitive and hypnotic, seeming to lull Ariana into a bizarre trance, so that she could no longer even think. The smoke drifting from the incense burners and pervading the tent appeared to have become thicker and ever more strongly scented. Its rich, alien perfume permeated her nostrils deeply, making it difficult for her to breathe. Her head swam, so that she felt strange and disoriented, even disembodied, as though she somehow surveyed the interior of the pavilion from a great distance beyond herself. After a long moment, Madame Polgár at last drew the shawl from the crystal ball, and as she did so, small blue sparks ignited and crackled in the darkness, as though they flew from her very fingertips.

"Gaze now—long and deep—into the crystal ball, and tell me what you see," she instructed Ariana.

As she had been directed, the younger woman leaned forward over the table to look into the crystal ball. Only moments before, it seemed, it had been as clear as the finest-wrought crystal bell. But now, much to Ariana's surprise, it was somehow no longer so.

"I…I see mist, *madame,*" she said slowly.

"Is that all?"

Even as Madame Polgár asked the question, inside the crystal ball the grayish-white brume that swirled like a gossamer veil on the wind drifted and parted to reveal a lake.

"*Mon Dieu,* 'tis the loch!" Ariana gasped out, stricken by the appearance of the lake that formed such a principal part of the dream, the nightmare, that had haunted her ever since she could remember.

So stunned was she to behold it in the crystal ball, in fact, that she did not hear the fortune-teller's own sharp intake of breath or realize how Madame Polgár now bent near eagerly.

"The loch?" the fortune-teller prompted softly.

"*Oui*…Loch Ness, 'tis called. 'Tis a lake in the Highlands of Scotland. I…I learnt about it in my lessons on geography with my governess, Mademoiselle Thibault."

"I see. And is it a very vast lake?"

"In length, *oui,* for it seems to be without beginning or end. But in width, *non,* for when the mist parts, I can spy the opposite shore."

"And what do you see there?"

"A…a forbidding old pale red-sandstone castle—a terrible place!"

"How do you know?"

"I—I don't know—except that despite its true color, it looks in certain lights as white and gruesome as old bones. So it—it must be enchanted somehow…and wicked!"

But then, recalling, of a sudden, all her mother's strictures to her about speaking of her nightmare to anyone, Ariana bit her lower lip hard and shook her now dully throbbing head to try to clear it. She felt dazed and confused, unsure of herself and her surroundings. She thought that perhaps she would awaken at any moment to discover that she was really abed and dreaming—a new, distorted version of her nightmare. With great difficulty she forced her gaze from the crystal ball, uncertain now whether she had actually seen the loch and the castle there or only imagined she had. The music played by the dwarf in the oblique corner had grown louder, the smoke wafting from the incense burners heavier, filling the tent with a spicy cloud. Frightened that she had spoken of elements of her nightmare, Ariana now wanted nothing more than to leave the marquee, but somehow, strangely, she seemed to lack any will of her own, to be held spellbound where she sat.

The gold bangles on her wrists jangling, Madame Polgár shifted the crystal ball back to its previous position on the table. Then she opened the ornate gilded box to withdraw a deck of tarot cards. These were beautifully and intricately painted, each one a small, magnificent work of art, and obviously well cared for, as though the fortune-teller employed them only on special occasions. She handed them to Ariana.

"Shuffle the cards three times, Daughter of Isis," Madame Polgár directed.

The deck felt stiff in Ariana's graceful hands, so that she had difficulty shuffling it. But at last she finished and returned it to the fortune-teller, who began to lay the cards out on the table in an ancient, complex pattern. When she was finished, she stared at them interestedly for a long moment. Then once more she spoke, her voice like the rasp of a hawk's talons against a sea cliff.

"The three kings you see among the cards represent three men whom you will meet in the future. Beware this one—" with one long bloodred fingernail, the fortune-teller tapped the King of Pentacles "—for the card is reversed, meaning he is corrupt and dangerous, so bodes ill for you. The King of Swords will be in some profession…a man of law, perhaps, or some other such field that requires thought and analysis, a designing mind. But whether he will prove friend or foe to you, I cannot say. But he who is represented by the King of Wands will be devoted to you. Trust him—if you must trust anyone at all—for he will watch over you, even unto death. For many perils lie in wait for you, Daughter of Isis, and a fateful journey will soon be in the offing, which will ultimately carry you across both sea and land to the lair wherein the dragon has for centuries abided. Long has it waited for your return—as have the brothers who are the sons. Even now, like a flock of ravens to a corpse-strewn battlefield, they are gathering from far and wide—and from a distant shore an interloper has come to reclaim that which belongs to the Ancient One. Like him, you will embark upon a dangerous search— yet what you seek is not what you will find. For of two hearts, only one will prove your own true desire. Cleave to that one, for the other will play you false in the end. In your hands you hold the key to your destiny. You always have. Use it wisely and well, Daughter of Isis…."

As Madame Polgár fell silent at last, Ariana glanced up from the cryptic cards arrayed upon the table to discover that the crone had mysteriously disappeared! The magnetic music had ceased, and the dwarf, too, was gone. It was as though he and his mistress had somehow vanished into the aromatic smoke saturating the pavilion. Bewildered and disturbed, feeling peculiarly as though she had slept for a hundred years and only just now awakened, Ariana slowly pushed the stool back from the table and rose, distressed to find that she was oddly weak and trembling. For a long instant, she grasped the edge of the table to steady herself, until, finally, her shaky legs regained their strength and steadiness. Then she fumbled her way from the tent, blinking her eyes as they were abruptly dazzled by the brilliant lights of the ballroom beyond.

"Oh, Ariana, you were inside the marquee for such a very long time!" Gabrielle cried upon spying her. "Far longer than anybody else! And you're looking quite pale and stunned, besides! What did Madame Polgár say to you? She's so uncanny that she's positively frightening, isn't she? Were you scared out of your wits?"

"*Oui,* do tell!" Joséphine demanded imperiously. "For we've all the rest of us shared our fortunes with one another, and so you must, as well—for we must know if you're going fall madly in love and marry the tall, dark, handsome man of your dreams! That is what we thought Madame Polgár would predict for us all—only, it wasn't. Such peculiar things she told us instead! Oh, was she not everything we said she was, Ariana?"

"*Oui,* she was…very mysterious, indeed," Ariana agreed, taking deep breaths to attempt to calm her nerves and clear her lungs of the smoke and incense from the tent. "So much so that I'm not quite sure what to make of her or all she told me."

"Well, what did she say?" Véronique inquired.

"So many things that, in truth, I hardly even know where to begin," Ariana replied, still uneasy that she had disobeyed her mother's warnings and discussed elements of her nightmare with the fortune-teller. "Besides which, it was all so very strange and cryptic that, as I said, I really don't know whether I can make heads or tails of it—or, if I can, what to think about any of it. However, the one part I'm certain of is that I'm soon to undertake a journey— over both sea and land, or so Madame Polgár told me." Deliberately, slowly regaining her composure, Ariana shrugged and laughed a little, trying to make light of the fortune teller's predictions. "For my own self, I shall believe it when I see it—for I cannot even begin to imagine leaving France!"

But the very next day, much to Ariana's dismay, instead of the protesters settling down, the situation only worsened. Barricades rose in every quarter of Paris, and the colonels of the national guard reported that their men were demanding that King Louis-Philippe dismiss the prime minister, François Guizot, from his post immediately. Following this announcement, an interrogation of the generals of the line elicited the most unwelcome and devastating information that not one commander would answer for his troops if the national guard sided with the multitudes of the city's citizens who were now taking up arms in the name of revolution and reform.

"Fire on the people? No! Fire on the people who pay us? We shall do nothing of the kind. If we have to choose between massacring our brothers and abandoning the monarchy, there can be no hesitation," an artillery officer stationed near the Hôtel de Ville was said to have emphatically declared when questioned about where his loyalties lay.

Finally grasping the seriousness of what confronted him, the king eventually saw no other choice but to agree to the people's demands and get rid of Guizot and his compatriots. The prime minister and his ministry were dismissed forthwith. Aides-de-camp and general officers, mounted on horseback, galloped throughout the streets of Paris to spread the news. When it reached the Petit Bourse, near the Opéra, the funds rose forty centimes in response. But still the protesters did not forsake the blockades they had erected earlier that day. The strongest and most creative of these, constructed between the Rue du Temple and the Rue St. Martin, was guarded by hundreds of ardent young men who insisted that they must have proof of Guizot's dismissal and guarantees of their own safety and freedom before they would abandon their barricade. Until all this arrived, they undertook, as a precaution, to post sentries and to prepare to bivouac for the night, although many lacked either food or the means to build a fire for warmth.

Guizot himself, highly aware of the loathing and contempt the people felt toward him, kept his town house, the Hôtel des Capucines, as securely protected as the protesters did the blockades, with a huge military force stationed both outside and inside. But the Hôtel de Lévesque had no such safeguards, and as the news of what was occurring in the city reached the household, Ariana could only be terrified for the safety of her family and their servants. It did not seem possible that it was only last night that her mother's masquerade ball had been held. This evening, to Ariana, the ball felt like a lifetime ago.

"What is happening in the city streets, Sophie?" she asked now of her maid, who had entered her bedroom, bearing a tray filled with a pot of hot chocolate, a delicate Sèvres cup and saucer, and an assortment of bonbons, cakes and small sandwiches. "I have heard the rabble marching outside, singing and shouting, and it all sounds so frighteningly near! Are the people still up in arms? Are they close to the Hôtel de Lévesque? Oh, they must be! I'm sure they must be!"

"Oui, mademoiselle." Nodding, Sophie set the tray down on a nearby table and began to pour the hot chocolate from the pot into the cup. "'Tis said that the protesters are calling for lights to be lit all over Paris, and that, as a result, all the grand houses around the Tuileries now have lamps or candles placed in their windows to appease the masses. Those who have refused to honor the protesters' demands are being threatened with the smashing of their windows, and in some places, rocks have been thrown to that end. The Ministère de la Justice would not heed the call for lights and was attacked by more than ten thousand men!"

"Oh, *non!*" Ariana gasped out, alarmed and stricken.

"I'm afraid 'tis true, *mademoiselle.*" Having finished doing the honors and handing her mistress the cup of hot chocolate, Sophie moved now to start lighting the lamps and to place them prominently at the windows. "The protesters broke the *ministère's* windows and set fire to the front door and sentry box. But do not worry, *mademoiselle.* Once 'twas learnt that the *ministère* was under assault, a body of cuirassiers and several detachments of the national guard were dispatched to the scene to restore order. They have formed a line across the Rue Castiglione, and no one is being allowed to pass now."

Ariana devoutly hoped that this would prove enough to quell the violence. But then, around ten o'clock, at the Hôtel des Capucines, where Guizot had also defiantly refused to light either lamps or candles, a bloody and hideous scene of carnage ensued. The large number of troops positioned around the hôtel had oc-cupied the pavement, compelling those gathered there onto the carriageway, which, like the boulevards' footpaths, was filled with hundreds of protesters, spectators and even idle promenad-ers curious to see what was taking place. For quite some time the demonstration was fairly peaceful, but then a phalanx of un-armed artists and students appeared, parading along the boule-vards and singing *"Mourir pour la Patrie."* Shortly thereafter, a gun was accidentally discharged, the bullet striking the leg of the horse ridden by the commanding colonel. Mistakenly believing that his troops were under attack, he at once gave the order to fire, and the fourteenth Regiment of Line raised their weapons to release a lethal barrage of musket balls into the crowd. A for-tunate few who witnessed the soldiers leveling their guns in preparation to fire had the swift presence of mind to drop to the ground and so were spared. But everywhere else, men, women and children from every walk of life fell where they stood, their blood spilling upon the pavement, the carriageway and the foot-paths. Panic set in immediately, and the thousands of people by now present at the Hôtel des Capucines fled in fear for their very lives in every direction, screaming and crying and calling for vengeance against their government, whose military would mas-sacre the populace in such a brutal, ruthless fashion.

Ariana, drawn by the sound of the terrifying shots to the French doors leading to her balcony overlooking the Rue St. Honoré, shivered as she discerned the fierce shouts of "To arms!" and "We are betrayed!" that rang along the boulevards, and she smelled the pungent scents of thick smoke, sweat born of fear, and bloodshed that filled the air. Then presently, as word trav-eled quickly through the city streets, she grasped the fact that all the violence she had heard had centered on the Hôtel des Capu-cines and that perhaps as many as a hundred citizens or more had been murdered there by the soldiers, after which a squadron of sword-wielding cuirassiers had charged, ignoring the futile en-treaties of the people to "Mind the fallen," and trampling the wounded and dead in their haste to assault the populace that they erroneously believed had begun the pandemonium by firing upon their ranks. Now, as the throngs of fleeing people poured into the boulevards from the area around the Hôtel des Capucines, from her vantage point at her French doors Ariana could spy hapless, horrified women clinging to walls, railings and trees, and even fainting upon the streets, while their fathers, husbands, lovers, brothers and sons tried desperately to drag them away from the scene of slaughter. Frantic parents snatched up their shrieking children to hurry away home with them. At the Hôtel des Capucines itself, as the crowd was dispersed, some semblance of order was at last restored, and a number of people turned their attention to the dying and dead, carrying the bodies of the populace to nearby houses and those of the uniformed national guards to their respective town halls. Several corpses, beyond the assistance of any physician, were loaded into a lumbering wooden cart, which was then, in a gruesome spectacle, hauled along the boulevards by a horde of angry men brandishing torches and sharp iron-headed pikes, and whose visages were ashen and grimacing in the gaslight cast by the street lamps.

The following day, after yet another portentously gloomy dawn gray and wet with drizzle had stolen over the glowering horizon, Ariana rose sometime after noon to the utterly shocking news that, as a direct result of last night's terrible catastrophe, King Louis-Philippe had abdicated his crown and throne, and that in the wake of this calamitous action, with France's future now so uncertain and perilous, her father had prudently decided to pack up his family and flee to England across the Channel, where they would be safe.

Her fateful journey and embarkation upon the dangerous search for her as-yet-unknown destiny, which Madame Polgár had predicted, had, it appeared, begun.

Book Two

The Locked Past

'Tis in my memory locked,
And you yourself shall keep the key of it.
—William Shakespeare
Hamlet [1600-1601]

The best prophet of the future is the past.
—George Noel Gordon, Lord Byron
Journal [January 28, 1821]

Chapter Six

Some Stories Told

What is life? A madness. What is life? An
illusion, a shadow, a story. And the greatest
good is little enough: for all life is a dream,
and dreams themselves are only dreams.

> —Pedro Calderón de la Barca
> *Life is a Dream [1195]*

And in this harsh world draw thy breath in pain
To tell my story.

> —William Shakespeare
> *Hamlet [1600-1601]*

The splendor falls on castle walls
And snowy summits old in story.

> —Alfred, Lord Tennyson
> *The Princess [1847]*

1848
*Oxford Street, Baker Street and Hatton Green,
London, England*

The morning after the brutal attack by the unknown assailants
who had set upon him in front of Mr. Quimby's town house, Malcolm awakened to discover that he was stiff and sore all over from
the beating he had received. Lying there in bed, dwelling intently on what had occurred the previous evening, he hoped fiercely
that the ruffians responsible felt even worse from the stout blows

he had given them in return. But then at last, knowing he could not continue to stay abed, no matter how bad he felt, he gingerly and with difficulty rose, glad when he performed his daily ablutions to see in the oval mirror above his washstand that at least his dark visage was unmarked. Otherwise, he would have been forced to come up with some innocuous explanation for the injuries, for he did not want his mother to learn what had happened last night. It would only upset and alarm her, as she would no doubt assume the worst—that he had been assaulted by their enemies.

But even after reflecting at length upon the incident, Malcolm himself was not so certain of that. It was quite true that, as the constable who had arrived on the scene in response to Nicolas Ravener's shouts had later in Mr. Quimby's town house observed, the attack had not appeared like the work of ordinary footpads bent simply on robbing him. But that did not necessarily mean that the Foscarellis had been involved. After all, was it really only sheer coincidence that he should have been set upon on the evening of the very same day that the two foreigners had come to Mr. Quimby's map shop? Or was there still some other, sinister connection of which he was as yet unaware? Malcolm did not yet know—and the fact that he did not disturbed him greatly. He felt almost angry with his mother for not enlightening him much sooner about their mysterious and troubled heritage. If she had not him left in the dark for so long, he would have been far better prepared to deal with the situation. But there was no help for that now. He would simply have to do the best he could to make up for lost time.

After dressing and breaking his fast, Malcolm left Hawthorn Cottage to make his way to the St. John's Wood omnibus station. Despite the fact that Mr. Quimby had told him to take his time this morning, he was nevertheless most eager to reach Quimby & Company (Cartographers & Map Sellers) at No. 7B Oxford Street. He wanted to ensure that he got all his work done as soon as possible, so that he would have plenty of time to eat luncheon with Mr. Quimby later that afternoon. Although Malcolm knew that his mother, had she been aware of his plans to tell their story to his employer, would have been shocked and horrified by the idea, he himself was cognizant of the fact that to stand any chance at all of reclaiming the past that had been stolen from him, he was going to need help. And certainly, at this point, his mother herself was in little or no position to provide it. Although she had finally, apparently, told him all she knew, it was patently clear to him that she had done so only to satisfy his curiosity and as a safeguard against their adversaries, making it plain that she did not wish him to embark on any scheme either to attempt to locate the Heart of Kheperi or to avenge his father's and Uncle Charles's murders. But one way or another, he *would* retaliate for those! Malcolm thought with grim determination.

By this time, the omnibus had reached its destination in Oxford Street. Disembarking from the crowded, ponderous public vehicle, Malcolm hurried into the premises of Quimby & Company (Cartographers & Map Sellers). After hanging up his coat and hat on the pegs at the rear of the shop and tucking his gloves and umbrella away on the shelf above, he made himself his usual cup of tea. But then, instead of lingering with Harry, Jem and Tuck before the cheerful fire in the main room, he told them that he had a great deal to get accomplished that morning, and he trudged upstairs to the workshop. Taking off his jacket and rolling up his shirtsleeves, Malcolm set to work, repairing and completing the drawing of the map on which he had labored yesterday and, distracted, had made so many mistakes. When it was finally finished, he observed with pride that he had done a good job of it, and he felt that Mr. Quimby would be pleased, even if the paper *was* worn a little thin in the one spot where he had been compelled to erase harder than he ought.

"Yes, indeed, that'll do. That'll do just fine, Malcolm," Mr. Quimby said, in fact, when he saw the map. "Why, I doubt that I could have done better myself! Lay it out on the table, and when Harry has eaten his luncheon, he can begin engraving the plates. In the meanwhile, you and I will nip up to my town house—for

I don't mind saying that after last night's unfortunate occurrence, I'm awash with curiosity to learn what 'twas that your mother imparted to you, which was evidently of such importance to you that you were driven to seek me out at such a late hour last evening—and at such miserable cost to yourself, as it turned out. I trust you are feeling at least slightly improved today and that your good mother has not learnt of the affair and so been unduly alarmed…?"

"No, sir. For you're right that it would only have distressed her—and for more reasons than you know. But these last belong to the story that Mother related to me yesterday and that I want very much to impart to you, Mr. Quimby. For to be honest, sir, I'm in dire need of advice and help, and I can think of no one else whom I would rather trust than you or whose counsel I would rather have than your own."

"Well, Malcolm, I'm truly flattered, and in that case, I devoutly hope I can live up to your expectations. So let us fetch our cloaks and hats and be on our way, then. For I confess that now I am even more consumed with curiosity than I was before!"

Once Malcolm and Mr. Quimby had collected their overclothes and departed from the map shop, the latter, over the former's objections, insisted upon hiring a hansom cab to convey them to his town house, "For 'twill be much quicker than walking, and even if you are only badly bruised and feeling slightly better today, Malcolm, I cannot think that even a brisk stroll in this cold and wet will be good for you after last night."

So without further protest, the younger man graciously consented to the older's plan, secretly relieved to be spared the walk—however short—in the wintry wind and drizzle to his employer's town house. A hansom cab was duly hailed, and presently Malcolm and Mr. Quimby were set down on the pavement outside the brick building that the elder gentleman called home. He let them in with his key, greeting Mrs. Merritt pleasantly when, hearing their arrival, she appeared in the foyer to assist them in divesting themselves of their coats, hats, gloves and umbrellas.

"I'm so glad you are joining Mr. Quimby for luncheon today,

Mr. Blackfriars," she declared as she bustled about cheerfully, hanging their overclothes on the hall tree, placing their gloves upon its shelf and their umbrellas in its stand. "'Tis so nice for him to have a bit of company now and then, I've always thought. I've instructed Polly to lay the table in the dining room, Mr. Quimby. I thought you would prefer to dine in there today, seeing as how Mr. Blackfriars was to be your guest."

"Yes, very good, Mrs. Merritt," Mr. Quimby replied, nodding with approval. "The dining room will suit us just fine. Is luncheon near to serving?"

"Yes, sir, 'tis all set out on the sideboard, ready and waiting."

"Excellent! Come along, then, Malcolm."

The two men made their way to the dining room, where they discovered that Mr. Quimby's cook, Mrs. Saltash, had prepared a steaming-hot vegetable soup, along with a nicely roasted chicken, tasty dumplings and carrots, a thick loaf of freshly baked bread and a delicious apple pie. Polly, the housemaid, served Malcolm and Mr. Quimby from the sideboard. Then, after instructing them to ring the bell should they require anything else, she bobbed a small curtsy and left them alone in the dining room to enjoy their meal. Once she had departed, Mr. Quimby spoke again.

"Now, Malcolm, if 'twill not interrupt your luncheon too much, I suggest you tell me your tale whilst we dine. Then, afterward, I can reflect upon the matter and determine if there is some way in which I can be of help to you—or at least if I can offer you any advice worth having."

So in between bites of his meal, Malcolm gave his employer an account of all his mother had told him yesterday, while Mr. Quimby listened intently, occasionally exclaiming at this or that and shaking his head with amazement, or interjecting a question or two. By the time Malcolm had finished his story, the two men had consumed their luncheon. Now they lingered over their coffee and apple pie.

"Well, I'm quite certain I don't need to tell you that I'm utterly flabbergasted by your tale, Malcolm," Mr. Quimby asserted, his shrewd pale blue eyes narrowed and thoughtful. "Why, do you realize that if the missing emerald still exists and were able to be located, 'twould undoubtedly be worth a fortune and make you a very rich man?"

"Aye, but still, I'm not getting my hopes up about that, sir. First and foremost, I want justice for the murders of my father and Uncle Charles!"

"Yes, but what you must understand, Malcolm, is that there are many kinds of justice—and an eye for an eye and a tooth for a tooth is not necessarily always desirable. There are other—and perhaps better—ways and means of dealing with the Foscarellis, as your father himself recognized. Now, do you have with you the crucifix your mother gave you yesterday evening?" At Malcolm's nod, the elder gentleman continued. "Do you mind showing it to me, or would you rather keep its appearance to yourself?"

"No, of course you may see it, sir." Withdrawing the cross from beneath his shirt, Malcolm slipped its chain from around his neck, then handed the crucifix to his employer. "I myself examined it at some length after receiving it from Mother, but for the life of me, I simply cannot determine that there is anything special or unusual about it."

"Hmm," Mr. Quimby mused aloud as he peered at the cross, turning it this way and that. "Nor do I spy anything that strikes me as particularly out of the ordinary about it, either. Therefore, we must take another approach and consult someone more knowledgeable in these matters than either you or I. Fortunately, I have a friend of long acquaintance who owns a jewelry shop in Hatton Garden. He is a Jew, and his name is Jakob Rosenkranz. If you have no objections, Malcolm, I believe we should take your crucifix to him and permit him to examine it. I give you my word of honor as a gentleman that he is an extremely judicious man—one who knows how to keep a secret and can thus be trusted not to speak of this affair to anyone else."

"I rely on your good judgment, Mr. Quimby," Malcolm responded slowly. "But I *am* curious. With all due respect, if your friend is a Jew, what can he possibly know about crucifixes?"

"More than you might suspect," the elder gentleman stated calmly, "for the cross is a very old symbol and not associated only with Christianity. Jakob is very learnt, so perhaps he will know something in this regard, which we do not, and which may be of help to us."

"Well, if that is the case, then, aye, by all means, let us inquire of Mr. Rosenkranz—for if there is, in fact, nothing remarkable about the crucifix, then I myself would fail to understand how it could be of any use to me—much less to hold the key that allegedly unlocks the mysteries of my family's legacy."

"Good. Then we are in agreement," Mr. Quimby observed, pleased. From his dark blue striped waistcoat he withdrew his ornate gold pocket watch to check the hour. Upon doing so, he sighed. "Unfortunately, 'tis much too late for us to visit Jakob today, for by the time we arrived at his establishment and concluded our business with him, we would not be able to get back to my own premises until closing—and there are all those plates that want engraving for Mr. Kenilworth's maps, and which we really must get on with. However, we could go tomorrow—and have luncheon at the Old Mitre tavern, in the bargain! What do you say to that, Malcolm?"

"That sounds like a fine idea, sir. And may I also say how deeply I appreciate all your advice and assistance in this matter."

"Oh, please, think nothing of it." With a simple, nonchalant gesture Mr. Quimby, blushing, modestly dismissed the younger man's thanks. "'Tis I who am deeply flattered to have been taken into your confidence, Malcolm. As you know, I adore puzzles— and what an intriguing mystery and grand adventure, this one is, eh?" The elder man beamed jovially with excitement. "Why, I haven't had this much fun since I was a child! So, at the moment, the only thing that troubles me is whether or not the attack upon you last night had anything to do with this business. I believe that, for the time being, we would be wise to assume that it did and to take steps accordingly…boxing, fencing and shooting lessons will do for a start. Gentleman John Jackson has been dead these three years past now, more's the pity, and of course, his boxing saloon closed down when I was almost as young as you are now. However, there are still some fighters who train aspiring pugilists, I know, and Domenico Angelo's grandson, Henry the Younger, still operates his fencing school in St. James's Street, I do believe. The original school was at Carlisle House in Soho Square, of course. But Angelo's son, Henry the Elder, moved it to the Opera House buildings, Haymarket, next to Old Bond Street, and then Henry the Younger moved it again to its present location. As for shooting—"

"I'm already quite an excellent shot, sir," Malcolm interjected. "My father taught me. We used to go hunting together. I've not got much practice in lately—"

"Then you must begin to do so at once!" Mr. Quimby insisted stoutly. "For if you ask me, these Italians, these Foscarellis, don't sound like a very pleasant sort of people at all…cardsharps and murderers…. Why, I shouldn't be at all surprised to find out they have long been mixed up with one of those secret assassination societies they have over there in Italy. Yes, we must take great care, Malcolm, and lay our plans well. Now, would you care for some more coffee or another piece of Mrs. Saltash's excellent apple pie? No? Well, then, let us smoke a cigar and have a small glass of port to warm us before we venture outside into the cold again, for from what I observe through the windows, 'twould seem that the rain is falling even more heavily now, and it doesn't appear that the wind has let up, either."

Rising from the dining table, Malcolm and his employer retired to the town house's cozy library, where a fire burnt brightly in the grate, and they enjoyed a pleasant smoke together, along with a good glass of port, before returning to Quimby & Company (Cartographers & Map Sellers). Once they were back at work, Mr. Quimby penned a short note to his friend Jakob Rosenkranz, informing him that he intended to call upon him at his jewelry shop on the morrow, around the luncheon hour, if it were convenient, and dispatched Tuck to Hatton Green with the message. Soon Tuck came back with a reply expressing Mr. Rosenkranz's availability at that time and the fact that he would be delighted to see his old friend, so was very much looking forward to their meeting.

Thus, the following day, shortly before noon, once more leaving Harry in charge of the map shop, Mr. Quimby again hired a hansom cab, and he and Malcolm set out for Hatton Green. This was a region famous for its impressive gardens and bounded by Holborn, Gray's Inn, Hatton Wall, and Saffron Hill Roads, the latter of which followed the course of the River Fleet, renowned for its mists, swampy banks and murky water. The land had originally belonged to the powerful Bishops of Ely, who, over the centuries, Mr. Quimby informed Malcolm as they rode along, had constructed an imposing palace and chapel dedicated to St. Etheldreda upon it, as well as a garden noted for its fine strawberries. But in 1576, not requiring the current bishop's permission, Queen Elizabeth had granted one of her favorite courtiers, Christopher Hatton, the lease of the bishop's gatehouse and fourteen acres of the bishop's grounds, as well.

"She set Hatton's annual rent for all this at a paltry ten pounds, ten cartloads of hay and a single red rose at midsummer," Mr. Quimby imparted to Malcolm. "Can you imagine?"

A cherry tree around which the Queen had reportedly danced the maypole with Hatton had thereafter marked the boundary between his property and the bishop's own. Hatton had been knighted a year later and become Lord Chancellor a decade after that, and when, in the 1650s, the gardens had been developed into an estate of houses and streets, the central of these last had been named Hatton Green in his honor. Now it was known for its jewelry shops, many of which belonged to Jews, and it was hard to believe it had once been home to Anglican bishops and a place where Queen Elizabeth had danced a jig with her courtier.

From Oxford Street, the hansom cab carrying Malcolm and

his employer to their destination of Jakob Rosenkranz's establishment wound its way along High Street to High Holborn and then Holborn itself, originally old Roman roads that culminated in Holborn Circus, which lay at the southern entrance of Hatton Garden. Here Holborn Bars, one of London's imposing and forbidding outer city gates, had once stood, although it had now long been torn down. To the west, in Gray's Inn Lane, were the Inns of Court, where the law was studied and practiced, and to the north, just off Hatton Green, was Leather Lane, a thriving street market where leather goods of all kinds were sold. Since Malcolm did not often have occasion to come to this part of London or its boroughs, he gazed around with interest at all the sights as the hansom cab made its journey to Hatton Green, finally pulling to a halt before a small, circumspect shop whose sign read Rosenkranz's Fine Jewelry. After disembarking from the vehicle, he and Mr. Quimby entered the place, a brass bell on the door tinkling discreetly as they did so.

Immediately a young man came forward to greet them. But he was quickly shooed away by another, older gentleman, whom Malcolm presently learnt was Jakob Rosenkranz.

The proprietor of the jewelry shop was a tall, lean, wizened man, with a pair of oval silver-rimmed spectacles that matched the color of his thin, wispy hair and long beard, and behind which glittered a pair of dark, penetrating eyes that darted ceaselessly around the premises, missing nothing. He was garbed wholly in sober black broadcloth, and he looked as though he were a hard taskmaster and perpetually bad tempered, to boot. However, Malcolm soon discovered that although prudent and exacting, Mr. Rosenkranz was nevertheless a scrupulously honest man who cheated neither his employees nor his customers, and who possessed a dry, waggish, razor-sharp wit that appealed to Malcolm's own sense of humor. In short, while the jeweler was not mean or stingy, neither did he tolerate fools gladly, nor would he be taken advantage of. After due consideration, Malcolm supposed that all these qualities must, in fact, stand his employer's friend in good stead, for he must deal with priceless gemstones and expensive metals every day, so must ensure that he had neither paste jewels nor adulterated alloys fobbed off on him.

"Jakob, how are you?" Mr. Quimby asked warmly, in greeting.

"The same as always…overworked, underpaid and freezing to death in this cold and wet!"

"Well, why don't you go on holiday, charge your customers higher prices and throw some more coal on the fire?"

"Because I can't go away and leave my shop unsupervised. Half my highborn clientele don't pay their bills as 'tis, because they're all living on their expectations. And if I toss any more coal onto the grate, the chimney is liable to get so hot that 'twill explode, and then where would I be?"

"In prison, I suspect, Jakob. I don't believe the authorities would approve of your blowing up a goodly portion of Hatton Green. Now, allow me to introduce to you my junior journeyman, Mr. Malcolm Blackfriars. Malcolm, this is Mr. Jakob Rosenkranz. Pay no heed at all to his infernal attitude of doom and gloom. It comes with the territory. If you or I make a mistake whilst drawing a map, we can simply erase it. If Jakob makes one, it shatters a costly or even invaluable gem."

"Quite so," the jeweler agreed, nodding. "Well, gentlemen, won't you step this way into my office? Aaron, Hezekiah, some tea for our guests, if you please."

While his two apprentices leapt to do his bidding and prepare the tea, Mr. Rosenkranz led Malcolm and Mr. Quimby toward the rear of the jewelry shop, where his private office was located. As Malcolm trailed along in the jeweler's wake, he gazed with interest around the establishment, noting that all the jewelry offered for sale was prudently locked up in glass-topped display cases and that the premises themselves were as clean and neat as Mr. Quimby's own map shop was. Once the gentlemen were in Mr. Rosenkranz's office, he bade them be seated in two bergère chairs before his desk, behind which he assumed his own seat. A silver teapot and its accoutrements were brought in on a matching silver tray carried by one of the two apprentices and carefully set down upon the desk.

"Thank you, Aaron, that will be all for now," the jeweler said, then, once the apprentice had gone, himself did the honors, pouring the tea into the delicate Meissen china cups arrayed on the tray.

"Milk or sugar, Mr. Blackfriars?" he inquired politely.

"Aye, both please."

When the teacups had all been handed out, along with small plates of biscuits from an ornate tin upon the tray, Mr. Rosenkranz spoke again.

"Now, Septimus, as pleased as I am to see you, my old friend, since you have brought Mr. Blackfriars along, I take it that your visit here today is not entirely a social call…?"

"No, 'tisn't. I want Malcolm to tell you a tale, Jakob, after which we shall want your opinion about something very important to him. But before he begins, I must have your word of honor as a gentleman that anything said here in your office this afternoon will go no further than the three of us without Malcolm's consent. I apologize if that seems cryptic, but the truth is that what we are dealing with is perhaps a matter of life or death!"

"Goodness! I am quite agog with curiosity now! Very well, then. You have my word, young Mr. Blackfriars, and as I suspect Septimus has already informed you, I will honor our agreement, so you need have no fear that I won't."

"Aye, sir, so Mr. Quimby has indeed told me."

That said, Malcolm related his narrative exactly as he had told it to Mr. Quimby the previous afternoon at luncheon, and also giving an account of the attack upon him outside his employer's town house, although making it clear that he did not know for certain whether this had had anything to do with the matter under discussion. Mr. Rosenkranz listened intently, now and then vociferating at this or that and shaking his head with astonishment or interposing a question or two. When Malcolm had finally finished his tale, Mr. Quimby once more spoke.

"So you see, Jakob, we would very much like for you to examine Malcolm's crucifix, and tell us whether or not there is anything at all unique or remarkable about it."

"Yes, of course. I shall be most happy to do so," the jeweler declared, his shrewd black eyes glittering with interest, curiosity and suppressed excitement. "But first, there is something I must show you." Rising from his swivel desk chair and taking a small ring of keys from the pocket of his black waistcoat, Mr. Rosenkranz unlocked a nearby cabinet, from which he withdrew a large silver strongbox. This he set squarely upon the desk, resuming his seat. "How long have you and I been friends, Septimus?" he queried.

"Why...for more years than I like to count! But since we were just lads, as well you know, Jakob."

"Yes...eleven or twelve years of age, were we not, when we first met? I don't think we can have been much older than that. Some young bullies had taken exception to the fact that I was a Jew," Mr. Rosenkranz explained to Malcolm, "and decided to beat me. They ambushed me at Smithfield Market, at the Bartholomew Fair, and perhaps I would have met a most untimely end there had it not been for Septimus and our friend Boniface Cavendish, who chanced to be passing by at the time. With rocks and sticks they bravely drove away the scoundrels who had set upon me, and so I was spared. But now, after hearing your tale, Mr. Blackfriars, I am put in mind of Friedrich von Schiller and his work *Wallensteins Tod*—which translates as *The Death of Wallenstein*. Do you know it?"

"Aye, sir, indeed I do."

"Then you will no doubt be familiar with the line 'There's no such thing as chance, and what to us seems merest accident springs from the deepest source of destiny.' This afternoon, all these years later, I am thinking that perhaps 'twas not chance, that 'twas no mere accident, after all, that Septimus and Boniface came to my rescue that day at the Bartholomew Fair. You may well wonder why that is, so now let me share with you my own curious story—handed down through my family for generations.

"As you are doubtless aware, Mr. Blackfriars, Jews have been persecuted throughout history, and my own family has proved no exception. Almost two centuries ago, in an attempt to better our lot in life, we immigrated to this country from what is now

Germany. But although we were jewelers by trade, we soon discovered that 'twas difficult to establish ourselves in that business here in London. For due to harassment and mistreatment in our homeland, we had come here with very little in the way of financial means. So in the beginning, my family scraped out a living principally as pawnbrokers—one of them in a tiny, cramped shop in Birchin Lane, not far from the Royal Exchange.

"One night, in the wee hours, this particular ancestor, Ezekial Rosenkranz, who owned the establishment at the time and lived in the small quarters above it, was wakened by a loud knocking on the front door below. Initially, as you may imagine, he was terrified by this, because naturally he feared that 'twas either the authorities, bent on arresting him for some unknown reason, or else blackguards who meant to do him some mischief, because he was a Jew. So at first, he attempted to ignore the sound, hoping that if he did not answer the door, whoever stood outside would go away. But instead, the pounding only grew even noisier and more demanding, and finally, afraid that his neighbors, too, would be roused from their beds, Ezekial became brave enough to dare to poke his head out the window, to try to determine what was amiss. He observed a single man below on the pavement, who, spying him, called up to him to come downstairs and open up the premises at once, insisting that 'twas a matter of life or death.

"Although still fearful, seeing no one else in sight, Ezekial at last acceded to the stranger's demand and went below to unlock the door. After glancing nervously up and down Birchin Lane, as though to be certain he was unobserved, the unknown man then hurried inside, issuing profound apologies for having wakened Ezekial at such an ungodly hour. Then, seeming to collect himself a little, he belatedly introduced himself as Westerfield, valet to the then Earl of Dúndragon, who was lodged at the nearby George and Vulture public house in St. Michael's Alley."

"No!" Malcolm and Mr. Quimby cried as one at this, utterly stunned.

"Yes, you may well express amazement, gentlemen—as I myself was equally astounded upon hearing Mr. Blackfriars's own narrative. But perhaps now you begin to realize why those deeply insightful words of von Schiller should have come to my mind, for what are the odds, I ask you, that Septimus and I should have accidentally become friends all those many long years ago, and that today he should chance to bring you here to my establishment, Mr. Blackfriars? Sheer coincidence? No, somehow I don't myself believe so. But I digress. So let me return now to my ancestor Ezekial, the pawnbroker, and to Westerfield, valet to the then Earl of Dúndragon. As you yourselves are already aware from the account of Mr. Blackfriars's mother, Lord Dúndragon had, whilst in his cups at Medmenham Abbey, embarked upon a ruinous game of piquet with the villainous Lord Bruno, Count Foscarelli and, having obliquely accused him of being a cardsharp, had been challenged to a duel at dawn for his pains. But what you don't know is that Lord Dúndragon had no intention whatsoever of keeping his disastrous appointment. Instead, he intended to flee to the Continent, and in dire need of money for his journey, he had dispatched his valet, Westerfield, to Ezekial's shop, to pawn what few possessions remained to him. These included a gold pocket watch, a gold signet ring and a silver crucifix."

Here both Malcolm and his employer once more uttered exclamations of surprise, but before either could voice any questions, the jeweler silenced them with an upraised hand.

"Wait—and you shall yet hear all, I promise you" he declared softly. Then, gathering breath, he continued with his own remarkable tale. "Now, during the ensuing transaction with my ancestor Ezekial, Westerfield expressed himself highly reluctant to part with the cross, for fear that his master should prove unable to redeem it later, and he finally asked Ezekial for a pen and paper, with which to write a note to Lord Dúndragon's younger brother and heir, Neill, then Viscount Strathmór, informing him of the whereabouts of the crucifix. Westerfield explained his desire by claiming that the cross was a highly prized family heirloom with sentimental value, but such was his immense agitation in connection with it that Ezekial quickly grew suspicious that there was a great deal more to it than that, and this feeling on the part of my ancestor only increased sharply minutes later. For when Westerfield at last departed from the premises, Ezekial, covertly watching him through the front windows, saw him viciously attacked by several dark-skinned foreigners, who had been lurking in the shadows, and forcibly dragged away into an alley, from which he did not afterward emerge. These men, of course, were undoubtedly hirelings of Count Foscarelli.

"Now, understandably, my ancestor became quite frightened that he should prove the men's next target, and believing that Westerfield—whether inadvertently or deliberately—had somehow involved him in some unknown but truly dangerous affair, he took both Westerfield's message to Viscount Strathmór and the crucifix itself, and furtively slipped from his shop, hurrying away to Petticoat Lane in the Jewish Quarter, where several of his relatives resided. There, in the house of his nephew, Ezekial painstakingly sketched a drawing of the cross, then carefully concealed both it and the crucifix itself beneath the floorboards. After that, he himself composed a letter to Viscount Strathmór, informing him of all that had occurred, instructing him as to when and where he could reclaim the cross and enclosing Westerfield's own short missive. As a precaution, Ezekial did not himself for many days afterward return to his establishment, but sent his nephew to watch it secretly instead—a wise move on his part, as it subsequently turned out, for during that time, his shop was broken in to and totally ransacked by Count Foscarelli's henchmen, and further, in the meanwhile, Westerfield's badly beaten corpse was discovered in the nearby alley.

"Eventually, my ancestor received a reply from Viscount Strathmór, and at the agreed-upon time and place they met, and the cross was not only redeemed, but also for a sum that was far more than what the crucifix itself was actually worth or had been pawned for, besides. By now, of course, the news was all over London that Lord Dúndragon had been shot and killed by Count Foscarelli in a duel at dawn at Green Park. 'Twas also widely known that the Italian had seized possession of all the

Ramsay estates in both Scotland and England, which Lord Dúndragon had foolishly wagered away during the calamitous game
of piquet. However, being the younger son, Viscount Strathmór
had never truly expected to inherit the Ramsay property in any
event, as, naturally, he had believed that his older brother, Lord
Dúndragon, would sooner or later marry and beget heirs. Thus,
needing to secure his own future, Viscount Strathmór had wisely
carved out a successful military career for himself, and a series
of prudent investments, besides, whilst not garnering him a fortune, had still ensured that he was comfortably settled and thus
able to handsomely reward my ancestor for both his honesty and
assistance.

"'Twas, in fact, this very money, combined with the funds
earned from the subsequent sale of his pawnshop, that enabled
Ezekial to establish Rosenkranz's Fine Jewelry here in Hatton
Green. So you see, Mr. Blackfriars, as strange as it may seem to
us both, the fortunes of your family and mine have long been irrevocably intertwined." Here the jeweler paused for a long moment. Then, with a second key on his key ring, he finally
unlocked the strongbox that he had earlier placed upon his desk.
After leafing carefully through all the sundry papers within, he
slowly drew forth a sketch—yellowed, creased and crumbling
with age—and handed it to Malcolm. "Is that your crucifix, Mr.
Blackfriars?" he inquired gravely.

"Aye…aye, 'tis indeed, sir! I'm almost sure of it!" Malcolm's
own voice rose with eager anticipation at the idea. Then, hastily
taking the cross from under his shirt and removing its chain
from around his neck, he handed the crucifix to the jeweler for
comparison to the drawing.

"Truly, despite everything, even now I can hardly believe the
two are one and the same—and certainly, I never in my life even
dreamt of holding the actual cross depicted by the sketch Ezekial
drew almost a century ago." Mr. Rosenkranz shook his head
slowly with amazement. "'Tis quite an expensive piece," he asserted as he scrutinized the crucifix carefully at some length. "For
'tis solid silver and not tin, of course, and the workmanship is ex-

quisite, as well. But aside from that, I do not immediately spy anything that would lead me to believe the cross is something more than what it at first glance appears. However, all that said, do not yet be downcast, Mr. Blackfriars, for appearances can be deceiving, and we all know the crucifix *must* be significant in some way, or else poor Westerfield would not, in all probability, have been murdered for it, nor Ezekial's pawnshop broken in to and ransacked for it, nor Viscount Strathmór so exceedingly grateful for its safe return. Further, the design of the piece is extremely intricate—and perhaps there is some obscure reason for that."

Opening one of his desk drawers, the jeweler brought forth his magnifying glass and peered through it intently at the cross.

"Ah." He sighed at last with great satisfaction, a small, triumphant smile playing about the corners of his thin mouth. "'Tis as I surmised. Here." He handed the magnifying glass to Malcolm. "Look closely at the pattern there, at the interwoven dogwood branches, with their flowers and thorns. Yes, there. 'Tis not clear in the sketch, which is only two-dimensional. But do you see? At the center of the garland of boughs, what initially seems like merely a twig or thorn is actually the Roman numeral one."

"Aye, so I see." Malcolm nodded, passing the magnifying glass to his employer, so that he could also study the design. "But what does it mean?"

"You said that your uncle Charles had a second crucifix, did you not?" the jeweler asked.

"Aye, a duplicate of this one, or so my mother told me."

"Oh, with all due respect to your mother, I myself doubt that it was an actual duplicate, Mr. Blackfriars," Mr. Rosenkranz insisted, shaking his head. "For if the crosses were precisely identical, why would they need to be numbered?"

"Quite so!" Mr. Quimby cried, plainly struck by this astute observation.

"Well, obviously, to tell one from the other—that is, which one belonged to my father and which one to Uncle Charles—or so I would have thought," Malcolm pointed out logically.

"Yes, that is true, also," his employer acknowledged, his enthusiasm of the previous moment now visibly dampened, his expression crestfallen.

"I see I failed to make myself perfectly clear. What I meant was, why the need to distinguish between duplicates in the first place?" the jeweler queried, his brow creased in a thoughtful frown. "I mean, if they are exactly alike, then what is the difference if one is two and two is one, or vice versa? Why number the crucifixes at all? If a man and his butler each have a key to his town house, does he number them one and two, when they both open the same lock?"

"Aye, I see what you mean now," Malcolm said slowly, reflecting upon the curious matter. "There is some reason for the numbers, then, of course, of which we are as yet unaware. Further, Count Foscarelli himself must indeed have had some good cause, of which we are also yet ignorant, however, to associate at least my own cross with the lost emerald. For otherwise, as you said, why would his henchmen have even bothered with assaulting and killing poor Westerfield, and with ransacking Ezekial's pawnshop?"

"Exactly!" Mr. Rosenkranz's dark face expressed his own triumph and satisfaction at this reasoning. "So I think we can be almost certain that however innocuous it may appear to us, the crucifix *is* still somehow the key to finding the Heart of Kheperi."

"Well, I'm quite sure I don't know what the two of you are so excited about," Mr. Quimby remarked glumly. "For if all that is indeed true—and I've no basis for assuming that 'tisn't— don't you see what it means? In all probability, it means that we shall undoubtedly need *both* crosses to locate the accursed emerald! So, do you know where the second crucifix is now?"

"No, unfortunately." Malcolm sighed heavily at the admission. "For after my mother and I parted from Aunt Katherine and her children that day at the George inn in Newcastle-upon-Tyne, we never saw nor heard from any of them again. 'Tis a matter that still distresses my mother deeply whenever she thinks of it."

"Yes, I can imagine," the jeweler put in sympathetically, "for nothing is more important than family. Still, 'tis a very great pity that the other cross has been lost, for 'twould no doubt assist us immensely were we able to compare the two side by side. Here, then, if I may be so bold, is what I propose, Mr. Blackfriars. If you and Septimus will do me the honor of allowing me to become part of your little coterie in this adventure, I will set about at once to make discreet inquiries about the second crucifix. We Jews are a rather tight-knit society, and many of us are jewelers, besides. So 'tis perhaps possible that I can learn something about the whereabouts of the other cross."

"Quite a most excellent idea, Jakob!" Mr. Quimby exclaimed, beaming. "I'm sure I speak for Malcolm, as well as for myself, when I say we would both be delighted to have you join our small ranks and grateful for any help you can provide."

"Aye, indeed, we would!" Malcolm chimed in appreciatively.

"Good." Mr. Rosenkranz was clearly pleased. "In that case, please permit me to make one other suggestion—and that is that the three of us together call upon Boniface Cavendish to take him into our confidence and enlist his aid, also. If you do not yet know him, Mr. Blackfriars, our friend Boniface is a bookseller by trade, with a shop in Old Bond Street. As such, he has stored in his head a lot of arcane knowledge from reading literally hundreds of books—much of that same knowledge utterly useless, I'm afraid, but still, 'tis entirely conceivable that he may know something about the legend of this mysterious missing emerald, the Heart of Kheperi, which your ancestor stole, and its curse upon your family."

"That's right!" Mr. Quimby interjected with renewed enthusiasm. "We must indeed make arrangements to meet with Boniface as soon as possible, Malcolm! He, too, is an honorable gentleman who can be trusted to keep his word, and heaven only knows what obscure volumes on Egyptian history he may have buried and moldering away in that dusty old bookshop of his—for, unfortunately, he is a pack rat of the highest order, I fear. Why, I don't believe he's ever thrown away anything in his entire life!"

Presently, it was agreed between the three men that Mr. Quimby would dispatch a note to Mr. Cavendish forthwith, to inquire about calling upon him on the morrow at his bookshop. Then, after the penning of this missive and its being carried away for delivery by the apprentice Hezekiah, Malcolm and his employer took their leave of the jeweler, feeling that their visit with him had proved extremely fortuitous and productive.

A slight distance from the jewelry shop, its entrance emerging between Nos. 8 and 9 Hatton Green, meandered a small narrow alley that led to the short street of Ely Place and to the Old Mitre tavern, to this last of which Malcolm and Mr. Quimby now made their way. Erected in 1546 by Bishop Thomas Goodrich of Ely for his servants, the public house had been demolished, along with the—by then—badly dilapidated Ely Palace, in 1772, when the Hatton line had died out, and the property, as well as the bishop's own, had reverted to the Crown, forfeited due to the large sums of money then owing to the monarchy for them. The tavern, however, had quickly been rebuilt, with a stone mitre from the palace's gatehouse being set into one wall as a reminder of its ancient heritage. Above its two separate dark wooden doors, placed amid a box of arched wooden windows that fronted on the alley, grew a mass of trailing ivy, and inside, the public house was equally as cozy, with two small wood-paneled bars. Within one of these Malcolm and his employer ate their luncheon, each longing fervently to discuss the topic uppermost in his mind, but dutifully refraining, lest others should overhear their conversation.

After that, a hansom cab returned the two men to Quimby & Company (Cartographers & Map Sellers), where they discovered waiting for Mr. Quimby a short reply from his old friend Boniface Cavendish—or, rather, from his senior clerk. For Mr. Cavendish himself, it appeared, had caught a chill from all the wintry cold and wet in London, and on the advice of his physician, he had gone away on holiday to the sunnier, drier Mediterranean until such time as he should be fully restored to his former good health.

Chapter Seven

Swept from Death's Path

Be not swept off your feet by the vividness
of the impression, but say, "Impression, wait
for me a little. Let me see what you are and
what you represent. Let me try you."

—Epictetus
Discourses

Ah, love, let us be true
To one another! For the world, which seems
To lie before us like a land of dreams,
So various, so beautiful, so new,
Hath really neither joy, nor love, nor light,
Nor certitude, nor peace, nor help for pain;
And we are here as on a darkling plain
Swept with confused alarms of struggle and flight,
Where ignorant armies clash by night.

—Matthew Arnold
Dover Beach [1867]

1848
The Pantheon Bazaar, London, England

Traveling from Paris to Calais and thence across the Channel
to Dover, Ariana and her family had finally arrived in London.
There, after spending some weeks lodged in an exclusive hotel,
they had taken up residence in one of the elegant town houses

to be found in beautiful Portman Square, in the fashionable Marylebone district.

Originally, the land on which Portman Square was situated had belonged to Sir William Portman, Lord Chief Justice to King Henry VIII. Subsequently passed down through the Portland family for generations, the sizable acreage had for the next two hundred years, however, remained largely fallow, being used principally for the wholly mundane purpose of pig farming. But at long last, in 1764, it had been developed by Henry William Portman, who had begun his residential project by laying the groundwork for the square itself, upon which graceful, imposing buildings by such renowned architects as Robert Adam and James "Athenian" Stuart had gradually been erected. The most famous of these, Montagu House, was located in the northwest corner of the square, which was constructed around a large, elliptical, tree-filled green park surrounded by a black wrought-iron fence to ensure the privacy of the square's upscale residents.

Montagu House had originally been built for Mrs. Elizabeth Robinson Montagu, a wealthy socialite and intellectual who, like her compatriot Mrs. Elizabeth Vesey, had made her mark with her establishment of "conversation parties," during which no gambling had been permitted, and literature had proved the primary thrust of the evening. These events had eventually come to be termed "bluestockings," after one of their frequent guests, Benjamin Stillingfleet. Allegedly so poor that he had not possessed the formal evening dress necessary for these assemblies, Mr. Stillingfleet had always appeared clothed in his informal day garments and blue worsted socks, this last of which had earned him the dubious but most often affectionate epithet of "Old Bluestockings" among the relatively close-knit coterie of illustrious attendees, which had included Dr. Samuel Johnson, Horace Walpole, Fanny Burney, Lord Lyttelton and even the king and queen.

Upon at last being comfortably ensconced at Portman Square, Madame Valcoeur, learning the history of the place, had at once decided that she would make her own mark in English society in the same manner as had Mrs. Montagu in the previous century. So, having been dutifully called on by virtually all the crème de la crème of London and warmly welcomed by them, the comtesse had enthusiastically set about to launch herself and her family into those exclusive, desirable circles by establishing her own salon. This scheme had proved an instant success, with the result that the Lévesques, although now well settled in England, had not suffered the social decline that sometimes befell other French émigrés. So, although Ariana was still occasionally homesick and missed all her childhood friends immensely, she did not lack for companions of her own class, being speedily taken up by a group of fashionable young ladies and made an object of homage by many of the handsome young gentlemen about town.

But still, despite all the unabashed, however well-intentioned, admonitions of her mother and the gentler, subtler prompting of her father, Ariana had yet to acquire any beau who truly suited her fancy. Now, sighing heavily at the thought, she turned from her bedroom window overlooking the park at the heart of Portman Square, feeling a wistful pang for the loss of her balcony at the Hôtel de Lévesque in the Rue St. Honoré. Although only eighteen, she knew that her parents were right and that she ought to be thinking of marriage and the securing of her future. Because he lacked a son, her father's title and estates in France would upon his death pass to a distant male relative. An heiress in her own right, however, Ariana herself would receive a monetary settlement in the form of a trust fund. So, barring any disastrous investments, she would never be poor. But nor, if she remained single, would her standard of living remain quite as high and luxurious as what she now enjoyed.

"I don't know why, but I feel very restless today," Ariana remarked now to her maid. "Let us go out, Sophie. The ceaseless drizzle of London has finally stopped, and 'tis such a fine spring day. We can go for a walk in the park or perhaps stroll down to Oxford Street to have a look in that Pantheon Bazaar we've heard so much about."

"Oh, *oui, mademoiselle*. That would be so much fun! Many

of the young ladies' abigails have told me that the bazaar has all kinds of trinkets and trifles at most reasonable prices, as well as an art gallery, a conservatory and even an aviary! Perhaps 'twill prove just the thing to lift your spirits, *mademoiselle*—for I know that sometimes, like me, you miss our homeland."

"*Oui*, 'tis true…I do. England is very different from France, is it not, Sophie? But at least here there doesn't seem to be nearly as much political turmoil—although I heard that six years ago, an attempt was made to assassinate Queen Victoria! I was surprised, for I thought she and Prince Albert were much adored by the populace. But it appears that is not the case in all quarters."

"*Non, mademoiselle.* There are many who dislike the queen and believe she should give up her crown and throne. But still, according to everything I have heard, that is not likely to happen. She has a good relationship with the prime minister and with Parliament. So you need not worry that we shall soon be compelled to flee from England, as we were France," Sophie declared firmly as she handed Ariana a fringed silk shawl to guard against the coolness of the spring breeze outside, along with a beautifully trimmed bonnet.

Both women now suitably attired for their excursion, mistress and maid went downstairs and let themselves out the front door of the town house. Then, after a brief but pleasant turn around the park, they started down Orchard Street toward Oxford Street and the Pantheon Bazaar. As they had not yet been in London above three months, they were still new enough to the city to gaze with rapt interest at all the sights, exclaiming over whatever caught their attention. Oxford Street itself was quite long and lined with shops of all kinds, being a particular favorite of florists and fruit vendors. But far and away one of its most popular attractions was the Pantheon Bazaar. This had, in 1772, begun life as a theater and a kind of indoor Vauxhall Gardens, serving as a venue for masquerades and balls. In 1791, it had evolved into an opera house, but unfortunately, this had burnt down the following year. It had reopened in 1795, but eventually, the kinds of entertainments it had originally offered had palled among the jaded highborn of London. Untenanted for some years, it had finally reopened yet again in 1812, as the Pantheon Theater. However, it was plagued almost from the start by great financial difficulties due to licensing irregularities, and at last, after only a few short years, damaged by a fire, as well, the theater had been compelled to close its doors. As a result, in 1814, it had been extensively remodeled and converted into the Pantheon Bazaar—and from the beginning, it had proved a worthy competitor to its principal rival, the Soho Bazaar.

Not far from the Cumberland Gate at the northeast corner of Hyde Park was the entrance porch to the Pantheon Bazaar, and after passing through this, Ariana and Sophie found themselves in a vestibule boasting a couple of unremarkable sculptures. From here, a flight of stairs led up to what Sophie, in her ignorance, had earlier termed the "art galley," but which mistress and maid now discovered was rather undeserving of that grand label, for it was, in reality, a series of rooms devoted to pictures of mostly mediocre quality, being painted largely by local artists and on the purchases of which the bazaar's proprietors received a commission. From these rooms, the upper floor of what was referred to as the "toy bazaar" was reached by another set of steps, which eventually gave way to a gallery overlooking the ground floor. From this vantage point, Ariana and Sophie saw that the entire bazaar was extremely tasteful and well laid out, with counters arranged in orderly fashion and displaying myriad wares. Hats, artificial flowers, gloves, hosiery, feathers, lace, jewelry and pocketbooks vied for space alongside cut-glass and porcelain ornaments, alabaster figures, cutlery, toys, books, sheets of music, photograph albums and a multitude of other items. Young women in plain, modest dress manned each counter, and the number of customers they were waiting on gave testimony to the bazaar's popularity among the *haut ton* of London, who, despite their riches, were, like their lower-class counterparts, still not averse to a bargain. At one end of the bazaar were the aviary, complete with caged birds for sale, and the conservatory, where was a wide variety of plants arrayed.

For the greater part of the afternoon, Ariana and Sophie

amused themselves by wandering among the counters on the ground floor, examining all the offerings and occasionally buying this or that, which especially appealed. Then, finally, exhausted by their shopping excursion and loaded down with bandboxes, a birdcage holding a pair of lovebirds from the aviary, and a potted plant from the conservatory, they decided to head homeward.

"Perhaps I should send for the carriage," Ariana said when, once outside on the pavement, she abruptly grasped the difficulty of their walking all the way back to Portman Square, laden with all they now carried. "Goodness! I didn't realize we had bought quite so much!"

"Hiring a hackney coach or a hansom cab would be much quicker, *mademoiselle*," Sophie suggested practically, "for then we would not have to try to find a messenger boy or to wait for the carriage to arrive from Monsieur le Comte's town house afterward, either. Shall I go and see if I can locate a hackney coach, *mademoiselle*—for in truth, I do not know if a hansom cab will have enough room for both us and all our purchases."

"*Oui,* that is an excellent idea! I'll stay here with our things."

"Will you be all right here alone for a few minutes, *mademoiselle?*" Sophie's face evidenced her sudden doubts as she thought of leaving her mistress's side.

"Of course. There are crowds of people all around, so 'tis highly unlikely that anyone would attempt to do me any harm with so many present to witness it—and there is a constable at the corner whom I can summon should I be in need of any assistance, besides," Ariana pointed out logically, touched by her maid's good nature, caring and concern. "So please don't worry about me, Sophie. I'll be fine."

"Very well, then. But pray do not leave this spot, *mademoiselle!* For I would be frantic if I returned to find you gone! I'll be back just as soon as I can."

With that, the maid disappeared into the masses of people thronging busy Oxford Street, while Ariana stood obediently outside the entrance porch of the Pantheon Bazaar to await her return with a hackney coach. But despite what she had told Sophie just moments before, now that she was actually alone on the pavement, Ariana discovered that she felt more exposed and vulnerable than she would have liked, standing there on her own, surrounded by all she and the maid had bought. She knew that, like Paris, London was rife with cutpurses and other scoundrels, and she fretted that perhaps one or more of these would swoop down upon the purchases, stealing some or all of them.

As a safeguard against this, she began to stack the bandboxes up neatly beside her, intending to place the birdcage atop them and the potted plant alongside to make it more difficult for any potential thief to take anything. As she concentrated on this task, however, Ariana suddenly felt strangely as though she were being furtively watched, and as the eerie sensation took hold of her, she glanced up swiftly from where she bent over all the bandboxes. Despite the relatively warm spring sunlight, she felt an abrupt frisson, and gooseflesh prickled her skin. Her eyes scanned her environs intently, but she saw nothing untoward, and after a moment she bit her lower lip hard, shaking her head at what she insisted to herself was no doubt naught save her own foolishness and nervousness. Still, this was not the first time since arriving in England that Ariana had felt as though she were being covertly spied upon, and now, still uneasy, she wished fervently that Sophie would come back, and that she had dispatched a messenger boy for her father's carriage, instead of approving the maid's suggestion that they hire a hackney coach to convey them home.

Nevertheless, determinedly returning her attention to the bandboxes, birdcage and potted plant, Ariana completed their arrangement to her satisfaction so that they would be safe from knaves. But so engrossed was she in this undertaking and in her own disquiet and puzzlement over feeling surreptitiously observed that it was several long moments before she recognized that a commotion had ensued in Oxford Street. However, finally it dawned on her that some contretemps was taking place, and she looked up to see, much to her shock and horror, that a run-away hansom cab was careering and careening wildly down the cobblestones. Surely the vehicle's solitary driver must have suffered a heart attack or apoplexy, she thought, dismayed and concerned, for he was slumped over wholly unresponsively in his seat up top, and even as she watched, a particularly violent sway of the unchecked equipage caused him abruptly to topple forward from his perch and tumble into the street, where he only narrowly escaped being squashed by one of the carriage's two high, churning wheels. Undeterred, the vehicle's single horse galloped on recklessly, dragging the hansom cab along awkwardly but dangerously behind it. Shouting warnings, a few bold men raced into the street to try to stop it, while women screamed and ran, snatching up their bewildered, bawling children to carry them away to safety. Other drivers in the wide but crowded street attempted to pull their own carriages, wagons and carts out of the way of the onrushing equipage, but some, hemmed in, were unsuccessful, and the now-wholly-out-of-control vehicle side-swiped and smashed them as it swept past precipitately.

For an instant, in all the pandemonium that had broken loose, Ariana was transported back to Paris and the night of the carnage that had occurred at the Hôtel des Capucines, when the soldiers had mistakenly opened fire on the protesters there. In some dim corner of her mind she knew she ought to step back into the vestibule of the Pantheon Bazaar, where she would be protected from the obviously terrified horse and the hansom cab as they continued their crazed, unbridled advance down Oxford Street, toward the Cumberland Gate. But instead, she seemed to be frozen where she stood, her eyes riveted to the unfolding scene of chaos and destruction, and her mind oblivious to the shrieking people who dashed past her, jostling one another in their haste to reach shelter.

Then, without warning, Ariana was struck brutally from behind, between her shoulder blades, and shoved hard out into the street, right into the path of the oncoming carriage. Losing her balance from the unexpected impetus, the wind knocked from her by the savage blow she had received, she stumbled and fell upon the cobblestones, scraping her palms painfully. Momentarily stunned and dazed, she shook her now-spinning head dully to try to clear it, to collect herself and her wits. Then, grossly hampered by her constricting corset and yards of crinolines and petticoats, she attempted desperately to struggle to her feet. As she did so, glancing up, Ariana was absolutely petrified to see that the unrestrained horse and the hansom cab were now barreling straight toward her. In seconds she would be crushed beneath the thundering hooves and roiling wheels—and killed!

Malcolm felt exceedingly frustrated that Boniface Cavendish had gone out of town and could not, it appeared, be expected to return anytime soon. Malcolm was eager to take some decisive action in connection with the vanished emerald and the two crucifixes. But although there was some talk among him, Mr. Quimby and Mr. Rosenkranz of consulting Mr. Cavendish's senior clerk for information about the Heart of Kheperi, in the end it was decided that even if the senior clerk proved trustworthy, the fewer outside their own little circle who learnt of the emerald and the crosses, the better.

For his own contribution to their enterprise, Mr. Quimby set himself the task of drawing and engraving several highly detailed maps of the area around Castle Dúndragon and Loch Ness over the centuries, while Mr. Rosenkranz conducted a discreet investigation into the crucifixes. In the meantime, Malcolm himself, his employer and the jeweler strongly advised, ought to begin at once to learn how to proficiently defend himself with not only his fists, but also pistol and sword. "For although we do not know for sure whether the attack upon you had anything to do with this business, you can be quite certain that an undertaking of this nature cannot be concealed forever and will thus eventually come to the attention of the Foscarellis—and once that happens, they will undoubtedly take steps to try to get rid of you, Malcolm!" Mr. Quimby declared soberly.

It was therefore arranged that during his luncheon break, on

Mondays and Wednesdays, Malcolm would commence boxing privately with an experienced pugilist, and on Tuesdays and Thursdays, fencing at Henry the Younger's L'Ecole d'Armes at No. 32A St. James's Street. At the weekends, he would practice with dueling pistols on his own, at the Red House tavern in Battersea Fields, exercising caution at this last, as the place had an extremely unsavory reputation and often attracted a rough clientele who both drank and gambled heavily, and engaged in illegal racing and shooting matches. For targets, the Red House sold pigeons for fifteen shillings per dozen, starlings for four shillings and sparrows for two shillings; and although in 1846, in response to public outcry about the dangerous and reprehensible character of Battersea Fields, Parliament had passed a bill to develop it into a royal park, it remained a popular haunt for shootists.

As there seemed nothing else he could do at this point, Malcolm threw himself into these various pursuits with a vengeance, more resolved now than ever to avenge the murders of his father and Uncle Charles. Somehow, the Foscarellis had undoubtedly discovered their true identities and known them to be in search of the priceless, accursed emerald, the Heart of Kheperi, so Lord Vittore, Count Foscarelli, had confronted them and killed them. It sickened Malcolm greatly to think that the Foscarellis should, for nearly a century or more, have been so obsessed with finding the lost gemstone that they would commit murder for it, and he became determined that they should not have it, that he would do everything in his power to locate it before they did.

Over the passing weeks, as both his boxing and his fencing lessons progressed, he recognized that his youth at Whitrose Grange had not been time wasted, for physically he had grown into a tall, broad-shouldered man with a lean, whipcord body and hard, strong muscles born of his years of labor at the tenant farm. This especially stood him in good stead with the big Irish prizefighter "Red" Rory Hoolihan, who trained him in the art of pugilism; and although he found fencing initially far more difficult, still, here, too, Malcolm discovered that his youthful exploits in the countryside surrounding Whitrose Grange came to his assistance now. Despite being a tall, powerful man, he was extremely agile and quick. Not for naught had he raced over rocky, wooded hillsides and along shingled, driftwood-strewn beaches all those long years ago, and his nimbleness and speed surprised many an unsuspecting opponent.

Of particular delight to Malcolm were his shooting sessions at Battersea Fields—not because he especially enjoyed the art, although he dutifully devoted his weekends to it, but because it was at the Red House tavern where he renewed his acquaintance with Nicolas Ravener. Following the assault upon him outside Mr. Quimby's town house, Malcolm had courteously called on the young man at the George & Vulture public house in St. Michael's Alley, where he was lodged, to thank him again for his aid that inauspicious night. Since that time, however, Malcolm had not had occasion to see Mr. Ravener. But ever since running into him at the Red House tavern, he had become good friends with him, learning that Mr. Ravener also often frequented not only the Red House tavern at Battersea Fields, but Henry the Younger's L'Ecole d'Armes and Red Rory Hoolihan's Boxing Saloon, as well. After that, the two men had made arrangements to meet regularly for practice at all three places, finding that because they were fairly evenly matched in both height and build, they were able to hone their skills even more expeditiously together.

Today, following one of these sessions at Henry the Younger's L'Ecole d'Arms, Malcolm was feeling particularly pleased with himself, for he believed he was finally making real progress at the art of fencing, although it would, of course, be many years before he could call himself a master. Adding to his sense of well-being was the fact that it was a relatively warm spring day, which he had been able to enjoy for quite some time that afternoon, having agreed that after his lesson had ended, he would, on his way back to Quimby & Company (Cartographers & Map Sellers), run an errand in Knightsbridge for his employer, thus negating the need to spare Tuck from the shop for that purpose.

Now, however, his fencing bout over and the errand, too, completed, Malcolm reluctantly turned his footsteps toward Mr. Quimby's establishment, meandering his way along Park Lane, on the eastern edge of Hyde Park, as though he were still an apprentice eager to be away from his place of employment for even a short while, instead of a junior journeyman, with all the perquisites and responsibilities of same. But then, as he reached the Cumberland Gate and turned on to Oxford Street, uncharacteristically dawdling and pausing now and then to gaze in the front windows of the shops lining the street, Malcolm slowly became aware that some kind of disturbance had arisen just ahead, and of a sudden, stricken by the chilling idea that something untoward had perhaps befallen his employer, he began to run toward Mr. Quimby's premises. He had not gone far, however, when he observed a horse harnessed to a driverless hansom cab hurtling crazily down the street and, directly in its path, a young woman struggling frantically to rise from where she had fallen on the cobblestones. At any moment she was going to be crushed beneath the horse and carriage, and killed!

Malcolm did not even stop to think of the danger to himself. He thought only of the helpless, terrified young woman. His heart pounding with fear for her, a rush of adrenaline abruptly surging through his entire body, he pelted into the street and, in one fell swoop, snatched her up and bolted with her to the sidewalk just as the horse and hansom cab raced by, the former at last breaking free from the shafts of the carriage and galloping on furiously, while the latter teetered precariously on its two high wheels for a moment before finally toppling heavily to one side, wood splintering and smashing. In some dark corner of his mind Malcolm was dimly aware of the sound of the equipage crashing, but his primary concern was for the young woman he held in his arms. She had fainted, he saw. Not knowing what else to do, he hailed a hackney coach that had pulled alongside the curb to avoid being hit by the unchecked vehicle, and carefully placed the young woman inside, then climbed in beside her, shouting at the driver to make haste to No. 7B Oxford Street.

The young woman did not stir, and now, as the hackney coach fought its way through all the panic and confusion from the curb and began slowly to rumble down the street, Malcolm feared that perhaps she had not simply swooned, but had suffered a heart attack and died, so great had her terror been. Efficiently he checked for a pulse, deeply relieved to find one, although it was fast and light. Nor did she appear outwardly to have suffered any injury. He wished he had a vinaigrette with which to revive the young woman, but since he did not, he contented himself with loosening her gown at the throat so that she could breathe more easily and ensuring that she was as comfortably situated in the carriage as was possible under the circumstances.

From beyond the hackney coach Malcolm could hear the sounds of shouts and constables' whistles being blown, of horses and vehicles clattering over the cobblestones and people chattering as order was gradually restored to the street. But inside the carriage all was quiet save for his and the young woman's breathing.

He studied her intently as the sunlight beaming in through the coach window fell upon her pale countenance, illuminating her porcelain skin and making it seem almost translucent, as though she were an angel. Her expensive, stylish bonnet tied under her chin had slipped from her head to dangle down her back, revealing a long, gleaming mass of raven ringlets that framed her face softly and matched the eyebrows that arched gently over her eyes. He wondered what color these last were, but since they were closed, he could tell nothing beyond the fact that she had the longest, thickest, sootiest eyelashes he had ever seen. Her cheekbones were high, finely molded and touched delicately with pink. Her nose was straight, classically chiseled and set above a full, rosebud mouth. Her long, graceful swan's throat sloped down to a bosom that rose and fell shallowly. The costly fringed silk shawl she wore wrapped around her had slid down her upper arms, and for an instant Malcolm imagined her shoulders bare and her breasts partially exposed, and he thought she was the most utterly gorgeous creature he had ever seen.

There was something about her very fragility and vulnerability at this moment that appealed deeply to him, making him long fiercely to protect her, and something about her beautiful, serene countenance that tugged at the edges of his long-buried memories. But these last evanesced before he could catch firm hold of them, so that in the end, he had only a strange, vague sensation that she reminded him somehow of someone…someone in a painting, perhaps, he thought, although he did not know for sure, for he had only a nebulous impression of mist and a face trickling with rain—or tears.

The hackney coach finally pulled to a halt at the curb before No. 7B Oxford Street, and after alighting, Malcolm paid the driver the fare, then lifted the still-unconscious young woman from the vehicle and swiftly carried her inside. Heedless of how Harry, Jem and Tuck crowded around, agog and curious, he called urgently for Mr. Quimby, and when the elderly gentleman appeared, at his direction Malcolm bore the young woman to the private office at the rear of the establishment and laid her gently on the settee therein.

"Tuck, fetch the medical kit," Mr. Quimby commanded, as Malcolm, sitting on the edge of the couch and chafing the young woman's hands, began to explain what had occurred. "There is a vial of smelling salts in it, I believe. Pray, continue, Malcolm. I did not mean to interrupt. You don't know who the young lady is, you say, or why she should have been all alone and in such a precarious position in the middle of Oxford Street?"

"No, sir."

"Well, no matter. Regardless of her identity, you did the right thing, of course, in coming to her aid and bringing her here. We'll see if we can't revive her, and then, hopefully, we'll learn who she is and whether there is anyone we can summon to look after her and convey her home. Ah, thank you, Tuck." Taking the medical kit his apprentice had retrieved, Mr. Quimby placed it on a nearby table. "Now, Harry, you take Jem and Tuck, and return to work—for only imagine the poor young lady's reaction if she were to awaken and not only find herself in unfamiliar surroundings, but also being peered at by a group of strange men! Why, she would undoubtedly swoon again! I shall call if you're needed." By this time, the elder gentleman had opened the medical kit, withdrawn the vinaigrette and handed it to Malcolm. "Uncork the bottle and wave it gently under the young lady's nose," he instructed. "That ought to bring her around."

"Aye, sir."

Malcolm did as directed, and moments later, much to his relief, the young woman at last stirred, moving her head slowly from side to side. A soft, low moan issued from her lips, and her eyelids gradually fluttered open to reveal eyes the rich violet color of amethysts, which stared up at him dazedly before filling with sudden panic and bewilderment as she became aware of her environs. Crying out, she struggled to rise, but gently Malcolm pushed her back down upon the sofa, speaking to her slowly and reassuringly, so that she would understand.

"No, please don't try to get up just yet, miss. You've had a bad shock, I fear, and need to recover yourself. But you're quite safe here, I give you my word of honor as a gentleman. Permit me to introduce myself. I'm Malcolm Blackfriars, and you're currently in the private office of my employer, Mr. Septimus Quimby. This is his shop, Quimby and Company, Cartographers and Map Sellers. Perhaps you've heard of it? We're located at Number Seven B, Oxford Street. You were nearly trampled underfoot by a runaway horse and hansom cab, and fainted in the street. I was able to remove you from harm's way in just the nick of time, and not knowing who you were or what else to do, I brought you here in a hackney coach directly. Do you remember any of that at all?"

Slowly the confusion in the young woman's frightened eyes started to dissipate, and finally she nodded.

"*Oui...oui,* I thought I was going to be killed! But then you came and rescued me! That was so brave of you, *monsieur!* But truly, I don't recall anything else after that."

"That's understandable. However, you needn't worry. Except for the shock to your senses at coming so near to death, you are quite unharmed." He paused, then, glad he had been taught the French language from birth, observed, "You are French, *mademoiselle.* Can you tell me your name? Have you been in England long? Do you have any family here to whom we could send a message, so they will not worry about you?"

Before the young woman could respond, however, the brass bell affixed to the front door of the premises clanged loudly. This sound was followed by a disturbance in the main room of the premises and a woman's voice raised anxiously but imperiously.

"Where is she? What have you done with my daughter, *ma pauvre petite,* young man? If you've harmed a single hair on her head, you'll be sorry, I promise you! I know she was kidnapped and brought here whilst unconscious, so do not think you can deceive me with any false tale otherwise! *Alors!* I demand to be taken to her at once—or else these constables here shall clap you in irons and haul you off to gaol straightaway!"

At that, Harry was heard stammering befuddled explanations and hasty reassurances before he worriedly appeared in the doorway of Mr. Quimby's private office, only to be summarily brushed aside by a tall, beautiful older woman accompanied by two policeman, a handsome, gray-haired gentleman and two ladies' maids.

"That is him, *madame!*" the younger of these last cried, pointing straight at Malcolm, who rose to his feet amid all the vehement reproaches, denials and general cacophony that instantly ensued. "That is the man who abducted Mademoiselle Ariana! I saw him putting her insensible body into a hackney coach and heard him shouting at the driver to bring her here!"

"*Quel monstre!*" Madame Valcoeur exclaimed with obvious

horror. "What have you done with my daughter, you beast? *Gendarmes,* arrest that man immediately!"

"*Non…non,* Maman!" Weakly Ariana managed to sit up on the settee at last, so that all those who had entered the private office could now see her, for she had previously been obscured from view by the relatively tall curved sides and arms of the ornately carved mahogany and upholstered couch. "Sophie is genuinely well-intentioned but, still, quite mistaken, I'm afraid. This is all only a dreadful mix-up, I assure you. I am not harmed, only badly shaken, and Monsieur Blackfriars did not kidnap me. Rather, he most courageously rescued me! Why, if not for him, I would have been crushed to death by an unrestrained horse and carriage in the street!"

"Is this true? Oh, *ma pauvre petite!*" Sweeping across the room, the comtesse enfolded her daughter protectively in her arms. "How I thank *le bon Dieu* that you are all right!"

"Ahem, ahem." Mr. Quimby cleared his throat audibly and at some length in order to gain the attention of everyone present. "Perhaps we should all sit down and try to discuss this matter calmly. Harry, please be good enough to bring some tea for our guests. Now, then," the elder gentleman continued, once the senior journeyman had, with considerable relief, disappeared to carry out his assigned task, "allow me to introduce myself. I am Septimus Quimby, the proprietor of this most excellent map shop, and this is my junior journeyman, Mr. Malcolm Blackfriars. My senior journeyman, Mr. Harry Devenish, is whom I just dispatched for the tea. May I now have the pleasure of knowing whom I am addressing?"

"*Certainement, monsieur.*" Monsieur Valcoeur now firmly took control of the situation from his previously utterly—however understandably—distraught wife. "I am Jean-Paul Lévesque, Comte de Valcoeur, and this is my wife, Madame Hélène, Comtesse de Valcoeur, and my daughter, Mademoiselle Ariana. Also, my wife's and daughter's ladies' maids, Madame Adélaïde Gauthier and Mademoiselle Sophie Neuville. I shall leave these two good constables to introduce themselves, and then I trust we may get down to the bottom of this unfortunate business, eh?"

The policemen dutifully introduced themselves. Then, over the tea brought in on a silver tray by Harry, Ariana recounted how, during the pandemonium engendered by the runaway horse and hansom cab, she had been accidentally shoved out into the street, where she had fallen. Following this, Malcolm told how he had swept her from harm's way and, because she had fainted, brought her to Mr. Quimby's shop, not knowing what else to do. After that, Sophie delivered her own narrative, explaining how she had returned with a hackney coach to the Pantheon Bazaar, only to see the unconscious Ariana being whisked away by Malcolm in another vehicle. Overhearing him giving the direction to the driver and mistakenly believing that her mistress was being abducted, Sophie had paid a passing boy on the street to watch their purchases, then instructed the driver of the hackney coach she had hired to journey posthaste to the Lévesques' town house in Portman Square, where she had raised a hue and cry.

"I am so very sorry." She wrung her hands quietly now, embarrassed and shamefaced. "I did not mean to cause any trouble. Truly, I did not!"

"*Non,* of course you didn't—so you're not to fret about that in the least, Sophie!" Madame Valcoeur insisted stoutly. "Under the circumstances, you did the right thing, and no one with an ounce of common sense would think otherwise. But now I must apologize to you, Monsieur Blackfriars, for my earlier remarks—for in my ignorance and upset, I abused you terribly, when I ought to have been thanking you from the bottom of my heart instead!"

"Also quite natural, *madame,* given the situation," Malcolm replied courteously. "So, please, think nothing more of it. I only hope this misunderstanding has now all been cleared up and that all has been forgiven and forgotten."

"You are indeed most kind and gracious, *monsieur.*" The comtesse eyed him with approval as she carefully took his measure. "We are inordinately grateful to you for saving our daughter's life and can never thank you enough. How can we ever repay you? If there is ever anything you need, Monsieur Blackfriars, if there is ever anything at all that Monsieur Valcoeur and I can do for you, please do not hesitate to let us know immediately. And if you and Mr. Quimby have no prior engagements, would you both also please do us the honor of dining with us a week from Thursday and joining us for our little conversation party afterward?"

This heartfelt invitation Malcolm and his employer both readily accepted with delight, after which Monsieur and Madame Valcoeur took their leave, carrying Ariana and their entourage away with them.

Chapter Eight

Madame Valcoeur's Salon

For in the time we know not of
Did fate begin
Weaving the web of days that wove
Your doom, Faustine.

— Algernon Charles Swinburne
Faustine [1866]

The glories of our blood and state
Are shadows, not substantial things;
There is no armor against fate;
Death lays his icy hand on kings.

— James Shirley
Contention of Ajax and Ulysses [1659]

To change your mind and to follow him
who sets you right is to be nonetheless the
free agent that you were before.

— Marcus Aurelius Antoninus
Meditations

1848
London, England

"Oh, Sophie, did you ever see such a handsome man as Monsieur Blackfriars?" Clasping one of the pillows from her bed tightly to her breast, Ariana whirled gaily and giddily around her bedchamber, her gossamer white wrapper and nightgown flowing and fluttering around her ankles. "If I had ever drawn a portrait of the man of my dreams, 'twould have looked exactly like him! I could scarcely believe it when I saw him bending over me right before I swooned in the street. In truth, I thought I must have already died, that the runaway horse and hansom cab had killed me, and that Monsieur Blackfriars was the angel sent down to earth to bear me up to heaven!"

"What nonsense you talk, *mademoiselle*," Sophie chided gently, but still she smiled as she plumped up the covers on Ariana's bed. "For Monsieur Blackfriars is hardly an angel—but a virile young man in his prime, and, *oui*, quite a handsome one at that, I agree. However, as your friend, I must also warn you that even if Monsieur Blackfriars has found much favor in your eyes and those of your parents, too, Monsieur le Comte and Madame la Comtesse are nevertheless most unlikely to look upon him as a proper suitor for your hand in marriage, *mademoiselle*, if that is what you are secretly wishing—and surely you must realize that, as well. You are the daughter of Monsieur le Comte and Madame la Comtesse, and Monsieur Blackfriars is only a drawer and seller of maps! He labors in a shop—and, worse, one that he does not even own, besides! A match between you would be deemed highly inappropriate for you, *mademoiselle*, however fortunate for Monsieur Blackfriars himself."

"I know…I know. But, oh, Sophie, now that I have seen him, I am quite certain I shall not be happy with anyone else but Monsieur Blackfriars, no matter what!"

"To the contrary. You can be sure of nothing of the kind, *mademoiselle*," the maid insisted firmly. "For in truth, at the moment you know little or naught about Monsieur Blackfriars beyond the fact that he was brave and daring enough to rescue you. But how do you know that fear for your life was his only driving motive? For all you know, he might be a scoundrel of the worst sort—a libertine or fortune hunter, perhaps, who saw an expensively dressed young lady in distress and who sought to gain for himself an opportunity that he would not otherwise have had!"

"*Non*, Sophie, that I cannot and will not believe—for this I *do* know. There was nothing in Monsieur Blackfriars's eyes that even hinted at coldness, calculation, or guile. Rather, he was all kindness and concern, with such an air of good breeding and such elegant, gentlemanly manners that 'tis difficult to believe he has spent the majority of his life apprenticed to a mere cartographer and map seller. Did I not know better, I should think him very well born, Sophie—and if you are honest, you would admit that you would, too."

Sighing, the maid allowed as how this was indeed so.

"But still, it does not change the fact that Monsieur Blackfriars is *in trade, mademoiselle!*" Sophie then observed gravely, although not unkindly. "I know how taken you are with him. But I would be remiss in my duty to encourage you where he is concerned. 'Tis you I must think of, and I just don't want you to get your hopes up, only to wind up disappointed and broken-hearted—for although Monsieur le Comte and Madame la Comtesse have invited Monsieur Blackfriars here to dine, 'tis only out of gratitude for his saving your life. You cannot think he will become a regular visitor here, *mademoiselle.*"

"Oh, I know you are right, Sophie. But still, I don't want to think about such things right now. So let me dream for just a little while. What possible harm can that do?"

"Perhaps none, *mademoiselle.* But on the other hand, perhaps a very great deal. Now, here is Fanny with your hot chocolate. Will you be wanting anything else before retiring?"

"*Non.*" Ariana shook her head as the housemaid, Fanny, set the tray she bore down on a nearby table, leaving Sophie to pour the hot chocolate.

"Thank you, Fanny. That will be all, then," Sophie said.

Bobbing a curtsy, the housemaid departed from the bedroom, followed shortly thereafter by Sophie herself. After the two women had gone, Ariana carried her cup and saucer over to the night table, then climbed into bed. But once tucked under the covers, she discovered that she was far too excited to sleep, despite the soporific hot chocolate she drank. Instead, she lay awake for a very long time, reliving in her mind the interlude when Malcolm Blackfriars had swept her from the path of the unchecked horse and hansom cab. She remembered looking up into his hauntingly handsome dark visage just moments before she had fainted and seeing the shaggy fall of his long glossy black hair, the breathtaking intensity of his heavily lashed eyes— the striking silvery color of Scotch mist—and thinking of the proud angel Lucifer, and of Congreve's lines of prose: "Has he not a rogue's face?…a damned Tyburn face, without the benefit o' the clergy." That was what she had unwittingly thought when she had gazed up at Malcolm Blackfriars, and it had both excited and frightened her.

In all her entire young life, no one had ever stirred her the way he had in just the brief time she had spent with him. Although she had not said as much to Sophie, Ariana had somehow sensed that beneath his gentlemanly facade lurked a deeply inherent wildness that now she struggled with difficulty to define. It was somehow as though while he lived and labored in the city, he would be far more at home in the country, she thought, and of a sudden, strangely, there rose unbidden in her mind an image of him garbed as a Highlander and tramping across the savage peaks and moors of Scotland. As, at last, her eyelashes fluttered closed and she drifted into slumber, this picture of him metamorphosed and merged in her brain with that of the young man Collie, who haunted her old recurring nightmare, sitting across from her in his small wooden fishing boat, the *Sea Witch,* with the Scotch mist winding its shroud around them and the dark peaty waves of Loch Ness lapping gently against the bow.

And for the very first time in her whole life, when the nightmare—and the terrifying, monstrous sea serpent—insinuated itself into her subconscious while she slept, Ariana did not scream. For when, finally, the great snake stealthily undulated its way toward her, Collie evanesced into the brume, and from it, in his place, Malcolm Blackfriars emerged, mounted bareback upon a foam-white seahorse and reaching down to snatch her from the gaping maw of death.

* * *

Malcolm had never before known time to pass so slowly. But now it did, the days prior to the forthcoming Thursday a week hence and dinner at the Portman Square town house of the Comte and Comtesse de Valcoeur seeming to creep by at an excruciatingly abated pace. He tried to concentrate on both his work and the quest he had undertaken to locate the Heart of Kheperi, but even this last failed to distract him from thoughts of Mademoiselle Ariana Lévesque. Although he had met other young ladies in the past, none of these had ever previously caught his fancy the way Ariana had in just the short time he had spent with her. Yet, with a sense of biting anger and wretched despair, Malcolm realized she was far beyond his grasp. Had he possessed either a title or a fortune, he might have aspired to court her. But as it was, unless he could somehow discover a way to reclaim the lost Ramsay estates in Scotland and England, he had nothing to offer Ariana—not even his own true name. With the exception of the time following his father's and Uncle Charles's murders, Malcolm had never felt so downcast, so bitterly aware of the unfortunate situation in which, through no fault of his own, he now found himself. Having laid claim to neither rank nor riches before, he had not, until now, rued their lack. But now he cursed his profligate ancestor Lord Iain Ramsay, once the Earl of Dúndragon, with a vengeance, for had Lord Dúndragon not gambled away the Ramsay lands, Malcolm might well now be both titled and wealthy, a desirable claimant to the hand of Ariana. But of course, he reminded himself, disheartened, there existed no means of redress for all that. So it was far better that he should focus his energies on locating the missing emerald, for it was priceless and would therefore restore his family's fortune, at least, if not their noble status or property. But so far, despite all the inquiries Jakob Rosenkranz had so discreetly undertaken, he had failed to learn anything about the lost gemstone, and Boniface Cavendish continued to be absent from his bookshop, so that Malcolm, Mr. Quimby and Mr. Rosenkranz had yet to have any conversation with him.

Now, at that frustrating thought, Malcolm inadvertently snapped in half the charcoal pencil he was employing to create the latest map he had begun drawing earlier that morning. As the pencil broke in two, he swore mightily under his breath and nearly flung the pieces into the dustbin. Then instead, sighing heavily, he took out his pocketknife and set about sharpening new points on one end of each bit and squaring off the other, so that finally, when he had finished, he had two good pencils, although their length was shorter than what he was wont to work with. Still, he would make do.

"Problems, Malcolm?" Mr. Quimby asked kindly as he appeared in the workroom.

"Aye. I owe you an apology, sir. I'm afraid I'm having a hard time keeping my mind on my job again. As a result, I broke my pencil and have only just now completed its mending. So I'm a trifle behind, but never fear. I shall get caught up once more presently."

"I have faith that you will—provided, of course, that a cascade of curly raven tresses and a pair of haunting violet eyes do not continue to distract you!" The elder gentleman's own pale blue eyes twinkled jovially at the thought.

"Is it that obvious, sir?" Malcolm queried ruefully.

"No. However, I flatter myself that I've come to know you very well over the years. Nor have I forgotten what 'twas like to be a young man in my prime, either. Mademoiselle Ariana Lévesque is a most beautiful young woman. A man would have to be either blind or a fool not to see that, and fortunately, you are neither, Malcolm."

"Even so, it does me no good to dwell on her, I know, sir— for she is far beyond my reach."

"Yes, well, as my old friend Boniface Cavendish is so very fond of saying, if our reach doesn't exceed our grasp, we have nothing left to strive for! Besides which, Malcolm, if we can get this tangled affair of your true heritage properly sorted out and locate the lost emerald, no one could say you were not a fit suitor for Mademoiselle Ariana, nor accuse you of fortune hunting where she is concerned. So do not be in despair just yet! The game may have been long afoot—but you and I have only just begun to play it!"

"Indeed, you are quite right, sir." Malcolm tried to be cheered by these resounding words of encouragement. "I fear I am too impatient—like a horse chafing at the bit or the hounds straining at their leashes before a hunt. I want to be doing something!"

"That's entirely understandable, of course. I confess to experiencing the same feeling ever since I learnt of this matter, even though I have no personal stake in it, the way you do, aside from the fact that I loathe treachery and injustice, and that because you are my junior journeyman, I feel a great sense of responsibility toward you. As you know, I never married—I was disappointed in love once, years ago, and proved too timid, I'm afraid, ever to risk my poor heart again—so I have no offspring of my own. Thus my apprentices and journeymen have always been my children, so to speak. But never you fear, Malcolm. The day for action *will* come, I'm certain of it! Meanwhile, we are wise to stay our hand and to lay our plans carefully in preparation for then, rather than to go off half-cocked. Your good father and Uncle Charles, I have no doubt, availed themselves of every safeguard, yet in the end fell prey to their adversaries, nevertheless. Therefore, we must prove even more cautious and cunning if we are to prevail against them. You are doing everything you needs must at the moment, so do not think you are not and blame yourself for inaction—and in the meantime, there is the pleasure of a very fine dinner and an agreeably stimulating conversation party with Monsieur and Madame Valcoeur and their lovely daughter to look forward to, eh, Malcolm?"

"Aye." The younger man nodded, attempting to smile.

"Then do not look so glum. For as Boniface is also fond of saying, if we can dream a thing, we can make it come true—and because we have neither of us been gifted, or cursed, with that talent known as Second Sight, we cannot know what the future holds in store. But we *can* do our best to make of it what we will, and as long as Mademoiselle Ariana does not become affianced, why, there is every reason for you to hope, Malcolm—and I, for one, see no good cause why you should not! Remember what I have taught you—'tis not clothes that make the man, but the man who makes the clothes! For there are many nobles who are not gentlemen—and equally as many gentlemen who are not nobles, as I hope and trust I myself may be a worthy example of. I may have neither title or great riches, but nevertheless, I do not feel myself inferior to any man. Now, let us see how far you have progressed with that drawing, for Harry must start engraving the plates soon if we are to finish that map before Mr. Greyson calls for it."

Much to his surprise, following his conversation with his employer, Malcolm found that the days not only passed more quickly, but also that he became far better able to immerse himself in his work, rather than allowing his own thoughts and tantalizing images of Ariana to absorb him. While he was aware that enchanting visions of her danced always at the periphery of his mind, he contented himself with the knowledge that he was shortly to see her in the flesh again and that there was at least the chance of his somehow attaining the wealth necessary to win her hand.

Then, finally, the night of the dinner at the elegant Portman Square town house of Monsieur and Madame Valcoeur arrived, and Malcolm was free to set aside his tasks at Quimby & Company (Cartographers & Map Sellers) and concentrate instead on the forthcoming affair. Disembarking from the omnibus at its stand in St. John's Wood, he practically raced home to Hawthorn Cottage. Once there, he paused only to greet his mother and remind her that he was going out for the evening before hurrying upstairs to his bedchamber. After bathing, he dressed carefully in his best suit, with a new neckerchief he had splurged on at a shop in Regent Street. He was not vain, but as he gazed at himself in the mirror over the mahogany gentleman's chest in his room, Malcolm fancied that he looked very well indeed. This opinion was shortly confirmed by his mother when he finally went back downstairs.

"Oh, Son," she cried softly when she spied him, "how extremely handsome you look—even if I do say so myself! That is a new neckcloth, isn't it? 'Tis most attractive—and you've tied it so beautifully, too! Why, even though you go into such company as to be found in Portman Square, I daresay there will be no man present who will surpass you in appearance!"

Malcolm smiled.

"You flatter me, Mother," he observed, although not without tenderness. "How I wish you were to accompany me!"

"You know that isn't possible, Son, that Madame Valcoeur's invitation did not include me, and even if it had, I'm afraid I would have been most uncomfortable, as it has been so long since I ventured into society. The last company I enjoyed was that of Uncle Charles, Aunt Katherine and their two children, and were I to go to Portman Square tonight, I would be reminded of that and grow very woeful, wondering whatever became of Katherine and her children after they returned home. It does so trouble and sadden me that I never heard from her again. I pray she is well, but, oh, Malcolm, in my heart I very much fear she is dead and has been so for these many long years past now. Otherwise, she would surely have responded to my many letters to her!"

Biting her tremulous lower lip softly, her eyes filling with tears, Mrs. Blackfriars turned away to conceal her emotions, but Malcolm was not deceived.

"I know Aunt Katherine would have got in touch with you if she could, Mother," he said gently. "And even if she has indeed lain in her grave for these many long years now, she would not want you to continue to grieve so for her."

"Aye, I know. 'Tis not knowing what happened to her that is so hard. I believe I could have some peace of mind if only I knew her fate for certain one way or the other. But there, it was a long time ago, and tonight is an evening for celebration and the future, not sorrow and the past. So you go on to Portman Square now, and above all, have a good time—because this is a rare and wonderful opportunity for you, Son! It never hurts to have friends in high places, and Monsieur and Madame Valcoeur cannot help but be grateful to you for so bravely rescuing their daughter from certain death—and at very great risk to yourself in the process! Oh, how I shudder even to think of it! So I shall not, but only be glad that both you and Mademoiselle Ariana are safe. Such a lovely name she has. It reminds me of that of Katherine's daughter, Ana. Do you remember? She had a longer name, of course, but I'm afraid my memory plays tricks on me nowadays, and I no longer recall what 'twas, for from the time she was born, she was always called Ana."

"Aye, I remember her—a brave, bonnie wee lass who tagged after me when I went fishing."

"Well, let us dwell no more on the past," Mrs. Blackfriars insisted again abruptly, smiling bravely as she fussed unnecessarily with Malcolm's jacket and tie, as though to distract herself from her unhappy thoughts. "Be off with you now—or Miss Woodbridge will soon be thinking I have quite forgotten all about her and our card game in the drawing room!"

"You had best return to her, then."

Bending his head, for he was now far taller than she, Malcolm dropped a light, affectionate kiss on his mother's brow. Then, after she had disappeared into the drawing room, he donned his hat, coat and gloves, and collected his umbrella, in case of rain. After that, he let himself out through the front door of Hawthorn Cottage, turning his footsteps from St. John's Wood toward Marylebone.

Now that spring stretched toward summer, the days had begun not only to grow warmer, but also to lengthen, so that the sun had not yet set when Malcolm started his roughly two-mile walk to Portman Square. Because he feared, in his eagerness, to arrive far too early at the town house of the Comte and Comtesse de Valcoeur, he forced himself deliberately to stroll in leisurely fashion along Park Road, around the southwestern edge of Regent's Park, toward the fashionable district of Marylebone. As he walked, he kept his wits about him and a sharp, wary eye on his surroundings, for although the attack upon him had not been repeated, still, he had not forgotten it or the fact that another such attempt could be made at any time. Ever since the night of the assault, in fact, Malcolm had had the strange but distinct sensation that he was being spied upon and followed, although he had not been able to discern by whom. Nor was this evening any different. Still, although he glanced around surreptitiously, he saw no one who looked either suspicious or familiar to him.

But even if someone *were* dogging his footsteps, he was unlikely to be set upon with any witnesses present, Malcolm reminded himself, and as it was such a fine evening, many people were out enjoying the park. At any other time, he would be doing the same. But tonight, Portman Square was his destination, and now, his anticipation spurring him on despite himself, he strode more briskly in that direction, finally reaching the elegant town house of the Comte and Comtesse de Valcoeur. After taking a deep breath in an effort to curb his rising excitement, Malcolm rang the brass bell, and in response, he was admitted to the town house by the butler, who greeted him pleasantly.

"Mr. Blackfriars, I presume? Won't you please come in, sir? We've been expecting you." Stepping into the elaborately beautiful foyer with its highly polished marble floor, Malcolm found himself efficiently divested of his hat, coat, gloves and umbrella. "If you'll follow me, please, sir. The family are gathered in the small drawing room. This way, sir." The butler, Butterworth, opened a pair of French doors off the foyer, then announced, "Mr. Malcolm Blackfriars."

Entering the small drawing room, Malcolm was immediately aware of having become the center of attention as all eyes turned toward him. For a moment he just stood there, awed by the magnificent room and the unfamiliar situation, and not quite sure what to do. But then his hostess came forward, and he collected himself and his manners. Bowing low over Madame Valcoeur's outstretched hand, he kissed it, and was instantly rewarded by her warm smile of approval.

"Welcome, Monsieur Blackfriars," she said. "We are so delighted that you could join us this evening. I believe that you know everyone here—except for Madame Polgár, of course. She is a talented clairvoyant, who, like my own family, has recently traveled to London from Paris. She was kind enough to pay me a call earlier this afternoon, so I invited her to join us for dinner. Madame Polgár—" the comtesse turned to the fortune-teller "—please allow me to present to you Monsieur Blackfriars. 'Twas he who saved our precious Ariana's life the other day in Oxford Street, for which we are all deeply indebted to him."

"How do you do, Monsieur Blackfriars?" Madame Polgár extended one hand to him, and Malcolm bowed low over it and kissed it, as he had done Madame Valcoeur's. "What a pleasure 'tis to meet such a brave, handsome young man."

"You are very kind, *madame,* but I am persuaded I did no more than what any other right-thinking man faced with the same situation would have done. Mademoiselle Ariana clearly required assistance, and most fortunately, I was in a position to provide it."

"Yes, Fate has a way of ensuring that one is always in the right place at the right time," the fortune-teller murmured enigmatically. "Tell me, Monsieur Blackfriars, are you a swordsman, by any chance?"

"Unfortunately, no, *madame.* Although I do study the art of fencing at Henry the Younger's L'Ecole d'Armes, I'm a cartographer by trade...the junior journeyman at Quimby and Company."

"Ah, yes. Mr. Quimby must be very proud of you."

"I am, indeed, *madame,*" the elder gentleman, who had arrived earlier, declared, from where he sat in a striped-silk wing chair before the ornately sculpted marble hearth, his feet propped up on a gout stool.

"Pray, won't you sit down, Monsieur Blackfriars?" Madame Valcoeur now indicated one of the brocade sofas in the room. "Will you have something to drink? Some hors d'oeuvres? How about everyone else? More refreshments?"

Taking the hint, the serving maids and footmen present dutifully refilled glasses and plates, and Malcolm soon found himself seated next to Ariana on a couch, a glass of sherry in one hand and a plate of appetizers balanced on his knees.

"'Tis very nice to see you again, *mademoiselle,*" he told Ariana. "I trust that you have now fully recovered from your ordeal."

"Oh, *oui, monsieur*—but I must thank you again for your bravery that day in rescuing me, for I know that had you not come to my aid, I would surely have been killed!"

"The loss of someone so beautiful would have been a very great tragedy, indeed. So I am glad I was able to prevent it."

Malcolm smiled gently at Ariana, feeling a strong sense of pleasure and satisfaction when color rose becomingly to her cheeks and her thick sooty eyelashes swept down modestly to veil her amethyst eyes against his gaze. She looked exquisite, he thought, in her pale lavender gown of lace and silk. Its ruffled décolletage displayed just an enticing hint of her full round breasts, and its trailing sash encircled a waist so slender that he felt he would be able to span it with his hands. Matching silk ribands were threaded through her glossy mane of long black ringlets that gleamed as blue-black as a raven's wing in the soft, glowing candlelight and firelight, in sharp contrast to her porcelain skin brushed delicately with rose upon her high cheeks and sweet lips. Morocco slippers encased her small feet, and with her graceful hands she plied a lovely lacy fan, although there was no coquettishness to the movements, only a shyness and vulnerability that touched him deeply and made him think that she had not been long out in society and was therefore not much accustomed to men.

"Madame Valcocur mentioned that you had only recently come to London from Paris," he observed. "How are you liking England and the city?"

"'Tis very different here, I find," she responded slowly. "More…settled, at least. Paris was in a state of uproar when we left there. King Louis-Philippe had just abdicated, and the revolutionaries and radicals had seized control of the city. So Papa thought that 'twas no longer safe for us there—because of what had happened before…the Reign of Terror before the turn of the century, I mean, when King Louis the Sixteenth and his queen, Marie Antoinette, were executed. So we came to London, to Portman Square."

"'Tis one of the most beautiful squares in all the city."

"Is it? I've not seen them all, so I wouldn't know. Papa chose it because of its proximity to Hyde and Regent's Parks, I believe. That's one of the things I enjoy very much here…walking in the park. If the weather's fine, I go for a stroll every afternoon. Do you like to walk in the park, as well, Monsieur Blackfriars?"

"Aye. My mother and I live in St. John's Wood, which is not far from Regent's Park, and of course, Quimby and Company is just right down the street from Hyde Park. Sometimes, weather permitting, I eat my luncheon there on one of the benches."

"Then perhaps I shall chance to see you there now and again." Ariana smiled.

"'Twould be my pleasure." Malcolm also smiled once more, for he recognized that Ariana, understanding that—despite how he had saved her life—this evening was most unlikely to reoccur, was telling him how they could meet again.

That must mean that she looked upon him with favor, he thought, for she did not seem to him to be the type of woman to encourage his attention, intending only to trifle with his affections.

But there was no time to speak further, for just then, dinner was announced. Everyone stood, and the gentlemen escorted the ladies to the dining room. There Malcolm discovered that although there were only six for dinner, the table was nevertheless elaborately set and that there were several courses that would be served. For the first time in his life, he had reason to be glad that although his parents had possessed neither titles nor riches, they had still been wellborn and well-bred, and had educated him appropriately—as though he were one day to be Earl of Dúndragon, instead of just a tenant farmer. Because of this, his manners at table were faultless, and he reached unerringly for the proper accoutrements for this course or that. He fancied that Monsieur and Madame Valcoeur, as well as Madame Polgár, were quite surprised and impressed by this, as though they had expected him to commit some faux pas and had prepared themselves to overlook it.

"Do you have family here, Monsieur Blackfriars?" the comtesse asked politely, curious.

"My father passed away several years ago, unfortunately. However, my mother is still living, and as she has not remarried I have thus far had no reason to establish my own residence. We share a small house—Hawthorn Cottage—in St. John's Wood."

"Oh, I'm so sorry. If I had known, I would have invited her to join us," Madame Valcoeur said, dismayed.

"No apology is necessary, so please don't trouble yourself over the matter, *madame*. Since Father died, Mother has not gone into society, but lived very quietly. She has her books and her music, her embroidery and her garden to entertain her, and she frequently plays cards with our housekeeper, Miss Woodbridge, also, in the evenings. That was, in fact, the order of business tonight when I departed from the house. So I believe she is content, although, of course, she still misses Father."

"She must have loved him very much."

"Aye, *madame,* she did."

"And your father…was he a cartographer, too? Is that how you became apprenticed to Mr. Quimby?" Madame Polgár's dark eyes glittered with inquisitiveness.

"No, *madame.* I'm afraid that the inheritance that ought to have been Father's—and thus eventually my own—was lost by our ancestors. So although in the end Father did come to manage land, he did so as a tenant farmer. But when he died, I was only sixteen, and as Mother could not run the farm on her own, we took up residence in Hawthorn Cottage."

"Yes, 'twas not long after that when Malcolm and I first met," Mr. Quimby noted, going on to explain how he had come to take Malcolm on as an apprentice.

"Well, 'twould seem that even from your youth, you have always been a man of inordinate courage and conviction, Monsieur Blackfriars." Monsieur Valcoeur nodded with approval upon hearing the tale. "We are so fortunate that you were at hand to save our daughter!"

"Indeed. A worthy friend—and foe!" the fortune-teller exclaimed. "You must permit me to read the tarot cards for you sometime, Monsieur Blackfriars—for I'll wager that you have quite a fascinating future in store."

"That may well be, *madame.* However, I prefer to believe that whatever was written in the stars at the time of our births can be changed through our own actions."

"And so it can be, *monsieur,* for that is why we were given the gift of Free Will, that we might have a hand in shaping our own destinies. Nevertheless, do not be so very quick to dismiss Fate—for it and Free Will are inextricably intertwined…two sides of one whole, like the two faces of the Roman god Janus."

"Ah, I see we have already found a stimulating topic for our conversation party this evening!" Like a child, the comtesse clapped her hands together with delight. "So let us speak no more of it until we are gathered in the drawing room with the rest of our guests, or otherwise, we will have exhausted the subject and have nothing left to say upon it for the remainder of the evening!"

Their hostess having made her wishes courteously but clearly known, those gathered around the table obediently directed their dialogue elsewhere, and the excellent dinner passed agreeably as the savory courses were served one after another. Finally, after dessert, the three ladies withdrew to the small drawing room, leaving the three gentlemen to linger over their port and cigars. But they did not do so for long, for presently, those invited to the conversation party started to arrive at the town house, and Monsieur Valcoeur rose from the table to perform his duties as their host. Malcolm and Mr. Quimby made their way to the small drawing room to join the ladies as the guests began to be announced by the butler and ushered into the chamber. Malcolm recognized the names and titles of many, although he knew none of them personally—until the butler intoned, "The Lady Christine Fraser and Mr. Khalil al-Walid."

At that, Malcolm was violently startled to observe that the latter guest was one of the two foreigners who had come to Quimby & Company (Cartographers & Map Sellers) several weeks ago and who had purchased the older maps of Scotland.

"Mr. Quimby," he whispered urgently to his employer, "'tis *them!* 'Tis those two foreigners who came to your map shop that day! See that dark gentleman in the Oriental robes, who has arrived with the Lady Christine Fraser and was announced as Mr. Khalil al-Walid…? And the other dark man behind them, who was not announced…that must be Mr. al-Walid's manservant!"

"Yes…yes, well, this is a very strange turn of events, is it not, Malcolm? Surely 'tis not just merely coincidence that Mr. al-Walid should be among the guests here tonight, do you not agree?" Mr. Quimby studied the two foreigners intently.

"I…I don't know, sir." Malcolm's handsome brow was creased in a thoughtful frown. "For under normal circumstances, you and I would not be here ourselves, and we do not yet know how Mr. al-Walid and his manservant came to be here…whether or not 'twas Madame Valcoeur herself who invited them."

As it eventually turned out, however, the nature of the comtesse's conversation parties was such that invited guests frequently brought others with them, knowing that all were welcome to attend, provided that they were well behaved and had interesting conversation to contribute to the party. This was the case where Mr. al-Walid was concerned. Lady Christine—who turned out to be one of the friends Ariana had made since arriving in London—had met the Egyptian while sojourning in Scotland, and having remained in touch with him after their return to England, she had asked him to Madame Valcoeur's conversation party.

"For Mr. al-Walid is a herpetologist, from Egypt. He is in search of the gigantic sea serpent that is said to haunt the waters of Loch Ness—and what could be more interesting or entertaining than that?" Lady Christine now inquired of those gathered in the small drawing room.

Hearing this, both their hostess and Ariana gasped, and the latter turned ashen and shivered suddenly and uncontrollably, as well.

"You are cold, *mademoiselle?*" Malcolm, noticing—as he had observed everything about her since entering the town house—how she shuddered, at once stood. "Please. Allow me to escort you to a chair nearer the fire, and perhaps your lady's maid could be summoned…to fetch a shawl for you?"

"*Oui,* an excellent suggestion, Monsieur Blackfriars. I fear that perhaps my daughter is not yet as fully recovered from her ordeal in Oxford Street as we had thought." Turning to one of the footmen, the comtesse directed that Ariana's abigail, Sophie, be sent for a shawl, while Malcolm saw that Ariana was comfortably settled in one of the wing chairs before the large marble hearth.

"There, you shall be warmer in a trice." He smiled reassuringly at her, trying to resist the urge he had to take her small, graceful hands in his own larger, strong ones and chafe them, in an attempt to bring some heat and color back to her.

"I'm sure I will. Thank you for your consideration, Monsieur Blackfriars. You are very kind." Then, turning to the others in the small drawing room, Ariana continued, "Pray, do not interrupt your discussion on my account. 'Twas only a momentary chill that I experienced, I assure you. Monsieur Blackfriars is right. I am already warmer here, by the fire. Please, Mr. al-Walid, won't you tell us about…your work?"

"Yes, for I myself am quite interested in hearing about it. Were the old maps you acquired in my establishment of any use to you during your quest, Mr. al-Walid?" Mr. Quimby queried pleasantly, his pale blue eyes wide and seemingly guileless, although Malcolm, who knew his employer well, was not deceived and could guess at the shrewd calculations now taking place in Mr. Quimby's mind, especially since learning that Mr. al-Walid was an Egyptian.

"Indeed, sir, I found them most valuable for my purpose, thank you." Mr. al-Walid's own face was inscrutable; his dark eyes were watchful and penetrating.

"Then…did you discover the monster of Loch Ness?" Madame Polgár questioned.

"No, unfortunately, *madame,* I did not. However, I am unde-terred and shall return in the future to Scotland to continue my search."

"Well, it sounds like a highly dangerous business to me," the fortune-teller remarked. "Have you considered, Mr. al-Walid, that this sea monster—if it truly even exists—could be the death of you?"

"There is always some risk involved in my field of study, *madame.* Nevertheless, I shall persevere in my endeavor."

"I believe you will. I'm certain you know that the snake is a very important spiritual symbol the world over, do you not, Mr. al-Walid?" The gold bangles on Madame Polgár's wrists jangled softly as she set her now-empty sherry glass to one side. "'Twas, of course, the chosen manner of death of your own Queen Cle-opatra…she who was the Goddess Isis incarnate in this life, the Divine Mother of us all. 'Tis Isis who—like the ubiquitous ser-pent—brings both life and death to us all. 'I, Isis, am all that has been, that is or shall be; no mortal man hath ever me unveiled.' That is the inscription to be found on her temple at Sais. Is that not so, Mr. al-Walid?"

"Yes, *madame,* that is correct." Mr. al-Walid nodded impas-sively. "You would appear to know a great deal about ancient Egyptian history and religion."

"That is because Madame Polgár is a talented clairvoyant, and as such, because of her interest in not only the future, but also the present and the past, she has studied the ancient Egyptians at some length," Madame Valcoeur explained.

"*Oui,* that is so," the fortune-teller agreed, "for the ancient Egyptians understood not only both life and death, but also the irrevocable intertwining of Fate and Free Will, which we dis-cussed briefly earlier, *madame,* and which I know that you wish to be the subject of your conversation party tonight. So we are indeed fortunate to be blessed with Mr. al-Walid's company this evening, for he will be able to give us a native's perspective of his country and its ancient inhabitants. So, tell us, Mr. al-Walid, is it not true that the ancient Egyptians revered the heart and believed it to be the fount of all human intelligence and emotions, from which Free Will springs?"

"Yes, they did, *madame,*" Mr. Al-Walid answered. "So much so, in fact, that although during the intricate mummification process employed by my ancestors, all the body's organs were removed and stored in canopic jars, the heart was instead always carefully preserved and, afterward, returned to its place in the corpse."

"I myself have also heard that the heart was often protected by a talisman or amulet called a heart scarab," Madame Polgár continued. "Do you know anything about that, sir?"

"I do, indeed, *madame.* For even today, the scarab beetle, which is the creature upon which the heart scarab was based, remains much venerated by us Egyptians. The talisman of which you spoke was placed over the heart of the mummy, to protect the deceased and his heart during his long journey to the Underworld. Over the millennia, there have been many such amulets discovered in our great pyramids and necropolises by both looters and archaeologists alike. The most famous of these was a heart scarab named in honor of the god Kheperi. So 'twas known as the Heart of Kheperi."

At that announcement, Malcolm, stunned, paused in the act of sipping from his glass of sherry, his heart beginning to hammer so hard and loud that he thought that, surely, everyone present in the small drawing room must hear it.

"What…what made that particular talisman so renowned?" Carefully he schooled his visage in a way that he devoutly hoped would display no more than a casual interest in the topic under discussion.

"Ah, well, you see, Mr. Blackfriars, legend has it that this amulet, the Heart of Kheperi, was cut from a huge raw emerald, so 'twas even larger than a goose egg, which in and of itself alone made it utterly priceless," Mr. al-Walid elucidated. "And then 'twas polished to perfection and suspended from a solid-gold chain. But what really made the Heart of Kheperi invaluable was the fact that 'twas rumored to possess the power of the god Kheperi himself and thus could, in the hands of one who knew how to wield it properly, bestow even immortality."

"*Non!* Such a thing is surely not possible!" Monsieur Valcoeur gesticulated dismissively. "For myself, I do not believe it!"

"I see that you are, as usual, still ever the skeptic, *monsieur.*" Madame Polgár frowned at him censuringly. "But even so, I tell you there are things in this world beyond our ken—for what are we but mere mortals? Except for those such as myself, gifted with extraordinary powers, we have little understanding even now of that which we cannot grasp with our own five senses. Why, during the Middle Ages, men still believed that the world was flat instead of round!"

"Quite so, *madame,*" Ariana said, from where she sat before the fire, wrapped in the fringed silk shawl that Sophie had brought her earlier. "For I have learnt as much during my lessons with my governess, Mademoiselle Thibault. But I am curious, Monsieur al-Walid, for you speak of this talisman, the Heart of Kheperi, as though it no longer exists. Has it been lost or destroyed, then? And if so, how could such a thing have happened to an amulet that must surely have been one of the greatest treasures of Egypt? Why was it not put into a museum, for safekeeping?"

"Now, there is a very bizarre tale, in truth, *mademoiselle.*" Mr. al-Walid now directed his attention to Ariana. "For legend has it that for centuries, the Heart of Kheperi was kept in a sacred place in the temple devoted to worship of the god Kheperi. But of course, nothing stays the same forever, and Egypt was no exception to the rule. Old pharaohs and priests died. New ones came to power, and with them often came new gods, as well. Temples that had fallen out of favor were destroyed, and new ones were built. And in the midst of all the winds of change that swept across Egypt over time, the Heart of Kheperi mysteriously disappeared and was lost for millennia. Then—so the story goes—one day, nearly two hundred years ago, a group of foreigners journeyed to my country, young men who were embarked upon what you call a Grand Tour. They traveled to Luxor, to the Valley of the Kings, where their intention, which they related to their native guide before he fled in fear from them, was to rob one or more of the tombs concealed in the valley. Eventually they broke into the burial chamber of the High Priest Nephrekeptah. This high priest had during his lifetime served in the Temple of Kheperi and was very powerful and esteemed, so the location of his grave had remained a secret until 'twas unwittingly stumbled upon by the young men, who also discovered the vanished Heart of Kheperi within—or so the tale is told."

"Why, are you saying that these young men *stole* the emerald?" Madame Valcoeur's face was visibly pale in the soft, glowing candlelight and firelight that illuminated the small drawing room, and she held one hand to her throat, as though greatly dismayed by Mr. al-Walid's narrative.

"One young man did so, *madame,* yes. The others lost their lives during a rare rainstorm that caused the valley to flood perilously whilst they were in the high priest's tomb."

"But how do…how do you know that this young man—what was his name?—actually found and took the Heart of Kheperi, *monsieur?* What proof have you of that? I mean, 'tis all only an old legend, after all, is it not?" Madame Valcoeur insisted.

"No, not quite, *madame.*" Mr. al-Walid shook his head. "The High Priest Nephrekeptah certainly existed, for there are ancient Egyptian texts that speak of him—and in fact, 'tis recorded that he was the high priest at the Temple of Kheperi when the priceless emerald so cryptically vanished. The young man who robbed his tomb was one Lord James Ramsay, Viscount Strathmór."

"Viscount Strathmór?" Lady Christine's lovely face wore an expression of rapt interest. "The title is Scottish—and the Ramsays are certainly a Scottish clan—but that particular viscountcy is very old and long ago fell into dormancy or even extinction at some point through lack of male heirs."

"Quite possibly, my lady. Not being knowledgeable about either Scottish titles or clans, I cannot say. I know only that Lord Strathmór somehow escaped from the high priest's tomb, eventually making his way to Cairo. There he struck up an acquaintance with an old blind priest at a temple, proceeding to question him about heart scarabs—much as Madame Polgár has done me tonight—and eliciting from the priest the story of the famous Heart of Kheperi."

"Still, that is hardly evidence of the emerald's existence, much less that Lord Strathmór actually stole it," Monsieur Valcoeur pointed out logically.

"That is quite true, *monsieur*," Mr. al-Walid conceded. "However, by circuitous means about which I know very little 'twas later learnt by the old blind priest in Cairo that Lord Strathmór did indeed possess the Heart of Kheperi, which he had pilfered from the high priest's tomb, from the very breast of the high priest's mummy itself!"

"If that is, in fact, so, then where is the emerald now?" Her narrowed dark eyes gleaming avidly, Madame Polgár leaned forward eagerly in her seat, her clawlike hands gripping the arms of her chair tightly.

"Alas, no one knows, *madame*—for it mysteriously disappeared again following Lord Strathmór's death. 'Tis presumed that his son and only child inherited the Heart of Kheperi, but what became of it after that is a complete enigma, I'm afraid."

"Well, I must say, Mr. al-Walid, that for a herpetologist, you yourself seem inordinately well versed in the history and religion of your country." The fortune-teller studied the Egyptian intently.

"Like yourself, *madame*, I have a keen interest in all things ancient and spiritual. They are not only fascinating fields of study in and of themselves, but as you yourself observed earlier, they are also related in one fashion or another to snakes. Thus it has always been my own belief that to fully understand the nature of the serpent, 'tis also necessary to grasp the creature's relationship with man."

The dialogue continued, moving now more specifically to the evening's chosen topic of Fate and Free Will, but for the remainder of the conversation party, Malcolm listened with only half an ear, the wheels in his mind churning furiously. Before he had left Hawthorn Cottage, his mother had told him that being invited to the town house of Monsieur and Madame Valcoeur presented a rare opportunity for him. But, surely, how little she had dreamt of just what kind! What were the odds, he wondered, that he should here again encounter Mr. al-Walid, discover that he was an Egyptian and that he was also very knowledgeable about and interested in the Heart of Kheperi? Surely all that was no simple coincidence! Surely the jeweler Jakob Rosenkranz had been right when he had quoted Friedrich von Schiller's lines: "There's no such thing as chance; and what to us seems merest accident springs from the deepest source of destiny."

More and more, Malcolm felt that he was being inexorably drawn into some long-tangled web of Fate—from which only the gift of Free Will would indeed save him, and he yearned ardently to discuss with Mr. Quimby everything they had learnt that evening. But the unexpectedly lively conversation party proved so interesting and entertaining to its guests that it did not finally break up until the wee hours, after which time it was far too late to have any discourse with his employer.

"Yes, yes, I am quite as anxious as you to go over tonight's events, Malcolm," Mr. Quimby declared, once the two of them had taken their leave from the town house. "But our little tête-à-tête will have to wait until tomorrow, I fear. For I'm afraid I am unaccustomed to keeping such late hours and have now grown so weary that I would scarcely have anything sensible to say at the moment. So I will see you in the morning instead. Plan on having luncheon again with me at my town house."

"Aye, I shall look forward to it, sir!"

Malcolm saw the elder gentleman safely into a hansom cab, then he himself turned his footsteps homeward. The moon and stars shone bright and silvery in the night sky, and they and the street lamps lit his path as he walked toward St. John's Wood and Hawthorn Cottage. He was so tired, and his head was in such a whirl, that he completely forgot to keep his wits about him and a wary eye on his surroundings. So it was that the sudden, brutal attack upon him caught him totally by surprise.

Only the abrupt, violent knocking of his hat from his head gave him any warning before rough hands attempted to jerk a hood down over his face, as they had during the previous assault upon him. But this time, although taken unawares, Malcolm—thanks to his many long weeks of training—was now much faster to react. Vehemently wriggling away from the strong hands that sought to restrain him and blind him with the hood, he struck out viciously with his umbrella at his assailants, jabbing and beating them savagely in a furious effort to drive them off. Fiercely they returned his blows, but it quickly became clear to him that the two scoundrels, while more than game for the fight, lacked the expertise he had now acquired.

After a moment, they wisely stepped back, so that Malcolm could see them clearly in the moonlight and lamplight that illuminated the street. Much to his astonishment, he saw that the two ruffians were wearing masks and dominoes, as though they had just come from a masquerade ball. But if so, it had taken place nowhere respectable, for their garments were dirty, patched and worn. The two men themselves had neither his own height or build, but were slight and wiry, as though they had long struggled and scratched for a living on the mean streets of London. Now, as they circled him charily, dancing lightly and deftly on the balls of their feet, he thought in some dark corner of his mind that they resembled nothing so much as the scarecrows that he had been accustomed to seeing in farmers' fields in his youth. One thing was certain—the two men were not the Egyptians Khalil al-Walid and his manservant, as Malcolm had previously half suspected.

The fact that they were strangers to him both reassured and, perversely, dismayed him. For on the one hand, it could be that they were nothing more than common cutpurses bent on robbing him—or, worse, cutthroats who intended to murder him so that they could strip his corpse at their leisure, divesting him not only of his jewelry and wallet, but also of his clothes and shoes. On the other hand, it might be that the two villains were employed by Mr. al-Walid and his manservant—or even by the Foscarellis—in which case, they surely meant to kill him and steal the all-important crucifix he wore around his neck! Malcolm knew that no matter what, he could not let that happen, and now, as his assailants suddenly moved in to renew their onslaught against him, he defended himself vehemently, as though he were a man possessed, employing both his umbrella and fists as he and the two scoundrels got down to the nitty-gritty.

Their terrible ferocity was horrifying. But there was no one present to witness it…no Nicolas Ravener to come to his rescue this time, no policeman hurrying to the scene, whistle shrilling. For the two knaves had chosen their spot well, picking a somewhat desolate place along the southwestern edge of Regent's Park, with only a few houses across the street and quite near Regent's Canal. The proximity of this latter was, in fact, especially worrisome, for Malcolm feared that if he did not prevail in the fray, the two rogues would pitch his insensate or even dead body into the waterway, where it would perhaps be some time before it was discovered. That morbid thought lent impetus to his battle, and although he sustained a number of punches to his own self, he still managed to deliver more than he received, using his umbrella to both stab and batter his assailants unmercifully, causing them to grunt and groan with pain.

Then, finally, one of the two scoundrels pulled a knife, whose long silvery blade glittered wickedly in the moonlight and lamplight. Malcolm's jaw set with grim determination, and knowing he must act fast, he tossed aside his umbrella and deliberately stepped into the armed attacker's swing, catching hold of the man's bony wrist. Frantically, he and his opponent struggled for control of the knife, while the other man grabbed up Malcolm's discarded umbrella and began to flog him about the head and back with it, until he thought that, surely, he was not going to prove victorious, but would within a matter of minutes be hammered to his knees and have his throat cut. Desperately, he agilely leapt and twisted to one side, his hands still wrapped around his adversary's wrists, and as he turned, Malcolm succeeded in pulling his foe off balance, so that the man lunged forward, staggering and accidentally driving the knife into his umbrella-wield-ing cohort.

Blood spurted in the semidarkness as, stricken and muttering angry, aghast curses, the stabber snatched his blade free, while the other man, gasping with shock and agony, dropped the um-brella and clutched his arm, where a dark wet stain now spread across his sleeve.

"I'm 'it, I'm 'it," he rasped, beginning to stumble away down the street.

"You'll pay fer that—jest like you'll pay fer everythin' else, Mapper! You owe us plenty—an' we won't be fergettin' it, nei-ther! Sooner or later, we'll collect what's rightly due us—an' you'll get what's deservedly comin' to you!" the other man spat to Malcolm, feigning drawing the bloody knife he held across his throat to emphasize his words, before hurrying away after his injured crony.

Breathing hard, now half bent over himself, hurting from the fearsome pounding he had taken, Malcolm watched his assail-ants warily until they disappeared into the long dark shadows. A few minutes later, his ears discerned the clip-clopping of a horse's hooves and the clattering of a vehicle's wheels on the winding road. As before, the two men had had transportation waiting for them, it seemed. After that, except for Malcolm's own harsh, panting breath and, in sharp contrast, the gentle, rhyth-mic lapping of the water in Regent's Canal against its banks, there was naught save silence.

After a time, certain his accosters had truly gone, Malcolm collected his hat and umbrella, angry that those he had bought to replace the first ones ruined by the two brutes would now themselves need to be replaced. Then, with difficulty, he contin-ued on to Hawthorn Cottage. Reaching it at last, he let himself in with his key through the front door, then painfully dragged himself upstairs to his bedchamber. There, wearily, he stripped and washed, then miserably crawled into bed. Finally, restlessly, he slept—haunted by nightmares and deeply troubled by the ep-ithet "Mapper." Obviously his assailants knew who he was and where he was employed. Conversely and most disturbingly, he had not a single clue as to their own identities or why they so plainly intended to kill him.

Chapter Nine

Mr. Cavendish's Bookshop

Soul of the age!
The applause, delight, the wonder of our stage!
My Shakespeare, rise; I will not lodge thee by
Chaucer or Spenser, or bid Beaumont lie
A little further, to make thee a room;
Thou art a monument, without a tomb,
And art alive still, while thy book doth live,
And we have wits to read, and praise to give.

—Ben Jonson
*To the Memory of My Beloved,
the Author, Mr. William Shakespeare [1623]*

For I bless God in the libraries of the learnt and for all the
booksellers in the world.

—Christopher Smart
Jubilate Agno [fragment]

The gods
Visit the sins of the fathers upon the children.

—Euripides
Phrixus [fragment]

1848
Old Bond Street, London, England

Much to his dismay, when Malcolm awakened in the morning
he felt as though all night long, while he had slept, someone had,

from a great height, repeatedly dumped a heavy cartload of bricks on him. He ached in every bone and muscle his being, and he could not repress a long groan of pain as he struggled mightily to haul himself from bed. Reaching his washstand and gazing blearily at his unshaven reflection in the mirror, he discovered to his further discomfiture that his left eye was swollen and bruised, and that his lower lip was split open. Plainly, there would be no hiding all this from his mother, and as he undertook his morning ablutions, he racked his brain frantically in an effort to think of some plausible explanation for his battered appearance.

By the time he got downstairs for breakfast, Malcolm had come up with what he hoped would be a believable account, which he was able to try out on Mrs. Peppercorn, when she spied him and gasped.

"Upon my word, sir, what happened to you?" she cried as he entered the cozy kitchen and sat down at the table. "I thought 'twas a respectable dinner and a conversation party at the town house of some French count and countess you were off to last night—and not a tavern brawl!"

"Aye, and so 'twas, Mrs. Peppercorn. Unfortunately, however, 'twas not until the wee hours that I was finally able to take my leave of the Comte and Comtesse de Valcoeur, and as 'twas so late then, rather than walk home, I decided to indulge in the uncommon luxury of hiring a hansom cab to convey me hither. Whilst getting into the vehicle, however, I slipped and suffered quite a nasty fall, inadvertently banging my face upon the step."

"Good Lord, sir! Why, 'tis a wonder you were not hurt even worse than you were!" Tsking over what she thought was the mishap Malcolm had experienced, Mrs. Peppercorn shook her head with concern. Then she turned to the scullery maid, who stood at the sink, washing dishes. "Lucy, don't bother with those right now. Instead, I want you to run straight down to the butcher's shop and buy a nice, fresh piece of steak for Mr. Blackfriars's black eye. That's the best thing for it, sir, for 'twill soon take the swelling out, and some of the bruising, as well!"

Although Malcolm tried to protest against this ministration, the cook would not hear of it, and the scullery maid was dispatched posthaste to the butcher's shop, while he applied himself to the morning paper and his breakfast. Presently Lucy returned with a piece of steak wrapped in brown paper and tied up with string, and taking it from the parcel, Mrs. Peppercorn handed it to Malcolm, insisting that he apply it to his injured eye. At last he agreed, thinking that it would be unkind not to humor her, since she had gone to so much trouble on his behalf. However, he soon discovered that the piece of steak, being fresh and cold, actually did have a soothing effect upon the pain in his eye, and by the time he had finished reading the morning paper and drinking a second cup of tea, he felt that the swelling, at least, had in some measure subsided.

"Yes, I was right. It *does* look slightly better now, Mr. Blackfriars." The cook nodded with approval as she studied him intently. "And at least you can tell your mother that you've applied a treatment, so she won't worry that you're about to lose your eye—for I know how she frets over you, sir!"

"She does, indeed, Mrs. Peppercorn. So I thank you for your assistance."

Rising from the table, Malcolm went upstairs to bid his mother good-morning, inwardly bracing himself for her upset when she saw him—which was considerable indeed. But finally he did manage to convince her that it was only an unwitting accident caused by his slipping on the step of a hansom cab that he had suffered—rather than his having been set upon by their enemies—and that he would be as right as rain again a few days hence.

"Well, if you had to stumble and fall whilst getting into a hansom cab, I can only be grateful that you were not badly hurt and that it did not happen *before* the dinner and conversation party at the Comte and Comtesse de Valcoeur's town house, Malcolm. Because, only imagine if you had been compelled to go there with a black eye and a split lip! Why…what an unfortunate impression *that* would have made!"

"Aye, I'll warrant Monsieur and Madame Valcoeur would not have been so delighted to see me in that case," Malcolm agreed, smiling ruefully.

"Did they look favorably upon you, Son? Oh, I cannot think that they did not, for your father and I took pains to ensure to the very best of our ability that you were raised as a gentleman—as you would have been if not for your wastrel ancestor Lord Iain Ramsay, once the Earl of Dúndragon."

"I do not believe that either Monsieur or Madame Valcoeur found any cause for complaint, Mother. So do not worry about that. Now, I must be away, or I'll be late for work. But I promise I will tell you all about the dinner and conversation party when I return home this evening."

"Yes, you must, for I am most anxious to hear everything," she said.

"I knew that you would be."

Although he felt slightly guilty for lying to his mother about how he had acquired his injuries last night, as he departed from her room Malcolm was still nevertheless glad that his interview with her had passed off so easily and that he had not been compelled to tell her what had really happened. For that would only have frightened her terribly and left her inordinately fearful that their enemies, the Foscarellis, had discovered their assumed identities and whereabouts, and he did not want anything to disturb his mother's peace of mind. She had, he felt, suffered more than enough over his father's and Uncle Charles's murders, as well as the inexplicable disappearance without a trace of Aunt Katherine and her two children.

Following his habitual omnibus ride to Oxford Street, Malcolm entered Quimby & Company (Cartographers & Map Sellers) to be greeted by the youngest apprentice.

"Gor, what 'appened to you?" Tuck asked, his eyes widening as he spied Malcolm.

"Happened, Tuck. You must try to remember not to drop your aitches—for you know what Mr. Quimby has told you…that nothing bespeaks a man's social class so much as his speech and

that even the lowliest born may aspire to be gentlemen and ladies, even though they possess no rank or riches. Now, if you
must know, I slipped and fell last night whilst getting into a hansom cab. Is Mr. Quimby in yet?"

"Yes, 'e's…he's back in his office."

Upon learning this, Malcolm made his way to the rear of the
establishment, knocked on his employer's open door and poked
his head inside.

"My God, what has befallen you, Malcolm?" Mr. Quimby
cried, aghast and rising from his chair.

"I regret to report that another attack was made upon me last
night, sir—and this time, I actually saw my assailants. There
were two of them, but unfortunately, I've no idea who they were,
for they were decked out in masks and dominoes." Malcolm went
on to describe the event as it had occurred.

"Mapper, you say that one of the blackguards called you?" The
elder gentleman's brow was furrowed in a thoughtful frown.
"Well, that's very odd, don't you think? I mean, if these were men
hired by the Foscarellis—or even the Egyptians—one presumes
that they would at least know you as Malcolm Blackfriars, even
if your own true name had not been revealed to them. But…Map-
per? I don't mind telling you that I find that exceedingly strange,
Malcolm—for 'tis an epithet that would almost appear to be somehow directed at your connection with my map shop, wouldn't it?"

"Aye, I hadn't thought of that, sir, but you're right," Malcolm
answered slowly. "Still, I can't imagine that I've somehow so angered a customer that he would set a couple of thugs on me."

"No, neither can I. So unless and until we can obtain further
information, it must remain a mystery, I'm afraid. In the meanwhile, you must stay on your guard at all times, in case another
such assault should be attempted. Thank goodness I insisted on
your taking lessons at Red Rory Hoolihan's Boxing Saloon and
Henry the Younger's L'Ecole d'Armes! For 'twould seem that
they stood you in good stead."

"They did, in truth, sir."

"Now, I know that you must be as eager as I am to discuss all that took place at Monsieur and Madame Valcoeur's dinner and conversation party last evening, and I also know I promised you luncheon today at my town house. However, there has been a change of plans, which I hope will prove agreeable to you, for I've already consented to it. Shortly after I arrived at the map shop this morning, I received a message from my old friend Boniface Cavendish. He has returned to England at last, and he wants to meet with us and Jakob this afternoon. Further, he has said he will provide luncheon for us all, and although I have no doubt that this will consist of sandwiches from a coffee stall, I did not wish to either offend or disappoint him by refusing his kind offer."

"No, of course not, sir. I will be very glad to meet with your friend Mr. Cavendish."

"Good. Then we can kill several birds with one stone, by informing Boniface of everything we have learnt thus far about your heritage and the Heart of Kheperi, and by sharing with him and Jakob all that occurred last night. They may be able to give us some insights into this peculiar matter of Mr. al-Walid—for believe you me, if that man is truly a herpetologist, I'll eat my hat! In search of a gigantic sea serpent, indeed! Why, what a complete absurdity!"

The morning after her mother's dinner and conversation party, Ariana awakened feeling as though she had hardly slept at all. She had spent a restless night, tossing and turning in her bed. She had been stunned to learn Mr. al-Walid's occupation—and even more shocked to discover that he had undertaken a journey to Scotland, to the Highlands and Loch Ness, in search of a great sea monster rumored to inhabit the lake. Ever since she could remember, her mother had told her time and again that no such creature actually existed beyond the realm of her own nightmare. Now, as she had last evening, Ariana felt a deep sense of utter confusion and hurt sweep over her, for it was as though her mother had betrayed her somehow, concealing from her the knowledge of the huge sea serpent that lived in the loch.

Even as the thought occurred to her, a knock sounded upon her door, and then her mother entered her room, bearing a tray laden with a pot of hot chocolate, warm crumpets and fresh fruit.

"Good morning, *chérie.* How did you sleep last night?"

"Not very well, Maman, I fear."

"Oh, dear, I was afraid of that—which is why I took your tray from Sophie so I could bring it in myself, and sent her away. I thought we might talk."

"About Mr. al-Walid and his field of study? About his search for the great sea monster of Loch Ness—which you always insisted to me did not truly exist?"

"*Oui,* for I suspected how you might be feeling after meeting Mr. al-Walid and hearing about his work." The comtesse set the tray down upon the night table and began to pour the hot chocolate from its Sèvres pot into its delicate, matching china cup, which, when full, she handed to Ariana. Then she sat down beside her daughter on the bed. "I do not blame you if you are angry with me, *ma petite.* However, I want you to know I did not precisely lie to you about the sea serpent. For although there are those who claim to have actually seen it, their tales are no more reliable than those of others who relate stories about silkies and kelpies and other such mythical creatures. There is, in fact, no proof, *chérie,* that this fabled sea monster is anything more than the figment of the Highlanders' wild imagination. And because you dreamt nightmares about it, and it terrified you, I thought it best to deny its existence altogether. I could see no point in frightening you even further by admitting that perhaps it *was* real."

"I do not say that you did not mean well, Maman, for I know full well that you did. But, oh, Maman, can you not see that I am not a child any longer? I am a woman grown—old enough to be married and to have children of my own! You can't go on protecting me forever! Why…don't you understand what a terribly sheltered life I have led already? 'Twas ages before I was permitted to make my debut into society like other young ladies, and even then, every ball, party, or rout to which I was invited was carefully looked into by you before I was allowed to attend. 'Tis no wonder I have not been able to find *un jeune homme* as you and Papa have wished!"

"Be fair, *ma petite,*" the comtesse insisted quietly. "There were many handsome young men in France who would have been happy to be your sweetheart. But if you are honest, you will admit that none of them found favor in your eyes. Nor have any potential suitors here in England attracted your notice—except, I think, for Monsieur Blackfriars. Is that not so, *chérie?*"

"Oh, do not speak to me about Monsieur Blackfriars—for I know that you will only say the same things as Sophie has already told me…that he is neither titled nor wealthy, so cannot be thought of as a suitable match for a young woman like me!"

"*Oui,* and all that is indeed true, *ma petite,* unfortunately. For otherwise, I should have no objections whatsoever to him, and neither would your papa, I do not think, for Monsieur Blackfriars is a very handsome and a surprisingly genteel and educated young man. But the world is not as we so often wish it to be, *chérie,* and the fact is that Monsieur Blackfriars has little or nothing to offer you beyond his own good name. *Alors!* What kind of life and future could you have, married to a mere map seller, for goodness sake?"

"At least I would be happy—and I have a fortune of my own, besides!"

"Money that your papa means to settle on you whenever you wed, *oui.* But I tell you this, *ma petite*—I know men, and Monsieur Blackfriars is not the man I believe him to be if, having somehow been prevailed upon to marry you in the first place, he would agree to live off your dowry. He may not be rich, but he is very proud and honorable—neither a profligate nor a fortune hunter, like so many of these young libertines to be found nowadays—and I tell you that he would not touch a penny of your funds, but would insist that you live on his own income."

"And would that be so very terrible, after all, Maman?"

"*Non,* perhaps not, *chérie.*" Madame Valcoeur's face softened. "Not if you loved him, and if he loved you. But having discerned the kind of man Monsieur Blackfriars is, I know he would not in all good conscience ask you to live such a life with him, when he is well aware of the life to which you were born and are accustomed. He would feel guilty and ashamed were he to beg you to settle for less. So set your cap for him if you must, *ma petite,* for I know the true heart has a will all its own and cannot be dictated to. But I warn you—unless something wholly unexpected happens to change Monsieur Blackfriars's status in life, if you are quite determined to have him, then you will almost certainly be doomed to heartbreak in the end. For my guess is that even if he loves you, he will not ask you to marry him, *chérie.*"

"Oh, Maman, I hope you are wrong! But still, deep in my heart, I very much fear that you are right," Ariana confessed sadly.

"I'm so very sorry…truly I am, *ma petite.* But as I observed earlier, there are many other handsome young men who would be suitable for you. So…may I ask, why Monsieur Blackfriars, *chérie?* What is it about him that has so captivated you and captured your heart at first sight, when so many others have tried and failed to win your hand?"

"I do not know, Maman—except that from the very first moment I saw Monsieur Blackfriars bending over me in Oxford Street and felt him sweep me up in his strong arms before I fainted, I have felt so strangely as though, somehow, I have known him all my life…that—oh, I know 'twill sound quite silly, Maman, but, well…he reminds me somehow so uncannily of the boy Collie in my dream…my nightmare…that 'tis almost as though the two are one and the same—" Ariana broke off abruptly, biting her lower lip. Then, shrugging her shoulders ruefully and woefully, she gave a little self-deprecating laugh. "But of course, how could that be? For Collie never actually existed, did he? He is nothing more than the product of my own childhood imagination, is he? For I've never really been to Scotland, to the Highlands and Loch Ness, have I? And since I can't believe I have been gifted with any real clairvoyant talent, like

Madame Polgár, Collie is therefore only a girlhood dream—and Monsieur Blackfriars is just someone who happens to resemble him a little, that's all. There. Now that I've spoken about it and sorted it all out properly in my mind, I shall dwell no more on any of it. And thus, in time, perhaps I will cease to dream about the boy Collie, or to think about Monsieur Blackfriars anymore, either."

"*Oui,* I believe that is best, *ma petite,*" Madame Valcoeur murmured mechanically, rising from the bed and turning away, her lovely countenance pale in the early-morning light that filtered in through the lacy curtains, and her gaze oddly stricken and deeply reflective.

Ariana, however—a peculiar lump in her throat, choking her, as she now bent determinedly over her breakfast tray and picked uninterestedly at its otherwise tempting contents—did not notice the strange, thoughtful expression on her mother's face. And would not have seen, anyway, through the blur of the tears that welled suddenly and unexpectedly in her violet eyes.

Once, a long time ago in the early seventeenth century, the area around Bond Street had been nothing more than open marshy countryside. But then in the latter half of the century a coterie of wealthy bankers and merchants had purchased the land from the Duke of Albemarle, and Old Bond Street had been laid out and named after Sir Thomas Bond, a close friend of King Charles II. Sometime after that, New Bond Street had been constructed, as well, and finally extended all the way to Oxford Street. Thus advantageously situated at the heart of the Mayfair district, bounded by Oxford, Regent and Piccadilly Streets to the north, east and south, respectively, and by Park Lane to the west, had Bond Street, by the middle of the eighteenth century, become one of the most fashionable places in the city, home to dozens of elegant, charming shops of all kinds. From nearby Grosvenor, Berkeley and Hanover Squares, as well as from farther afield, the *haut ton* of London society had flocked to the street, and this had not changed over the years.

Cavendish Bookshop was happily situated at the intersection of New Bond, Old Bond and Grafton Streets, and was a small, outwardly unassuming establishment whose oak front door opened into an interior that was positively crammed to bursting with books. In fact, as he, Mr. Quimby and Jakob Rosenkranz stepped inside the shop, and the ubiquitous brass bell affixed to the front door chimed, Malcolm thought he had never seen so many books in his entire life. From floor to ceiling were wooden shelves stacked high with books of every description—some massive tomes bound with leather, and others small chapbooks that were little more than pamphlets, and still others of every size and kind in between, all appearing to have been shelved with little rhyme or reason, just shoved in wherever they would fit. The whole effect was such that the premises appeared to be unbelievably tiny, crowded and untidy—and the shelves themselves were, Malcolm observed, layered with dust.

Now, as he gazed around the shop, utterly fascinated by it, he witnessed the approach of someone he presumed must be Boniface Cavendish himself—a man who was neither short and stout, like Mr. Quimby, nor tall and lean, like Mr. Rosenkranz, but somewhere in between, and quite one of the most eccentric and remarkable gentlemen Malcolm had ever before spied. This was because Mr. Cavendish's appearance could, even by the kindest of persons, have been described only as wild. His gray hair stuck up oddly in every direction from his head, as though it had seen neither a brush nor a comb for days, and his baggy clothes were so rumpled that they looked as though he had slept in them for weeks. His silver-rimmed spectacles, which were shoved up on his brow, badly needed polishing, and pipe tobacco and ash dusted the front of his wrinkled shirt.

"By heaven, where the devil have you been?" he greeted them in a voice that boomed. "I expected you fully half an hour ago!"

"No, your note distinctly said half-past noon, Bonny. I'm quite sure of it, and 'tis just now half past." Mr. Rosenkranz's own voice was querulous, and after shutting up his pocket watch, at which he had glanced to determine the time, he frowned at his friend censuringly.

"Did I? Why, I could have sworn I said noon on the dot! But no matter. You're here now, and I see you're as peevish as ever, Jakob! Had no luncheon yet, I expect."

"No, of course not, for you promised us luncheon here—although I doubt that we shall get anything more than a sandwich, and it had better not be ham, Bonny, for you know I don't eat pork!"

"Oh, yes, quite right, quite right...bless me if I hadn't clean forgotten that luncheon was to be on me today. Danny! Tim! Where are you, lads? Oh, there you are. Take some clean mugs, and run down to the coffee stall...get us all some coffee and sandwiches and whatever else may be served there today. Now, Septimus, my old friend, I trust you are in a better mood than Jakob—and that *you* have no objections to ham!"

"Yes, indeed—and none at all, Bonny. Now, please, allow me to introduce to you my junior journeyman, Mr. Malcolm Blackfriars. Malcolm, as I'm sure you've already realized, this is Mr. Boniface Cavendish, the proprietor of this bookshop."

"I'm very pleased to meet you, Mr. Cavendish," Malcolm said.

"Any friend of Septimus's and Jakob's is a friend of mine. So please call me Bonny. Well, won't you come into my office, gentlemen? For I don't mind telling you that I'm quite awash with curiosity to learn what has been happening here in my absence—for I've a nose for things and can tell there must be something most unusual afoot! Otherwise, Jakob, at least, would not have deigned to agree to luncheon from a coffee stall, I feel certain—for 'tis not at all in keeping with his jeweler's image, you know!"

"You are quite mistaken, Bonny. I've nothing against luncheon from a coffee stall and often frequent one myself on highly busy days," Mr. Rosenkranz protested crossly. "'Tis simply that I am prohibited from eating pork, because I'm a Jew."

"Bless me if I hadn't forgotten all about your dietary restrictions, too! Well, have no fear on that account, Jakob. For you shall have watercress, then, or something else equally as inoffensive," Mr. Cavendish went on cheerfully, unabashed, as he led the way to his private office at the rear of his establishment. "And then you may be comfortable with your conscience—and well fed, besides! For Mrs. Potter has nothing but the very best watercress at her coffee stall—or so she assures me!"

The bookseller, Malcolm quickly gathered, was as absent-minded as he was gregarious and disheveled, and his office, when they entered it, gave testimony to that fact, for it was a complete mess, with books and papers stacked everywhere, as though Mr. Cavendish quite inattentively laid anything and everything down wherever he happened to be at the time. In addition, the room was strewn with sundry and even bizarre knickknacks, which included a brain preserved in a large jar and a big stuffed horned owl whose moth-eaten feathers appeared to be molting. As a result, Malcolm could now well see why Mr. Quimby had declared that he did not believe the bookseller had ever thrown away anything in his entire life.

After hastily removing precariously teetering piles of books and papers from the sofa and chairs within, then taking a huge square handkerchief from his breast pocket and violently beating the cushions with it to tidy them, Mr. Cavendish bade them all be seated, seemingly oblivious of the clouds of dust he had stirred up with his actions. Instead, assuming his own chair behind his desk, he beamed at them all jovially and proceeded to add to the office's musty atmosphere by lighting his pipe, puffing on it with obvious pleasure and causing curling tendrils of smoke to waft through the air.

"Now, tell me everything," he insisted eagerly, "for unless I miss my guess, whilst I've been away, recovering my good health and soaking up the sunshine in the Mediterranean, the three of you have embarked upon some grand adventure!"

"Indeed, we have, Bonny," Mr. Quimby confirmed, nodding. "But before you can be made privy to any of it, we must have your word of honor as a gentleman that you will speak of this matter to no one besides ourselves, without Malcolm's consent."

"Ah, 'tis a mystery…a secret, then, is it? Better and better!

Of course I give you my word. Now, say on, Septimus. For to quote the wise immortal bard, I am 'like greyhounds in the slips, straining upon the start. The game's afoot.' But…what game is it? Something to do with young Mr. Blackfriars here, obviously—or he would not be present. Has he discovered a long-lost treasure map, moldering away in your shop, Septimus?"

"There is nothing at all—including a long-lost treasure map— *moldering* away anywhere on my *own* premises, I assure you, Bonny, although, most regrettably, I cannot say the same about *yours.* Now, do be still, whilst Malcolm tells you his tale—and then you and Jakob both shall hear about the strange and unsettling events that occurred last evening, as well, and that resulted in Malcolm's bruised appearance today. For believe me, the plot, as they say, thickens!"

Before any more could be said, however, Mr. Cavendish's clerks, Danny and Tim, returned from Mrs. Potter's coffee stall. It was only in the past five years or so that coffee stalls had become exceedingly popular, so that they now numbered upward of three hundred in the city. The vast majority of these were nothing more than springbarrows, with two or sometimes four wheels, often brightly painted, and they were owned and operated primarily by women, who sold coffee that had usually been adulterated with chicory, to make it go further. Some coffee stalls, although not many, also peddled tea and, very rarely, hot chocolate. In addition to coffee, one could generally also buy slices of bread and butter, currant cake, ham sandwiches, bunches of watercress and boiled eggs at coffee stalls. The price of all this was only a pence or two per item ordered, so that coffee and a relatively good, however simple, luncheon could be had for far less than a shilling. But because the proprietors of the coffee stalls bought all their supplies in bulk, their profit was still normally two hundred percent—providing that they acquired a good location and had the necessary funds to set up shop to begin with, so that they did not have to borrow money to get started.

Danny and Tim had purchased plenty from Mrs. Potter's coffee stall, so that there were not only mugs filled with steaming-hot coffee, but also several ham sandwiches and slices of bread and butter, along with bunches of watercress for Mr. Rosenkranz and anyone else who desired it, two dozen boiled eggs, and thick, generous helpings of freshly baked currant cake. While Malcolm and the others apportioned the luncheon and began to eat their meal, he related his story, up to and including the events of the previous night. As both Mr. Quimby and Mr. Rosenkranz had been, Mr. Cavendish was astonished and riveted by the narrative, so that at the end of it, for a long moment, he could only sit in his chair in silence, shaking his head with amazement. Then finally he spoke.

"Well, quite frankly, Mr. Blackfriars, I'm truly astounded by all you've told me, for in truth, although I jested with Septimus about your being hot on the trail of some long-lost treasure, I genuinely never expected to hear anything like this! Be that as it may, however, I do believe I can actually be of some small assistance to you in your quest for this missing emerald, the Heart of Kheperi." Lost in thought, the bookseller drummed his fingers on his desk. "Now, let me think where the book I've now been put in mind of by your utterly fascinating tale might be…whether I shelved it under history or some other category…hmm… Aha!"

Suddenly bolting from his chair, Mr. Cavendish excitedly disappeared without warning into his bookshop, where they soon heard him calling to his clerks and rummaging through his shelves, then muttering under his breath to himself and cursing when a stack of books accidentally toppled over, several falling from their perches and hitting him on the head.

"Bonny really does need a keeper, you know, Septimus," Mr. Rosenkranz observed dryly. "For you mark my words—one of these days, he is going to do himself or someone else some mortal injury in this thoroughly disorganized bookshop of his. He and his customers shall be buried under a pile of rubble—and undoubtedly shan't be discovered for weeks!"

"Hush, Jakob," Mr. Quimby chided softly. "*You* know he means well, and that he has a heart of gold, besides, underneath that invariably crumpled exterior of his. Why, he would give you the very shirt off your back if you needed it!"

"Well, thank heavens I don't—for it could stand a good washing, starching and pressing! Oh, I know he is the very soul of kindness, Septimus. But...well, really, must he always be so very...*chaotic?*"

"I heard that, Jakob!" the bookseller exclaimed as he reentered his office victoriously. "But never you mind. I take no offense. No, indeed, I don't—for why, I ask you, should a man cavil at the truth, especially when 'tis related to him by his oldest and dearest friends? Higgledy-piggledy I am and shall probably always be. I freely admit it. But what, after all, has whether or not the shelves in my shop are often slightly disarrayed to do with the grand scheme of things? Do you think the world shall come to an end tomorrow because there is a book out of place in my humble establishment? *I* know where everything on my premises is—and more important, when it comes to knowing books and what is between their covers, there is no one who surpasses me! So, now, cease your cantankerous grumbling, Jakob—for in truth, you never mean anything by it, anyway, and both Septimus and I know that. You just like to complain on principle in order to keep everyone on their toes, and I am certainly on mine, I assure you. For here is the very tome I sought—and now we shall learn all about this tomb-robbing Lord Dúndragon's only son and heir, Lord Robert Roy Ramsay, the ninth Earl of Dúndragon!"

Triumphantly waving the book he held in both hands, Mr. Cavendish resumed his seat and plunked the weighty tome down upon his desk.

"What is that you have there, Bonny?" Mr. Quimby leaned forward in his chair to peer at the title of the book. "A history of the Clan Ramsay?"

"No—a history of secret societies." Opening the tome, the bookseller started to leaf through the voluminous pages, until at last he cried out with satisfaction. "I knew it! I knew it! There.

What did I tell you? I never forget anything I have read in a book!"

"Which is exactly why you can't remember anything else!" Mr. Rosenkranz remarked sourly. "But never mind about that now. Just what, precisely, is it you've found, Bonny?"

"An obscure passage about Lord Rob Roy Ramsay, the ninth Earl of Dúndragon. Yes, you see? 'Twas Mr. Blackfriars's saying that Lord James Ramsay, the eighth Earl of Dúndragon, was killed by his only son and heir during a tragic hunting accident that jogged my memory, so I recalled that I had read that bit of information somewhere previously. After that, it only remained for me to figure out where. 'Twas here…in *The Enlightened Ones, A History of Esoteric Orders,* by Sir Walter Hutcheson. Here. Listen to this." Mr. Cavendish pointed to the ornately printed page, moving his finger along beneath the sentences as he continued. "Sir Walter wrote that after the eighth Lord Dúndragon's untimely death, the ninth Lord Dúndragon was so greatly distraught at having, however unintentionally, caused his father's demise that he turned more and more to the spiritual side of life and the study of arcana and esoterica. You must remember that this was the pursuit of many famous and wellborn men over the centuries…Dr. John Dee, Paracelsus, Nostradamus, Leonardo da Vinci, Sir Isaac Newton and so forth. So, in and of itself alone, there was and is nothing very remarkable about all this. In addition to which, the Earls of Dúndragon were Scottish, and Scotland had long been a hotbed of, among other things, Knights Templar activity. And here in England, of course, there were various pseudomonastic orders such as the Knights of St. Francis, founded by Sir Francis Dashwood and now better known as the Hellfire Club. But here…here is the really interesting part. Eventually, like Sir Francis, the ninth Lord Dúndragon established his own pseudomonastic order, which he called the Order of the Sons of Isis—after the Divine Mother Goddess of the Egyptians. Further, the order, which comprised thirteen 'brothers' or 'monks' in number, was believed to worship an 'Egyptian version of the philosopher's stone,' carved in the shape of a scarab beetle, sacred to the Egyptian god Kheperi, and thought, if wielded properly, to be able to bestow immortality upon whoever possessed it!"

"The Heart of Kheperi!" Malcolm exclaimed, his heart racing.

"So 'twould seem." The bookseller nodded, his hazel eyes gleaming with excitement.

"Does the book say what became of the emerald, Bonny?" Mr. Quimby asked.

"Unfortunately, no. However, it *does* state that after four of the so-called brothers of the Sons of Isis themselves met most bizarre and tragic, untimely deaths, the order abruptly disbanded, and the brothers scattered."

"At which point, one presumes, the Heart of Kheperi vanished." Mr. Rosenkranz sighed heavily at the realization.

"The ninth Lord Dúndragon and the remaining eight brothers must, like the eighth Lord Dúndragon, have decided that the emerald truly *was* accursed, as 'tis claimed, and concealed it somewhere for safekeeping, until they could better understand its power," Malcolm speculated, thinking aloud. "Then they had the two crucifixes fashioned, which are somehow the key to the location where they hid the Heart of Kheperi."

"Oh, great heavens!" Mr. Quimby groaned, suddenly smacking himself on the forehead and shaking his head with dismay. "Don't you see? Counting Lord Dúndragon, there were *nine* brothers left. *What if there are nine crosses…a ninefold key, as 'twere?*"

Chapter Ten

Rendezvous in the Parks

Over hill, over dale,
　　Thorough bush, thorough brier,
Over park, over pale,
　　Thorough flood, thorough fire.
I do wander everywhere,
Swifter than the moon's sphere;
And I serve the fairy queen,
To dew her orbs upon the green;
The cowslips tall her pensioners be;
In their gold coats spots you see;
Those be rubies, fairy favours,
In those freckles live their savours.
I must go seek some dewdrops here,
And hang a pearl in every cowslip's ear.

　　　　　　　　　　　—William Shakespeare
　　　　　　A Midsummer Night's Dream [1595-1596]

1848
Hyde Park and Kensington Gardens, London, England

All weekend long, Ariana had wrestled with her heart and mind, trying to persuade herself that there was no such thing as love at first sight and that she could not therefore be in love with Malcolm Blackfriars. She was strongly attracted to him, yes—but that was only because he bore a striking resemblance to the boy Collie in her dream…her nightmare…in which she envisioned herself as being filled with happiness, excitement and delight as she tramped at Collie's side through the wet autumn woods, then huddled in his small fishing boat, the thrilling sound of his low voice washing over her. But however real he might seem to her, Collie did not truly exist. Instead, he was only a figment of her imagination—upon which she had now imposed Malcolm Blackfriars's own dark, handsome visage—and she must accept that.

She would think no more about Malcolm Blackfriars, Ariana resolved sternly. But much to her dismay, that soon proved easier said than done, and finally, on Monday afternoon, she could bear no longer the agony of not ever seeing him again.

"Sophie, the sun is shining, and 'tis such a fine, beautiful day outside that I should like to go for a walk," she declared to her abigail, turning from the window of her bedchamber overlooking the square below. "Run downstairs and tell Monsieur Montségur to prepare an alfresco luncheon for us, and we will take it to Hyde Park and eat it there. Won't that be fun?"

Sophie, however, as she glanced up from where she sat on the upholstered bench at the foot of Ariana's bed, was not deceived by the look of wide-eyed innocence on her face.

"*Mademoiselle,* this idea of yours wouldn't, by any chance, have anything to do with the fact that Monsieur Blackfriars told you at Madame Valcoeur's dinner and conversation party last week that he sometimes eats his own luncheon in Hyde Park, would it?"

"Well, and what if it does?" Ariana tossed her head, annoyed, a stubborn pout beginning to form about the corners of her mouth. "Am I to refrain from ever going there again and enjoying a stroll or a picnic because of that? Besides, 'tis quite a large park, you know, so 'tis highly unlikely that we shall even meet Monsieur Blackfriars there. And anyway, it doesn't matter if we do—for you know I spoke to Maman about him, and that she has not forbidden me to see him."

"*Oui,* that is true," the maid agreed, nodding, as she finished the last of the stitching she was doing to repair the hem on one of Ariana's gowns, then tied a knot in the thread and bit off the end. "For Madame Valcoeur is wise in the ways of affairs of the heart, and thus knows that had she forbidden you to see Monsieur Blackfriars, you would only have become all the more determined to do so and would have met with him secretly, given the chance. This way, you are spared any subterfuge—and Madame Valcoeur is not made to spy upon her own daughter."

"Now you have caused me to feel very guilty, Sophie!" Ariana accused.

"I'm sorry, for that was not my intention, *mademoiselle.* 'Tis simply that I do not understand this pursuit of a man with whom you can have no future—especially when you have so many other handsome young gentlemen from which to choose. Why, had I as many prospective suitors as you, I should count myself most fortunate—and not waste my time pining over one without either a title or wealth to recommend him!"

"Monsieur Blackfriars has many other fine qualities—and rank and riches are not everything, Sophie."

"You say that only because you have never lacked either, *mademoiselle.* Were you suddenly to change places with some poor woman on the street, you would know better! Oh, I do not claim that being nobly born or possessed of a fortune engenders happiness, mind you, for we both know that is not necessarily true. But still, a title opens doors that would otherwise remain firmly closed in your face, *mademoiselle,* and money ensures that you will never wind up destitute, in a workhouse or worse!"

"*Bon Dieu,* Sophie! You sound almost like one of the revolutionaries or radicals in Paris!"

"Well, although I do not at all agree with their violent methods, *mademoiselle,* that does not prevent me from knowing there is still a great deal of truth in at least some of what they have to say. 'Tis, in fact, not right that some should have so very much, whilst others have so very little. Further, when men—and women, too, for that matter—cannot find honest work and grow too poor to support their families, to properly feed and clothe their children, then they have nothing left to lose and so become dangerous to the rest of us. Why, even Monsieur Valcoeur has said as much, for I myself have heard him."

"*Oui,* so have I. But, Sophie, what can be done? Everyone cannot have a rank or riches."

"*Non,* but they *can* have a decent life, with a fair day's wages for a fair day's work."

"You are an idealist, Sophie, and not a realist, I fear—or else you would know that even so, there would still always be those who wanted more than their fair share and so who would never be satisfied with their own lot in life, however comfortable. That is the nature of men and the way of the world, unfortunately. But…enough of such talk! Monsieur Blackfriars is scarcely a pauper—and even you must admit, Sophie, that he committed not one single faux pas at Maman's dinner and that he held his own with everybody present at her conversation party afterward."

"*Oui,* in that regard, you are right. He behaved the perfect gentleman, I cannot deny. Very well, then. I will go below and tell Monsieur Montségur to prepare an alfresco luncheon for us, and then we shall go for a stroll in Hyde Park, and dine there, as well, so you can moon over Monsieur Blackfriars if we should chance to meet him, or else return home deeply downcast if we do not. Either way, I just hope you know what you are doing, *mademoiselle*—and that you will not be doomed to heartache in the end!"

But now that she had succeeded in getting her own way, Ariana refused to have her spirits dampened by the thought that Malcolm would not, after all, be present in Hyde Park, and soon she and Sophie, dressed in their best walking clothes and trailed by two footmen carrying a blanket and a woven picnic hamper laden with their alfresco luncheon, were making their way down Portman Street, toward Oxford Street and Park Lane. Upon reaching the Cumberland Gate, the procession continued along the main road that wound directly through the heart of Hyde Park, to its Serpentine River, and there, not far from its edge, Ariana directed the footmen to spread the blanket and to begin unpacking the picnic basket.

Her heart was pounding and her palms were sweating, for as

she and the others had strolled through the park, she had indeed spied Malcolm, and now, as she settled herself upon the blanket, spreading her skirts prettily about her and adjusting her parasol just so to shield her from the sun, she saw that he was walking toward her. At the sight, she felt her hammering heart lurch erratically in her breast, and for one wild instant she feared she was about to swoon.

"Don't you dare faint, *mademoiselle!*" Sophie hissed.

"I wasn't going to," Ariana lied.

"You were!"

"Hush, you goose! He'll hear you!"

After this whispered exchange, nothing more was said in this regard, for just then, Malcolm approached, dashingly doffing his top hat and bowing low to Ariana. As the bright yellow sunbeams glistened on his glossy black hair and a crooked, engaging smile split his lips, she felt her breath catch in her throat, as though her corset were laced far too tightly, and her pulse fluttered and raced.

"Monsieur Blackfriars…what an unexpected but pleasant surprise!" Tilting her head up to gaze at him, Ariana flashed him a bright sunny smile of welcome. Then, observing his injured face, she exclaimed, "Oh, my goodness! You've been in some dreadful tavern brawl!"

"No, not at all, *mademoiselle,* I do hasten to reassure you," Malcolm rejoined quickly. "I'm afraid my somewhat sad appearance is due only to my having slipped and fallen upon the step of a hansom cab after leaving your parents' town house last week. And unfortunately, now that they are healing, the injuries that I sustained actually look much worse than they truly are." He paused for a moment, then continued, "I was just about to eat my luncheon when I spied you and your small entourage strolling through the park. And then, of course, I could not dine until I had spoken to you and told you again how very much I enjoyed the dinner, the conversation party and the company at your parents' town house. Will you please do me the honor of conveying my sincerest thanks once more to both Monsieur and Madame Valcoeur for having me as their guest?"

"Of course. But…are you dining alone here in the park, Monsieur Blackfriars? If so, then won't you please join me and Mademoiselle Neuville? For in truth, it seems that our cook has packed enough for an army!" Ariana blushed at the admission, knowing that Sophie had badgered Monsieur Montségur, their cook, to prepare food sufficient that Malcolm could eat with them, if they found him at the park.

"I wouldn't want to impose—"

"*Non,* really, 'tis no imposition at all, I assure you. Besides which, I am most interested in hearing your opinion of something that was brought up at the conversation party last week, *monsieur.*"

"Then, in that case, aye, I would be delighted to join you and Mademoiselle Neuville."

So saying, Malcolm sat down upon the blanket, while Sophie, having sent the two footmen away to occupy themselves elsewhere until needed, served up the luncheon, filling the delicate china plates with thin slices of cold roast beef, chicken and ham, generous helpings of two different salads, a variety of cheese and fruit, and thick slabs of freshly baked bread, liberally spread with butter. Then Malcolm uncorked the wine, pouring it into the crystal glasses and handing one to each woman before taking his own. After that, he, Ariana and Sophie consumed their meal, speaking of polite, inconsequential generalities as they did so. Then, once she had finished her luncheon, Sophie tactfully announced that she was going to take a leisurely walk along the Serpentine River, where she could best admire the graceful swans that floated upon the gently rippling waves and the dashing riders who galloped past on horseback along Rotten Row, which road lay beyond the water's southern edge.

"Acquiring horses for riding in the park is something Papa has not yet taken care of since we came to England," Ariana noted wistfully as she watched her abigail tossing bread crusts to the ducks that waddled along the river's shore. "But I hope he shall soon do so. Do you ride, Monsieur Blackfriars?"

"Aye, although I have not done so for several years now."

"Then perhaps when Papa arranges for mounts for us, you

would do me the honor of riding with me here in the park, *monsieur?* I am sure there could be no objection to your borrowing one of our horses occasionally for that purpose."

"Maybe not, *mademoiselle*—although, again, I would not want to impose, to take advantage of your parents, or to trespass on their kindness and generosity to me. I am…fully aware of the great divide in our stations in life. I understand why I was invited to dinner and to the conversation party afterward, but however much the idea appeals—because, if I may be so bold, 'tis a means of furthering my acquaintance with *you, mademoiselle*— I do not expect to become a regular visitor at your parents' town house in Portman Square."

"But you…you must not be so very certain of that, *monsieur,*" Ariana insisted quietly. "For if there is one thing I have learnt these past few months, 'tis that we may actually be sure of very little in this life. You see, before we came here to England, I had a…somewhat sheltered upbringing, and although I was aware, from things Papa said and that the servants whispered about, too, that the revolutionaries and radicals were fomenting discord in Paris, I had no idea that the seeds of rebellion they sowed would produce such fruits as they did, that the prime minister, François Guizot, would be dismissed from his post, or that King Louis-Philippe would abdicate his crown and throne the day after that. Instead, whenever I happened to think about my life at all, I believed that it would flow on as steadily and serenely as the River Seine—although, to be honest, I confess I did now and then long for some change and excitement in my days," Ariana admitted, smiling ruefully. "But even when, one night at a masquerade ball held by my parents, Madame Polgár read the tarot cards for me and told my fortune, saying that I was soon to travel over both sea and land, I did not believe her. Yet, only a few days after that, here I was, just as she predicted."

"Then…you think she is a genuine clairvoyant—and not merely a talented fraud?" Malcolm asked.

"I…I am not sure." Ariana frowned thoughtfully. "Knowing the wholly unsettled and even, as it turned out, dire political state of Paris, she could no doubt easily have guessed that Papa might take Maman and me away from France, to England, where we would be safe. But Madame Polgár also spoke of many other things to me that night…strange, even cryptic things—including the fact that I would meet three men in the future. She called them the King of Pentacles, the King of Swords and the King of Wands. *You,* I know, Monsieur Blackfriars, she must believe to be the man whom she described as the King of Swords, because she asked you that evening if you were a swordsman, remember?"

"Aye, I do—but of course, as I said, although I do study at Henry the Younger's L'Ecole d'Armes, I'm hardly a master at fencing."

"*Non,* but you *are* a cartographer, which requires thought and analysis, a designing mind, and those are traits of the King of Swords—or so Madame Polgár imparted to me. So, you see, *monsieur?* How could she have known about you before I myself had ever even met you? That is why I think she must at least have *some* true clairvoyant ability."

"Aye, that would indeed seem to be the case, then. Did she say anything else about this King of Swords?"

"*Non.*" Ariana shook her head. "Except that she could not tell whether he would prove a friend or a foe to me."

"Then let me set your mind to rest at once, *mademoiselle,*" Malcolm said earnestly. "For this, I promise you—no matter what, I will never be your foe, but always your friend."

"I believe that you will, *monsieur*—and I am very glad of that, for although I now have many acquaintances here in London, I still have but a few true friends, I think. Lady Christine Fraser, whom you met the other evening, is perhaps one. But 'tis indeed…comforting to know that I could count on you, if ever I should stand in need of a friend."

"But surely you've no cause for worry on that score, *mademoiselle!*" Malcolm was surprised and even distressed by the sudden gravity and uncertainty of her expression.

"I don't know—for now that you have come into my life, I cannot help but wonder about the King of Pentacles, whom

Madame Polgár also told me about when she read the tarot cards for me. For she warned me that he was corrupt and dangerous, and that he boded ill for me!"

"And have you indeed met such a man?" Malcolm was highly disturbed by this prediction.

"*Non,* thank goodness! At least, not yet—and I devoutly hope I never do, either!"

"Well, if you do, *mademoiselle,* you must tell me at once," he urged, "and I will do whatever I can to protect you from him."

"Thank you, *monsieur.* That eases my mind a great deal. Now, although 'tis my own turn not to wish to impose upon *you,* I would still very much like to ask you, Monsieur Blackfriars, what you thought of Monsieur Khalil al-Walid and his field of study. Are you familiar with Scotland? With the Highlands and Loch Ness? Do you believe that Monsieur al-Walid is right and that there is some titanic sea serpent that lives in the lake?"

"I know of Scotland, aye, and the Highlands and Loch Ness, too, *mademoiselle,*" Malcolm replied slowly, "because of course at Quimby and Company we have many maps of that region— three of which I sold to Mr. al-Walid myself, when he came to the map shop prior to embarking upon his alleged search for the fabled sea monster. To be honest, however, I am not quite sure what to make of Mr. al-Walid. He could be nothing more than what he claims…a herpetologist whose specialty is indeed the study of snakes, and who seems to take a genuine and consider- able amount of interest in the ancient history and religion of his own country, besides, and about which he is unquestionably highly knowledgeable. But although this is not the first time I have heard it said that some great sea serpent inhabits Loch Ness, I'm afraid I cannot say whether or not 'tis true. But now I am curious. Why do you ask, *mademoiselle?*"

"Oh, no pressing reason, *monsieur.*" Ariana shrugged lightly, as though the matter were of no real importance to her. Then, spying the expression of puzzlement and concern on his face, she reluctantly went on, "In truth, 'tis undoubtedly quite silly on my own part, I do assure you. But 'tis simply that…well, ever since I was a child, I have had a disturbing dream—a terrifying nightmare, really—about…a-a sea monster in a lake, so I just wondered if such creatures actually do exist, that's all."

"I don't think anyone truly knows the answer to that question, *mademoiselle,* although belief in such creatures has certainly persisted for millennia. 'Twas the practice of ancient cartographers, in fact, when they did not know what lay beyond a land or sea, to write 'Here be dragons' across that portion of the map. So 'tis entirely possible, I would imagine, that at some time or another in the long-distant past, cartographers did not know what lay beyond Loch Ness, and so they inscribed 'Here be dragons' on that part of a map of Scotland, and because of that, it mistakenly came to be believed that a gigantic sea serpent lived in the lake."

"Why…*oui,* I never knew that about maps before, but I suppose your conjecture could well be so, couldn't it? Then…do you believe that Mr. al-Walid is off on a wild-goose chase?"

"Well, Mr. Quimby certainly thinks he is!" Malcolm laughed. "He has called Mr. al-Walid's quest for a sea monster in Loch Ness a complete absurdity!"

"Did he really?" Ariana laughed then, too, immensely cheered by this. "I like your Monsieur Quimby very much, indeed. He seems to me to be an eminently sensible, down-to-earth sort of fellow."

"Oh, he is. And since he's also extraordinarily good-humored, he would be quite delighted, as well, to know that his thoughts about Mr. al-Walid's work had made you laugh. Do you know…that's actually the first time I've heard you laugh? 'Tis a lovely sound. You should do it more often."

As Malcolm spoke, the intensity of his gaze in that moment was such that Ariana felt her heart beat fast, as though she had run a very long way and could not now catch her breath. Other equally strange sensations were coursing through her being, as well, so that she felt hot and flushed, giddy and faint. An electric tingle radiated through her breasts and prickled its way down to the very core of her, a kind of stimulation she had never before experienced and that both excited and confused her. Worst of all was the sudden heat and moisture that she felt between her thighs, so that she wondered suddenly if her monthly had begun.

"Well, 'tis—'tis growing late, and I must return home," she announced in a rush, and started repacking the picnic hamper.

"Aye, I must get back to work, too. Here. Let me help you with that."

On his knees now, handing her their now-empty plates and glasses, Malcolm bent close to her, so near that Ariana could smell the clean, exhilarating, masculine scent of him…sandalwood shaving soap and vetiver cologne—both exotic essential oils with rich woodsy fragrances—and the faint aroma of smoke from equally exotic cheroots, she thought, and the bouquet of the wine he had drunk at luncheon. Mingled with all this was the warm redolence of the late-spring sunshine soaked up by his dark skin and the salty tang of the light sheen of musky sweat that had resulted. Without warning, Ariana felt an unbidden, almost overwhelming desire to wrap her arms around him and draw him even closer, to lay her head upon his shoulder and bury her face against his broad chest.

She hardly knew him. In some dim corner of her mind, she recognized and acknowledged that fact. Yet, still, somehow, she felt as though she had known him all her life. All during luncheon and afterward, she had spoken so easily with him, as though he were an old friend, even an old lover. Of a sudden, she remembered the eerie sensation she had experienced in the pavilion that night when Madame Polgár had foretold her future…that the fortune-teller had walked along the banks of the River Nile in Egypt during the time of Queen Cleopatra. Had not Madame Polgár said that evening that each soul journeyed through many lifetimes? Was it possible, Ariana wondered now, that she had known Malcolm Blackfriars before, in another place, another time, far distant from here and now? Was that why she was so strongly attracted to him, felt she had fallen in love with him at first sight?

Shutting the lid of the picnic basket, he stood and held out one hand to assist her to her feet. When, after a moment, she laid her palm in his, Ariana felt his fingers close around hers warmly, sending an unexpected tremor through her body, such as she had experienced once as a child, when she had, with a stout branch, struck a tree trunk a hard blow.

"Thank you for the luncheon, *mademoiselle*." Malcolm spoke, still clasping her hand gently but firmly in his. "The food and wine were excellent—and the company even more delightful. If you should choose to stroll this way again this week, I would be pleased to return the favor by bringing a picnic hamper of my own to share."

"I could walk here once more on Thursday, *monsieur*," she murmured, deliberately choosing a day toward the end of the week, so as not to seem too eager or too bold—all the while longing to say that she would stroll through the park every single day, if need be, to see him again.

"Then I shall see you then. *Au revoir, mademoiselle*." Bowing, Malcolm lifted her hand to his lips and kissed it lightly.

"*Au revoir, monsieur*," she said.

Then, after he had reluctantly taken his leave of her, she stood and watched him until he was out of sight, tremulously pressing her mouth to the back of her hand, where he had kissed it.

Although he might have been out of sight, in the days that passed with what seemed, to Ariana, excruciating slowness, Malcolm was never out of her mind. She thought about him ceaselessly, and in her vivid, impassioned daydreams she imagined endless different, adventurous scenarios in which, by one means or another, he was suddenly catapulted to her own status, became possessed of both a title and fortune, so that there was no longer any impediment to his courtship of her. She told no one of either her daydreams or desires, however, although, even so, she suspected that they were still no secret either to her mother or to Sophie. For the latter continued to chide her about Malcolm and her lack of any real future with him. Strangely enough, however, her mother said little or nothing in this regard, which, although immensely bewildering to Ariana, was nevertheless such a welcome relief to her that she did not seek to question it.

Instead, on Thursday she dressed carefully in one of her most flattering walking gowns and set out again for Hyde Park, with Sophie at her side.

"You are wasting your time with poor Monsieur Blackfriars and headed straight for a broken heart, *mademoiselle*," the abigail declared as they strolled down Portman Street toward the park. "What is wrong with the Earl of Netherfield, pray tell?"

"*Bon Dieu,* Sophie!" Ariana exclaimed, exasperated. "Why, the man is at least fifty years older than I am—and quite ugly, besides!"

"Still, he has both rank and riches, so that if you married him, your future would be assured."

"I doubt it—for he has already buried two wives and would probably dodder on to outlive me, as well!"

"I am only thinking of you, *mademoiselle*," the maid pointed out reproachfully.

"Then do not imagine me wed to such a one as the Earl of Netherfield—for even if he were a king, I could not bear such a match! Now, let me hear no more of this nonsense! I have set my cap for Monsieur Blackfriars, and I will have him if I can."

"Then you will spend the rest of your days as poor as a church mouse, I fear."

"Hardly that, Sophie, for as I've told you before, Monsieur Blackfriars is not a pauper."

"*Non,* but still, his annual income can scarcely be enough to maintain more than just a small cottage, with perhaps one or two servants. What is that—compared to what you would have as the Countess of Netherfield?"

"But in the latter case, I would also have Monsieur Netherfield!"

"Well, perhaps you could put a sack over his head."

"Sophie!" Still, despite herself, Ariana could not help but

laugh, and her abigail laughed, too, so that in the end, they were a merry pair as they passed the Cumberland Gate and entered Hyde Park, making their way to the Serpentine River.

There they discovered Malcolm waiting for them. Clearly, he had come prepared to please, for he had already spread a blanket on the ground for them to sit upon, and in the center was a picnic basket, beside which sat Malcolm, reading and waiting. Leaping to his feet upon spying the two women, he bowed to them and then kissed Ariana's hand, the warmth of his mouth sending a thrill coursing through her.

"Mademoiselle Ariana, what a pleasure to see you again!" he said, smiling.

"The pleasure is mine, Monsieur Blackfriars," she replied, smiling back at him.

In that moment, for the two of them, it was as though the world spun away and there was only the place where they stood together, their eyes locked on each other, her hand in his. In some dark chasm of her mind Ariana was aware of the sounds of the people who walked or rode in the park, of the hoofbeats of the horses that galloped past, of the calls of the swans and ducks that floated on the serene waves of the Serpentine River, and of the gentle lapping of the water against the shore. Yet all this paled into insignificance in the face of the drumming of her heart—so loud that she thought Malcolm must surely hear it—and the lightness of her breath. How long she and he would have remained thus, Ariana did not know. But at last the magic spell that seemed to have been cast upon them was broken when Sophie tactfully cleared her throat to remind them of her presence. Reluctantly, then, Malcolm released Ariana's hand and bade her and Sophie be seated on the blanket. Then he knelt beside them and started to unpack the picnic hamper, setting out the china plates and crystal glasses.

Upon seeing all this, Ariana covertly shot her maid a triumphant look, which said that, clearly, Malcolm not only appreciated the niceties in life, but was also able to provide at least some of them. But Sophie only shook her head mutely, as though to reply that a sufficient amount of fine crockery was hardly enough to live well on. However, it was soon seen that Malcolm's cook, Mrs. Peppercorn, had gone to as much trouble as Monsieur Montségur had previously to prepare a feast that was bound to win favor from even the most discerning gourmet; and after Malcolm filled and then handed Ariana and Sophie their plates, they began to eat their alfresco luncheon with enthusiasm, remarking on the tastiness of the food.

"Our cook, Mrs. Peppercorn, will be delighted to hear your praise," Malcolm told them, "for she takes a great deal of pride in her work—as do the rest of the small staff at Hawthorn Cottage. I chose the wine myself. However, Miss Woodbridge, our housekeeper, was responsible for the flowers, and Nora and Lucy, our housemaid and scullery maid, made their own contributions, as well, by selecting the linens and polishing the silver."

"It sounds as though you and your mother are most comfortably situated at Hawthorn Cottage, Monsieur Blackfriars," Ariana observed.

"Aye, we've lived there for many years now—ever since we first came to London, in fact."

"That was after your father died?"

"Aye."

"And do you never think of establishing your own household?"

"Now and again, aye, of course. However, in the end, I've always decided—and my mother has agreed—that there is really no need to spend the money rather than save it, unless and until I should marry. For I think a wife would perhaps prefer to have her own home and not lodge with my mother, although she is a very good and gentle woman."

"I'm sure she is. I would enjoy meeting her sometime."

"I know she would like that very much, too." He paused, then continued, "If you've finished your luncheon now, Mademoiselle Ariana, would you care to take a stroll along the Serpentine with me?"

"*Oui,* you go ahead, *mademoiselle,*" Sophie insisted. "For the last time we came to the park, 'twas I who enjoyed the pleasure of walking along the Serpentine and feeding the ducks. So today, if Monsieur Blackfriars has no objections, I will clear away the dishes and repack the picnic basket for him instead."

"Thank you, Mademoiselle Neuville. That would indeed be most appreciated," Malcolm said gratefully.

Rising, he extended one slender but strong hand to Ariana, assisting her to her feet. Then, taking with them what remained of the bread from their luncheon, so that they could feed it to the ducks, they made their way to the Serpentine River and began to meander along its bank. As they strolled along, Malcolm broke the crusty bread into small pieces, tossing some to the ducks themselves and handing other bits to Ariana to throw. Presently, he and she were surrounded by a dozen or more ducks, who quacked and waddled about them eagerly, snatching up the bread. Tilting her parasol to shield her from the sun, Ariana moved nearer to the Serpentine's edge, intent on casting some of the bread upon the water for the beautiful, graceful swans who floated on the waves, their cygnets in tow. But much to her shock and horror, as she drew closer to the shore, one of the swans suddenly reared up terrifyingly in the water, spreading its wings and beating them violently, and lowering and extending its head, hissing as fiercely as an angry snake at her as it swam toward her swiftly.

"Ariana!" Racing to her side, Malcolm grabbed her hand and pulled her away from the Serpentine's bank so rapidly that she had to run to keep up with him. "Hurry! Hurry!" he urged savagely, and only when they were well away from the water's edge did he finally pause to allow her to catch her breath.

"Mon Dieu!" Ariana gasped out as she rasped hard for air, her heart pounding frantically. "I…I don't think I've…ever seen anything…quite so frightening…as that. What happened? Was it…was it…something I did?"

"Aye." Malcolm nodded. Then he explained, "You got too near the swans' cygnets. So the cob moved to defend its young, whilst the pen hurried them from beyond your reach. 'Tis never a good idea to try to feed swans who still have cygnets."

"I—I didn't know. I—I thought swans were peaceful birds."

"Under normal circumstances, they are. But as you saw just now, cobs are highly protective of their families and grow extremely—even viciously—aggressive when they feel that their pens and cygnets may be threatened. In such situations, cobs are terribly dangerous, for their wings are inordinately powerful. With them, they can actually kill a small child—and even break an adult's back or neck, as well."

"I hadn't realized that before. So naturally, 'twas quite a dreadful shock and truly terrifying to me to see what I believed to be such a serene creature abruptly turn into such a-a monster!"

"Aye, I can well imagine. But that's why I had to drag you away so quickly. If the cob had attacked you, you might have been severely injured—or even killed!"

"Then it seems I must once more thank you for saving my life, Monsieur Blackfriars."

"No, please…'twas nothing more than what anyone else would have done, I assure you."

"Maybe so. But still, I thank you, *monsieur.*"

"You're welcome, *mademoiselle.* Now, shall we walk this way instead, toward Kensington Gardens, so we may avoid the swans and their cygnets?"

"*Oui,* that would be nice. The trees and flowers are all so very lovely this time of year, are they not? And Kensington Gardens reminds me a little of the Jardin des Tuileries back home."

"Do you miss Paris very much?"

"Not nearly as much now as I did when we first came to London." Ariana did not add that this was because of her meeting Malcolm, but the implication was there, and she thought he understood it, for he smiled with pleasure at her.

"I'm glad you are no longer so homesick," he told her as they began to walk in the direction of Kensington Gardens.

Hyde Park and Kensington Gardens had eventually grown to be two separate parks, divided by the Serpentine River and the Long Water, and now reunited by the bridge that, in 1826, had been built over the watercourse. In earlier centuries, spectators had watched hangings at the Tyburn Tree from the park, which, along with the gardens, had proved such a haven not only for pic-nickers, promenaders and riders, but also for duelists, highway-men, thieves and other such rogues that Rotten Row had become the first street in London to be lit with street lamps at night, in an attempt to deter crime. But no such scoundrels plagued the park and gardens now as Ariana and Malcolm wandered across the bridge, past the west end of the tree-lined Rotten Row and into Kensington Gardens themselves. Here, she and he followed pleasant, winding avenues that led them through the gardens, along the Long Water and at last toward the Basin or Round Pond, which lay before the imposing redbrick Kensington Pal-ace, set back and separated from the gardens by black, gilded wrought-iron gates.

As Ariana and Malcolm strolled along the dirt paths, each was vibrantly aware of the other and of their proximity, how her arm was tucked lightly into the crook of his own as he escorted her through the gardens. They might have been lovers, Ariana thought, and wished wistfully, fervently, that they were, that there could be something more between them than just the friendship that had so unexpectedly budded between them and that they now so tentatively and carefully cultivated.

She did not know that Malcolm, too, harbored thoughts such as these, that he was, in fact, consumed with inner conflict—wanting to love and possess her, yet painfully cognizant of the fact that as matters currently stood, he had little or nothing to offer her, not even his own true name. Not for the first time, he cursed with a vengeance his ancestor Lord Iain Ramsay, once the Earl of Dúndragon, who had drunkenly gambled away the Ramsay es-tates in both Scotland and England. If not for that, Malcolm would perhaps now be both titled and wealthy, a superior suitor for Ariana's hand in marriage. Instead, as it was, he could only bite his tongue to keep from telling her how much he ardently ad-mired and desired her. For what good would it do to speak of his feelings for her? he wondered bitterly. How could she possibly return them, when her own station in life was so high above his?

No, the most for which he could hope was her friendship, Malcolm thought with despair. Almost, he wished he had never even met her—for the fact that she was so very near to and yet so very far from his reach was sheer torment to him. From the first, he had memorized every smallest detail of her lovely countenance, so that he did not even have to look at her now to know the way in which the bright sunbeams that slanted beneath the tilt of her ruffled silk parasol illuminated her fair porcelain skin and made her heavily black-lashed violet eyes shine like amethysts in her face, or how color bloomed like dusky roses in her cheeks, matching the hue of her vulnerable rosebud mouth, with its bee-stung lower lip. Fiercely he ached to kiss her, to wrap his hands in her mass of gleaming raven-black tresses, to bury his dark visage between her full round breasts, to inhale deeply the sweet, fragrant-lily scent of her, and to claim her as his own.

But he said nothing of this as they stood before the Round Pond, watching the youngsters who, beneath the observant eyes of the governesses and nannies who accompanied them, sailed their small model boats upon the water.

Instead, he declared, "If we should happen to walk this way again, *mademoiselle,* I will have to bring one of my own model boats, and then we can sail it here if you like—although perhaps, after all, such a pastime is only for children."

"*Non,* indeed not, *monsieur,*" Ariana countered gaily, smiling at him, "for I was even now thinking how much fun 'twould be to indulge in it! Do you have many model boats, then?"

"No, not anymore…just a few that I built shortly after my mother and I came to London. The rest were all…destroyed during a terrible fire at the farmhouse in which we lived before that. That was the night my father died and how we came to lose the place."

"What a tragedy! I'm so very sorry." Ariana bit her lower lip tremulously with sympathy for his loss and grief. "Then perhaps you would prefer not to sail one of your model boats here, after all, if it brings back such unhappy memories."

"No, please don't worry about that, *mademoiselle,* for 'tis only happy memories I have of my model boats and sailing them upon the streams of the countryside I used to tramp and explore as a lad, and of the real boat I had then, too—a small old fishing boat I used to row out upon the lake that our farmhouse, which was set upon a hillside, overlooked."

Hearing this last, Ariana abruptly went deathly still and pale, and a chilling frisson tingled up her spine, causing her to shiver violently despite the warm summer sun that shone down brightly upon the gardens. For surely, she reflected in some nebulous crevasse of her mind, it was more than just sheer coincidence that Malcolm should have described the very scene that she had seen time and again in the dream, the nightmare, that had haunted her ever since she had been a child—and in which she and the boy Collie traipsed down the wooded hillside from the farmhouse in which they lived and rowed out in his small fishing boat, the *Sea Witch,* to the heart of Loch Ness.

"Is…is something wrong, *mademoiselle?* Have I…have I said something amiss?" Malcolm inquired tentatively, puzzled and concerned as he observed how ashen Ariana's face had become beneath her parasol.

"*Non,* 'tis just a-a…sudden migraine, I fear." To lend credence to the lie that impulsively tumbled from her lips, she pressed one delicate, graceful hand to her head. "It has come on so very swiftly and unexpectedly that I've grown rather faint and ill, I'm afraid."

"Then let us return to Mademoiselle Neuville at once, and we shall find a hackney coach or hansom cab to convey you home as quickly as possible." Courteously taking Ariana's arm in his again, Malcolm began to walk back with her to the northern shore of the Serpentine River, where they had left Sophie with the picnic basket. "You must let me know if the pace I have set is too fast for you, *mademoiselle,* in your current condition."

"*Non,* 'tis…'tis fine," Ariana insisted, trying hard to recover her wits and composure. "So please do not be anxious on my own account, *monsieur.* I am sure I shall be better presently, for no doubt my headache is only the result of too much sun. So tell me, did your…did your fishing boat have a name?"

"Aye." Malcolm nodded, smiling fondly a little at the memory. "I called her the *Sea Witch*."

Chapter Eleven

The Masqueraders

Things are seldom what they seem,
Skim milk masquerades as cream.
> —Sir William Schwenck Gilbert
> *H.M.S. Pinafore [1878]*

And, after all, what is a lie? 'Tis but
The truth in masquerade.
> —George Noel Gordon, Lord Byron
> *Don Juan [1823]*

> All the world's a stage,
> And all the men and women merely players:
> They have their exits and their entrances;
> And one man in his time plays many parts.
> —William Shakespeare
> *As You Like It [1598-1600]*

1848
Portman, Hanover and Grosvenor Squares, London, England

"Maman, please, tell me the truth! Have we ever been to Scotland, to the Highlands, to Loch Ness?" Ariana demanded as, the following day, she and her mother sat in the morning room of the town house in Portman Square, having breakfast.

"Why…*non, chérie*. Why…why do you ask?"

"Because of something Monsieur Blackfriars told me yesterday in Kensington Gardens."

"I did not know that you had seen him again, Ariana." Slowly ceasing to stir her cup of hot chocolate, Madame Valcoeur laid her silver spoon upon the china saucer.

"Perhaps not. However, you did not forbid me to do so, Maman."

"*Non,* but I did not precisely encourage you, either, *ma petite.* Still, that is neither here nor there. If you enjoy Monsieur Blackfriars's company—and it seems that you do—then your papa and I are not averse to your being friends with him, of course. He is, after all, an undeniably handsome, intelligent, personable young gentleman, to whom our only objection could be that he has neither a title nor a fortune to recommend him as a prospective suitor for you. But as you see, that has not blinded either me or your papa to those good qualities that he does possess. And if I am honest—and I hope that I am—I must confess that I find myself rather…curious about Monsieur Blackfriars…I suppose because of your own interest in him. So, pray tell—what is it he said to you that has caused you to ask me yet again about Scotland, about the Highlands and Loch Ness?"

"He told me…Maman, he told me that when he was a lad at the tenant farm where he lived before his father died, he had an old fishing boat, which he used to row out upon a lake—exactly as the boy Collie does in my dream…my nightmare. But there's still more, Maman! The name of Monsieur Blackfriars's boat was the *Sea Witch*—just like Collie's! Now, what do you think about that?"

The comtesse did not immediately answer, however, for while listening to her daughter, she had suddenly choked on the hot chocolate she had sipped from her cup. Abruptly banging the cup down upon the saucer, she coughed so violently that Ariana grew alarmed.

"Maman!" Rising from her chair, she ran to her mother's side. "Maman, are you all right? I'll ring for help!"

"*Non…non,* I'm fine, really. My hot chocolate just…went down…the wrong way, that's all. I just…need a moment…to catch my breath. There. You see? I am…better already. So, now, what is it that you were saying to me, *chérie,* about Monsieur Blackfriars? Please tell me again…slowly, so I can understand the significance of what you are trying to impart to me."

At her mother's urging, Ariana repeated her words.

"So you see how very confusing all this is to me, Maman," she declared once she had finished relating again her narrative about the two fishing boats and their identical names. "I feel…I feel more and more strongly that, somehow, Monsieur Blackfriars and the boy Collie are one and the same. But if we have never been to Scotland, to the Highlands and Loch Ness, then how is that possible? Unless, of course, I am experiencing déjà vu or have even been gifted with some small clairvoyant talent, like Madame Polgár—except that instead of seeing the future, I see the past."

"But, Ariana, Monsieur Blackfriars did not identify the lake on which he used to go boating as Loch Ness—and the *Sea Witch* must be a fairly common name for vessels, besides. So I believe that you are perhaps reading more into all this than is truly warranted. It could simply be nothing more than sheer coincidence, you know."

"I don't think so, Maman. I don't know why, but I just don't. Oh, how I wish there were some way in which I could find out the truth one way or another! For if Monsieur Blackfriars *is* the boy Collie in my dream, my nightmare, then it *must* be that I have somehow glimpsed a piece of his past, and I would like very much to know why."

"Did…did Monsieur Blackfriars tell you anything else that might have led you to such a conclusion as this, *ma petite?*" Madame Valcoeur inquired, now studiously buttering a crumpet.

"Non." Ariana shook her head. "He said only that the farmhouse in which he lived before coming to London had burnt down. Most tragically, his father also died that night—in the terrible fire, I presume, although Monsieur Blackfriars did not clarify that point."

"I see," the comtesse said slowly. "But, *chérie,* you have never spoken of the farmhouse burning down in your dream or mentioned any man in it who could conceivably be the boy Collie's father. So, whether you want to admit it or not, there *are* differences in your nightmare and the story of Monsieur Blackfriars's youth, about which he told you. And as I pointed out to you earlier, he only mentioned a fishing boat and a lake. He did not say they were in Scotland, much less the Highlands and, specifically, the area around Loch Ness."

"I know…I know. But still, Maman, I cannot shake the conviction that, somehow, Monsieur Blackfriars and Collie are one and the same."

"Well." Madame Valcoeur shrugged lightly, as though dismissing the odd affair. "'Tis a mystery to me one way or the other. However, I still say you are reading much more into the matter than is actually called for, Ariana, and I certainly hope you will not speak of it to anyone else. For you know, *ma petite,* I believe I would find it most disturbing to learn that you were clairvoyant, like Madame Polgár. Sometimes, I confess, she makes me very uneasy."

"Then…why do you have anything to do with her?" Ariana asked, greatly surprised by her mother's admission. "How did you meet her, anyway, Maman?"

"She passed by Valcoeur one day—in her coach. That dwarf, Dukker, who accompanies her everywhere, was driving. They had lost their way and stopped at the gates to ask for directions. By chance, your papa and I happened to be returning home at the time, and after taking Madame Polgár's measure and that of her horses and carriage, too, I invited her up to the house. 'Twas quite a warm day, you see, and she had traveled many miles, she said, and so was not only weary from her long journey, but also hungry and thirsty. Dukker had taken a wrong turn, she told me, so they had missed the wayside inn at which she had intended to rest and dine. She partook of luncheon with me, and I found her fascinating, I'll admit, for she is not only clairvoyant, but also very learnt, as you know. We became friends and have remained so. But still, she sometimes upsets me with all her questions and predictions."

"Well, then, Maman, the truth is that you scarcely know anything about her at all!" Ariana cried. "Why, in reality, she could be nothing more than an impostor, who has most unscrupulously taken advantage of your good nature and hospitality!"

"*Non,* for your dear papa, of course, is not nearly as trusting as I am, and so he conducted a discreet check into her background. She actually is who she claims to be—Tzigana, Madame Polgár. Her husband was a Romanian count or baron of some sort—really, I forget which—who was tragically killed in a duel or an accident or something of that nature. For political reasons they had left their homeland and were living abroad at the time, just as we are now, and after his death Madame Polgár found herself at loose ends, so decided to travel. Evidently she is descended from a long line of clairvoyants—ancestors who were Knights Templars or Freemasons or something of that ilk—and through them, she has ties to both France and Scotland. So I presume that's why when she, too, came to believe that France was no longer safe, she journeyed here to England. I believe she intends to go to Scotland eventually."

"Perhaps that's why she seemed so interested in Monsieur al-Walid and his search for the fabled sea serpent of Loch Ness," Ariana suggested thoughtfully.

"I don't know. I confess that I found Mr. al-Walid a very strange, unnerving man, and I thought Madame Polgár's apparent interest in him most peculiar! Now, please, Ariana, do not start in about that sea monster in Loch Ness again! You know very well how this dream, this nightmare of yours disturbs me, and really, I have heard quite enough about it for one day!"

"Very well, then, Maman." Ariana sighed with resignation. "Monsieur Blackfriars told me that Monsieur Quimby said Monsieur al-Walid was off on a wild-goose chase, anyway!"

"Well, I'm very glad to hear it! Monsieur Quimby seems a most reasonable, educated man, and if he does not believe that the sea serpent truly exists, then I am quite certain it does not!"

* * *

In the weeks that passed, summer drifted languidly toward autumn, and when she was not otherwise occupied, Ariana spent as much time as she could with Malcolm.

On a Monday, which was when the regular sales at Tattersall's took place, her father had visited the horse auction at No. 10 Grosvenor Place, and there he had bid on and bought three fine mounts for riding. Ariana had been slightly bemused by this, as although her father rode, her mother seldom did, so that it would have seemed that only two horses were required. But still, for whatever reasons unknown to her, her father had purchased three. Even more curious was the fact that one of these was a high-spirited black stallion—most certainly not a suitable mount either for her mother or for her, and her father himself always rode the big bay gelding he had acquired. For Ariana herself, there was a delicate, graceful white mare. So it was that the black stallion was ridden solely by Malcolm, whenever he found time to accompany her on jaunts in Hyde Park.

The stallion suited him, Ariana thought, and she secretly wondered if her father had bought it specifically with Malcolm in mind. But still, why he would have done such a very strange thing she could not fathom, and at last she decided that the whole idea was only wishful thinking on her own part. Malcolm himself, she sensed, was highly torn over the stallion. He was scrupulous about not taking advantage of her parents and her, but even so, once persuaded to make use of the stallion, he could not conceal his utter delight at being mounted upon it, galloping along Rotten Row.

In such moments, there was something so wild and free about him, so thrilling and exciting, that Ariana was not the only one powerfully attracted to him. More than once, she spied female promenaders eyeing him both appreciatively and covetously, and at such times she felt not only a fierce surge of pride at being by his side, but also such an intense jealousy that she was almost ashamed of herself, for she was not usually given to that unpleasant emotion. Still, any ruffled feathers she might otherwise have experienced were quickly smoothed by the fact that Malcolm had eyes only for her, so that she hoped against hope that he was falling in love with her, as she was him. Never before had she met a man who so enchanted her, and had he been able to accompany her to the various social functions she attended and pay proper court to her, she would have been ecstatic. As it was, however, her high spirits could be dampened only by the fact that Malcolm did not move in her own circles, so that he was never invited to the parties, routs, soirées and balls that, with the arrival of autumn and the Little Season, increasingly occupied her evenings.

Tonight, in fact, she was to accompany her parents to a masquerade ball being held by the Marchioness of Mayfield, and although over the past days Ariana had attempted to persuade Malcolm to go with them, he had courteously but firmly refused.

"Mademoiselle Ariana, you must understand—even as I do—that whilst 'tis one thing for me to enjoy an alfresco luncheon in Hyde Park, a stroll in Kensington Gardens, or even a gallop along Rotten Row with you, 'twould be quite another thing entirely for me to attach myself to you and your parents in order to attend a ball to which I myself have not been invited," he had told her. "Therefore, I must decline your own invitation, however kindly intended."

Swallowing hard to force down the lump of disappointment in her throat, Ariana had nodded and attempted to smile.

"I *do* understand, *monsieur,* of course—only, I wish…I wish society were different, that a man were judged solely on his merits or lack of them, rather than whether he is of noble birth or possesses a fortune or by any other such yardstick. For in truth, such things are so seldom the true measure of a man's worth, I am discovering more and more."

"No, perhaps not," Malcolm had agreed. "But unfortunately, that is the way of the world in which we live—and in reality, I am not so sure that those such as Karl Marx and Friedrich Engels, who, as you know, foment revolution and radicalism wherever they go, have the right of it, after all. However much we may wish it, *mademoiselle,* all men are not created equal—although I do agree that they should all be given equal opportunities to better their lives if they can. But the truth is that the rebellious lots who overthrew King Charles the First of England and your own King Louis the Sixteenth of France proved no better rulers than the monarchs they disposed of. So I'm not sure what the answer is—except that those who govern ought to be the best and the brightest among us, and even then, I suspect that there would always be those who objected to such leaders, anyway, and aspired to take their places."

"*Oui,* I said something quite similar myself to Sophie." Ariana had paused, then continued, "Well, if you will not go to Madame Mayfield's masquerade ball, then at least consent to race me to the end of Rotten Row!"

"You're on!"

At that, laughing, Ariana had urged her white mare, Gossamer, to a gallop, and Malcolm had set his heels to the sides of the black stallion, Caliginous, to keep pace. Side by side, then, the two horses had thundered down the wide dirt path toward the bridge that spanned the Serpentine River. But in the end, the mare could not outdistance the stallion, so that Malcolm had beaten Ariana to the finish. Finally pulling the mare to a halt, she had gasped both with excitement and for breath as, her eyes sparkling from the thrill of the chase, she had gazed at Malcolm and tried to draw air into her lungs. This last had grown even more difficult when, for one wild instant, she had thought he was going to lean over and kiss her. But then, much to her disappointment, he had seemed to recover himself, and reining in the snorting and prancing Caliginous, he had said that they must get the horses back to her father's stables, which were located in the mews behind the town house in Portman Square.

"*Mademoiselle,* you must hurry and finish dressing." The sound of Sophie's voice abruptly jolted Ariana from her reverie. "For 'twas Fanny who just now knocked at your bedroom door, to say that a message has arrived from Monsieur le Comte and Madame la Comtesse d'Eaton. They have been unexpectedly called out of town—an illness in the family—and so they wish for us to take Mademoiselle Christine to the masquerade ball with us. Further, it has been arranged that, afterward, she is to come back here to stay for several days, until her uncle and aunt return home."

"Oh, that will be fun, won't it, Sophie? For Christine is the best friend I have in London, and whilst she is here, 'twill be almost like my having a sister. I've always longed for a brother or sister, you know."

"*Oui, mademoiselle.* But hurry now," the abigail urged, "or else we shall be more than just fashionably late to Madame la Marquise's masquerade ball. For on the way, we must go by Hanover Square now, to collect Mademoiselle Christine and her trunks."

With her maid's deft assistance, Ariana swiftly completed her toilette. Because for the marchioness's masquerade ball only a mask and domino were required, her costume was not elaborate, consisting merely of the feathered-and-beaded white visor she wore over her face and the simple, loose, matching cloak that covered her white ball gown. At last she was ready. After descending the sweeping curved staircase to the black-and-white-marble-tiled reception hall below, she discovered that both her parents and her mother's lady's maid, Madame Gautier, were to travel in one coach to the marchioness's town house in Grosvenor Square, while she, Sophie, Christine and Christine's own abigail, Miss Innes, were to take another.

"For otherwise, even if we were all able to fit into one carriage—which I myself doubt—our ball gowns would be monstrously crushed," Madame Valcoeur insisted. "And I will not attend such an affair as Madame la Marquise's, wearing a crumpled frock!"

"Most assuredly, *I* would never dream of asking you to do such a thing, *ma chère.*" As he spoke, Monsieur Valcoeur's voice was suitably grave and respectful, but his eyes twinkled merrily, so that Ariana knew he was teasing her mother.

"Oh, into the carriage with you, *monsieur!*" the comtesse cried, shooting him a censuring look, which, however, had little or no effect on her husband, since she could not repress the fond smile of amusement that curved her lips at his badinage. "And watch that you do not squash my dress!"

Ariana and Sophie climbed into the coach behind that of Monsieur and Madame Valcoeur. Then the small procession set out down Orchard Street toward Hanover Square, where they picked up the Lady Christine Fraser, her maid, Miss Innes, and her baggage.

"Ariana!" Christine smiled brightly from behind her feathered-and-beaded dusky-rose half mask as she settled herself among the plump velvet squabs of the carriage. "I hope you don't mind the arrangements my uncle and aunt made with your parents, for me to stay with you for a while. I'm afraid Uncle Owen and Aunt Phoebe feared they might be gone for quite some time—for Uncle Owen's cousin is very ill—and that, as a result, I might grow lonely in their absence."

"*Non,* not at all. In fact, I am quite looking forward to your company."

"Well, that's all right, then. We shall be very merry together this evening at Lady Mayfield's ball—and afterward, too, for as long as I may remain with you in Portman Square. Jane—" she directed her attention to her abigail "—did you remember to bring my jewel case?"

"Yes, my lady."

"Excellent for I should have been *extremely* distraught had it been left behind! Oh, look how the fog has thickened outside! I hope 'tis not going to rain!"

"I believe that 'tis only misting, Christine," Ariana said, peering through the dark windows of the carriage. But then, even as she spoke, she observed droplets of rain begin to trickle down the panes. "*Non,* I tell a lie, for it has started to drizzle."

"Well, I hope we shan't get too wet, then! Jane, did you remember to bring my umbrella?"

"Yes, my lady."

"Good. Then we needn't worry—unless, of course, it really starts to pour."

But by the time they reached the town house of the Marchioness of Mayfield, only mizzle still fell from the opaque evening sky.

Originally a hundred acres of meadowland and marshland lying on the outskirts of London and where a sprawling, boisterous fair had once been held every May, Grosvenor Square was composed of a considerable grid of wide straight avenues, with a large plaza at its heart, which square was home to numerous imposing, elegant town houses surrounding a big oval park. Now, as the Lévesque party drew to a halt before the grand town house of the Marchioness of Mayfield and Ariana and the rest descended from the carriages, she observed that street lamps glowed all around, softly illuminating the magnificent plaza and its equally splendid park in the light, brumous rain. The leaves of the deciduous trees in the park had turned red and gold with autumn; some had already fallen from their branches and now, brown and curled, whispered and rattled with each breath of the soughing wind across the square. The fog that blew inland from the sea and rolled off the River Thames had grown even heavier, drifting ghostily over the plaza and park, where it played will-o'-the-wisp among the trees and the long shadows they cast beneath the hazy silver moon.

In stark contrast, the town house of the Marchioness of Mayfield was well lit, shining like some bright faery castle in the darkness, and like toy soldiers, footmen outfitted in livery and bearing umbrellas lined either side of the front door, to shield the marchioness's guests from the mizzle as they made their way from the pavement to the town house. Beneath this artificial canopy Ariana and the others trod, to be admitted at last into the reception hall, with its gleaming expanse of snow-white marble and its grand, sweeping staircase. There the butler greeted them politely, relieved them of their coats, then led them to the regal, mirrored ballroom and imperiously announced them. The marchioness then received them, after which they were free to join in the festivities under way.

Like the front of the town house, the ballroom was bright with lights, the flames of its many shimmering crystal chandeliers reflecting in the countless gilt-edged mirrors that covered the walls. In the minstrels' gallery the orchestra played, and dancing couples thronged the highly polished parquet floor, a colorful, rippling sea of visors and dominoes. Here and there, other costumed guests clustered in groups or sat upon the brocade chairs aligned against the walls. At one end of the ballroom, long tables covered with pristine white cloths groaned beneath the weight of large, ornate solid-silver trays boasting an array of delectable hors d'oeuvres and equally huge, elaborate solid-silver bowls brimming with tart punch.

Talking and laughing together, Ariana and Christine pressed their way into the crowd, and soon they were surrounded by friends, and their dance programs were filled. Determinedly throwing herself into the spirit of the ball, Ariana danced until she thought her feet could dance no more. But despite her attempt at gaiety, always at the back of her mind was an awareness of the fact that Malcolm was not present and of her own disappointment at his absence. For it was him with whom she longed fervently to dance, and as a result, her partners were rendered faceless not only by the half masks that concealed their features, but also by her own lack of interest in them. At last, as the evening wore on, she wearied of them altogether, grew tired of making polite conversation and smiling at their jests, of discouraging their flirtations and fending off the unwelcome advances of the bolder among them. Pleading fatigue and excusing herself from her latest partner, she wove her way through the guests to the long tables laden with food and drink, where she found Christine sipping from a cup of punch.

"Christine," Ariana inquired after a moment, "who is that man standing over there, in the flamboyant crimson mask and matching domino, who keeps staring at us?"

"Where?"

"Over there...by the tall potted plant."

"Oh, my God!" Christine cried, clearly shaken as she spied

the man who was watching them. "I didn't know *he* was going to be here—or else I would not have come!"

"Why? What's wrong? Who is he?"

"Viscount Ugo—and I most earnestly warn you, Ariana, that if you are wise, you shall have nothing whatsoever to do with him, for he is a most dissolute, wicked and treacherous rake!"

"Do you actually know him, then?"

"Yes, unfortunately! We have met occasionally in the past, for his family, the Foscarellis, are from the Highlands, as my father's family, the Frasers, are."

"But...Foscarelli? That is an Italian name, surely." Ariana's brow was knitted in a puzzled frown. "So Viscount Ugo's family immigrated to Scotland from Italy?"

"Yes...around a hundred years ago—and there hangs a strange, depraved tale! As diabolical as the Foscarellis themselves are and have always been! One of Viscount Ugo's ancestors, Lord Bruno, Count Foscarelli, immigrated here to England, actually, rather than to Scotland. 'Tis claimed that he was compelled to leave his homeland because of some dreadful scandal or another. But just exactly what that entailed, I don't believe that anyone has ever really known. At any rate, whilst in Florence, he had evidently become friends with Sir Francis Dashwood, who, during the last century, founded that infamous Hellfire Club. So Count Foscarelli traveled to England, where he fell in again with his crony Sir Francis and began patronizing Medmenham Abbey, which is where the Hellfire Club held its meetings—usually two or three times a year, I think. Anyway, during one such meeting, Count Foscarelli got into a high-stakes game of piquet with Lord Iain Ramsay, once the Earl of Dúndragon—which was a rather substantial earldom in the Highlands—and Count Foscarelli won everything Lord Dúndragon owned...all the Ramsay estates in both Scotland and England. I'm speaking of the Dúndragon branch of the Clan Ramsay, of course—for the family are only distantly related to the Ramsays of Dalhousie, I believe. Afterward, Lord Dúndragon claimed that Count Foscarelli had cheated him, and as a result of the accusation, they fought a notorious duel in Green Park, during which Count Foscarelli brutally shot and killed Lord Dúndragon."

"*Non!* How perfectly awful!" Ariana exclaimed.

"Well, naturally, 'twas for poor Lord Dúndragon!" Christine declared irreverently, and then grinned. "Although I don't think anybody really cared, for I believe he was a fool and a wastrel of the worst sort. So that's how the Foscarellis came to possess Castle Dúndragon, along with other Ramsay property, and of course they must still have land in Italy, one presumes, since they have continued to use their Italian titles. The Earl of Dúndragon's title long ago fell into abeyance or possibly even reverted to the Crown, I think, for lack of a Ramsay heir."

"Lord Dúndragon had no children, then?"

"No, only a younger brother—Viscount Strathmór."

"The same Viscount Strathmór that Monsieur al-Walid told us about that night at Maman's conversation party?" Ariana inquired, much startled. "The one who stole that priceless emerald from the tomb of that Egyptian mummy?"

"No, that was another, earlier Viscount Strathmór. The Viscount Strathmór that I'm talking about was, as I said, Lord Dúndragon's younger brother, and although, unlike Lord Dúndragon, he had heirs, what became of them, I don't know. 'Tis rumored in the Highlands that they fled for their very lives, that if they had not, the Foscarellis would have murdered them all!"

"But…why?"

"Because of that emerald—the Heart of Kheperi! By this time, of course, it had long vanished, just as Mr. al-Walid told us that evening. But Count Foscarelli apparently mistakenly thought Lord Dúndragon had it, and that's why he lured him into the ruinous game of piquet to begin with and cheated him at cards—so he could get his hands on it. Like many others, he believed that the emerald has the power to bestow immortality on whoever wields it."

"Oh, but surely that is only an old, superstitious legend, Christine! I simply can't imagine that anyone would commit murder over it for that reason!"

"You're wrong, Ariana," Christine insisted gravely, her beautiful face abruptly draining of color. "They would—and have! But I daren't say any more just now, for much to my deep distress and apprehension, Viscount Ugo is unquestionably headed our way, and he might overhear our conversation. Pretend you don't see him, and then perhaps he will leave us alone!"

"But if you despise and fear him so much, why do you not simply give him the cut direct and refuse to speak to him?"

"No, that would be extremely unwise—for as I told you before, he is a wholly sinister young man, and so 'twould be very dangerous to offend or cross him. I did not know he was in London. He must have come to town at the start of the Little Season. Had I been aware of that—and of the fact that the marchioness had invited him to her masquerade ball—I would have stayed home!"

Christine said nothing further in this regard, however, for just then, Viscount Ugo reached them. Clicking his heels together smartly, he swept them a low bow, then kissed the back of Christine's graceful hand as she reluctantly extended it to him.

"Signorina Christine, what a pleasure to see you again," he murmured smoothly, appearing not to notice the visible shudder that ran through her at his touch or, if he did, mistaking it for desire and delight. "Will you introduce me to your friend? I don't believe we've met."

"Certainly. Mademoiselle Ariana, may I present to you Lord Lucrezio Foscarelli, Viscount Ugo. Lord Ugo, this is Mademoiselle Ariana Lévesque. She and her parents, le Comte and la Comtesse de Valcoeur, came to London from Paris just this past spring, after King Louis-Philippe abdicated."

"How do you do, Monsieur Ugo?" Ariana said, politely proffering her hand.

Was it just her imagination, or did the Italian pause as though greatly startled of a sudden by the introduction to her? If so, he recovered quickly, and a moment later she felt sure that the odd impression was nothing more than her own wild, vivid fancy, whipped up by Christine's narrative and a trick of the candlelight.

"Very well, indeed—now that I have met you, *signorina,*" Lord Ugo rejoined, smiling in what Ariana thought was a highly predatory fashion, his teeth flashing whitely in his dark visage, beneath his crimson visor. From behind the narrow slits of this last, his glittering black eyes raked her with ill-concealed interest and speculation, so that abruptly she felt an icy shiver creep up her spine, prickling the fine hairs on her nape. "How are you liking London?"

"I was quite homesick at first, but now I find I am liking it very much, after all."

"And what, if I may be so bold as to inquire, has proved the cause of this sudden change of heart? Dare I venture to guess that a prospective suitor has entered the picture?"

"If one has, that surely is my own affair, Monsieur Ugo."

"Aha!" He threw back his head and laughed—an eerily demonic sound that sent another strange chill through Ariana. "How sweetly the lady puts me in my place and tells me to mind my own business!"

"Not at all, *monsieur.* I merely pointed out the obvious. Now, if you'll please excuse me, duty calls, I fear—for I believe I see my mother beckoning me from across the room, so I must attend her."

"Of course. 'Twas a pleasure meeting you, Signorina Ariana."

She wished she could say the same, but since she could not, Ariana said nothing, simply nodding instead. Then she turned to her friend, who stood silently, watchfully, by.

"Are you coming, Christine?"

"Actually, Signorina Christine, if you could spare me a few moments of your time…?" the Italian interjected, importuning. "There is a small, private matter I would discuss with you."

"Yes…all right, my lord," Christine agreed slowly, reluctantly.

Under the circumstances, Ariana was loath to leave her friend alone with Viscount Ugo. Still, short of being rude to the Italian and dragging Christine away, there was nothing else she could do. She had already excused herself on the pretext of speaking with her mother and so could not now do an about-face and remain with her friend and Viscount Ugo, especially when he had made it clear that her company would now constitute an intrusion. So, instead, she left the two of them standing there together, threading her way through the throng, highly disturbed by all Christine had told her about the Foscarellis and about Viscount Ugo himself. As, frowning and strangely unnerved, Ariana dwelled at length on him, it suddenly occurred to her that there had been something peculiarly familiar about the Italian, which had not been immediately apparent to her, because like everyone else present, he was wearing a half mask and domino. But now she realized that it was almost as though she had met him before somewhere, although she felt sure that was not the case, and the fact that she could not think why she should believe she knew him niggled and gnawed at her worrisomely.

She was so deeply troubled and engrossed in her reverie, in fact, that, not watching where she was going, she accidentally stumbled hard into one of the marchioness's guests.

"Oh, *pardon, monsieur!*" Ariana blurted out, much discomposed and mortified. "I'm so terribly sorry. Please forgive me." Then, glancing up at the tall dark handsome man she had so forcefully bumped into and who was garbed in an unremarkable black visor and plain black domino, she inquired tentatively, "Monsieur Blackfriars…? *Non,* my apologies, *monsieur.* I thought you were someone else, but now I see I was mistaken." For upon closer inspection, she observed with great disappointment that the eyes that peered out at her from behind the stranger's half mask were a striking shade of sapphire-blue—not the elusive, changeable misty silver color of Malcolm's own.

"Do you speak of Mr. Malcolm Blackfriars, my lady? Is he a friend of yours, then?" the stranger asked, much to her surprise.

"*Mais, oui, monsieur,*" she answered, with keen interest now. "Do you know him, also?"

"Indeed, yes, my lady. Malcolm and I are very good friends. Since we have that in common, pray, please permit me to introduce myself. I am Nicolas Ravener, at your service, my lady." He bowed low before her.

"I am Mademoiselle Ariana Lévesque."

At that, it seemed to her that Mr. Ravener's dark visage abruptly turned quite pale beneath his visor, and to her utter shock and bewilderment, a muttered oath broke from his lips.

"A thousand pardons, *mademoiselle,*" he then said, in a rush. "But I've just now spied someone with whom I must speak at all costs and without delay. 'Twas a pleasure meeting you, but now I beg you will excuse me!"

As she stood there distressed and rendered speechless by his incomprehensible behavior, Mr. Ravener rudely hurried away and, staring after him, Ariana saw him push his way heedlessly through the crowd, apparently in hot pursuit of Viscount Ugo, who was just now disappearing through a pair of the mullioned French doors that opened onto the terrace and well-tended, private gardens at the rear of the marchioness's town house. Even more perplexed, and intensely curious now, as well, Ariana impulsively hastened after the two men.

Reaching the French doors, she slipped out into the night, taking care to remain hidden in the shadows, so that neither Mr. Ravener nor Viscount Ugo should see her. As the autumn air was chilly with mist and mizzle, few others had sought the gardens' moonlit beauty, preferring the warmth of the blazing hearths in the marchioness's drawing, card, billiard and smoking rooms instead. So there was no one about save for Ariana and the two men. From her vantage point on the terrace, she now observed the Italian pause on one of the garden paths and light a cheroot before continuing his solitary stroll. But much to her surprise and astonishment, instead of catching up with him, Mr. Ravener covertly hid himself behind a large topiary dolphin, so that it was evident that he spied upon Viscount Ugo and, contrary to his words to Ariana, had little or no intention of speaking with him. Rather, as the Italian probed deeper into the gardens, Mr. Ravener followed him furtively. Likewise, her Moroccan slippers barely whispering upon the stones as she descended from the terrace and trod swiftly along the garden paths, did Ariana now pursue the two men, shivering uncontrollably beneath her domino, which provided little protection against the cool night air and drizzle, and taking care to use the various ornamental trees and shrubberies for concealment.

In this manner did she finally reach the heart of the gardens, where there rose a tall stone fountain, whose waters spewed into a sizable round deep fishpond beneath. Here the Italian halted, puffing with evident contentment on his cigar and, obviously deep in thought, gazing unseeingly at the fish that swam in the pond.

Now, as Ariana watched through a small gap in a boxwood hedge, her heart hammering in her breast, Mr. Ravener slowly crept from behind the trunk of a maple tree, and to her everlasting shock and horror, before she could issue a warning, he brutally attacked the clearly unsuspecting Viscount Ugo. Grabbing the Italian from behind and strongly pinning his arms to his sides, Mr. Ravener jerked open Viscount Ugo's crimson domino, sending its buttons flying and clawing viciously at the Italian's throat. The two men struggled briefly but desperately together for what, to Ariana, seemed an eternal moment, during which time she stood frozen with cold and petrified with fright, morbidly riveted to the savage scene, before Mr. Ravener finally shoved Viscount Ugo violently into the fishpond, then fled as though the hounds of hell harried hard his heels. Fortunately, the loud splash the Italian made as he struck the water covered the small, unwitting cry of dismay and fear that emanated from Ariana's throat as she witnessed what happened.

Then at last, still terrified but managing at last to collect her wits, seeing that Viscount Ugo was unharmed, briefly flailing wildly about in the fishpond before finally staggering to its stone edge, she turned and ran as fast as she could back to the bright lights and safety of the marchioness's town house.

Chapter Twelve

Thieves in the Night

Lay not up for yourselves treasures upon earth,
where moth and rust doth corrupt,
and where thieves break through and steal:
But lay up for yourselves treasures in heaven.

—The Holy Bible
The Gospel According to St. Matthew

A certain man went down from Jerusalem to Jericho,
and fell among thieves.

—The Holy Bible
The Gospel According to St. Luke

The day is for honest men, the night for thieves.

—Euripides
Iphigenia in Tauris [c.412 B.C.]

1848
The Strand and the Adelphi Wharves, London, England

The day after the eventful masquerade ball held at the Marchioness of Mayfield's grand town house in Grosvenor Square, Malcolm—blissfully unaware of all that had occurred there—spent the whole of the Saturday afternoon at the notorious Red House tavern in Battersea Fields, target shooting with Nicolas Ravener. Afterward, at precisely six o'clock in the evening, the two of them were seated at a table at the Caledonian Hotel in Robert Street, just off The Strand, where, for two shillings and sixpence each, they enjoyed a pint of porter and the *table d'hôte,* an ordinary supper served daily and with little fanfare. As he sipped from his jar, Malcolm felt slightly guilty, for of late, having devoted the majority of his spare time to Ariana, he had not only somewhat neglected his training at Red Rory Hoolihan's Boxing Saloon and Henry the Younger's L'Ecole d'Armes, as well as his target practice, but also his friend, Mr. Ravener. Until tonight, Malcolm had not seen him for several days, the last occasion being at Red Rory Hoolihan's Boxing Saloon. There Malcolm had been working out all his many frustrations on a weight bag, punching it so hard that it was a wonder the worn canvas had not split open.

"Your jabs are quite savage today, Malcolm," Mr. Ravener had observed at the time. "Is something troubling you?"

"No…aye—my blasted principles, Nicolas!" Ceasing his violent blows to the bag, Malcolm had smiled ruefully. "I've become friends with a lady—and no, before you ask, 'tis not a courtship, although, in all honesty, I wish 'twere. But unfortunately, her station in life is so far above my own that unless there is some drastic change in my circumstances, there can never be any thought of marriage between us, however much I may desire it. The lady is to attend a masquerade ball at the town house of the Marchioness of Mayfield on Friday, so that gives you a good idea of the kind of society in which she moves. She wanted me to accompany her, but as I, of course, was not invited by the marchioness—who is unquestionably unaware of even my very existence!—I was compelled to decline. But I tell you, Nicolas, for one wild moment I confess I *was* terribly tempted to don a mask and domino, and to slip into the marchioness's town house, so I could hobnob with all the *crème de la crème* of London— for I have it on the best authority that everybody who is anybody in town will be present!"

"Well, then, why don't you?" Mr. Ravener had inquired, grinning. "Go, I mean? After all…an affair like that? Who would know? For you've no need to present a gilt-edged invitation at the front door to get past some stuffy old butler and gain admittance to the town house. No, just slip past the mews, over the garden wall and in through one of the rear doors…that's the ticket, Malcolm! For since everyone will be in disguise, once the marchioness's masquerade ball is under way, nobody will ever even recognize you or know you weren't properly invited! After all, what is one more guest in a costume, among hundreds likewise garbed?"

"Good God, Nicolas! You sound as though you've done something like that before!"

"Yes…once or twice, when I thought 'twas expedient—and I don't mind admitting it, either. For fortune favors the bold, Malcolm—and ever since I was orphaned at the young, impressionable age of twelve, I've had to fight and scrape for everything I've ever got out of this life!"

"I see. I'm sorry. I didn't know you'd had it so rough."

"Yes, well, I don't usually talk about my past."

"Or your present, either," Malcolm had remarked shrewdly. "For do you realize, Nicolas, that in all the months since I made your acquaintance, you've never once until now mentioned your family, your friends, what you do to earn a living, where you reside, or anything else of a personal nature? No, I'm not chiding you, and I really don't want to pry. Your business is your own, after all. But still, I can't help but be curious, you know."

Mr. Ravener had shrugged lightly, dismissively, in response.

"That's because there's simply nothing much to tell, I assure you. My parents died, leaving me an orphan, as I've just now told you. I've always been something of a solitary soul, so I've no friends aside from you. I'm a gambler by trade, actually—which is how I come and go just as I please and answer to no master save myself, and also why I box, fence and shoot. In my profession, one cannot be too careful. And I'm currently lodged at the George and Vulture public house, in St. Michael's Alley. Is there anything else you'd care to know?"

"No—but thank you for satisfying my curiosity."

"Don't mention it."

Now, recalling the conversation, it occurred to Malcolm that, being a gambler—and clearly a daring one at that—Nicolas was undoubtedly acquainted with all kinds of people from all walks of life, and that he might therefore prove useful in the quest for the missing Heart of Kheperi. Aside from being unable to court Ariana properly, Malcolm's chief cause of bedevilment was the fact that so little progress had been made in this connection. Mr. Quimby had completed various maps of the area around Castle Dúndragon covering the past few centuries, but so far, nothing more concrete than that had been accomplished. Jakob Rosenkranz had still not learnt anything with regard to the whereabouts of the second crucifix, which had belonged to Malcolm's murdered uncle Charles. Nor had Boniface Cavendish turned up anything else about Lord Rob Roy Ramsay, the ninth Earl of Dúndragon, or the mysterious order—the Sons of Isis—that he had founded. Malcolm had declared his intention of returning to Scotland, to the Highlands and Loch Ness, with the goal of trying to discover the identities of the original twelve unknown members of the order and of attempting to trace their descendants. But even Mr. Quimby's largesse, it appeared, had limits, for when Malcolm had announced his design, his employer had stated firmly that he could not be spared from the map shop for such a length of time as that. So, knowing that Mr. Quimby had already been more than generous with him, Malcolm had, however reluctantly, abandoned his scheme, agreeing to his employer's proposal that Mr. Cavendish—who knew a great deal more about ancient manuscripts, anyway—undertake the task of investigating the order.

"For it may be that Boniface can, in the London Library, find whatever information we seek, buried in some musty, moldering old text they've got locked away there," Mr. Quimby had said. "And of course, there are Dr. Williams's Library, in Cripplegate, and Sion College and the reading rooms, as well—although I'll admit I don't believe that the latter would be of any use whatsoever to us."

So, as he ate his supper and chatted with Mr. Ravener, Malcolm mulled over in his mind the idea of taking him into his confidence and requesting his assistance in the search for the lost emerald. But in the end, he decided that this was perhaps too serious a step to make without first consulting Messieurs Quimby, Rosenkranz and Cavendish, so reluctantly he held his tongue.

Following their meal, Malcolm and Mr. Ravener, being at loose ends, then determined to see the new first-night plays at the Theatre Royal, Adelphi, in The Strand, not far from Robert Street. Originally named the Sans Pareil, the theater had been founded nearly half a century ago by a washing-blue merchant, John Scott. In addition to peddling his "Old True Blue" for bluing stockings, linen and cottons, and for dyeing silk, tiffany and gauze, Mr. Scott had sold magic lanterns. He had also had a daughter with a passion for the stage and who had thus aspired to a career as an actress, and at last, in support of her ambition, the doting Mr. Scott had remodeled the back of his warehouse in The Strand, turning it into a theater for her. Eventually, this had proved so successful that he had replaced the ramshackle building with a proper new one, which had, over the passing years, finally changed both owners and names, with the old house front facing The Strand having a gin-palace facade constructed less than a decade ago.

Since its inception, the theater had been famous for its productions of melodramas, comedies, burlesques and totally outrageous farces, and tonight was no exception to that rule. Malcolm and Mr. Ravener paid two shillings each to sit in the pit and watch the performances. As the theater doors opened at half-past six in the evening and the curtain rose at seven, they had already missed the first play of the evening, *The Wreck Ashore; or A Bridegroom from the Sea,* a two-act melodrama. But they were in time to see the three-act comedy *Paul Pry,* with the well-known actor Edward R. Wright in the starring role, and as Malcolm laughed along with the rest of the crowd, he was able for a time to forget all the frustrations that plagued him so deeply. Afterward, he and Mr. Ravener remained for the one-act farce *Shocking Events,* which followed. Then they departed from the theater, companionably making their way to an oyster-house on Adelphi Street for a late-night drink and bite to eat.

Finally, however, as the hour stretched toward midnight, Malcolm pushed back his chair and rose from the table.

"'Tis growing late, Nicolas, and I must get home and to bed. I have to rise early on Sundays, to accompany Mother to church. I'd offer to share a ride in a hansom cab with you, but if you are lodged at the George and Vulture, then, of course, we go in entirely opposite directions. So I'll bid you good-night now."

"Yes—besides which, I want to finish this drink before I take my leave here. 'Twas a most enjoyable day and evening. Take care, and I'll see you next week at Red Rory's or elsewhere. Good night, Malcolm."

After shrugging on his cloak in the smoky, dimly illuminated interior of the rowdy oyster-house, Malcolm departed from the premises, walking briskly up Adam Street toward The Strand, where he knew he would be much more likely to find a hansom cab at this hour of the night. But then, upon reaching The Strand and in the process of hailing a passing driver, he suddenly realized that in the semidarkness of the oyster-house he had mistakenly taken Mr. Ravener's coat instead of his own. Being of approximately the same height and build as his friend, Malcolm had not discovered his error until he raised his arm to flag down the hansom cab, so that a gust of wind blown inland from the nearby River Thames had caught the capes on the back of the cloak, making them flap like a raven's wings of a sudden. His own coat was plain, lacking the fancy capes that increased the cost of the garment. Cursing under his breath, he turned on his heel, retracing his steps toward the oyster-house in Adelphi Street and hoping that Mr. Ravener had not yet left the place.

The street lamps along the pavement glowed softly in the mist that drifted in from the sea and the River Thames, and the chilly autumn air was quiet, save for the soughing night wind and the light pitter-patter of the cold drizzle that sprinkled from the dark, hazily mooned sky. As Malcolm approached Adelphi Street the brume obscured his vision, so it was the sound of violent blows and grunts of pain that reached his ears in the stillness of the evening that alerted him to the fact that trouble lay ahead. Some instinct warning him, he quickened his pace until he ran down Adam Street, at whose end, breaking free of the fog at last, he spied Mr. Ravener engaged in a desperate struggle with two masked men wearing dominoes, one of whom flashed a knife whose long, sharp silver blade gleamed menacingly in the nebulous moonlight. Mr. Ravener himself was not defenseless, however. He always carried with him a silver-knobbed walking stick upon whose head was engraved a rampant winged dragon, and now Malcolm observed that the cane concealed a lethal small sword, which Mr. Ravener had drawn and was laying about him skillfully, to good purpose, holding his attackers at bay.

Still, Malcolm's heart lodged in his throat, for as he raced toward the scene he saw that his friend had been driven out onto the Adelphi Wharves, which jutted out over the River Thames and where there was not much room to maneuver deftly. Finally gaining the docks, Malcolm smashed his umbrella, which he had not bothered earlier to unfold against the mizzle, down hard on the head of the nearest assailant, leaving the one with the weapon to Mr. Ravener.

"Gor, Tobe, 'tis t' Mapper!" the unarmed man cried as he stumbled about from the force of Malcolm's onslaught.

"Kill 'im, Badger!" the one called Toby snarled. "Don't let 'im get away!"

As he heard the names of his two opponents, Malcolm was momentarily stupefied, for in that instant the years fell away and, horrified, he realized he was battling none other than the pickpocket Tobias "Toby" Snitch and his thieving accomplice, Dick "Badger" Badgerton, Mr. Quimby's former ne'er-do-well apprentice. No wonder they wore masks and dominoes! They must have been spying on him for quite some time and, not wanting him to see their faces when they had previously attacked him, for fear that otherwise he would recognize them, manage to escape from them and somehow track them down afterward, they had disguised themselves in costume. Further, what better way to flee from the police, if necessary, than by passing themselves off as mere masquers wandering to or from a public ball, rather than betraying themselves as a pair of thieves bent on moving up to mayhem and murder?

But plainly, as Malcolm had feared when he had first heard the sounds of the conflict, they had, because of his mixing up of the coats, mistaken the unsuspecting Mr. Ravener for him in the darkness.

Now, in some dim corner of his mind, as he fought with Badger urgently, Malcolm wondered how many years the two men had spent in prison after appearing at the then-new Central Criminal Court and being sentenced for their crimes against his employer. When had they got out, and how long had they plotted their revenge against him? For they must have come to hate him bitterly during their stint in gaol, since if not for him chasing down Toby, the two of them would never have been caught that long-ago day when they had schemed to steal Mr. Quimby's purse. Still, their time could have been much worse, Malcolm knew. They had, in fact, got off somewhat lightly, since because Badger had been apprenticed to Mr. Quimby, both he and Toby had been incarcerated in City Bridewell, a former royal residence, which, following the Reformation, King Edward VI had turned into a penitentiary for rebellious apprentices and vagrants, most of the previous palace having burnt down during the Great Fire of London in 1666. Still, although in the past decades attempts had been made at prison reform and the rehabilitation of inmates, Malcolm was aware that more often than not, incarceration hardened rather than reclaimed those unfortunate enough to be gaoled, and now he knew this to be the case for Toby and Badger. He now understood that because of their trying to yank a hood down over his head during their previous assaults upon him, they had surely intended to kidnap, torture and then finally murder him. His death would have been extremely unpleasant, the result of their dire vengeance—and still might be.

For Badger was strong, wiry and quick from having lived such a hard life, and even though Malcolm was taller, heavier and equally as nimble, it was nearly all he could do to hold his own, especially since his umbrella had broken when he had clubbed

Badger over the head with it, and now Malcolm had only his own fists for self-defense.

"Coat pocket, Malcolm!" Mr. Ravener rasped as he lunged, feinted and parried with his small sword against Toby's swift, skillfully slashing and twisting blade.

For a minute, Malcolm did not comprehend. Then, abruptly, he grasped the fact that one of the pockets in his friend's cloak, which he had so unwittingly confused with his own in the oyster-house, must contain something that would aid them in their fight for their lives. Dodging Badger's hammering blows, he searched Mr. Ravener's coat pockets frantically, his hand at last closing over something cold and steely. Withdrawing the small but deadly pistol invented a few short decades ago by Henry Deringer, Malcolm fired it at point-blank range at his adversary. For what seemed an interminable instant, he thought he must have missed, because Badger just stood there, looking wholly stunned but uninjured. But then, almost as though in slow motion, his thin, weaselly visage drained of color in the pale moonlight and his hands clutched his chest, blood seeping between his fingers as he staggered back. In that moment, a memory of Uncle Charles in what Malcolm knew must have been the last seconds of his life flashed eerily into his mind, and somehow, the fact that he wore a caped greatcoat now, just as Uncle Charles's murderer had then, seemed the bitterest of ironies.

But there was no time to ponder it now—for much to Malcolm's horror, as Badger lurched spasmodically around the pier, gasping and groaning in agony, blood bubbling from his chest, he stumbled without warning into Mr. Ravener, violently knocking him from the wharf into the River Thames before toppling in himself. With thunderous splashes they hit the water, going under, while Malcolm stood upon the dock, aghast and hideously torn, the now-spent pistol in his hand and Toby just a few yards distant, his fingers still wrapped tightly around the handle of his wicked blade.

"You done kilt Badger, Mapper—an' now you got to pay fer that!" Toby growled.

Thinking rapidly, making a split-second decision that he

hoped would save both his friend's life and his own, Malcolm suddenly flung the useless pistol at his foe's head. Then, as Toby ducked to avoid being struck by the hurled weapon, Malcolm barreled straight into him, the impetus sending them both over the edge of the pier.

The River Thames was so dark and cold as he plunged into it and felt it engulf him that it blinded Malcolm and took his breath clean away, so that for an instant he thought wildly that he was going to drown. But then finally, gasping for air, he broke the black moonlit surface, treading water and scrambling for his bearings, searching desperately for Mr. Ravener. Spying him choking and bobbing on the waves, Malcolm swam toward him and caught hold of him. Then, hauling his friend with him, he sliced through the water toward the embankment and the Salisbury Stairs. The latter were just a few short yards away, but to Malcolm it seemed an eternity before he managed to reach them and drag his friend up the steps. Turning Mr. Ravener over, he pumped him hard on the back several times, until his friend began to cough, water sputtering and trickling from his mouth.

"Nicolas…Nicolas! Are you all right? Can you stand?"

"Yes—if you will…kindly offer me…your assistance."

But once Malcolm got Mr. Ravener to his feet, he saw that a dark patch of blood stained his friend's waistcoat.

"You're hurt!"

Mr. Ravener nodded weakly.

"The…bloody little bastard…managed to…stick me."

"Can you walk? I've got to get you to hospital, and I daren't leave you here in this condition, because I don't know whether or not Toby Snitch can swim. I hope he can't and that he's drowned. But I daren't take the chance that he hasn't, because if he's still alive, he'll probably come up either the Salisbury Stairs or the York Build Stairs. Those are the closest places around here where he can get over the embankment, and if he does manage to accomplish that, he'll finish you off whilst I'm trying to flag down a hansom cab."

"I can walk—but I...won't go to hospital. Take me...to the George and Vulture."

"Don't be a fool, Nicolas! You've lost a great deal of blood! You need a doctor!"

"I'll...take care...of myself. Just get me...to the inn."

"I refuse to stand here quarreling with you!"

So saying, his friend's arm slung over his shoulders, Malcolm half carried Mr. Ravener down Adam Street to The Strand, there hailing a passing hansom cab. Knowing that the driver might refuse to take them if informed that Mr. Ravener was wounded, Malcolm intimated that his friend was terribly drunk and that, as a result, they had accidentally fallen into the River Thames while staggering along its embankment. He gave their direction as Cochrane Street, St. John's Wood, promising the driver a bonus if they were got there quickly.

"I told you...to take me...to my lodgings," Mr. Ravener protested weakly once they were inside the vehicle and it had drawn away from the curb, rumbling over the cobblestones toward Charing Cross and Cockspur and Regent Streets.

"You're in no condition either to argue or to look after yourself. If you won't go to hospital, then I insist you come to Hawthorn Cottage, where you'll be well cared for until you recover! 'Tis *my* fault that you were attacked to begin with. Had I not erroneously donned your coat instead of my own in the oyster-house, Toby and Badger would never have mistaken you for me." As he spoke, Malcolm peeled away his friend's soaked cloak, waistcoat and shirt in order to see for himself what damage had been done. A short but nasty gash in Mr. Ravener's side was exposed to his anxious gaze. "I've got to staunch this blood. Otherwise, you're liable to bleed to death before I can get you home and summon a physician."

Tearing away strips of his own wet shirt, Malcolm made a makeshift padding and bandage, wishing he had ignored Mr. Ravener's demurring and instructed the driver to deliver them straight to the nearest hospital. But the way his friend, despite his condition, had objected to this idea had caused Malcolm to feel as though if he persisted in it, Mr. Ravener would become so agitated or even angry that he might turn physically violent and do himself some further harm when Malcolm was compelled to restrain him.

Still, the longer he dwelled upon how far distant Hawthorn Cottage yet was—for the hansom cab had just now swung from Regent Street onto Oxford Street—the more concerned Malcolm grew about his friend. The temporary ministrations to his injury now completed, Mr. Ravener slumped listlessly against one corner of the vehicle, his eyes closed, his face ashen, his breathing shallow and rapid, and his teeth chattering. He was shivering uncontrollably from his sodden clothes, his wound and the cold, and Malcolm knew that shock was setting in swiftly. He feared horribly that his friend would lose consciousness and die—and without even a brandy or a blanket to warm him. Suddenly pounding with his fist upon the box, Malcolm shouted up to the driver that he had changed his mind, to take them posthaste to Portman Square, and a few minutes later, upon arriving there, he bore Mr. Ravener from the vehicle, directing the driver to wait at the curb. Then, not caring that it was now nearly two o'clock in the morning, he rang the front bell of the Lévesque town house ceaselessly and beat upon the door, until at last it was opened by the butler, Butterworth.

"Mr. Blackfriars!" he exclaimed, plainly shocked by the two men's appearance.

From behind the butler in the reception hall could now be heard the startled, frightened voice of Madame Valcoeur and, in response, her husband's own soothing, reassuring one before he stepped forward to address the butler.

"Well, who is it, Butterworth? What is amiss that the whole household has been roused at such a late hour?"

"'Tis Mr. Blackfriars, my lord—" the butler began.

"Please," Malcolm interrupted, gazing past Butterworth to where he could now spy the comte and the comtesse standing in the reception hall—and Ariana, as well, who, upon hearing Malcolm's name, had paused in the middle of descending the grand staircase, one delicate hand held to her throat, and behind her, the Lady Christine, whom Malcolm had met at the comtesse's conversation party. "Please. You said that if I ever needed any-thing…anything at all…I could come to you. My friend Mr. Ravener was attacked this evening. He's badly hurt—"

"Oh, *mon Dieu!*" Madame Valcoeur cried with obvious dis-tress. "Of course you must bring him in at once!"

There then followed such a shouting of orders and a flurry of activity that Malcolm could scarcely believe it. Footmen ap-peared, to carry Mr. Ravener upstairs to a sumptuous bedcham-ber, where he was stripped, put into a warm nightshirt and bundled up in bed. Housemaids ran to and fro, fetching pots of hot tea and warm snifters of brandy, as well as washcloths, tow-els, soap, basins of steaming water, bottles of antiseptics and other necessities. Additional footmen were dispatched to sum-mon the surgeon and to bear a message to Mrs. Blackfriars, to let her know that her son's friend had been injured and that, as a result, the two men would be staying the night at Portman Square. The driver of the hansom cab was paid and awarded a substantial bonus, besides. Malcolm was installed in a room ad-joining the one in which Mr. Ravener had been placed, and was given clean dry clothing to change into. After he had finished washing and dressing, he was then escorted to the library, where he had a crystal snifter of warm brandy pressed upon him by Monsieur Valcoeur.

"The doctor has come and is upstairs now, attending to your friend Mr. Ravener," the comte uttered soberly. "So you need not be concerned about him for the moment. However, as I'm sure you already know, he has lost a lot of blood, and his condition appears very grave. Can you tell us now what happened? You said he was assaulted?"

"Aye," Malcolm replied, then went on to explain everything, beginning with the day he had pursued and caught Toby Snitch and ending with the night's dire events.

"Oh, you must feel terrible, Monsieur Blackfriars," Ariana ob-served sympathetically, once he had completed his tale. "To think poor Monsieur Ravener should be in such a wounded state due to confusion about the coats on your own part and a case of mistaken identity on that of his attackers! But then, at least 'twas nothing at all—as I initially feared—to do with that dreadful, wicked man Lord Lucrezio Foscarelli, Viscount Ugo!"

Much to her astonishment, the effect of her words upon those assembled in the library was as though she had dropped a bombshell. For a moment, everyone present gaped at her, and a deathly silence fell upon the room, which was finally broken by Christine.

"Good Lord, Ariana! Whatever would make you believe that Lord Ugo might have assaulted poor Mr. Ravener?" she asked.

"Because right after you had introduced Monsieur Ugo to me last night at Madame la Marquise's ball and I had left the two of you standing there together, talking, I was so unnerved by all you had told me about him and his horrid family that I'm afraid I wasn't watching where I was going, and I ran squarely into Monsieur Ravener—literally!"

"Mr. Ravener! He was at the marchioness's town house last evening? Are you quite sure, *mademoiselle,* that 'twas he?" Malcolm inquired, as greatly startled by this piece of news as he had been by the wholly unexpected mention of the Foscarelli name.

"*Mais, oui, monsieur*—for at first I…I mistakenly believed that 'twas you I had accidentally stumbled into. You and Monsieur Ravener are of a similar height and build, you see, and you both have black hair and dark skin, so there is actually a great deal of resemblance between you. And of course, Monsieur Ravener was wearing a mask and a domino. So 'twasn't until I saw that his eyes are blue instead of gray that I realized my error. But before that, I had addressed him by your name, so he was aware that I knew you, and then, naturally, after that he introduced himself to me as a friend of yours."

"I see," Malcolm said slowly. "But that still doesn't explain why you initially thought Mr. Ravener had been set upon by Lord Ugo."

"*Non,* but that was because whilst we were speaking and becoming acquainted, Monsieur Ravener suddenly—and, *oui,* most rudely—abruptly excused himself and hurried after Monsieur Ugo, who was going out through the French doors into the gardens. I—I confess I was curious, and so I followed them and—oh, I know 'twas terrible of me! But I spied upon the two men in the gardens, and so I witnessed Monsieur Ravener sneak up on Monsieur Ugo and attack him from behind!"

"What?" Malcolm expostulated, incredulous.

"*Oui,* I'm afraid 'tis true, Monsieur Blackfriars, for as I told you, with my own two eyes did I see him do this awful thing. He and Monsieur Ugo struggled briefly—and then Monsieur Ravener pushed him into the fishpond at the center of the gardens! 'Twas all so very upsetting and—and even frightening that I waited only to be certain Monsieur Ugo was all right, that he had not sustained some injury, had not knocked himself unconscious by hitting the stone fountain that rose from the middle of the fishpond and thus would doubtless wind up drowning, before I ran back into the town house."

"I am…truly stunned by your story, *mademoiselle.* For I cannot even begin to imagine why Mr. Ravener would have committed what, on the face of it, seems such a dastardly, cowardly act!" Malcolm was, in fact, deeply bewildered by—and suddenly, despite himself, even highly suspicious of, too—his friend's motives and behavior. "I myself did not know he was even aware of Lord Ugo's existence, much less was acquainted with him or that there is evidently bad blood between them for some reason as yet unknown to me. Still, I feel certain Mr. Ravener must have had good cause for his actions, and I assure you, I will find out what it is!"

"If and when you do, Monsieur Blackfriars, I pray you will not mention my daughter's name in connection with the affair," Madame Valcoeur entreated, her lovely face pale. "For surely there is no need to involve her in it. And, Ariana—" she turned to her daughter "—although I do not know what all Christine told you about le Vicomte Ugo, you should indeed be made aware of the fact that his reputation, and that of his family, is…most unsavory. Therefore, I must positively insist that you have nothing whatsoever to do with him in the future. Is that clear?"

"*Oui*, Maman." She nodded, swallowing hard, for she could never before remember her mother speaking to her so sternly.

"*Très bon*. Now, here is Dr. Whittaker. So let us discover his opinion of poor Monsieur Ravener's condition and whether or not he is even expected to survive the night."

Book Three

The Ninefold Key

Lars Porsena of Clusium
By the Nine Gods he swore
That the great house of Tarquin
Should suffer wrong no more.
By the Nine Gods he swore it,
And named a trysting day,
And bade his messengers ride forth
East and west and south and north,
To summon his array.

      —Thomas Babington, Lord Macaulay
      Lays of Ancient Rome [1842]

Yet some there be that by due steps aspire
To lay their just hands on that golden key
That opes the palace of Eternity.

      —John Milton
      Comus [1634]

Chapter Thirteen

An Invitation To Remember

The bell invites me.
Hear it not, Duncan; for it is a knell
That summons thee to heaven or to hell.

—William Shakespeare
Macbeth [1605-1606]

What beck'ning ghost, along the moonlight shade
Invites my steps, and points to yonder glade?

—Alexander Pope
Elegy to the Memory of an Unfortunate Lady [1717]

Though her mien carries much more invitation
than command, to behold her is an immediate check
to loose behavior; to love her is a liberal education.

—Sir Richard Steele
Tatler [1709-1711]

1848
Portman Square, London, England

Mr. Ravener did not die. But in the days that followed, he was extremely ill, for as a result of his having been stabbed by Toby Snitch, he had lost a considerable amount of blood, and an infection born apparently, the physician Dr. Whittaker surmised, of his wound's subsequent exposure to the water of the River Thames—filthy with sewage—set in with a virulence, so that a fever seized hold of him, causing him to grow delirious.

Realizing how his friend's life hung in the balance and how deeply worrisome that was to him, Madame Valcoeur kindly suggested to Malcolm that he take up residence in the Lévesque town house until Mr. Ravener should prove fully recovered from his injury. Malcolm was inordinately grateful for the offer, and the morning after the attack he rose rather earlier than usual, having spent a restless night, gnawed not only by anxiety about his friend, but also by the fact that he, Malcolm, had ruthlessly shot a man. Although it was true that, given the chance, Dick "Badger" Badgerton would undoubtedly have murdered him, still, Malcolm was haunted by the thought that he had killed him. For he felt certain that he had, in fact, done so, that wounded as Badger had been by the point-blank-range gunshot, he could not possibly have survived the dark cold water of the River Thames and hauled himself up any of the stairs along the embankment, even had he known how to swim, which Malcolm doubted. Toby Snitch, however, was another story entirely, and the fact that he might have lived to escape also tormented Malcolm.

Now, after immersing and thoroughly scrubbing himself in the bathtub in the well-appointed bathroom that adjoined his bedchamber, Malcolm dried himself with a large fluffy towel. By means of the various other toiletries that had been so thoughtfully provided for his use, along with the bar of soap and the sponge he had employed during his bath, he cleaned his teeth and combed his hair. Despite everything, he could scarcely contain his curiosity and amazement as he gazed around first the luxurious bathroom and then the equally magnificent bedchamber he had been allotted. So this was how those who moved in the highest circles of society lived, he reflected, and he felt himself beset at once by a combination of envy, wistfulness and despair—for the sight of what the titled and wealthy so casually enjoyed on a daily basis brought home to him more forcefully than anything else had done just how vast the divide between his own station in life and that of Ariana truly was. Bitter anger at his ancestor, the desperate, dissolute Lord Iain Ramsay, once the Earl of Dúndragon, again filled Malcolm's heart and mind, and he grew more determined than ever to find the priceless missing emerald that might at least restore his family's riches, if not their rank.

In the bedroom he discovered that sometime last night, while he had so fitfully slept, his own garments had been carefully laundered and pressed, and restored to him. After putting them on, he knocked gently on the adjoining door to Mr. Ravener's own bedchamber, then, without waiting for a response, entered to spy Ariana standing next to his friend's bedside, wringing a wet washcloth out over a porcelain basin that sat upon one of the two night tables. Glancing up at Malcolm, she smiled faintly, holding one finger to her lips.

"He's sleeping—although not well at all, for he's become delirious with fever, I fear, which Dr. Whittaker, did, however, indicate would probably be the case," she whispered, so as not to disturb the patient. "We are to do our best to try to keep fluids down him, so he doesn't dehydrate, and also to keep him cool in the event that the fever should rise dangerously high. I'm so very sorry about your friend, Monsieur Blackfriars, for even though he did assault Monsieur Ugo from behind, I'm quite sure now that you were right and that he must have some good cause for having done so. For 'tis the strangest thing—once or twice in his delirium Monsieur Ravener has called me 'Maman' and clutched my hand, seeming to take solace from my presence. So I believe that perhaps he must have a French mother or else calls her by the French word for *mother*, at least, and that he must love her very much, indeed. And of course, no man who clearly adores his mother so dearly can be all bad. For my own sweet *maman* has always said to me that how he treats his mother is one of the truest measures of a man —and of how he would treat me, too, were I ever to become his wife."

Unspoken between the two of them—although the words hung heavily and portentously in the air, nonetheless—was the fact that Malcolm cherished his own mother and that that fact had not escaped Ariana's notice. In that moment, as he gazed at her beautiful countenance filled with such hope, tenderness and concern, it was all Malcolm could do to hold his tongue, to keep from blurting out that were Ariana to consent to marry him, he would indeed cherish her equally as dearly as he did his mother. But instead, he explained, "Mr. Ravener is an orphan, unfortunately, both his parents having died when he was but twelve years old."

"Oh—but then, that makes it even worse, doesn't it, that he should be calling for her now? For if only she were still alive, we could send for her instead of deceiving him—for I confess that although it has made me feel a trifle guilty, I have not disabused him of the notion that I am his mother, fearing that the realization that I am not would only upset him. Does he have any other family, do you know? An uncle or an aunt, perhaps, with whom we ought to get in touch?"

"No, not that I'm aware of." Malcolm shook his head. "In truth, from certain things he has said to me, I believe that Mr. Ravener is actually quite alone in all the world."

"Well, I am most sorry to hear that," Christine announced, entering the bedroom in time to overhear these last words. "And 'tis not exactly true, anyway. For personally, I don't care how Mr. Ravener did it! Any man brave enough to attack the villainous Lord Ugo, no matter how he did so, is a friend of mine!" She paused, then continued, "I knocked on the door, but I guess 'twas so softly that you did not hear me. Sophie has charged me most severely with the task of prying you away from Mr. Ravener's bedside, Ariana, for she says you sent her away quite decidedly last evening and sat up with him yourself instead all night long. So I've offered to take over your vigil here—none of us is attending church this morning—and you're to go downstairs with Mr. Blackfriars to the morning room, for breakfast. Sophie says you've not yet eaten."

"No, I haven't—and to be honest, I'm famished, and I'm sure Monsieur Blackfriars must be, as well. So, *oui,* I shall leave Mr. Ravener in your care for now. But if he should call out again for his mother, Christine, you must promise to send for me immediately—for he has somehow in his currently disordered state of mind confused me with her, and I believe he will grow quite agitated if I am not here to comfort him."

"Yes, all right, I promise. Now, do be away before Sophie herself should appear—for under her rather unassuming facade, she is really a veritable tyrant, so that I fear for my well-being if she should think I've not carried out her instructions to me! Not at all like my dear Jane, who is very meek and mild, with seldom ever a cross or imperious word to anybody!"

Descending the grand staircase to the reception hall, Ariana led Malcolm to the morning room, where they discovered breakfast laid out in silver chafing dishes arrayed upon the sideboard, with two each of the household's footmen and maids standing by, ready and waiting to serve them. From the staff present, Ariana learnt that her father had already risen and dined, then, on what he had declared was urgent business, departed from the town house. Her mother, deeply fatigued and distressed by last night's occurrences, still lay abed, sadly afflicted with a migraine. So Ariana and Malcolm had the morning room to themselves, and as they seated themselves together at the table, she could not help but think that such their married life would be, if she should ever wed him. She was wholly unaware, however, that the same thought was uppermost in Malcolm's own mind, except that he was envisioning her in the kitchen at Hawthorn Cottage and comparing its plain old wooden table to the elaborately carved one of expensive Honduras mahogany, at which he now sat. No, he mused with highly grievous regret, he could not in all good conscience ask Ariana to make such a sacrifice as that for the likes of him—especially when he could not even offer his own true name.

Following breakfast, Ariana retired to her bedchamber to rest and recover from having stayed up all night, nursing Mr. Ravener, while Malcolm hurried home to inform his mother in person of all that had occurred last evening. After reassuring her of his own well-being and escorting her to church, he packed a bag and went back Portman Square. On the following Monday morning, after spending the night at the Lévesques' town house, he again returned to Hawthorn Cottage to check on his mother. Then he hastened to the ominbus stand in St. John's Wood, where he caught the public transport, hoping he was not going to be late to work at Quimby & Company (Cartographers & Map Sellers).

But "You're late!" Harry cried as Malcolm entered the premises. "And 'tis no use thinking you can sneak by with its going unnoticed, Malcolm, for Mr. Quimby is already here…although I daresay that since you seem to come and go as freely as you please these days, perhaps he will let you off, after all, even though you're only the second-best journeyman at this establishment—the first being myself, of course!" the senior journeyman insisted, his usually cheerful face grim.

"Look, Harry," Malcolm began, comprehending at once the senior journeyman's fears, "will you believe me when I tell you that I've quite unexpectedly developed a number of serious personal problems, with which Mr. Quimby is helping me? For I give you my word of honor as a gentleman that that is indeed the case—and that I am not currying favor with our employer, with the goal of obtaining either your own job or Mr. Quimby's establishment whenever he decides to retire."

"'Tis true what you say, then? You're not after my place here at Quimby and Company? Or the shop, either?" Harry asked, still slightly suspicious.

"No." Malcolm shook his head. "And if you'd spoken with either Jem or Tuck, who, unlike either of us, board here on the premises, you'd know that I've put in long hours after closing here to try to make up for whatever time I've missed during the day. I've got troubles, Harry—and that's the God's honest truth—not the least of which is that Badger and his friend Toby mistakenly attacked one of my friends Saturday night, thinking he was I. They damned near murdered him!"

"Good Lord! Are you talking about Dick Badgerton and Tobias Snitch?" Harry's face now evidenced his astonishment and horror.

"Aye. They must have been released from City Bridewell and been plotting to avenge themselves against me ever since. Worse, I'm quite certain I killed Badger—and perhaps Toby, too. But I won't know for certain unless and until the bodies are discovered by the authorities. We all four of us fell into the Thames, off the Adelphi Wharves, and whilst I was able to save my friend, Mr. Ravener, I didn't see what happened to either Badger or Toby—although I presume that they both drowned. As I say, I'll know more if and when their corpses are fished from the river. Now, I must make Mr. Quimby privy to all this, so I would appreciate it, Harry, if you could get started on engraving all the intaglio plates for Mr. Pettigrew's maps this morning, and I'll come give you a hand just as soon as I've finished speaking with our employer."

"Right." Harry nodded, now looking rather shamefaced. "I'm…I'm very sorry I suspected you of being after my position here, Malcolm. I ought to have known better."

"Aye, but that's all right. I understand."

As he headed toward Mr. Quimby's office at the rear of the map shop, Malcolm was sober as he thought of all he had to report to his employer this morning.

"Good God!" Mr. Quimby expostulated upon learning of Saturday night's events. "Do you mean to tell me that all these assaults upon you had absolutely nothing whatsoever to do with either Mr. al-Walid or the Foscarellis? That they have all been the infamous, revengeful work of Dick Badgerton and Tobias Snitch all along? Well, upon my word, Malcolm! I confess I'm completely flabbergasted by this news—really, I am!—for in truth, I've given no thought at all to either of those two scoundrels since the day they were locked up in City Bridewell! So…Badger is dead, eh? Well, I can't say as how I'm much surprised, for once I discovered what an unpromising, bone-idle, thieving young scamp he was, I feared that in the end he would come to no good, despite all I tried to teach him! But still, after all is said and done, I can't help feeling just a little sorry for him, poor rascal, for after all, he came from a poverty-stricken family who all wound up in the workhouse, Fleet or Marshalsea debtors' prisons, or else dead. Still, Badger had an opportunity here to break that vicious cycle and escape from all that. But he threw it away, turning to a life of crime instead. So I suppose that ultimately I grieve for the loss of what he might have been—instead of what he eventually became." The elder gentleman paused, reflecting and shaking his head sadly. Then he continued.

"Well, Malcolm, I'm very sorry to say that although we can be relatively certain Badger will bother you no more, I don't believe we can be equally as sure about Toby Snitch. He was unharmed, you say?"

"Aye, as nearly as I could tell, sir. But still, 'twas relatively dark on the wharves, with only the street lamps on Adam and Adelphi Streets to cast any light at all there, and Mr. Ravener's quite good with a sword. So he might have pinked him, I don't know—and I'll not get a straight answer from Mr. Ravener one way or another unless and until his fever breaks and he recovers from his delirium."

"That's a pity…a very great pity, indeed," Mr. Quimby declared, still shaking his head. "For as you must be yourself, Malcolm, I'm extremely interested to hear why he attacked this Foscarelli fellow, Viscount Ugo—and from behind, no less! If you'll forgive me for saying so, that doesn't speak very highly of your friend, Malcolm—even if, like you, he *does* have some good reason for bearing the Foscarellis a grudge."

"No, I know that on the face of it, it really doesn't, sir. But still, by his own admission, Mr. Ravener was orphaned at the age of twelve, has lived a hard life ever since and earns his wages as a professional gambler. So he takes his opportunities as he finds them. And the truth is that under the circumstances, I'm not so sure I wouldn't have done exactly the same thing in his place. Further, the longer I've dwelt on the affair, sir, the more I've become convinced that 'twas never actually Mr. Ravener's intention to *murder* Lord Ugo. I mean, if he'd wanted to kill him, I feel quite certain he could have, having taken him by surprise in that manner. Why, he could have stabbed him in the back with that small sword he had out Saturday evening in his own defense. But what did Mr. Ravener do instead? He pushed Lord Ugo into the marchioness's fishpond! Really, the longer I ponder that, sir, the more it seems to me that that was the act of a man who feels such contempt for Lord Ugo that he felt as though the viscount were beneath slaying, if that makes any sense to you."

"It does, indeed. Well, so you are temporarily lodging at the Lévesques' town house!" Mr. Quimby abruptly changed the topic, his pale blue eyes twinkling both shrewdly and merrily. "How fortunate that Portman Square was rather nearer than Baker Street Saturday night, eh, Malcolm? So you are to enjoy at length the delightful company of the Comte and Comtesse de Valcoeur—and of their beautiful daughter, Mademoiselle Ariana…? You must be happy about that, even in the midst of your concern for your friend poor Mr. Ravener."

"To be honest, I'm of two minds about the matter, sir," Malcolm reluctantly confessed. "For unless I can locate the Heart of Kheperi and restore my family's fortune, if not their titles, what do I have to offer Mademoiselle Ariana? Why, at this point, I could not even bestow my true name upon her! So I am in great despair over all that. But still, aye, despite how it torments me, I am glad to be in her presence. We shared breakfast again together this morning."

"Well, personally, I urge you to make the most of your time there with her and her parents, Malcolm—for do you know? I have the strangest feeling there are mysterious forces at work—Fate, that peculiar fortune-teller Madame Polgár would no doubt insist—and that things are beginning to happen in regard to the lost emerald, even if we ourselves do not yet comprehend them. For Jakob tells me that he believes he is growing ever closer to discovering who fashioned your crucifix, as well as the second one that belonged to your uncle Charles, and Boniface is buried in ancient manuscripts at the London Library and elsewhere, hot on the trail—or so he claims—of the Sons of Isis, the order founded by your ancestor Lord Rob Roy Ramsay, the ninth Earl of Dúndragon."

"All that *is* good news!" Malcolm was much cheered by the information imparted to him by his employer. "Although I still believe that we are not naught save mere pawns of the gods, but that, instead, we can grab Destiny in our fists, and bend and shape it with our own Free Will."

"That's the spirit, Malcolm!" Mr. Quimby clapped his hands together briskly, his round face beaming. "Now, how are the intaglio plates for Mr. Pettigrew's maps coming?"

"Harry—I hope—has got started on them already this morning. So if you'll excuse me now, sir, I'll go upstairs and help him, or we'll never get them finished within the fortnight!"

"Silence! Silence!" Madame Polgár ordered sternly, her eyes closed and one hand upheld regally until the wildly babbling dwarf at last fell mute. "There. That's much better," she declared, slowly opening her eyes and lowering her hand. "For I simply cannot make heads or tails of what you are saying when you gibber away in that nonsensical fashion, Dukker! Now, where have you been? You've been gone since Friday evening— and I was beginning to think you had been taken up by the Watch or else were lying injured or even dead in some dark alley. No— do not start chattering like a magpie again, Dukker! Take deep breaths—and try to calm yourself. For I can tell from your jabbering that something of import has occurred, but I cannot determine what 'tis if you do not speak slowly and distinctly."

"*Oui...oui, madame.* I will try to talk more plainly. 'Twas like this. You will remember that after we had arrived in the carriage of Monsieur and Madame Alvaston at the masquerade ball of the Madame la Marquise de Mayfield last Friday night, you instructed me to wait for you in the mews at the rear of the town house?"

"I'm not an idiot, Dukker! Naturally I recall my directions to you—except that, clearly, you disobeyed them, for most provokingly, you were nowhere to be found when Monsieur and Madame Alvaston and I departed from the ball!"

"*Non, madame.* I apologize for not having followed your orders, but whilst I was frittering away my time in the loft of the mews, I observed from the window an incident in Madame la Marquise's gardens below, which struck me most forcibly. Le Vicomte Ugo appeared, and as he strolled through the gardens, smoking a cigar, I saw that he was being covertly followed by a second man. At first I thought 'twas Monsieur Blackfriars. But then later I realized that 'twas none other than his friend Monsieur Ravener. Unbeknown to both Messieurs Ugo and Ravener, they were being spied upon by yet a third person—Mademoiselle Ariana!"

"Indeed? *Oui,* this is all quite fascinating to me—for as you know, anything that concerns Monsieur Ugo and Mademoiselle Ariana interests me greatly. So, pray, continue, Dukker. What happened next?"

"Why, you will never guess, *madame!* Monsieur Ravener crept up on Monsieur Ugo and attacked him from behind—and Mademoiselle Ariana watched Monsieur Ravener all the while and never once cried out a warning to Monsieur Ugo! After a brief but violent struggle, Monsieur Ravener pushed Monsieur Ugo into the fishpond at the center of the gardens, then fled. As Monsieur Ugo—who was angry but not injured—attempted to extricate himself from the fishpond, Mademoiselle Ariana herself, instead of helping him, hurried back to the town house. Now, what do you think of all that?"

"I think you did quite well, indeed, to have observed the incident, Dukker."

"Thank you, *madame*" The dwarf beamed proudly at the fortune-teller's praise. "Now, to continue. At that point, I believed that 'twould be prudent of me to leave my post at the mews and to follow Monsieur Ravener. For of course, up until the moment of his assault upon Monsieur Ugo, it did not appear that he had any acquaintance at all with either him or Mademoiselle Ariana."

"How very quick-witted of you, Dukker! I only hope that this time, unlike the last occasion when you took matters into your own hands, your impulsive actions proved less hazardous and more successful!"

"*Oui, madame,* they most assuredly did. For fortunately—unlike that day in Oxford Street, when I accidentally shoved Mademoiselle Ariana far too hard, so she stumbled out into the street and fell down right in the path of that runaway horse and hansom cab—this time, everything went according to my intentions."

"Well, I am very glad to hear it—for I tell you, Dukker, my heart nearly stopped in my breast that day when you informed me of what had befallen poor Mademoiselle Ariana, since for one wholly hideous instant I was horrified that she was dead, that you had killed her! And as you know, that would have proved highly disastrous to all our plans!"

"*Oui, madame.* Anyway, as I said, I followed Monsieur Ravener—which is why I was not at my post when you departed from Madame la Marquise's town house last Friday evening, and also why I have been absent for the past few days."

"And what did you learn about this Monsieur Ravener? Is he a player or isn't he?"

"I'm afraid I do not yet know, *madame.* He is certainly a professional gambler, for after he made good his escape from Madame la Marquise's gardens, he went to the Cockerel Club, a gaming hell that is known for the high stakes that are wagered in its card and hazard rooms. He then returned to his lodgings at the George and Vulture public house. On Saturday he spent the entire day with Monsieur Blackfriars, target shooting at the Red House tavern in Battersea Fields, after which the two of them dined together at the Caledonian Hotel in Robert Street, then attended the plays at the Theatre Royal, Adelphi, in The Strand." The dwarf paused, gathering breath. Then he went on, "Now, here is the interesting part, *madame.* Once Messieurs Ravener and Blackfriars left the theater, they went to an oyster-house on Adelphi Street. When the hour grew late, Monsieur Blackfriars departed—except that I thought that 'twas Monsieur Ravener, for the two men had somehow got their cloaks confused in the oyster-house, and Monsieur Blackfriars was wearing Monsieur Ravener's coat. So I mistakenly followed Monsieur Blackfriars, thinking, of course, that 'twas Monsieur Ravener. But then, abruptly realizing the mix-up that had occurred, Monsieur Blackfriars turned and retraced his footsteps toward the oyster-house, and then what did I see? On the Adelphi Wharves, Monsieur Ravener was locked in mortal combat with two masked men! The upshot was that Monsieur Blackfriars immediately ran to Monsieur Ravener's assistance—and in the end, all four men wound up falling from the docks into the River Thames, one of the two masked men, I am almost certain, killed by a gunshot Monsieur Blackfriars fired at point-blank range from a small pistol he took from Monsieur Ravener's cloak!"

"Oh, good God, Dukker!" Madame Polgár cried, aghast. "Never tell me that both Messieurs Blackfriars and Ravener are dead, as well—that they drowned in the Thames!"

"Non, madame." The dwarf shook his head, emphasizing his words. "Fortunately, they are both still alive. However, Monsieur Ravener is in a very bad way, I fear, having been wounded by one of the two masked men—the one Monsieur Blackfriars did not shoot, for the pistol only fired one shot, you see. But what do you think, *madame?* Instead of taking Monsieur Ravener straight to hospital, Monsieur Blackfriars flagged down a hansom cab and directed it to carry both him and Monsieur Ravener to the town house of Monsieur le Comte and Madame la Comtesse de Valcoeur in Portman Square. For that is where they went—and there they are still!"

"Is that so? Oh, you have done well, Dukker…exceedingly well, indeed," the fortune-teller announced, nodding thoughtfully. "For all this information is quite valuable to me…*oui,* 'tis…for now I begin to see the hand that Fate has thrust so ironically into this affair." For a long moment, as she contemplated all she had learnt from the dwarf, Madame Polgár fell silent, drumming her fingers absently on the arms of her chair. Then she muttered to herself, "I wonder if they know…perhaps not, but surely, 'tis only a matter of time now…." After that, suddenly recalling herself to the present, she instructed, "If Monsieur Ravener is as ill as you say, Dukker, then there will be naught happening at Portman Square for the time being. Therefore, I want you to go instead to Berkeley Square, to the town house of Monsieur Ugo, and keep a close eye on him. 'Twas undoubtedly he who set those two masked men upon Messieurs Ravener and Blackfriars, and whilst they and the rest are but pawns in the dangerous game we play, Monsieur Ugo is our mortal enemy, and we must learn how much he already knows and what he is about!"

In the autumn days that passed with a flurry of falling leaves and drizzle, Ariana and Christine took turns nursing Mr. Ravener through his illness until at last, his fever broke and he began slowly but surely to recover. However, for quite some time, although he chafed at his confinement, he was still very weak and unable to leave his bed. So Malcolm continued to reside at the Lévesques' town house in Portman Square, and not only was there no suggestion made that he depart from it, but when his own good conscience finally compelled him to bring up the subject himself, he was informed quite decidedly by both Monsieur and Madame Valcoeur that they would not hear of it until his friend was wholly restored to his former good health.

"For I am quite sure that your presence here is a great comfort to Monsieur Ravener," the comtesse insisted firmly. "For now that he is on the mend, he longs to be up and about, and I fear he would prove even more unruly and determined to leave his bed before he is fully recovered were you not here to keep him company when you can, Monsieur Blackfriars. Further, if I am honest, I must confess I have my own selfish reasons for detaining you. I have always longed—that is to say…Ariana is…our only child. I had hoped to have other children, of course, but unfortunately, 'twas not to be. So despite the sad circumstances that brought about your and Monsieur Ravener's temporary residence here in Portman Square, still, it has done my heart immeasurable good to have you both here, and to have Christine, as well. You cannot even begin to know, Monsieur Blackfriars, how much enjoyment the sight of you four young people talking, reading, or playing cards together in the evenings at Monsieur Ravener's bedside has given me. Why, when I see you all together, such joy and peace swells within me that 'tis almost as though, somehow, all the wrongs of the world have been put right again. So, please, do not think of departing from us just yet—and further, when Monsieur Ravener is well enough that he can leave his bed to join us at the dining table, I would very much like to invite your mother here to supper, so I can meet her. For she has been the very soul of kindness and generosity to share you with us during this difficult time, and I would like to thank her for that."

"I know I speak for Mother herself when I say she would be deeply honored to make your acquaintance, Madame Valcoeur," Malcolm replied gravely, not knowing whether to laugh or to cry at the comtesse's words, which had overwhelmed him.

For of course, in the face of them, he could have no thought of leaving the Lévesques' town house at the moment, since to do so could only appear churlish, rude and ungrateful. Still, the idea of continuing to stay tormented him unbearably, for with each passing day he knew he was falling ever deeper in love with Ariana. Being ensconced at Portman Square had given him a rare opportunity that, under usual circumstances, most men would never have had—he had been able to live with the woman he desired above all others, without actually having yet wooed and won her as his bride. And residing in the same house with her on a daily basis had shown him more plainly than anything else could ever have done just exactly what kind of a wife she would make him—and Malcolm had seen that she would prove everything he had ever hoped for and dreamt of in his bride. She was beautiful, caring, generous and kind—yet with a surprising passion, willfulness and stubbornness that had let him know there was fire beneath the ice. She had utterly bewitched him with her highly expressive amethyst eyes, which could glow with tenderness and concern one minute and then sparkle with irrepressible gaiety and good humor the next.

Every evening when he returned from Quimby & Company

(Cartographers & Map Sellers) to the Lévesques' town house, he would listen intently for the tread of Ariana's light footsteps upon the grand staircase—never knowing how, with equal concentration, she herself would strain to hear the sound of the front door opening, which would signal his arrival—and when he would glance up from the reception hall to spy her descending the steps, he would inhale sharply, each time struck anew by the force of her sheer loveliness and desirability. At such times, Malcolm ached fiercely to claim her as his, and bitterly cursed his ancestor Lord Iain Ramsay, once the Earl of Dúndragon, who had so recklessly and uncaringly caused all of his descendants to be disenfranchised from what rightfully ought to have been their birthright and inheritance.

"Maman has just now told me that you are to remain with us at least a little while longer, Monsieur Blackfriars," Ariana said, interrupting Malcolm's reverie as she entered the small drawing room. "I am so very glad to hear it, for I fear that it would prove increasingly difficult to keep Monsieur Ravener abed, where he belongs, were you not here to help entertain him in the evenings. Like you, he frets about taking advantage of our hospitality—although I have assured him repeatedly that he is most welcome here—and he continues to worry about his lodgings at the George and Vulture, even though I have informed him that that was one of the first things Papa took care of the morning after the attack. For you know that Papa himself went to the public house to retrieve Monsieur Ravener's belongings and discharge the reckoning there, in addition to speaking to the authorities about both Dick Badgerton and Tobias Snitch, and their terrible assault upon you and Monsieur Ravener."

"Aye, I know." This last had, in fact, lifted a great burden from Malcolm's shoulders, for when Badger's body had finally been hauled by some passing lightermen from the River Thames, the subsequent inquest had returned a verdict of accidental drowning, for there was no hard proof that the shot Malcolm had fired was what had actually killed Badger. So Malcolm's only worries now were that he did not know what had become of Toby, nor what, if any, sum of money Monsieur Valcoeur had laid out to ensure a cursory investigation and quick closing of the case involving Badger, and when prodded for information about this last, the comte had merely shrugged and said the matter was of no importance. "But still, what you must understand, *mademoiselle*," Malcolm now went on to Ariana, "is that, like me, Mr. Ravener is very proud. Both of us are men accustomed to making our own way in the world and to paying our own bills, neither expecting nor accepting charity from anyone else."

"But under the circumstances, 'twas not charity at all, but a kindness to have taken Monsieur Ravener in that night—and to have continued to care for him ever since. For 'twas a miracle that he did not die, Dr. Whittaker has told us, and even though Monsieur Ravener is now out of danger, he is still very weak and regains his strength but slowly. So you must not either of you think that I or my parents perceive you as interlopers who seek to take advantage of us and our largesse, Monsieur Blackfriars. We know that is not the case at all, that both you and Monsieur Ravener are men of the world, with your own means, and that 'tis due only to the attack upon Monsieur Ravener that you are here at all—although both I and my parents have been only too happy to help, for no matter what, there is no way we can ever repay you for your having saved my life that day in Oxford Street. So you see, Monsieur Blackfriars, 'tis not you who are in our debt, but we who are in yours!"

"I give up, *mademoiselle*…really, I do!" Laughing, Malcolm raised his hands, as though he were surrendering to a hooligan. "Indeed, both Madame Valcoeur and you have importuned me so prettily that 'twould be exceedingly boorish of me to do anything else but stay."

"Good!" Ariana smiled, clapping her own hands together, her eyes dancing mischievously. "I confess I hoped that would prove the case! Do you think that was wicked of me?"

"Very! However, you are easily and quickly forgiven, for I know that you thought only of Mr. Ravener and keeping him abed until he recovers his former good health."

"*Oui,* there was that," Ariana agreed slowly, suddenly blushing, for the truth was that her concern for Mr. Ravener had been but a part of her reason for wishing Malcolm to remain at the town house. "But if I am honest with you, Monsieur Blackfriars, then I must admit that 'twas also for your own sake that I wished you would stay. For I…I do so enjoy your company!" she declared in a rush, flushing even more furiously.

"As I do yours, *mademoiselle,*" Malcolm rejoined softly, longing savagely in that moment to take her in his arms, to kiss her passionately and to ask her to marry him. "I wish…I wish things were…different between us."

As they had spoken, each had unconsciously moved nearer to the other, so that now they stood so close together that Ariana felt sure Malcolm could hear the wild hammering of her heart in her breast, the result of the boldness both of her own admission and of his response. In truth, she had so relatively little experience with men that she had not until this instant been certain he cared for her more than just as a friend. The knowledge that he did caused a multitude of tumultuous emotions to burgeon within her. Foremost among them were hope and despair—hope that he would talk to her of a future together, and despair that he would not. For his words had been most carefully and gentlemanly chosen, designed to acknowledge the feelings that lay between the two of them, while gently informing her that any relationship beyond friendship could not be pursued, that the gulf between them was too wide to bridge.

"As I told you once before, things can change, *monsieur,*" Ariana now observed quietly.

"Aye…we can always hope for that, *mademoiselle.* But in the event that they should not, I would not want to deceive you into believing that I care naught about the vast divide in our stations in life—because I do."

"I—I understand, and I thank you for your honesty, *monsieur.*" Forcing herself to blink back the sudden tears that brimmed in her compelling eyes and to smile brightly, however tremulously, she then asked abruptly, "Will you come now for our evening game of cards with Monsieur Ravener and Mademoiselle Christine?"

"Aye—although what good 'twill do, I'm sure I don't know! Mr. Ravener is such an expert that the rest of us scarcely stand a chance against him!"

To spare her any further distress, Malcolm pretended not to notice how her eyes glistened momentarily with unshed tears, although the sight wrenched him sorely, making him feel both guilty and ashamed that he had, however briefly and obliquely, given in to his desperate yearning to let her know how much he loved and desired her. Until now, while he had been certain of his own feelings for Ariana, he had not been sure of hers for him. But her tearful eyes and brave smile spoke to him more eloquently than even words would have done of the fact her heart, too, was at risk, as surely as his own; and despite everything, at the realization, Malcolm felt such a surge of joy, coupled with desolation, that he was beside himself with frustration at the situation.

"*Oui,* but since Monsieur Ravener is a professional gambler, 'tis only to be expected that he should prove superior at cards," Ariana pointed out logically as the two of them walked from the small drawing room toward the reception hall and its grand staircase. "So we need none of us feel any inadequacy on our own parts at the fact that we so very seldom prevail over him at whist or loo or piquet. I daresay that were the tables reversed, Monsieur Ravener would not do nearly as well at drawing a map or embroidering a handkerchief!"

"Aye, well, whilst I am willing to give him the benefit of the doubt when it comes to artistic skill—for Mr. Ravener is a man of many talents, I think—I do believe I can safely agree that fancy needlework is not numbered among his accomplishments!" Malcolm laughed again.

"What is so funny?" Christine cried from the top of the steps. "Do the two of you play cards this evening or not? For Mr. Ravener is most insistent that he shall no longer remain abed unless he is given yet another opportunity to fleece us all at loo!"

"Perhaps we shall fleece Monsieur Ravener, instead!" Ariana called up to her, smiling. "For Monsieur Blackfriars and I have just been plotting our strategy in that regard. So do you return now to Monsieur Ravener and advise him that he had best be on his guard—that 'tis only because he has been so ill that we have played so leniently with him before, permitting him to win. But now that he is better, there shall be no holds barred!"

Grinning, Christine disappeared into Mr. Ravener's bedchamber to relay this sally, knowing how provoked he would be at the thought that the three of them might have been allowing him to win at cards, because he had been so very sick. And indeed, she was quickly proved correct in her deduction.

"Let me win…?" Mr. Ravener scoffed from where he sat propped up amid all the pillows on the bed. "Why, the very idea! Despite my having been bound to this bed—wholly against my own will, I might add, threatened with dire consequences by you and everyone else in this household should I attempt to rise from it—I assure you that my skill at cards has scarcely been affected by my current condition, Lady Christine! I have won fair and square—and so I shall prove by winning again this evening! Now, do Mr. Blackfriars and Lady Ariana join us or not?"

"We do indeed, Nicolas," Malcolm said as he followed Ariana into the bedroom. "And may I say how glad I am to see you in such high spirits! You are much improved in health these past few days."

"I am well enough to have left this bed, I tell you, and I simply cannot continue to lie here, idling my time away, recuperating. For one thing, I have…urgent business affairs to attend to," Mr. Ravener insisted.

"Indeed? And would those have anything to do with Viscount Ugo, Nicolas?" Malcolm inquired with studious casualness as he began to draw the small card table up against the bed and to set three chairs around it for himself, Ariana and Christine.

"Viscount Ugo…?" Mr. Ravener asked, after a long minute. With seeming uninterest in the topic, he reached for the deck of cards that lay upon the night table next to him and began to shuffle it expertly. "I'm afraid I am not acquainted with him and therefore cannot imagine why you should think I would have any pressing business with him, Malcolm."

"Can you not? Well, then, perhaps I was mistaken." Malcolm shrugged lightly, as though the matter were of no real importance. Then he assisted each woman into her chair before assuming his own seat at the card table. "'Tis merely that whilst you lay ill and delirious with fever, I heard a rather…peculiar tale about a…slight altercation having taken place between you and Lord Ugo at the Marchioness of Mayfield's masquerade ball…something to do with a fishpond, as I recall." He raised one devilish eyebrow inquisitively.

"From whom did you hear such an account?" Mr. Ravener queried slowly.

"'Twas I who told Monsieur Blackfriars," Ariana interjected before Malcolm could answer, and ignoring the fact that her mother had not wished her to become involved in the affair. "For I was in the gardens that night when you pushed Monsieur Ugo into the fishpond! So I witnessed your assault upon him!"

"I see." A muscle twitched visibly in Mr. Ravener's jaw. Then he announced, "I ought never to have introduced myself to you. However, once I realized you were Malcolm's friend, it appeared that I could hardly do otherwise. You're right, *mademoiselle*. 'Twas indeed I in the gardens with Lord Ugo that evening. I had hoped to avoid having to explain the—what must seem to you all at the moment—rather cowardly event, so that is why I initially disclaimed any acquaintance with him. Besides, 'twas true what I told you. He and I have never been formally introduced, so I don't actually know him."

"Then why on earth did you attack him—and from behind, no less!—then shove him into the fishpond, Nicolas?" Malcolm demanded.

"My reasons are my own, and for the time being, Malcolm, I'm afraid I can tell you nothing more than that—except, of course, that they are excellent ones and that I did not at the time intend Lord Ugo any real injury. I could have killed him, you know. So, surely, the fact that I merely dunked him in the fish-pond demonstrates my lack of malevolence toward him!"

"To the contrary, the manner in which Mademoiselle Ariana described the incident made me believe that you hold Lord Ugo in such extraordinary contempt that you felt he was beneath your slaying him!"

"Yes, well, that may be. However, the fact remains that I did him no real harm—other than to his pride and dignity, of course. Therefore, you must acquit me of having any evil designs against him."

"Let us agree instead that I shall reserve judgment one way or another until I know more about the matter," Malcolm stated gravely. "Now, do you intend to deal the cards—or only shuffle them all night?"

The cards were dealt for loo, and as the play commenced, no more was said about either Viscount Ugo or the incident that had occurred in the gardens at the rear of the marchioness's town house the night of the masquerade ball. Still, unbeknown to the others, each of the four of them seated at the card table remained preoccupied by the matter, and as a result, the game failed to engage their attention in the way that it usually did. After a while, as though even he could not bring himself to concentrate on the play, Mr. Ravener pleaded fatigue and, after a moment, graciously accepted Christine's offer to read aloud to him until he fell asleep. Taking the hint, Malcolm and Ariana departed from the bedchamber, retiring to the music room, where she played the pianoforte and Malcolm, seated beside her on the bench, turned the pages of the sheet music for her. In this manner they passed the rest of the evening together, until at last, reluctantly, they bade each other good-night.

When Mr. Ravener was finally well enough to leave his bed and join the Lévesques at the dining-room table, Madame Valcoeur kept her promise to Malcolm and invited Mrs. Blackfriars to supper. At the time, little did the comtesse dream how this would throw everyone—including herself—into a quandary of the highest proportions, casting the Blackfriars household and her own into such a frenzy of activity that one would have thought both the Lévesques and the Blackfriarses were about to hobnob with royalty. At the Lévesque town house in Portman Square, all the housemaids were set diligently to washing windows and sweeping hearths, to dusting furniture and mopping floors, while in the kitchen, the cook, Monsieur Montségur, labored furiously to prepare an array of fancy dishes. Hawthorn Cottage, in Cochrane Street, was equally as busy as a beehive as Miss Woodbridge and Nora were put to the unaccustomed task of refurbishing Mrs. Blackfriars's best gown, adding new trim and mending the hem, then cleaning and pressing the frock, in preparation for their mistress's coming social engagement.

"Oh, isn't it exciting, ma'am?" Nora gushed to Mrs. Blackfriars as they worked on the dress.

"Yes." Mrs. Blackfriars nodded, smiling. "I confess I feel just like a young lass again, about to attend my first ball!"

In truth, she was not only nervous about going into society again, but also intensely curious about the Lévesques—particularly about Ariana. Over the years since Mrs. Blackfriars and Malcolm had moved to London, there had been more than one young woman whom he had brought home to Hawthorn Cottage for her to meet. But in the end, his heart had not proved deeply engaged by any of them, and so, much to her despair, he had never wed. Eventually she had grown to think that perhaps he felt he labored so hard and such long hours at the map shop that he could not fully devote himself to a wife and marriage. Now, however, she sensed that Ariana had changed all that, that Malcolm had fallen desperately in love with the young lady. But given the vast difference in their stations in life, how he hoped to win Ariana's hand and heart, Mrs. Blackfriars did not know. Still, she herself secretly believed that Monsieur and Madame Valcoeur did not find him completely objectionable as a prospective suitor for their daughter, or otherwise, they surely would not have invited her, his mother, to dinner. After all, they need not have issued the invitation. So the fact that they had done so would seem to indicate their approval of Malcolm, and this was a puzzle to Mrs. Blackfriars.

So it was that as the evening of the forthcoming affair at the Lévesques' town house in Portman Square inexorably approached, her excitement, nervousness, expectation and curiosity only increased, until she felt as though she did not know whether she were coming or going. When she examined her best gown, she thought that perhaps it was not fine enough for the grand occasion and that she should have arranged for a new one, even though there had been no time to do so, and the frock she intended to wear was only a few months old, besides. Upon learning that Monsieur and Madame Valcoeur would dispatch their own carriage for her, Mrs. Blackfriars grew even more flustered, for she had never envisioned such an honor and courtesy being paid her; and the night of the dinner, when the Lévesques' coach at last arrived to call for her and Malcolm, for a moment, as she stood at the gate of Hawthorn Cottage, preparing to enter the vehicle, she could only stare at it, awestruck by its magnificence and that of the four matching grays harnessed to it.

Mrs. Blackfriars knew that had her husband, Alexander Ramsay, lived and proved able to reclaim his family's legacy, her own lifestyle would have been equally as luxurious as that of which she was now provided a first glimpse. Yet what she felt in that instant was neither bitterness nor regret over what had been denied her—for despite their modest means, she and her husband had been inordinately happy together—but, rather, anguish for their son and only child, that perhaps his own hopes for happiness would be forever dashed because he possessed neither a title nor a fortune with which to tempt Ariana.

"Mother…?"

The sound of Malcolm's voice abruptly jolted Mrs. Blackfriars from her reverie, and she became aware of the fact that one of the footmen had disembarked from his post at the rear of the equipage to open the door and let down the steps for her. Flushing slightly with embarrassment at the idea that she had stood there gaping like a schoolgirl, she quickly ascended into the carriage and settled herself amid the plush red-velvet squabs within. Malcolm climbed in to sit beside her, then the footman shut the door and resumed his position at the back of the coach. The driver clucked to the team, and with a small lurch the vehicle rolled forward, heading from St. John's Wood toward Marylebone.

Inside the equipage, Mrs. Blackfriars and Malcolm spoke but little, preoccupied with their own thoughts and gazing out the brumous windows trickling with rain. With the advent of evening, the street lamps had been lit, and they glowed hazily along the streets, illuminating the fronts of shops and houses alike. Mrs. Blackfriars studied the passing scenes with interest, for since she had come to trust and have confidence in her household staff, it was seldom that she went into the city anymore, or even beyond the confines of St. John's Wood, and although she had not expected that time had stopped, still, she was vaguely startled by all the changes she observed. Until now, she had not realized how far progress had traveled in little more than a decade, and she resolved that she must get out more.

As the carriage drew nearer to Portman Square, the houses grew increasingly grander, so that she not only admired them, but also felt more than a little daunted by them. There was a great deal to be said, after all, she thought, for the cheerful coziness of a Whitrose Grange or a Hawthorn Cottage, and so, although the large, imposing houses impressed her, she felt no envy of their owners. Still, as the coach turned from Gloucester Place into Portman Square, she could not repress a small exclamation of delight at the sight of the large oval park at the heart of the square, for although autumn now sped toward winter, and many of the deciduous trees had lost their leaves and stood naked in the moonlight and lamplight, she could still see what a pleasant place it would be to walk in when the weather permitted.

Finally, after halfway circling the park, the vehicle came to a halt before one of the biggest town houses in the square, and Mrs. Blackfriars knew that this must be the home of the Lévesques.

"Oh, how lovely 'tis!" she remarked as she descended from the equipage.

"Aye." Beneath the umbrellas held over them by the footmen to protect them from the drizzle, Malcolm nodded. "'Tis one of the most beautiful houses fronting the square, I think."

He rang the front bell, and presently the butler, Butterworth, opened the door to admit them. After greeting them politely, he ushered them through the opulent reception hall to the elegant small drawing room beyond, announcing them, then closing the French doors behind him as he exited the chamber. For an instant, Mrs. Blackfriars and her son stood poised on the threshold of the room, gazing at the multitude of faces within, which had turned to look with interest at them. Then, before anyone could speak, as her suddenly startled, stricken eyes alighted on one particular countenance amid the crowd, Mrs. Blackfriars's own visage turned ashen.

"Katherine!" she cried with both joy and incredulity.

Then the small drawing room seemed slowly to spin about her before a merciful blackness swirled up to engulf her, so that she knew nothing more.

Chapter Fourteen

Family

Oh let us love our occupations,
Bless the squire and his relations,
Live upon our daily rations,
And always know our proper stations.

> —Charles Dickens
> *The Chimes [1844]*

Happy families are all alike;
every unhappy family is unhappy in its own way.
> —Leo Nikolaevich Tolstoi
> *Anna Karenina [1875-1877]*

Then felt I like some watcher of the skies
When a new planet swims into his ken;
Or like stout Cortez when with eagle eyes
He stared at the Pacific—and all his men
Looked at each other with a wild surmise—
Silent, upon a peak in Darien.

> —John Keats
> *On First Looking into Chapman's Homer [1816]*

1848
Portman Square, London, England

Fortuitously, as Mrs. Blackfriars sank into a swoon, Malcolm had the presence of mind to catch her. Sweeping her up, he carried her to the sofa and laid her down gently, while Ariana, observing that her mother was in no position to do so, quickly ordered several of the housemaids and footmen present to bring smelling salts, a washcloth and a basin of water, and to instruct the cook, Monsieur Montségur, to hold dinner back at least half an hour. Then she ran to Malcolm's side to assist him with his mother, leaving her own mother to her father. For when Mrs. Blackfriars had fainted, Madame Valcoeur, her own face abruptly blanching, had also cried out softly, slumping in her wing chair, and there she still sat, murmuring to herself and clearly in a state of shock and high agitation. Torn between his duties as both host and husband, Monsieur Valcoeur now hovered over his wife, gently chafing her hands and speaking to her soothingly, interspersing his comments to her with expressions of concern to Malcolm and Ariana for Mrs. Blackfriars. The Lady Christine, seeing everyone thus occupied, moved swiftly to direct other housemaids and footmen to pour glasses of brandy, ratafia and sherry, and to pass them around, while, from his own wing chair before the fire, as though he were a predatory hawk stalking some prey, Mr. Ravener watched the entire tableau silently and thoughtfully.

At last the application of a vinaigrette beneath her nose brought Mrs. Blackfriars back to consciousness, and her eyelids fluttered open. For a moment, her eyes were filled with confusion, and it was obvious that she did not know where she was.

"Are you all right, Mother?" Malcolm asked, his dark visage expressing his anxiety for her as he assisted her into a sitting position on the couch.

"Yes…yes." Mrs. Blackfriars moaned gently, one hand pressed to her brow to keep in place the cold wet washcloth he had earlier laid there. "I'm—I'm fine…'twas just such a—such a…shock to me to see Katherine standing there…no…no, not Katherine," she corrected herself now, staring as though mesmerized at Ariana. "I see that now, for she was my age—and you, *mademoiselle,* are not yet twenty, I'll wager. Yet you look so very like her that I can scarcely believe it! How can that be…? I—I don't understand…."

Much to the surprise of everyone present, it was Mr. Ravener who answered, first brazenly dismissing all the servants, then solemnly swearing Christine to secrecy.

"Now, Mrs. Blackfriars, pray forgive me for being so seemingly mysterious and clearly bold, but may I inquire as to whether or not you speak of Katherine de Ramezay? Please," he continued when she was plainly hesitant to reply, "you need have no fear of telling me the truth—for if 'tis indeed her of whom you speak, then I would have you know that she was my mother and, further, that I have since beginning to recover my health suspected that the young lady whom Malcolm and I know as Mademoiselle Ariana Lévesque is, in reality, my long-lost sister, Ariana de Ramezay! Now it only remains for me to discover whether you are our aunt Elizabeth Ramsay and your son, Malcolm, our cousin—although I'll admit I already feel certain of that!"

"Oh, *mon Dieu!*" the comtesse suddenly cried, shaking her head and one hand flying to her mouth. Then, astounding everyone with her bombshell, she asserted, "'Tis so, in truth—and I knew it! I knew it! Oh, *ma chère* Elizabeth—how I hope I may call you that!—please do not be afraid, for you are among friends here, I promise you! For my own husband, Jean-Paul, is Charles de Ramezay's cousin. That is how we came to have Ariana, you see. We are her godparents."

"Maman…now 'tis I who don't understand…. What are you and Monsieur Ravener saying?" Ariana's lovely, earnest countenance was filled with utter bewilderment and dismay. "I am Ariana Lévesque—not de Ramezay so how I can be this woman to whom Monsieur Ravener refers? How can I be his sister—and Monsieur Blackfriars our cousin?"

"That is a very long story, *chérie,*" Madame Valcoeur said, sighing heavily, "and, I confess, 'tis more than past time that you were told it, I fear—only, I was so afraid for you, Ariana, and what might become of you if ever you learnt the truth, that I persuaded your papa that we should keep silent to protect you. But now we must speak of all—and tell you how you came to us thirteen long years ago. But first, Jean-Paul—" she turned to her husband "—please instruct Fanny to inform Monsieur Mont-ségur that he should not serve supper until nine o'clock, as even half-past eight will be too early now, I think."

As, at the doors of the small drawing room, the comte gave instructions to the housemaid he had summoned, the comtesse herself paused for a long moment, gathering breath. Then, once her husband had finished his dialogue and closed the drawing-room doors again, she went on, addressing her daughter.

"You are indeed Ariana de Ramezay, *ma petite,* for your real parents were Charles and Katherine de Ramezay, le Comte and la Comtesse de Jourdain, and as I have said, Charles was Jean-Paul's cousin, Charles's father and Jean-Paul's mother having been brother and sister. What happened was this, Ariana. When your own brother, Nicolas, was twelve years old and you were but five, your parents decided to travel to Scotland, to the High-lands, where they had learnt that Alexander and Elizabeth Ramsay were lodged at a place called Whitrose Grange, overlooking Loch Ness."

Here Ariana gasped, stunned.

"Then my dream…my nightmare…'tis not just my imagina-tion, as you always insisted to me, Maman, but a real memory!" she accused.

"*Oui,* I believe so—although since I do not know for certain, that will be something for Elizabeth and Malcolm to address. In fact—" she now addressed the two of them "—perhaps you will be good enough to continue the tale from this point."

So Mrs. Blackfriars and Malcolm, now recovering from their astonishment and confirming their own true identities, explained all that had occurred at Whitrose Grange—how Malcolm's father, Alexander Ramsay, and Nicolas and Ariana's father, Charles de Ramezay, had been sneaking across Loch Ness to Castle Dún-dragon, in search of the Heart of Kheperi; how their real identi-ties must have been discovered and they themselves murdered by Lord Vittore, Count Foscarelli; how the Grange had caught fire and burnt that same night; and how Malcolm and the rest had fled.

"But what happened to Katherine and her two children after

we left them at the George inn that day in Newcastle-upon-Tyne, I never until this moment knew," Mrs. Blackfriars declared softly, her eyes brimming with tears. "I wrote to her—many times—at a secret address we had arranged between us. But when I never heard from her again, I feared she must be dead."

"Yes, I'm afraid she is—and has been for these past thirteen years now, Aunt Elizabeth," Nicolas confirmed gently. "She took ill on the voyage home to France, as did I...some fever that swept the ship, so that by the time we arrived at Calais, many aboard were extremely sick. Maman was afraid we would both die and that there would be no one left to care for Ariana, who had been spared the illness. So Maman wrote a letter to Monsieur and Madame Valcoeur, and she paid a family who had been on board the ship, and was then traveling overland in the direction of Valcoeur, to deliver both the missive and Ariana to them. In the meanwhile, Maman and I found lodgings in a cheap public house in Calais, not far from the docks." He shrugged lightly, dismissively. "'Twas not much of a place, I fear, for because we were both of us so very clearly feverish, there were not many who would open their doors to us. Since I was not, however, as sick as Maman, after getting her settled in a room I dragged myself through the streets, in search of a physician. But even after he had agreed to come, there was little he could do to save her. Some days later, she died."

"Oh, Nicolas, I am so very sorry!" Mrs. Blackfriars began quietly to weep.

"As am I," the comtesse declared tremulously, her own eyes spilling over with tears. "For upon Ariana's arrival at Valcoeur, Jean-Paul left at once for Calais. But by then, you and Katherine were nowhere to be found. 'Twas as though the earth had swallowed you both up, and since we knew from Katherine's note to us that she and you were terribly ill, we believed that the fever had claimed both your lives. Until that night when Malcolm brought you here, injured, to Portman Square, we never knew that you had survived, Nicolas. But that evening when I spied you standing with Malcolm on our doorstep, I saw that you were the spitting image of Charles at that age, and since from many things Ariana had previously told me, I had already begun to suspect Malcolm's own true identity, I hoped and prayed that you *were* our own long-lost Nicolas—and now, thanks be to *le bon Dieu,* you are! So, please, tell us how you lived, how you came here to England and how you managed to locate Malcolm."

"How did I live? Like any other street urchin, I'm afraid," Nicolas said carelessly, not wishing to distress his relatives. "You must have some idea what port cities are like. After Maman breathed her last, some of the other people who were staying in the room—for the tavern was one of those places that rented beds and even space upon the floor for a few centimes a night— helped me to bury her. She had to be interred in a potter's field, of course, for by then we had precious little money remaining, and naturally, with Maman dead and myself underage, I had no means of accessing any of Papa's bank accounts. It has been one of the greatest ironies of my life—knowing that all of Papa's money has just been sitting idle in banks, whilst I have been forced to scratch and scrape for a living! And I did—for of course, after what had happened to Papa and Uncle Alexander, and all that Maman had told me about our family legacy before she died, I trusted nobody and was terrified to tell anyone my real name. Since de Ramezay and Ramsay both mean 'from the Raven's Isle,' I changed my surname to Ravener and, to avoid detection by our enemies, passed myself off as an English lad who had been pressed into service on a merchant vessel and, to escape, had jumped ship at Calais." He fell silent for a long moment, remembering. Then he continued.

"Of course, because Maman had been born and bred in Scotland, I had spoken English, as well as French, fluently from the cradle, so there was no difficulty with my posing as an English lad, and the fact that others thought me such and did not know I spoke French as well as they frequently worked to my advantage, besides. So somehow I managed to survive and, eventually, by becoming a professional gambler, even prospered. But over the years I never forgot what had occurred at Whitrose Grange or the story Maman had related to me about our family history and the Heart of Kheperi, and so, when I had finally grown to manhood and had sufficient funds, I left France and came here to England, to London. Originally, 'twas my intention to journey on from England to Scotland and the Highlands. But then something totally unexpected took place. I started into Quimby and Company to purchase a map of the city—and through the front shop windows I recognized Malcolm behind the counter. Being sixteen and thus almost grown at the time of our fathers' murders, he had not changed nearly as much as I, which is why, I presume, he did not also know me when first we met.

"Still, I did not immediately present myself to him. One's memory sometimes plays tricks on one, and I wanted to be sure about his identity, especially after I discovered that he was calling himself Malcolm Blackfriars. So instead, I followed him and learnt everything I could about him. When I saw Aunt Elizabeth at Hawthorn Cottage, I was certain I was right about the two of them. Unfortunately, however, the evening on which I had intended to reveal my own true identity to Malcolm was the night he was, I believe, first set upon by the two dastardly men who also later attacked me—the thieves Tobias Snitch and Dick 'Badger' Badgerton."

"Malcolm!" As she stared at her son, Mrs. Blackfriars's gentle face expressed her shock and distress at this information. "You said nothing of this to me!"

"No, at the time I didn't want to worry you, Mother. But presently you shall know all, I promise you. Now, pray continue, Nicolas."

"Well, you see how 'twas. I did not wish to tell you the truth about myself in front of either the constable who had arrived on the scene or your employer, Mr. Quimby, who had taken us all into his town house, following the assault upon you, in which I had intervened. So I was compelled to introduce myself to you as Nicolas Ravener instead, and then afterward, I decided that perhaps 'twas best to maintain the charade a little while longer—

at least until I could learn who had set upon you and why. After all, 'twas always possible that if I had found you, our adversaries had, too, and in such a situation, I could have been of a great deal more use to you did they not connect me with you beyond a chance friendship."

"Aye, I see." Malcolm nodded, reflecting. "In your place, I would probably have done the same thing—and at least now I comprehend your actions toward Viscount Ugo, why you did not simply slay him outright that night in the Marchioness of Mayfield's gardens. You must believe he possesses a crucifix—that is why you tore open his domino to claw at his throat—which means that there are indeed more than two crosses, as Mr. Quimby surmised."

"Mr. Quimby! Oh, Malcolm, have you told him our story, then?" Mrs. Blackfriars asked, horrified.

"Aye, Mother, I have."

"But you promised me to keep silent and do nothing—"

"To the contrary, Mother, if you will remember correctly, I made no promise of the kind, and thank God I didn't! For otherwise, we would surely have little or no hope at all of reclaiming our family's lost legacy!"

"Well, you must all be aware that I am…wholly stunned and confused by this entire tale." Ariana's countenance was pale, and her eyes were troubled and perplexed. "So at this point, I have no idea what you are talking about. What does a crucifix have to do with recovering the missing emerald, the Heart of Kheperi?"

"Unfortunately, I do not yet know exactly," Malcolm answered. "However, I will try to explain." Reaching beneath his shirt, he drew forth his own cross, which he wore around his neck, and showed it to Ariana. "Once I had given Mr. Quimby the chronicle of our family's history, he suggested that we take this crucifix to a friend of his, a jeweler named Jakob Rosenkranz, who has a shop in Hatton Green." Amid the others' cries of amazement at hearing the account, Malcolm then went on to detail Mr. Rosenkranz's own narrative about his ancestor Ezekial Rosenkranz, who had owned the pawn shop in Birchin Lane, which had been visited by Westerfield, the valet of Lord Iain Ramsay, once the Earl of Dúndragon. "So you see, we know that this cross is Number One and that there is at least one other, which belonged to Uncle Charles, and which I presume is Number Two. Do you have that one, Nicolas?"

"No." Mr. Ravener shook his head. "Maman hung it around Ariana's neck before sending her to Monsieur and Madame Valcoeur."

"But I have no such crucifix," Ariana insisted.

"*Mais, oui, chérie,* you do," the comtesse stated. "Jean-Paul has it under lock and key in a secret compartment in the desk in his study, for we knew from Katherine's letter to us that 'twas of the utmost importance and that we must guard it with our very lives."

"I will go and fetch it now." So saying, the comte left the small drawing room to enter his study, returning a few minutes later with the intricate silver cross, as well as an ornate magnifying glass. "You will have to do the honors, Malcolm," he declared, handing both the objects to him, "for I fear my eyesight is not what it used to be."

Drawing near the lamplight, Malcolm carefully examined the crucifix with the aid of the magnifying glass.

"Aye." His voice rose with excitement. "This is indeed cross Number Two! See how the Roman numeral two is woven into the dogwood and thorns there." He pointed this out to Ariana as she bent close to him to inspect the crucifix.

"*Oui...oui,* so I see."

"Now I must have a look at the back." Turning the cross over and once more peering at it through the magnifying glass, Malcolm read aloud, "'Wisdom 19:1-2.'" Glancing up, he inquired, "Do you have a Bible at hand, Madame Valcoeur?"

"*Certainement.* But please, won't you and Nicolas both call me Aunt Hélène? I know I am, in reality, some sort of cousin by marriage to the two of you, but Aunt Hélène would be so much easier, I think."

"I would be honored, *madame*...that is, Aunt Hélène." Malcolm smiled warmly at her.

"And I, as well, Aunt Hélène," Mr. Ravener said, also smiling, however wanly, for he was not yet as fully restored to his former good health as he would have wished, and coming downstairs for the first time this evening had tired him far more than, at the moment, he was willing to admit.

"Good." Then, taking up the family Bible from a nearby table, the comtesse paged through it, finally finding the chapter and verse she sought. "'But the godless were assailed by merciless anger to the very end, for God knew beforehand what they would do; how, after letting His people leave and hastening their departure, they would change their minds and set out in pursuit,'" she quoted aloud.

"Which, unfortunately, doesn't seem to be of any more help in locating the Heart of Kheperi than the chapter and verse from Revelation, which is inscribed on the back of my own crucifix." Malcolm sighed heavily. "So let us leave that puzzle for the moment. For I would very much like to know from you, Nicolas, why you suspected that there were more than two crosses and why you believed that Viscount Ugo might have one."

"Ah, well, there are several reasons for that—the first being that I never forgot Papa's own crucifix, which Maman had given to Ariana for safekeeping. At the time, Maman said that it ought to have come to me after Papa's death, but that she and I were both so ill that she could not take the risk that the cross would be forever lost, and therefore Ariana must have it instead. The problem with that—and my own inability not only to retrieve it, but also to present myself to Monsieur and Madame Valcoeur when I had recovered from the fever that took Maman's own life—was that following her penning of the missive that accompanied my sister, Maman fell into a delirium, so 'twas often difficult to make heads or tails of what she was trying to tell me. So until the very night of the Marchioness of Mayfield's masquerade ball—which, obviously, I attended uninvited after Malcolm had told me everyone who was anyone in London would be present—and my chance meeting with Ariana there, during which, like Aunt Elizabeth, I was immediately struck by her resemblance to Maman, I did not actually know where or to whom my little sister had been sent."

"Oh, *mon cher* lad, if only you *had* known," Madame Valcoeur murmured, shaking her head sadly. "For we would have opened our doors and our hearts to you, just as we did Ariana— for as your poor *maman* knew, although I longed for children, I could not have any of my own. And of course, you would not recollect your own christening, at which Jean-Paul and I stood proudly as your godparents, or—your being only seven years old at the time—even Ariana's own christening, where we were again so honored. So I am not surprised that you did not remember us."

"That is not precisely true, Aunt Hélène," Mr. Ravener averred, "for I *did* vaguely recall my having an uncle Jean-Paul and an aunt Hélène— and when Malcolm brought me here and I saw the two of you, I recognized you both at once, although I was too ill from my wound and loss of blood to take up the matter then. But being only a child when last I'd seen you and having known you only as Uncle Jean-Paul and Aunt Hélène, what I could not remember was your surname or your titles. So I had little or no means of trying to trace you. You could have lived anywhere in France, and even in Paris you would have been known by your titles, rather than your Christian names. But even so, I did eventually make my way to Paris to attempt to track you down, and although I was unsuccessful, I did not count the journey a total loss—for 'twas there that, in a high-stakes game of piquet, I acquired a crucifix that I judged to be a duplicate of Papa's own."

"No!" Malcolm's face evidenced his incredulity and excitement at this report. "But…where is this cross now, Nicolas? 'Twas not found upon your person the night I brought you here, injured."

"No, 'twas not. For 'twas—and still is, I devoutly hope!— concealed beneath the floorboards of my former apartment at the George and Vulture public house." Mr. Ravener's voice was wry. "Which is precisely why I was so violently opposed to being taken to hospital or otherwise removed from my lodgings!"

"Oh, *sacrébleu!*" Monsieur Valcoeur expostulated. "Malcolm and I must go and fetch it as soon as possible!"

"Yes." Mr. Ravener nodded gravely. "For as much as it pains me to confess it, I am still not well enough to do so myself—and although I'm quite sure Viscount Ugo has no idea who attacked him that night in the marchioness's gardens, he will certainly not have been idle in trying to learn my identity and then perhaps surmising that I was after any crucifix he might have, as well as growing suspicious that I might also possess one myself. And in that case, he might also—as I myself did—take an interest in the George and Vulture. Having heard from Maman a disjointed tale about Lord Iain Ramsay, once the Earl of Dúndragon and a member of the so-called Hellfire Club, and not knowing whether he had ever possessed a cross and, if so, if 'twere the same one that had belonged to Uncle Alexander, I had some vague notion that Lord Dúndragon, if he had indeed ever owned a crucifix, might, for safekeeping, have concealed it at the George and Vulture prior to his infamous duel with Lord Bruno, then Count Foscarelli. Many of the Hellfire Club members had lodged at the tavern when in London, I had learnt from casual inquiries here and there. So that is why I originally took rooms there. I know that the inn's proprietor thought me quite difficult and querulous, for I was constantly complaining and requesting to change to a new apartment, until I had searched them all most carefully—to no avail, however. But Lord Ugo, should he himself undertake such an exploration, would not come up equally empty-handed, since I have secreted my own cross there. The fellow from whom I won it, by the way, seemed to know nothing about it and thus to think 'twas of no importance. He was in his cups at the time of our game and mumbled something about having had it from a dying friend who'd had no heirs and who had told him 'twas quite valuable. But he'd since taken it to a jeweler and learnt 'twas worth no more than the silver and workmanship—or so he mistakenly believed."

"But of course," Malcolm mused aloud, "such an event as that is only to be expected—given the fact that Mr. Quimby believes there are actually nine crucifixes."

"Nine!" Ariana exclaimed.

"Aye, a ninefold key, as 'twere—for after we'd seen Mr. Rosenkranz, we then shared the entire tale with his and Mr. Quimby's friend Boniface Cavendish, who owns a bookshop in Old Bond Street."

"Oh, Malcolm!" Mrs. Blackfriars chided, much distressed by this news. "Why, 'tis a wonder the whole of London doesn't know our true identities and family's history by now! Oh, Son, what have you done? I warned you how extremely dangerous our foes, the Foscarellis, are! How they will stop at nothing—not even murder!—in their quest to find the lost emerald, the Heart of Kheperi!"

"Aye, well, that may be, Mother, I do not deny it. However, I assure you that Messieurs Quimby, Rosenkranz and Cavendish are all most trustworthy gentlemen, who have given me their word of honor to respect my confidences and who may thus be safely entrusted with our secrets. Indeed, 'twas Mr. Cavendish who uncovered the fact that after Lord James Ramsay, the eighth Earl of Dúndragon—who stole the accursed emerald from the high priest's tomb to begin with—was tragically killed in a hunting accident by his own son, that same son, Lord Rob Roy Ramsay, the ninth Earl of Dúndragon, inherited the Heart of Kheperi. Understandably grief stricken over having, however unintentionally, caused the death of his own father, he turned to spiritualism and founded a pseudomonastic order called the Sons of Isis—"

"The Sons of Isis!" Ariana gasped out, stunned. "Oh, *mon Dieu!* I—I think that must be what Madame Polgár was speaking of that evening when she read the tarot cards for me and told my fortune!"

"Why? What did she say?" Malcolm leaned forward eagerly in his seat upon the sofa. "For Mr. Quimby and I have been highly interested in learning whatever we can about her ever since that night of Aunt Hélène's conversation party, when Madame Polgár expressed such a fascination with Mr. al-Walid's account of the Heart of Kheperi."

"Well, 'twas shortly before we left Paris...Maman—oh, I hope I may still call you that!" Ariana glanced hesitantly at the comtesse.

"I would be so very proud and honored if you did, *ma petite*." Sudden tears of joy mingled with sadness brimmed in Madame Valcoeur's eyes. "For although, as you now know, I am not your true mother, you—unlike Nicolas—were so very young when she died that I am still the only *maman* you have ever really known."

"*Oui,* that is so. For although ever since learning all this tonight, I have tried hard to recall both my real parents, I am afraid their images elude me—that they are but vague impressions and shadows in my mind—and I did not guess that Monsieur Ravener...Nicolas...was my brother, either, although I am glad 'tis so." She smiled at Mr. Ravener.

"As am I." He smiled back at her gently.

"Anyway, to continue, 'twas the evening of Maman's own masquerade ball, at which it had been arranged to have Madame Polgár present to entertain our guests by predicting their futures, that she said something to me about the Sons of Isis—or at least, now I think that must be what Madame Polgár meant. I was one of the last to enter her pavilion, and 'twas all very strange and cryptic. But I do recall that she told me I was going on a fateful journey, across both sea and land, to the dragon's lair— Oh, I've just this moment realized that must be Castle Dúndragon! For that day on the lake, Collie, you said that Dúndragon translated as 'Fortress of the Dragon.' Remember?"

"Aye, I do." A smile tugged at the corners of Malcolm's mouth. "No one has called me by my childhood diminutive of Collie for years, Ana. Even now I find it difficult to believe that you are that same brave, bonnie wee lass who went fishing with me that day in the *Sea Witch*."

At his words, Ariana blushed deeply, for she had not until now recognized that she had employed the nickname.

"I'm sorry...Malcolm."

"No, 'tis quite all right. Collie will do."

"As will Ana."

"Good. Now, about the Sons of Isis…?"

"Oh, *oui*, Madame Polgár told me that the dragon had waited for centuries for my return, as had the brothers who were the sons—by which she surely referred to the Order of the Sons of Isis, don't you think? She said that even now they were gathering from far and wide, like ravens to a corpse-strewn battlefield. That an interloper would try to take what had belonged to the Ancient One—the high priest's emerald, of course! That I would embark upon a perilous search, and that I held the key to my destiny in my own hands and always had—the crucifix, I'll wager! Oh, she must be a true clairvoyant, for how else could she possibly know all that?"

"Actually, she might be a descendant of one of the original brothers of the Sons of Isis," Malcolm explained soberly. "In a book on the history of pseudomonastic orders, Mr. Cavendish discovered that there were twelve members of the Sons of Isis—thirteen, in reality, counting its founder, Lord Dúndragon himself. They were claimed to have worshiped a priceless emerald carved in the shape of a scarab beetle—the Heart of Kheperi. But after four of their number died strange, untimely deaths, the other nine members evidently decided that the emerald was accursed, as has been said, and they apparently buried it somewhere until they could better understand its alleged power. Then they had the crosses made, which are somehow the key to its location, and disbanded. So if there are indeed nine crucifixes, as Mr. Quimby has theorized, then obviously they have been handed down to descendants of the original brothers of the order for more than a century and a half—which would, of course, easily explain why the missing emerald has never been found, particularly if one does, in fact, need all nine crosses to locate it."

"*C'est impossible!*" the comte declared adamantly. "Surely these pseudomonks were mad to have conceived such a bizarre plan!"

"More than likely they intended to reunite at some point to recover the emerald themselves, Uncle Jean-Paul," Mr. Ravener observed astutely, "and hit upon their scheme to prevent one or more of them from doing so without the others. I don't believe they ever meant for the matter to go on the way it has—or for the Foscarellis to have become so lethally obsessed with the Heart of Kheperi, either. That entire family must be rife with insanity, inculcating each successive generation with the same fixation on obtaining the emerald, whatever the cost!" He paused for a moment, reflecting. Then he continued, "No doubt you have all wondered why I did not insist that Christine leave us before I began my questions of Aunt Elizabeth. The reason for that is simple. During the past few weeks I have lain ill, I have had several long conversations with Christine. I was curious, you see, about why she despises Lord Ugo so…whether 'twas merely his wicked reputation or something more. Finally she told me that she believes that Lord Ugo and his father, Lord Vittore, Count Foscarelli, were responsible for the deaths of her parents."

"My parents were…killed ten years ago, when I was only eight years old—and after hearing your stories tonight, I am now more certain than ever that 'twas Count Foscarelli and Lord Ugo who murdered them." Christine spoke quietly. "I lived in the Highlands then, for 'twas only after my parents died that I came to London, to stay with my uncle and aunt. But before then, my parents and I had gone to visit them, and 'twas one night when we were returning home to Scotland from England that our carriage was set upon—by highwaymen, we thought. Our driver tried his best to outrun them, but shots were fired, and both he and our footmen were hit. Finally our coach was run off the road and overturned, killing both my parents, too. After that, the door to the vehicle was wrenched open, and some instinct warning me, I pretended to be dead, as well. A man reached inside…a stranger. I dared not glance up from where I lay in my dead mother's lap—for she had attempted to shield me during the accident—so I could not see his face. But he spoke in a foreign language—Italian, I now think—to another man who waited on horseback just beyond the carriage. The first man fumbled at the throat of my father's cloak, then violently tore his crucifix from his neck. The cross Father wore that evening was, as I recall, identical to the two crucifixes I have seen here tonight, and I know that he had said 'twas very precious—a key to unlock a great mystery—and that 'twas to be mine someday. So I now believe that perhaps one of my ancestors must have belonged to this order…this Sons of Isis…and that was how Father had acquired the cross—and why the Foscarellis murdered him for it!"

"If that is true, then Mr. Rosenkranz was right to have quoted von Schiller to me," Malcolm noted thoughtfully, "and there is indeed no such thing as chance, and what seems to us merest accident does, in truth, spring from the deepest source of destiny! For why else should you have become Ariana's friend and be here tonight, my lady? I cannot believe that all that was sheer coincidence, but rather Fate, which Madame Polgár says inevitably thrusts its hand into the affairs of men—and which I say we must fight with our own Free Will! So the Foscarellis have yet additional murders to answer for! And we now know, as well, that they have at least one crucifix—whilst we ourselves have three!"

"Provided you can retrieve mine from the George and Vulture," Mr. Ravener pointed out.

"*Oui,* that we will do—straightaway," Monsieur Valcoeur insisted.

"Aye—and quite possibly Madame Polgár has a cross, as well," Malcolm speculated. "We do not yet know. But if so, then that accounts for the whereabouts of at least five, and perhaps Messieurs Quimby, Rosenkranz and Cavendish can assist us in locating the other four. Do you think Mr. al-Walid may have one?"

"The Egyptian about whom Christine has spoken to me?" Mr. Ravener queried. "Possibly. However, from what she has said, I believe that 'tis far more likely that he is trying to trace the descendants of the original brothers of the Sons of Isis. When she met him in the Highlands, 'twas at the Church of St. Andrew, in the village not far from Castle Dúndragon. Christine had gone to see the priest, Father Joseph, there, who is an old friend of her family. At the time, Mr. al-Walid was going through all the church records. Now, why would a herpetologist, whose field of study is snakes, be doing something like that, I ask you?"

"I don't know, but regardless, I think he bears watching, that he at least knows a great deal more about all this than he has so far let on." Lost in contemplation of all he had learnt, Malcolm drummed his fingers on one arm of the sofa. "Perhaps we should take some aggressive action and see what happens as a result."

"What did you have in mind? I could easily break in to both Madame Polgár's and Mr. al-Walid's lodgings and search them," Nicolas suggested.

"Were you fit, aye," Malcolm agreed, not even pretending to be shocked and determinedly ignoring his mother's own small cry of alarm and dismay. "But at the moment you're not yet back up to snuff, and besides, we have no guarantee that Madame Polgár, if she even possesses one of the crucifixes at all, does not wear it upon her person. The same is also true of Mr. al-Walid. No, Nicolas, I had something else entirely in mind…."

During dinner, which was finally served at nine o'clock, it was agreed that Mrs. Blackfriars and Malcolm would temporarily take up residence at the Lévesques' town house, and a message to that effect was promptly dispatched to Hawthorn Cottage. Then, once the meal was finished, the ladies all retired to the small drawing room, leaving the gentlemen to their port and cigars, after which Monsieur Valcoeur and Malcolm planned to retrieve Nicholas's cross from the George and Vulture. Ariana's head was in a whirl, for so much had been revealed to her that evening that she could scarcely take it all in. Even though, somehow, she had felt all along that Malcolm and the boy Collie in her dream, her nightmare, *were* one and the same, to have that fact confirmed was nevertheless still startling to her. Even more shocking was the knowledge that Monsieur and Madame Valcoeur were not her true parents, but rather, relatives and godparents who had taken her in following the deaths of her own real father and mother. That information had wholly rocked Ariana's world, making her feel as though all her life she had lived a lie and had now lost her own identity. Yet…she had gained a brother, Mr. Ravener, in the process. So she could not be completely sorry about all she had discovered.

"Ma pauvre petite," the comtesse murmured now as she gazed at her adopted daughter. "I would not blame you if you hated me and your papa now."

"Oh, *non,* Maman! That I could never do! 'Tis just that all this has been…so upsetting and confusing. I suppose that if I am honest, I must admit that I feel…guilty, somehow, at experiencing so little sorrow over the deaths of my true parents. I *am* saddened by the fact that I never really knew them, cannot even recall their faces, and that they seem like strangers to me—especially when I know they must have loved me very much for my mother to have sent me away the way she did, to ensure that I would be safe."

"Yes," Mrs. Blackfriars put it in. "You're right, Ariana. Charles and Katherine *did* love you deeply, with all their hearts, so I know they would not have wanted you to grieve for them, and that, further, they would understand why they are now only distant memories to you. After all, you were only a five-year-old child when they died. So you cannot be expected to remember them clearly—or to think any less of Jean-Paul and Hélène, who have long stood in their stead and loved you, too, and done very well by you, indeed."

"Malcolm told me that you are very kind and good, Aunt Elizabeth, and now I see that is so, in truth." Ariana paused, reflecting. Then she went on, "Oh, how I wish I knew what Papa and Malcolm and Nicolas are discussing in the library! I just know it must have something to do with the Foscarellis and this business of the Heart of Kheperi, and therefore, it must be something wholly dangerous!"

"Yes, I fear that is indeed the case," Christine agreed, biting her lower lip anxiously. "And 'tis most worrisome to me! Nicolas…Mr. Ravener…is not yet well enough to exert himself in this affair, and I fret that he shall be wounded again—or even killed!"

"You like him very much, don't you, *chérie?*" Madame Valcoeur asked, causing Christine to flush furiously. "Oh, do not be embarrassed by that, for I believe that Nicolas adores you, as well. Otherwise, he would scarcely have admitted you to our family's secrets. 'Twould be an excellent match, for he is not at all poor, you know. After Charles was murdered and Nicolas disappeared, Jean-Paul was next in line to inherit the county of Jourdain, through his mother, who was, of course, a de Ramezay. The county of Valcoeur, naturally, was his through his own father. But now that Nicolas has been found, Jourdain will revert back to him, for he is its rightful comte. So your uncle and aunt could have no objections to him on that score, and certainly Jean-Paul and I would not oppose such a marriage."

"Thank you, *madame.*" Christine smiled tremulously. "I hope…I hope that when my uncle and aunt return, Nicolas will speak to them."

"Oh, I hope so, too, Christine!" Ariana hugged her friend. "For then I will have gained not only a brother, but also a sister! And I have always so longed for siblings!"

"And for a husband, as well, *ma petite?*" the comtesse prompted archly, causing her daughter to blush as deeply as Christine had just moments ago. "Malcolm's position is rather more uncertain than Nicolas's, I fear. For even if Lord Bruno, Count Foscarelli, *did* cheat Lord Iain Ramsay, once the Earl of Dúndragon, at cards more than a century and a half past, thereby robbing Malcolm of his own inheritance, 'twas all so long ago that I don't see how anything could be proved at this late date to set matters aright."

"No, but—" Christine broke off abruptly. Then she continued slowly, "The thing is…I—I wouldn't want to get anyone's hopes up, but Father Joseph, who, as Nicolas told you, is an old friend of my family and the priest at the Church of St. Andrew in the village that lies just beyond Castle Dúndragon, told me that Mr. al-Walid made some…rather peculiar inquiries whilst at the village church, not just about the records there—the usual births, marriages and deaths—but also about legal matters that have naught to do with the Church…solicitors and last wills and testaments and such, particularly in connection with Lord Somerled Ramsay, who, as I understand it, was Lord Iain Ramsay's father and the Earl of Dúndragon prior to him."

"Why...whatever can that mean?" Ariana wondered aloud, puzzled. "Why would Mr. al-Walid be interested in anything like that?"

"Well, Father Joseph declared that there had been gossip in the village ever since he could remember that the Foscarellis—who are much hated by the villagers, by the way—had no true legal claim to Castle Dúndragon, even if Lord Bruno, Count Foscarelli, *had* won it at cards!"

"Yes, during their furtive forays across Loch Ness, Alexander and Charles had learnt that information in the village, as well," Mrs. Blackfriars confirmed. "But unfortunately, they could never determine what might have prompted the reports, whether 'twas just wishful thinking on the part of the villagers, who, as you said, loathe the Foscarellis, or whether there actually *was* some legitimate basis for the rumors."

"But if there were, then—"

"As Christine observed, you must not get your hopes up, Ana." Mrs. Blackfriars interrupted Ariana gently. "However it came about and whether rightly or wrongly, Malcolm has been deprived of his inheritance and could never lay any legal claim toward recovery founded solely on the idle tittle-tattle of a handful of disgruntled villagers. Without any solid proof that could be placed before the courts, nothing can ever be done toward that end."

"Perhaps not. But I still think 'tis most odd that Mr. al-Walid should have been asking such strange questions," Ariana insisted stoutly. "For I don't see what he would have to gain by it!"

"No, neither do I. 'Tis simply one more anomaly in the bizarrely twisted legacy of the Clan Ramsay of Dúndragon, I'm afraid." Mrs. Blackfriars sighed heavily.

"That may be." Madame Valcoeur spoke, nodding. "However, under the circumstances, neither I nor Jean-Paul would raise any objections should Malcolm wish to become a suitor for Ariana's hand. He is a good man, and part of our family, and so I feel certain that something could be arranged."

"Even so, he is…extremely proud—and accustomed to making his own way in this world, besides," Mrs. Blackfriars pointed out. "Although he is very circumspect and so has not said as much to me in so many words, I know he cares deeply for Ana. And, my dear child—" she turned to Ariana "—nothing would give me greater happiness than to have you for my daughter. You are so like Katherine, not only in appearance, but also in temperament, I think, and she was a wonderful woman, the best friend I ever had. But I hope I may be forgiven if I speak frankly. I fear that Malcolm will not be persuaded to follow his heart when he can offer you so little at this moment, in comparison to what you already have. Truly, I believe that—even more than gaining revenge for his father's murder—is what has driven him to take up the hazardous quest at which both Alexander and Charles failed. I have already lost my husband. I would not want to lose my son, as well."

"Nor would I care to lose Nicolas, when we have only just found him again," the comtesse said gravely. "But, *ma chère* Elizabeth, on the other hand, Malcolm and Nicolas are both bold, virile men in the prime of their lives—and we cannot reasonably expect them to stand idly by whilst the Foscarellis attempt to crush us all, as they surely *will* try—which is why I am so glad you have agreed to stay with us here in Portman Square for a while, where you will be safe! They must indeed be quite mad, as Nicolas claimed. Why, they have already murdered Alexander and Charles, and Christine's parents, too! So 'tis clear they will stop at nothing to achieve their evil ends, such is the hold this accursed emerald, this Heart of Kheperi, has on them. Oh, *le bon Dieu* knows that 'tis a malevolent gem indeed to have caused such great wickedness and sorrow to so many! How I wish that Lord James Ramsay had never stolen it from the ancient tomb of that Egyptian high priest to begin with! But there, as much as one may wish to, one cannot change the past. So we can only go forward—and even were Malcolm and Nicolas *not* to undertake any search for the missing emerald, for myself, I still do not think the Foscarellis would cease to be a threat to any of us, for in my opinion, they simply cannot conceive of anyone lacking their own greed to possess it and whatever mysterious power it may be imbued with!"

Deeply unsettled by the evening's revelations, Ariana dreamt again that night—her old nightmare, in which she went fishing with Malcolm in his little boat, the *Sea Witch,* upon the waters of Loch Ness. But this time, in some dark chasm of her mind, she realized that it was not just a dream, but a real memory, which had somehow got distorted by gruesome images born of her own instinctive fear that day when, through the drifting veils of mist, she had spied Castle Dúndragon perched like a predatory vulture upon the craggy promontory that jutted out into the lake.

Now, in her dream, she saw the strange dark boy who stood upon the parapets begin his slow, riveting metamorphosis into the titanic sea serpent, and she was terrified as she observed that this time he wore a visor as crimson as blood upon his face, identical to the half mask that Viscount Ugo had sported at the Marchioness of Mayfield's masquerade ball. Ariana opened her mouth and screamed again and again, but much to her horror, no sound emerged from her throat as the great sea monster towered over her menacingly, its seemingly endless, foreboding maw gaping wide.

And then all was darkness and silence.

Chapter Fifteen

The Madhouse and the Séance

The lunatic, the lover, and the poet,
Are of imagination all compact:
One sees more devils than vast hell can hold,
That is, the madman; the lover, all as frantic,
Sees Helen's beauty in a brow of Egypt:
The poet's eye, in a fine frenzy rolling,
Doth glance from heaven to earth, from earth to heaven;
And, as imagination bodies forth
The forms of things unknown, the poet's pen
Turns them to shapes, and gives to airy nothing
A local habitation and a name.
Such tricks hath strong imagination,
That, if it would but apprehend some joy,
It comprehends some bringer of that joy;
Or in the night, imagining some fear,
How easy is a bush supposed a bear!

—William Shakespeare
A Midsummer Night's Dream [1595-1596]

There sighs, lamentations and loud wailings resounded
through the starless air, so that at first it made me weep;
strange tongues, horrible language, words of pain, tones of
anger,

voices loud and hoarse, and with these the sound of hands,
made a tumult which is whirling through that air forever dark,
as sand eddies in a whirlwind.

—Dante Alighieri
The Divine Comedy [c. 1310-1320], Inferno

1848
*Cavendish and Portman Squares, and Southwark,
London, England*

A few days after the highly revelatory supper at the Lévesques'
town house in Portman Square, not only Messieurs Quimby, Rosenkranz and Cavendish were extremely surprised to receive an invitation to that residence, but so, too, was Madame Polgár. However,
unlike the three men, the fortune-teller was suspicious, as well.

"What do you think, Dukker?" Her golden eyes glittered
speculatively in the firelight, like those of a vigilant hawk who
has spied some prey. "We have been invited once more to dinner and a conversation party at the town house of Monsieur and
Madame Valcoeur, within the fortnight. The invitation is worded
innocuously enough, but still, I wonder…"

"Do you believe that you have overplayed your hand, *madame?*" the dwarf queried, his brow knitted in a thoughtful
frown. "That Monsieur and Madame Valcoeur now suspect you
of being more than just a mere fortune-teller?"

"Perhaps." She nodded slowly. Then she shrugged. "But then
again, perhaps not. We shall not know one way or the other
without accepting the invitation and seeing what we can learn."

"Under the circumstances, do you think that is wise, *madame?*
For if all is now known in the Lévesque household, then it could
be that they intend to do you some mischief!"

"*Non*…they are not that sort—except, possibly, for Messieurs
Blackfriars and Ravener. For 'tis a high-stakes game we play,
Dukker, and I do not believe that either of those two young men
cavil at that. After all, Monsieur Blackfriars did not hesitate to
shoot an assailant at point-blank range, did he? Nor could Mon-

sieur Ravener have survived as a professional gambler on the mean streets of Calais, Paris, London and elsewhere the way he has were his a cowardly nature—for from what you have discovered from the servants' gossip at the town house of Monsieur and Madame Valcoeur, my suspicions and deductions about Monsieur Ravener have, of course, been proved quite correct. No, unless I miss my guess—and I so very seldom do—he and Monsieur Blackfriars are most worthy opponents who bear watching. Still, even so, they can perhaps be turned into our allies, However, that is not at all the case with Viscount Ugo. *He* is our mortal enemy, Dukker, and we must never forget that."

"He spies upon us, *madame,* even as we spy upon him."

"*Oui,* I am afraid he and his father have learnt far more about us than we would have wished. Still, that cannot be helped. Forewarned is forearmed, and we are on our guard against them, are we not, Dukker?"

"*Oui, madame.* They will not obtain what they seek, I swear it!"

"Good! But still, remember my words to you, what I wish you to do in the unhappy event that some misfortune befalls me."

"*Oui,* I do not forget, *madame.*"

"Then all will be well. Now, before we go out to the theater this evening, I must meditate for a while, Dukker. So go and get your harp, and play something appropriately soothing for me."

Rising from the chaise longue she had previously occupied, Madame Polgár moved to sit in a red-velvet wing chair before the hearth, with its gleaming mantel of ebonized wood and where the fire burnt cheerfully in the grate. Now that winter drew nigh, the small town house she had taken in Henrietta Street, not far from Cavendish Square, was often cold and drafty, and as she had grown up in the Romanian country of Wallachia, she was accustomed to a much warmer climate. So she felt the chill acutely, especially now that she was so old. For although, over the years, she had taken good care of herself and was thus well preserved, she *was* old—far older than most people ever realized.

So even her very bones seemed to ache with the cold, and she longed for her homeland, which she had not seen for more than twenty-five years now, ever since she and her husband had emigrated due to the political unrest and rebellion that had seized their country. In that time, following her husband's death, she had traveled far and wide, spurred on by a cryptic narrative she had, as a child, been told by her grandmother.

In the beginning, Madame Polgár had given scarce credence to the tale, for her grandmother had been an outsider, fair and pale, a stranger from high, wild mountains in a faraway land, who had married into the family after having met and fallen in love with Madame Polgár's grandfather while touring the Continent. Even after her marriage, there had always been something strange and distant about the Lady Sibyl Macbeth, as though a part of her were still in the Highlands, where she had been born and bred. She had been blessed with "second sight," as she had called it, and this gift she had passed down to her granddaughter, Madame Polgár.

Now, as the fortune-teller stared at the crepitant blaze in the hearth and felt its warmth permeate her being, she knew that the story her grandmother had related to her had been true. Before her golden eyes, the flames that crackled and sparkled on the grate appeared to dance like fiery faeries in the crystal ball that perched upon its gold stand atop a nearby table, which she now drew slowly toward her. Per her instructions to him, Dukker had fetched his harp, and now he sat on a cushion in one shadowy corner, plucking its strings softly. The eerie, haunting melody he played wafted like the draft through the chamber and like the mist that swirled inside the crystal ball as Madame Polgár gazed into it deeply.

But try as she might, the fortune-teller could not focus her concentration tonight, and so in the end she saw nothing in the crystal ball but the whorling brume that told her naught. At last, sighing heavily, she gave up the attempt. It was almost as though a veil had been drawn over her future, or even as though she were to have none at all, she thought—and suddenly shivered violently, as though a goose had just walked over her grave.

* * *

Dukker ran and ran until he thought his lungs would surely burst. He had never been so terrified in his entire life. His protector, Madame Polgár, was gone. She had been kidnapped by means of an extremely clever ruse employed by their enemies— and despite all his vigilance, he had not seen it coming until it had been too late to save her. So in the end, he could do naught but manage his own escape, knowing that if he did not, he could be of no further assistance to her, would stand little or no chance of rescuing her. Since the previous night, when the daring abduction had been carried out, he had operated on sheer adrenaline. But now, as at last he slowed his steps in order to catch his breath and to carefully scrutinize his surroundings, the full horror and import of what had occurred struck him, and he nearly wept. He should have been more alert, he thought, and he blamed himself bitterly for the hideous misfortune that had befallen the fortune-teller. But neither his tears nor his self-recrimination would help her, Dukker knew, and finally, after forcing himself to take several deep breaths, he pulled himself together.

Now confident that he was not being followed, he slipped covertly through the long wintry evening shadows until at last he stood before the Lévesques' town house. Glancing about warily, he rang the front bell loudly and repeatedly, and finally, in response, the door was opened by the butler, Butterworth, who stared down his long nose at Dukker, as though it were some obnoxious creature and not the dwarf who stood without.

"One ring would have done—and as I'm sure you're well aware, the likes of you should use the rear entrance, besides," the butler intoned haughtily, preparing to slam the door in Dukker's face.

"*Non!* Wait! Wait! I—I must see Madame Valcoeur at once!" the dwarf babbled, nearly hysterical at the thought that he would be summarily denied admittance to the town house. "'Tis a matter of life or death! Madame Polgár has been kidnapped!"

However reluctantly then, Butterworth allowed him to step inside.

"Wait here," the butler ordered tersely, "and don't touch anything!" Then he vanished from the reception hall to summon his mistress.

In due course, the comtesse herself appeared in the reception hall, her lovely face pale and filled with shock and concern at her butler's report.

"What is it, Dukker? What's wrong? Butterworth has said that Madame Polgár has been abducted! Is that true?"

"*Oui, madame!* And there is no time to be lost, for not only her sanity, but also her very life is at stake!" The dwarf prattled on nervously and excitedly until, with an upraised hand, Madame Valcoeur stopped him.

"*Bon Dieu!* This is terrible news!" she exclaimed. "I can scarcely believe it! But you must calm yourself, Dukker—for I can hardly understand anything you say when you jabber away in that fashion. There. That's much better. Now, come with me, for if you wish help, then 'tis best that Monsieur Valcoeur and Messieurs Blackfriars and Ravener, who, fortunately, are also here tonight, are made privy, as well, to this matter, and since time would seem to be of the essence, 'tis best that you tell your story only once, so that all necessary action can be taken as soon as possible."

Leading him into the small drawing room, the comtesse bade the dwarf be seated. Then she directed him to relate his tale as quickly and succinctly as possible. Relieved that she had taken him seriously, rather than having him cast out of the town house, Dukker sat down gingerly on the edge of a chair, clutching to his chest a small ornately gilded box, and starting to stammer out his tale to those present.

"Well, there is s-so much to relate in regard to the events that led up t-to the kidnapping o-of Madame Polgár that I—I hardly even know where to begin! And perhaps you already know a great deal of what I would impart—in which case, 'twould no doubt be best just to describe what happened last night. I—I don't know. Oh, 'tis like this—some time ago, Madame Polgár embarked upon a d-dangerous quest that caused her to acquire some formidable foes…the Foscarellis. Perhaps you have heard of them? 'Tis they who abducted her! This terrible act took place last evening, after Madame Polgár and I had left the theater. We had been t-to see an Italian opera at the Covent Garden Theatre, in Bow Street. When we came out, we hired a hackney coach to convey us home, for Madame Polgár keeps no carriage of her own in the city. But unbeknown to us at first, the growler we entered was not a genuine vehicle duly licensed by the commissioners, but, rather, one deceptively employed by the Foscarellis for the sole purpose of kidnapping Madame Polgár."

"Oh, *non!*" Madame Valcoeur cried. *"La pauvre madame!"*

"Oui, madame," the dwarf agreed sadly. "But initially, I am ashamed to say, we were wholly taken in by this most clever ruse, not suspecting at all that the hackney coach was not what it seemed. 'Twas only when it did not go in the direction of Madame Polgár's town house, as we had advised the driver, that we realized our peril. From where I stood at my post at the rear of the growler, I shouted at the driver that he was going the wrong way. But much to my horror, he not only ignored me, but also laid his whip to the backs of the horses, until the vehicle clattered so rapidly along the streets that I was nearly pitched from my perch! At that moment, some men on horseback appeared, as well, to surround us, and that was when I truly understood our danger and that Madame Polgár was being abducted! She recognized that, too, for she began to cry out for me to save myself. But when I would have leapt from my post onto the pavement, one of the men on horseback plucked me from my perch and slung me facedown over his saddle, so I could not escape. In this manner was I borne along to the mews behind the town house of the Foscarellis, at Berkeley Square. But I am very strong, and fortunately, once there, I was able to squirm free of my captor's grasp and get away. However, I did not run off, but only tricked Madame Polgár's kidnappers into believing I had, so they ceased to search for me. Then, once they had given up the chase, I secreted myself in a place where I could watch all the comings and

goings at the town house, and the next day my vigil was re-warded when I spied Madame Polgár being bundled into a car-riage. On foot, I followed the coach to see where she was taken—and 'twas to Bedlam! The Foscarellis have locked her away in that madhouse!"

"Oh! She must be got out at once!" the comtesse declared, visibly distraught as she turned imploringly to her husband and Malcolm and Mr. Ravener.

"*Oui, ma chère,* of course she must," the comte responded stoutly. "Nicolas, are you well enough to accompany Malcolm and me?"

"I am."

"Then let us make haste in this affair! Ariana, you and Lady Christine look after your mother and Madame Blackfriars in our absence—and make sure Dukker does not depart from this household before our return!"

"But I want to go with you, *monsieur!*" the dwarf protested vehemently, springing to his feet.

"*Non,* you will remain here, and wait!" Monsieur Valcoeur rejoined sternly. "For now I tell you that all of us here have quite a good idea of what kind of quest your mistress has been em-barked upon and that has resulted in her becoming a target of the Foscarellis. Therefore, you will only be a hindrance to us, because you are known to them as her servant and, by accompa-nying us, would only alert them as to our intentions to rescue Madame Polgár. As 'tis, we can only hope you were not followed here and spied entering the house!"

"*Non, monsieur,* I was most careful to ensure that I was not!"

"For all our sakes, I hope that is the truth! Now, sit yourself back down, and do not stir from that chair until our return. Ari-ana…your *maman* and Madame Blackfriars—"

"*Oui,* Papa."

Shouting for his carriage, the comte abruptly strode from the small drawing room, Malcolm and Mr. Ravener hard on his heels, leaving the four females and the dwarf to sit in anxiety and momentary silence. This last was soon broken, however, as Ariana and Christine set about offering the two older ladies glasses of ratafia and sherry to soothe them, and to direct the servants to prepare food and drink for Dukker.

Bedlam, as it had come to be popularly known, had been founded in 1247, in Bishopsgate Street Without, by Simon Fitz-Mary, an alderman and sheriff of London. Originally it had served as a priory for the Order of St. Mary of Bethlehem. But as it had now long been notorious as a lunatic asylum, its history was not unfamiliar to either the men who now set out for it or the women and the dwarf who remained behind. From at least as early as 1329 there had been a hospital attached to the priory, initially constructed for the treatment of the poor who were either ill or else who simply had nowhere else to go—thus its name, Bethlehem, which meant "House of Bread." But sometime around the turn of the century it had begun also to take in mental patients, for in 1405 a report of a royal commission had addressed the state of the insane who were confined there, and those who had been judged cured and discharged from the establishment had been given a tin badge to wear upon one arm and thereafter been licensed to beg. In 1375 the place had become a royal hospital, seized by King Edward III on the pretext that it was an alien priory, and in 1547, during the dissolution of the monasteries, King Henry VIII had formally bestowed it upon the city. By 1674, its old premises having grown wholly filthy and untenable, the hospital had been transferred to new quarters at London wall and Moorgate, in Moorfields. But unfortunately, the new building had been constructed on an old London ditch packed with unstable rubbish, so that by 1799 it had become necessary to shore up and underpin the walls. At length, in 1812, the lunatic asylum had been moved again, to a massive, loftily domed, three-story redbrick edifice on Lambeth Road, in St. George's Fields, which structure and grounds had been established partially on the old gardens of the infamous Dog & Duck public house, and now comprised several acres. Until around the beginning of the current century, it had been the custom to charge visitors a penny for admission to the hospital, and as many as a hundred thousand people a year had paid for the privilege of being entertained by viewing the lunatics manacled and chained like wild beasts there. Now, however, this practice was strictly prohibited, and visitors were permitted entry only four days a week, by order of the hospital's governors, and this only to see relatives or friends who were inmates there.

"I truly hope Madame Polgár is unharmed." Malcolm spoke grimly as Monsieur Valcoeur's imposing carriage clattered its way along the city's labyrinthine streets, past Parliament, and across the Westminster Bridge, into the opprobrious district of Southwark.

"*I* hope the Foscarellis have not now obtained her crucifix, if indeed she had one," Mr. Ravener declared, more practical than sympathetic. "And it seems that they, at least, believed she did, or else they surely would not have gone to such lengths as this to get their hands on her."

"I don't think she would still be alive, even locked away in a lunatic asylum, if they had got her cross out of her," Malcolm pointed out logically.

"No. However, we don't know that she *is* actually still alive. After all, we have only the dwarf's word for it, and although I don't believe he lied to us about Madame Polgár's kidnapping or her having been transported to Bedlam, 'tis possible that even now she could be gasping her last breaths in that madhouse!"

"I fear that you are right, Nicolas." With his elaborately engraved gold-knobbed walking stick, the comte beat on the box above them, shouting to the driver, "Hurry, man, hurry! For we have not a moment to lose!"

At last the coach jolted to an abrupt halt before what was now the Royal Bethlehem Hospital, and Monsieur Valcoeur, Malcolm and Mr. Ravener quickly alighted from the vehicle, to make their way beneath the portico with its six Ionic columns, which supported a splendid pediment above, into which were set the Royal Arms and, underneath, a motto devoted to King Henry VIII. Once inside the lunatic asylum, the three men found themselves in an entrance hall whose chief claim to fame was two amazingly lifelike statues in Portland stone, entitled *Melancholy* and *Raving Madness,* and carved by the Danish-English sculptor Caius Gabriel Cibber. Originally, they had stood over the gates of the old hospital at Moorfields, but had been transported from there to the new edifice. The statues were screened by curtains, which were normally drawn only upon public occasions. But Malcolm and Mr. Ravener had no hesitation in furtively glancing behind them while the comte engaged in conversation with the warder, who, at their threat to summon the police, had reluctantly admitted them. Also on display were several iron manacles and chains, a reminder of the lunatic asylum's cruelly abusive history before investigatory committees had compelled drastic changes in its policies and treatment of patients.

"That sly warder is still giving Uncle Jean-Paul a difficult time," Mr. Ravener observed quietly. "I suspect that his palm was well greased by the Foscarellis not to allow anyone access to Madame Polgár."

"Well, then, let us do a little greasing of our own," Malcolm suggested meaningfully, also under his breath.

Before leaving the Lévesques' town house, knowing the unsavory suburb into which they were headed, like the footmen who had accompanied them hither, the two men had wisely taken the precaution of arming themselves with pistols, which they had concealed beneath their coats. Now, suddenly drawing their weapons, they strode forward boldly, the folds of their cloaks swirling about them eerily in the soughing draft that snaked into the entrance hall. One man on either side, they seized the unsuspecting but recalcitrant warder roughly from behind, pressing their pistols warningly against him.

"Now, you will either escort us posthaste to wherever you are restraining the elderly woman brought here today by the Italians, or you will suffer a most unpleasant fate!" Malcolm growled softly, jabbing the cold hard muzzle of his weapon into the warder's side to emphasize the threat. "And don't try to cry out or to pull the wool over our eyes, either! I've already shot one man—and I assure you, I won't hesitate to shoot another!"

"Y-y-yes, yes…all right, all right. I won't try anything, I swear! Come this way, then, if—if you please," the warder stammered, his beady, cunning eyes now fearful and darting nervously from one man to the other.

Bedlam's three stories, beneath which was also a basement, consisted of a center structure and two principal wings, although, over the years others had been added to enlarge the building. Each floor was divided into galleries, which housed the patients, and the edifice itself was fireproof, and heated by both air and water, so that as the little procession wound its way stealthily along the long halls, Malcolm was surprised by the warmth within. The only visible signs that he and the rest were not in an ordinary structure were the fireplaces, which were railed in, and the bone, rather than metal, knives in possession of the inmates. He was not sure what he had expected to find in the lunatic asylum, but it was certainly not the billiard and bagatelle tables installed for the male patients or the pianos supplied for the female patients. Even at this relatively late hour, those inmates not abed were engaged at working at their trades, which included knitting, embroidery and tailoring. Others read newspapers and periodicals, or played games.

Finally, with a key on the huge iron ring at his waist, the warder opened the door to a small cell. Dimly illuminated by the flickering light cast by the lamps affixed to the walls of the corridor, the tiny room displayed walls and a floor lined with cork and India rubber to protect deranged patients from violently injuring themselves. But far from being frenzied, Madame Polgár was alarmingly sedate, slumped in one corner, her head lolling listlessly.

"Sacrébleu!" Monsieur Valcoeur hastened to her side. Then, after a moment, glancing up from his examination of the hapless woman, he announced soberly, "She has been beaten and drugged. Give me a hand here with her, one of you!"

Suspecting that despite his claims of fitness, Mr. Ravener was still relatively weak, Malcolm pocketed his pistol, then ran to the comte's aid, lifting the unconscious Madame Polgár to carry her from the cell. With the others leading the way, he bore her swiftly along the galleries and down the stairs of the hospital, then got her into the carriage outside. Turning the terrified warder loose at last, Mr. Ravener and Monsieur Valcoeur climbed in after Malcolm. Then, with his cane, the comte rapped smartly on the box, and with a lurch the team harnessed to the coach started forward, hooves clip-clopping on the cobblestones and the vehicle's wheels chuntering as they picked up speed.

This time, Monsieur Valcoeur's driver did not need to be told to hurry. He had not been at all happy about venturing into Southwark, particularly at this late hour. A poor, horribly crowded district filled with three-story tenements crammed to overflowing with families, cockroaches, lice and fleas, the place was a veritable dung heap, crawling with maggots and flies of the worst sort. Noisy, filthy, lined with wooden wharves and stairs from the River Thames, it was home to a squalid sprawl of ramshackle warehouses and foul industries such as breweries, coke ovens, glassworks and potteries, all of whose chimneys ceaselessly belched dirty smoke and soot into the air, so that all the buildings were streaked black with grime. From the River Thames itself wafted the obnoxious stench of sewage, and in the streets was the fetid stink of manure from the horses, cattle, pigs and sheep that were regularly driven to the street markets and which smell mingled ironically with the lingering aroma of the freshly baked pies peddled by the piemen from their carts during the day. Had it been broad daylight, merchants would have been hawking their wares, and the deal porters, who carried incredibly heavy loads of wood or deal at the docks, would have been hard at labor, as would the mudlarks, the children who daily stood waist-deep in the mud along the River Thames, in search of chips of timber and chunks of coal that had spilled from the barges and that the urchins could sell for a few pence. But now only prostitutes, cutpurses, cutthroats and gin-soaked drunks roamed the streets and skulked in the alleyways. While Monsieur Valcoeur, Malcolm and Mr. Ravener had been inside the lunatic asylum, the driver had kept a sharp eye out, and the armed footmen at their posts at the rear of the vehicle had likewise kept a close hand on their pistols to deter thieves and other assailants. Now, however, such was the haste with which the equipage traveled along the hazily lighted streets that the footmen were compelled to hang on to their perches tightly to keep from being flung off.

Through the carriage's foggy windows trickling with drizzle Malcolm could scarcely even see the dimly glowing street lamps, such was the "pea soup"—the blanket of mist, combined with smoke and soot—that permeated Southwark, and he marveled at the driver's speed, although only briefly. For his main worry was for Madame Polgár, who was clearly not at all well. The comte had covered her with a lap robe against the cold and tried to get a few sips of brandy down her throat from the silver flask in his coat pocket, and he now chafed her hands. But otherwise, there was little that could be done for her until they reached Portman Square and could summon Dr. Whittaker. Once or twice she moaned softly, so that Malcolm knew she was in pain, but still, she did not open her eyes, not even when the coach jerked and swayed precariously after hitting a bump in the road. As the vehicle rumbled over Westminster Bridge, and Malcolm spied the River Thames below and the lighters and barges that plied its water, conveying cargo and coal to and from the docks, he breathed a sigh of relief, for he knew that the equipage had left Southwark behind and was now on safer ground. Beside him on the seat Nicolas, too, seemed to relax slightly, although, still, he kept a wary glance upon their surroundings.

Finally the carriage reached Portman Square. After depositing its passengers at the front of the Lévesques' town house, the driver guided the coach around to the mews at the back, both he and the footmen vastly relieved to have suffered no misfortune this night. The comte leading the way and Nicolas following behind, Malcolm carried Madame Polgár inside to the small drawing room, where, amid the upset cries and queries of the four ladies and the dwarf, he laid her down gently upon the sofa. At the sight of his mistress alive and breathing, Dukker was momentarily beside himself with joy, thanking everyone profusely and, in between, trying to speak to the fortune-teller. But she did not respond, and presently, as Monsieur Valcoeur shouted for Dr.

Whittaker to be fetched, the dwarf realized she was not unharmed, and his face fell, his ebullience abruptly dissipating.

"Is she—is she going to be all right?" he asked anxiously.

"I don't know." The comte shook his head. "She has been abused, obviously—although not as badly as I at first feared—and also drugged, which is what has rendered her unconscious, I think. We will know more after Dr. Whittaker's arrival. In the meanwhile, I suggest that we remove her upstairs to a bedchamber, where she can be made comfortable."

"Oui, mon cher," Madame Valcoeur agreed, clearly greatly distressed over the maltreatment her friend had suffered. "I've already instructed the servants to make a room ready."

Thus, in due course was Madame Polgár settled into a bedchamber at the Lévesques' town house and examined by Dr. Whittaker, who reported that although she had indeed been misused, her injuries were not mortal, the worst of these consisting of three fingers that had apparently been deliberately and viciously broken.

"C'est monstrueux!" The comtesse was completely horrified by this news.

"Quite so, *madame*." The surgeon's voice was grave. "However, as I said, Madame Polgár should make a complete recovery. My only concern is that she is not a young woman, so I do not know what kind of a strain this deeply unfortunate episode may have placed upon her heart. I've not dispensed her a sedative, for I do not know what sort of drug she was given, although I suspect some opiate, and so dare not risk an overdose. However, when the effects of it have finally worn off, you may administer one or two teaspoons of laudanum from the bottle I've left upon the night table, as she requires to diminish her pain."

Once the doctor had departed from the town house, Sophie and Lady Christine's own abigail, Miss Innes, were assigned the task of watching over the fortune-teller, while the others, including Dukker, again gathered in the small drawing room. The dwarf had wished to remain with his mistress, but as it was plain that seeing her in such a dire state was distressing him terribly, he had been limited by the physician to brief visits. So now Dukker perched once more on the chair he had previously occupied in the small drawing room, his visage disconsolate and his hands still hugging to his chest the little gilded box he had brought with him to the town house. Ariana's heart went out to him, for although the fact that Madame Polgár should have a dwarf for a servant seemed most bizarre, he was clearly devoted to her.

Now that the fortune-teller had been well taken care of, Monsieur Valcoeur, Malcolm and Mr. Ravener were at liberty to impart the story of her rescue, which they recounted at some length, awing and dismaying the four ladies.

"Oh, Collie!" Ariana cried, at hearing all the details of the scheme that had been enacted and that, although ultimately successful, had still disturbed her. "What if you and Papa and Nicolas had been attacked in Southwark or by the inmates at Bedlam and—and even killed? I—I could not have borne that!" Then, blushing furiously at her outburst, she bit her lower lip and cast down her eyes in embarrassment at the thought that she had betrayed her heart to all present, that her concern had been especially for Malcolm.

"I am far more worried about you, *mademoiselle,* and Lady Christine, as well," he declared, his brow furrowed in a troubled frown and his heart filled with both love and fear for Ariana. "For if the Foscarellis would assault poor Madame Polgár in such a dastardly fashion, then what might they do to the two of you? They are, of course, already aware that Lady Christine is involved in this affair, and although, having already stolen her father's crucifix, they may believe she is of no further use to them, the same cannot be said about you, Ana, should they ever suspect that you, too, have some knowledge about this matter."

"We are on our guard against the Foscarellis, Malcolm," Mr. Ravener asserted reassuringly.

"So were we." Dukker spoke chillingly from where he sat numbly in the corner. "But still, in the end, that did not help Madame Polgár...."

* * *

Malcolm's hand felt strong and warm around Ariana's own fragile one, which was chilled to the bone. Together, with all the others assembled in the mirror-lined ballroom at the Lévesques' town house, the two of them sat at the huge round table that Madame Valcoeur had earlier that evening caused to be erected in the middle of the chamber. The table itself had been covered with a cloth of fringed scarlet silk, and at its heart stood a pair of heavy, ornate candlesticks, one gold, the other silver, and each about eight inches tall. In the gold candlestick burnt a fat white candle, and in the silver an equally fat black candle. Save for these, the fires that blazed in the great Parian hearths at either far end of the ballroom, and the pale wintry moonlight that streamed in through the three pairs of French doors set into the wall adjoining the terrace beyond, no other light illuminated the chamber, and the effect of that which did, reflected endlessly in the many mirrors affixed to the walls, was somehow eerie, atavistic and otherworldly.

At the transitory head of the round table sat Madame Polgár, clothed in a regal feathered-and-bejeweled turban and flowing robes that matched the color of the tablecloth. Having, during the days that had passed since her abduction by the Foscarellis, learnt from the comtesse that her invitation to the promised dinner and conversation party at the Lévesques' town house had been prompted by the idea of finagling her into conducting a séance, the fortune-teller had ultimately declared herself well enough to rise from her bed to keep the engagement, rather than compelling it to be put off.

"But, *ma pauvre* Madame Polgár, I fear that you are not at all yet fit," Madame Valcoeur had protested at this announcement. "Whilst 'tis true that the bruises from the cruel beating you received are fading, your poor fingers have required splinting and are not at all mended."

"I do not need them for a séance, only for the tarot cards, which I shall not employ, and now that we no longer have any secrets from each other, I wish to make amends for having sought to steal your daughter's inheritance, the crucifix I hoped she would have," Madame Polgár had insisted. "For…long had I suspected her true identity, having learnt that Monsieur Valcoeur was the cousin of Monsieur Charles de Ramezay, le Comte de Jourdain, and having discovered from the old nurse at Valcoeur that you yourself could bear no children of your own, *madame*. That afternoon in Oxford Street, as you are now aware from our previous conversations the past several days, Dukker truly intended only to knock Mademoiselle Ariana down, so he could take from her any necklace she might be wearing. He never meant to shove her so hard that she fell into the path of the unchecked horse and hansom cab. Still, you might have lost her that day, and 'twould have been my fault. But then, what an ironical hand Fate thrust into this affair, eh, *madame?* For only look at the long chain of events required for Dukker to have pushed your daughter—and for Monsieur Blackfriars to have been present at the scene to save her life! What would Lord James Ramsay, once the Earl of Dúndragon and who stole the Heart of Kheperi in the first place, think of all that? I wonder. For we so seldom understand, you see, how our actions may affect the lives of others even centuries after we are dead and buried in our graves, that time itself is an infinite tapestry and each of us the interlaced threads of which 'tis woven. And now my own thread has reached its length and shall soon be snipped, I believe. So I will conduct the séance, and in this way, perhaps I can atone for all my sins, which are many. I was greedy for the power of immortality the Heart of Kheperi is claimed to be able to bestow. But now, as death draws nigh, I know that it, too, serves a purpose and that only by experiencing it can I grasp what that is. That is why I could not see my future in the crystal ball—for no mere mortal can unveil Isis."

Besides the fortune-teller, Malcolm and Ariana, arrayed around the table were Monsieur and Madame Valcoeur, Mrs. Blackfriars, Mr. Ravener, Lady Christine, and Messieurs Quimby, Rosenkranz and Cavendish. Dukker sat upon a cushion in one corner of the ballroom, his dark curly head bent to his harp, his fingers plucking a haunting melody upon its strings. The assembly had debated including the enigmatic Mr. al-Walid in their séance. But finally, uncertain of his goals, they had deemed it unwise at this point to let him know how much they had thus far discovered about the keys to unlocking the mystery of the priceless missing emerald that had been stolen from his homeland.

"Is everyone ready to begin?" Madame Polgár inquired now, her bearing majestic, her voice strong, even though she felt that her body was extremely old and frail and would this night betray her before she had accomplished her chosen task. But still, knowing the power of the mind over that of the body, she deliberately fought her weakness and triumphantly held it at bay. "Are we all holding hands? Good. Then we shall attempt now to contact the other side—that of those who have passed through death's door, as we all must someday pass, each in our turn— and to speak with Lord Robert Roy Ramsay, the ninth Earl of Dúndragon. Whilst I try to establish a link with the spirits, all of you at this table must remain silent. However, should I succeed in breaking through and reaching Lord Dúndragon, then you may each ask him one question, and if he so chooses, he will answer, and although 'twill be I who seems to speak, remember that, in reality, I will but serve as the medium, the instrument through which Lord Dúndragon will be able to communicate with us. Now, then, let us begin…."

Long afterward, until the day she died, Ariana would never recall exactly what the fortune-teller said and did at the round table at which they had all gathered. Instead, she would recollect only misty images and impressions, as though seen through a glass darkly or through a silhouetted vignette. Foremost in her consciousness was the feel of Malcolm's hand clasping her own tightly and, on her other side, the hand of her newfound brother, Mr. Ravener, grasping hers with the equal love and tenderness that had sprung up at once between him and her, as though they had not been parted for the past thirteen years, but had grown up together as they ought. So despite the fact that the fires crackling in the two hearths did little to dispel the chilliness of the large ballroom, the coldness, fear and uncertainty that crept through Ariana as the séance got under way was combated by the warmth of the closeness and caring that radiated toward her from both Malcolm and Mr. Ravener.

Outside, the rain that had begun earlier to fall now drummed more strongly upon the black slate roof and against the mullioned windows, and the wind whispered and moaned, and tapped and rattled the panes. On cat's paws, the gray-white fog slunk in from the sea and the River Thames, padding through the gardens and up the stone steps of the terrace at the rear of the town house, and brittle brown leaves blown from the deciduous trees rustled and whorled like the skirts of Gypsies dancing beneath the moon. Inside, Madame Polgár's imperious voice echoed in the still, empty chamber as she importuned the gods and the spirits, intoning ancient words and muttering what sounded like incantations. All this was accompanied by occasional wild flickerings of the candles and strange rappings upon the table. And then, at last, quite clearly, she spoke.

"Is that you, Lord Rob Roy Ramsay, once the Earl of Dúndragon? Are you with us?"

After a long, taut moment, her eyes closed, her head lolling on her neck, she answered her own questions. But much to Ariana's shock, the voice that now issued from the fortune-teller's throat was startlingly deep and masculine.

"Ayc, I be Lord Dúndragon of auld. Who is it summons me from t' other side?"

"'Tis those who seek the truth and who search for what has long been lost. We request your help in our quest. We want to ask you some questions. Will you answer?"

"If I can."

"Good. Now, listen—and on your oath of honor, respond well and truly."

"I give ye me word to do so."

"Lord Dúndragon—if such you are indeed—did you found an order called the Sons of Isis?" Monsieur Valcoeur glanced both skeptically and suspiciously at Madame Polgár, for although he had agreed to take part in the séance, he still secretly thought it foolish hocus-pocus.

"Aye, for t' sons o' t' widows, as Horus was t' son o' t' widow Isis, after t' death o' his father, Osiris."

"How—how many in number were you?" Madame Valcoeur queried faintly as she stared at the fortune-teller, simultaneously mesmerized and repelled by the seemingly disembodied voice that emanated from her throat.

"Thirteen."

"What was your primary purpose?" Behind his spectacles, Mr. Quimby's pale blue eyes were wary, and yet riveted to the unfolding tableau.

"To learn how t' use t' key to unlock immortality."

"And did you succeed?" Mr. Cavendish inquired curiously, frankly fascinated.

"Nay—for we couldna ken t' magick o' t' stone."

"What stone? Do you speak of the lost emerald, the Heart of Kheperi?" Despite his obvious distaste for the proceedings in which he had only with the greatest of reluctance consented to participate, Mr. Rosenkranz could not conceal the sudden note of eagerness in his voice.

"Aye, 'twas an Egyptian philosopher's stone. Me father had wrongly stolen it from a tomb in t' valley known as t' Gateway to t' Kings. It had been born o' t' god Kheperi an' belonged to a supreme high priest devoted to his worship. 'Twas said to possess t' ability to bestow immortality on those who wielded it. But in truth, 'twas accursed!"

"How do you know?" It was the Lady Christine who now spoke.

"Four o' our brothers died—horrible, untimely deaths—because o' t' stone!"

"What did you do with it after that? Did you destroy it?" Ariana asked, fearful for her own personal reasons that perhaps the emerald no longer existed

"Nay, for 'twas far too valuable an' powerful for that. So we locked it away, as it had kept t' knowledge o' its power locked away from us."

"Where did you lock it away?" Mr. Ravener asked grimly.

"In a place where 'twould be safe fore'er, if need be."

"Where?" Malcolm demanded.

"'Twas so long ago now—"

"Where?" he repeated urgently. "Tell us! *Tell us!*"

"In t' place o' t' ninefold key…"

As those present heard these prophetic but cryptic words, the table at which they all sat in a circle, holding hands, began eerily to tremble before them. Then, of a sudden, it rocked violently, gave a great heave and levitated itself from the floor. At the same time, the wind outside started to huff and howl, as though a pack of hellhounds barked and bayed in the gardens.

"Oh, what is happening? What is happening?" Mrs. Blackfriars cried, half rising from her chair, terrified.

"'Tis t' stone…t' accursed stone!" the spirit of Lord Dúndragon warned direly. "Beware! Beware! Remember to whom t' Heart of Kheperi belongs!"

Echoing weirdly in the ballroom, his seemingly disembodied voice burgeoned with the roar of the wind, which now turned the full force of its strange, abrupt fury on the town house, blasting the French doors open wide, extinguishing the fires and the two wildly wavering candles within and, as a dark, drifting cloud occluded the inscrutable face of the moon, plunging the chamber into utter blackness.

Chapter Sixteen

A Matter of Love and Death

Behold a pale horse: and his name that sat
on him was Death, and Hell followed with him.
—*The Holy Bible*
The Book of Revelation

For we wrestle not against flesh and blood,
but against principalities, against powers,
against the rulers of the darkness of this world,
against spiritual wickedness in high places.
—*The Holy Bible*
The Book of Ephesians

Set me as a seal upon thine heart, as a seal
upon thine arm: for love is strong as death…
—*The Holy Bible*
The Song of Solomon

1848
The Lévesque Town House, Portman Square, London, England

Nobody knew, at first, what had occurred, that it was only the
suddenly unbridled wind that had caused the French doors to
blow open wide, dousing the fires and candles and casting the
ballroom into darkness. So for a moment, all those assembled
for the séance feared that they were perhaps under attack by their
enemies, the Foscarellis. As a result, everyone leapt from their
seats at the round table, and instinctively Malcolm swept Ariana

into his arms to protect her from whatever might threaten them, while at the same time calling out to his mother, to ensure her own well being.

"Don't worry, Malcolm!" Mr. Quimby answered amid the shouts of the men and the screams of the women. "She is safely here with me and Mr. Cavendish."

But still, Ariana—crushed so close against Malcolm that she could hear his heart thudding in his chest—could feel that, despite his employer's reassurances, the tension did not leave his body. His strong muscles were hard and taut beneath her hands as she clung fiercely to him, ignorant of what was happening, afraid of the worst. Her own heart pounded so savagely, she thought that it might burst in her breast, but whether solely from trepidation, she could not have said. For she had never before been held by a man in this fashion, and in truth, the adrenaline that now surged through her body was born of a mixture of both fright and excitement. Despite her apprehension, she felt the warmth of Malcolm's embrace seep through her, in the way that a beeswax candle melts slowly from its flame, and the musky male scent of him permeated her nostrils as she breathed in and out—quick, shallow gasps for air, as though her corset were laced far too tightly. He had one hand wrapped in her hair, pressing her head to his chest, and the other encircling her securely as he peered into the blackness, attempting to determine if there were any menace to them and, if so, whence it emanated.

But at the cries and shrieks of those gathered in the ballroom, the servants had come running, and now, the coattails of their livery flapping in the wind, the footmen closed all the French doors, while the housemaids, their pinafores and skirts whipping about them wildly, lit the sconces affixed to the walls of the chamber.

"Oh, *madame! Madame!*" Spying the fortune-teller sprawled in her chair, her head resting against its back, her eyes closed, Dukker rushed frantically to her side, clutching one of her hands in his and beginning to chafe it anxiously. "Speak to me, *madame!*"

Alarmed, Mr. Cavendish, who was nearest at hand, also hastened to Madame Polgár's side. He felt for a pulse, then bent to lay his head against her breast. Then, rising from his examination of the fortune-teller, he shook his head sadly.

"Madame Polgár is dead," he announced softly. "I am afraid that her abduction some days ago and the mistreatment she received at the hands of the Foscarellis, as well as the séance tonight, simply proved too much for her, and her heart could not stand the strain. She is gone."

"*Non, non!* She can't be!"

Much to the consternation and sympathy of those present, the dwarf suddenly flung himself upon his deceased mistress and started to sob uncontrollably, shaking her pitifully and begging her to open her eyes.

"Oh, Malcolm!" Ariana breathed, greatly distressed and her eyes beseeching.

Together, then, they drew Dukker away gently from the body of his mistress, speaking to him kindly and attempting to console him as they led him from the ballroom, Madame Valcoeur and Mrs. Blackfriars trailing in their wake, the former deeply upset and the latter, as a result, not only offering solace to her newfound friend, but also quietly making suggestions as to what orders ought to be issued to the staff.

"*Oui, oui…*whatever you think best, Elizabeth." Madame Valcoeur wept into her lacy white handkerchief. "Oh, *la pauvre* Madame Polgár! Just before the séance she told me that she was going to die, you know. Oh, I should never have let her go through with it! I knew she wasn't yet at all well, thanks to those evil Foscarellis—may they rot in hell! I should have insisted that she remain in her bed upstairs, instead of allowing her to conduct the séance. For it has killed her!"

"No, Hélène, really, you mustn't blame yourself. Madame Polgár was, I think, very old, and she had been abused and terrorized by the Foscarellis. 'Tis exactly as Mr. Cavendish said. Her heart simply gave out from the strain of it all. Now, please sit down, and let me ring for some tea—or would you prefer hot chocolate?"

"I've already directed the servants to bring both, as well as some coffee, Aunt Elizabeth," Ariana asserted as she entered the small drawing room, followed by Malcolm and the others who had been assembled for the inauspicious séance. "Collie and Nicolas have had to put Dukker to bed and to sedate him—for naturally, he was most wrought up. They have given him some of the laudanum that Dr. Whittaker prescribed for Madame Polgár. I hope Dukker will rest quietly now for a time. I know that her death has proved a terrible shock to him, and, indeed, to us all."

"Yes, the séance and its unfortunate culmination were an experience I would not at all care to repeat." Mrs. Blackfriars shivered a little and, as she settled herself in a chair before the marble hearth, drew her shawl more closely about her.

"And aside from the death of Madame Polgár, of course, the worst thing about the entire affair is that I don't believe we actually learnt anything from it!" Mr. Ravener frowned as he reached into his jacket pocket, withdrawing a slim gold case, from which he extracted a cheroot. Then, obtaining permission from the ladies to smoke, he lit up, inhaling deeply.

"Oh, but I don't believe that's true at all, my good fellow!" Mr. Cavendish protested. "In fact, to the contrary, I think we learnt one highly important piece of information, at least!"

"What, Bonny?" Mr. Quimby queried, curious.

"We discovered that all the original brothers of the Sons of Isis were the sons of widows! For remember what Lord Dúndragon told us, that he had founded the order for 'the sons of the widows, as Horus was the son of the widow Isis, after the death of his father, Osiris.'"

"Aye...aye, that's right, sir!" Malcolm agreed, nodding excitedly, from where he sat next to Ariana on the sofa.

"Oh, I don't know how all of you can be speaking about the matter of that accursed emerald now, with *la pauvre* Madame Polgár lying dead in the next room!" the comtesse moaned.

For the fortune-teller's body had been removed from the ballroom to the large drawing room, there to be washed and otherwise prepared for burial by the Sisters who—Madame Polgár having been a Catholic—had been hastily fetched from the Chapel Royal of France, in Little George Street. Dr. Whittaker had also arrived, to examine the fortune-teller's corpse and sign an official certificate as to the cause of death, which he deduced as heart failure. This certificate would be used to register the death with the Registry Office the following morning. Last but not least, an undertaker had been summoned to handle all the funeral arrangements, and a leaden coffin had been ordered, which, once Madame Polgár's body was placed within it, would be set on trestles within the large drawing room, with candles burning all around, until the burial could take place.

"Ma chère." Monsieur Valcoeur now addressed his wife. "I'm confident I speak for everyone present when I say that our discussion of this business does not indicate a want of delicacy on our parts, but, rather, demonstrates a certain amount of both practicality and precaution. Except for our seeing that Madame Polgár is decently interred, there is nothing more any of us can do for her now, for she is in the far more capable hands of her Maker. Further, although she may, in truth, have been too weak to be subjected to the strain and excitement of the séance, the real cause of her demise lies on the doorstep of our adversaries, the Foscarellis—and knowing what kind of men they are, we would be most foolish, indeed, not to take any and all steps necessary to recover the lost emerald and to protect ourselves against them!"

"Oui, I know that you are right," the comtesse conceded, and tried to pull herself together.

So the conversation continued at some length. But then, finally, as the hour grew late, those gathered in the small drawing room began one by one to take their leave. Malcolm and Ariana offered to sit the first vigil with Madame Polgár's corpse, but Madame Valcoeur demurred, insisting that it was her own duty and that she would not shirk it. So instead, they sought the cozy comfort of the library, for a quiet tête-à-tête.

"Poor Madame Polgár." Ariana sighed heavily as she gazed out the library's misty, rain-bespattered windows, which overlooked the gardens at the rear of the town house, now bleak and barren with autumn's fading into winter, the trees naked and shivering in the wind. The dark cloud that, earlier, had obscured the moon had drifted on across the night sky. "I do wish, now, that she had not agreed to conduct the séance!"

"She was a grown woman, Ana, who ultimately made her own decisions." Coming up behind her, Malcolm laid his hands boldly but gently upon her shoulders, a tender, reassuring caress. "We can none of us blame ourselves for that. By her own admission to your mother, Madame Polgár had foreseen her own demise...perhaps she even frightened herself to death with her own séance. Who knows?"

"'Twas so terrifying!" Beneath his lightly stroking hands Ariana shuddered unwittingly. "That deep voice that spoke from her mouth! Surely that was not her own, not something that was feigned! And that strange rapping upon the table, the way the table itself trembled, then suddenly rocked so violently and heaved up from the floor to float above us! Oh, she *must* have been a true clairvoyant, Collie! For how else could she have done all those things?"

"I don't know." He shook his head. "I confess I am as mystified by it all as you. Further, both your father and Mr. Rosenkranz having been highly skeptical of Madame Polgár's supposed talent, after her body had been removed from the ballroom they examined the table, its cloth, the candlesticks, all the French doors and even Dukker's harp most carefully, only to report that they could discover nothing—no mechanical devices, no strings, or any other apparatus—that would lead them to believe she employed some trickery to deceive us."

"Then she really *was* a genuine clairvoyant and not a fraud!"

"So 'twould seem."

"Then Lord Dúndragon *did* speak to us!" Turning suddenly in his arms to face him, Ariana said, "Oh, Collie, I'm so afraid, so worried about what our future might hold in store for us—or not," she added softly, significantly. "After everything we've learnt about this emerald, this Heart of Kheperi, I've come more and more to feel that Lord Dúndragon was right to say 'tis accursed and that we should beware of it! Only look at the evil hold it has taken of the Foscarellis! *They* are the ones who ought to have been locked away in Bedlam—not poor Madame Polgár! I'm frightened of the risks that both you and Nicolas—and even Papa—seem prepared to take to find the emerald. You could all wind up hurt—or even killed!"

"The Foscarellis may be evil. They may even be insane, as Nicolas has insisted. But they are not gods, Ana. They are mortal men who have gone on as long as they have because they are wholly unscrupulous, without conscience or compassion. But they can be beaten—and by God, I intend to beat them!"

"It upsets me to hear you talking this way, Collie. I—I don't want anything to happen to you."

"I'll be all right, Ana. So don't you worry about that. 'Tis *you* I'm concerned about. I know I've little or no right to dictate to you, but I do wish you'd stay close to home for a while. For the Foscarellis will no doubt investigate anyone and everyone who was connected to Madame Polgár, and they've already proved they will not balk at abduction."

At the thought of somehow falling into the hands of the Foscarellis, Ariana shivered again, feeling suddenly as cold as the frigid wintry air that blew its cloudy breath upon the frost-limned garden beyond the windows of the library.

"'Tis difficult to believe that they are not shunned by society," she said, "that despite their unsavory reputation as a family, they are still invited into all the best homes here—just like that of the Marchioness of Mayfield. People are surely aware of the rumors about them."

"Aye, I would imagine so. But on the other hand, rank and riches open many doors that would, under ordinary circumstances, remain closed—and sometimes a dubious reputation can work in one's favor. Women, particularly, are often attracted to rakes, libertines, fortune hunters and other ne'er-do-wells, especially if such men are both handsome and charming."

"Well, I suppose that honesty compels me to admit that le Vicomte Ugo is both of those things," Ariana confessed. "Still, even if Christine had not warned me against him, I would not have liked him. He reminded me of a—a snake! That horrible sea serpent in my recurring dream…the nightmare about which I told you that afternoon in Hyde Park. Collie…do you believe that perhaps on that day we went fishing on Loch Ness, I actually spied Monsieur Ugo on the parapets of Castle Dúndragon? That I sensed then that he was wholly wicked and intended us some harm? For children are often far more sensitively attuned to people and nature than adults, I think."

"Aye, that's true, so perhaps you did."

"So much has happened to us since that day. Sometimes I can scarcely take it all in. 'Tis hard to believe that 'twas little more than a decade ago that you and I went fishing together on the lake. Still…what an impression that day must have made upon me! For I have dreamt of it ever since—yet I recall nothing at all about the murders of my own real father and yours, or the burning of Whitrose Grange!"

"You must not blame yourself for that, Ana. You were only a five-year-old child at the time. 'Tis no doubt possible that the events proved so confusing and traumatic for you that your mind repressed your memories of them, blocking them from your consciousness. For only think what it must have been like for you—to lose both your father and mother so close together, and your brother, Nicolas, besides, and to have been sent away to Uncle Jean-Paul and Aunt Hélène, who although relatives and your godparents, must still have been like strangers to you at the time."

"Yet, until recently, I never dreamt of all I had lost—except for you, Collie. 'Tis as though in the face of all the changes that swept like a violent hurricane through my young life, I clung to you fiercely. Somehow I must have sensed all the dangerous undercurrents of the brewing tempest about to tear my family apart forever, and you must have seemed like the eye of the storm to me, represented refuge for me. That must be why I never forgot you, but remembered you all these long years."

"As I remembered you, Ana. For that afternoon I took you

fishing upon Loch Ness was the last happy day I ever knew at Whitrose Grange—because that night our fathers were murdered, and the Grange was burnt. The following morning, we left it behind forever." Malcolm paused for a long moment, reflecting, recollecting his joyous boyhood days at the tenant farm, when he had known nothing about the Foscarellis, and his life had been sheltered, serene and sweet. Then he continued, "We have come a long way since then, haven't we, Ana? And you've grown from a brave, bonnie wee lass into an even more courageous and beautiful young woman."

"I'm flattered, of course. But you're wrong, you know, Collie," she replied gently, with a small, wry smile, as she turned from the library windows to face him. "For although I do try to be brave, deep down inside I'm not courageous at all, I don't think—but, rather, terribly frightened of the Foscarellis and…and about our future."

"I shall never let anything happen to you, Ana! I swear it!"

Without warning, at Malcolm's words there was between him and her a moment as highly charged as the electric atmosphere before a storm, a portentous moment when her wide, expressive eyes—filled at once with fear, uncertainty, longing and, most of all, love—locked with his own, and she glimpsed within his gaze a plethora of raw, naked emotions he could no longer conceal. Bitterness and anger over the past, pain and regret over the present, apprehension and doubt over the future, and, most of all, desire and love for her…all these abruptly irrepressible feelings now flickered one after another in his smoldering eyes, evidencing his severe inner conflict. Hard he fought his own better nature—but, in the end, at long last lost. Ariana had but a split second to recognize and savor her gladness and triumph before he suddenly crushed her to him and, with a desperate hunger and release of all his hitherto pent-up yearnings, kissed her as though there would be no tomorrow, but was only the here and now.

She had never before been kissed by a man, and none of her daydreams and fantasies had prepared her for the reality of it—for the way in which his hands would tangle almost roughly in her hair, tilting her face up to his and holding her still for his on-slaught, how his lips would claim hers with such atavistic ardor, and how his hard, strong body would meld itself to her own soft, fragile one, so that she trembled uncontrollably against the length of him. Emotions and sensations she had seldom ever before experienced now coursed through her wildly, making her head spin and driving all thoughts save those of him from her mind. And then, after a moment, she ceased to think at all, could only feel as, with his mouth, he swallowed the little whimpers and moans she unwittingly made, and wakened her to her first knowledge of passion.

But then at last Malcolm remembered that he was a gentle-man and that he was taking liberties with an innocent young woman to whom—however much he might wish to wed her—he could offer little or nothing. However reluctantly, he forced himself to break off the kiss and to release her.

"I'm…I'm sorry." He struggled visibly to get himself under control, a muscle throbbing in his set jaw. "I had no right to do that. It shouldn't have happened. However much I may wish I were, I am not in a position to ask you to marry me, Ana."

"Oh, Collie!" Ariana's voice was filled with anguish. "Must your pride stand in the way of our happiness?"

"I am no fortune hunter—and I cannot live on your dowry, Ana. 'Tis already bad enough that—as I now realize—suspect-ing my true identity, your father purchased the black stallion, Caliginous, for my own use, especially when he and your mother owe me nothing, to say nothing of whatever sum of money he must have laid out to save me from perhaps going to gaol for shooting Badger and knocking him and the still-missing Toby into the Thames. Nor can I ask you to sacrifice your own way of life, and all to which you are accustomed, to live the kind of life I could give you. I am not a rich man. Un-like your brother I have no unexpected county or earldom awaiting my reclamation of it. My own inheritance was lost—foolishly wagered away more than a century and a half ago—and there is no hope of recovering it. I am a cartographer, and as such, the most I can strive for is my own establishment some day."

"That is enough for me, Collie. I do not ask for more."

"Perhaps not. Still, I know that you must have many other suitors who could give you far more than I."

"But none who could give me what I desire most—happiness. Only you can do that, Collie."

"Damn it, Ana! You put me in a deuced awkward position when you say things like that!"

"As the saucy minx no doubt intends!" Mr. Ravener declared, stepping from the shadowy rows of bookcases that lined the library. "Please forgive me—for truly, I did not at all mean to eavesdrop. Christine having retired for the night, I but came to the library for a book, hoping that reading for a while would quiet my mind so I could sleep. But I guess I was more tired than I realized, for I had no sooner begun to read than I fell into a doze in my chair here in the library and only just now awoke. I did not intend to disturb your little tête-à-tête. Still, upon awakening, I could not help overhearing, and recognizing that I was no longer alone, I meant to make my presence known to you both at once. However, once I grasped what was happening between you, I deemed an earlier interruption even more inappropriate, so felt compelled to wait for a…er…lull in the proceedings."

At that, Ariana flushed with mortification, recognizing that her brother had witnessed her kissing Malcolm.

"You are shameless, Nicky!"

"If I am, put it down to the life I have been forced to lead. No, I don't resent you, Ana." He answered the unspoken question in her eyes. "In truth, nothing has made me happier than to find you alive and well cared for by Uncle Jean-Paul and Aunt Hélène. For as our dying *maman* realized, 'twas far better that I, not you, should have been left to survive on the mean streets. But having successfully managed to do so, I do not now apologize if I am sometimes lacking in those qualities thought necessary of a gentleman. So, rather than equivocate, I will speak bluntly. You and Malcolm are obviously very much in love, as all in this household are aware, since we would have to be blind not to see it. And although you may not recognize it, Ana, 'tis much to Malcolm's credit that he has pointed out the difficulties of such a match to you. But, Malcolm, have you considered at all the danger to Ana if you *don't* marry her?"

"Whatever do you mean, Nicolas?" Malcolm's brow knitted in a troubled frown.

"As the daughter of our *maman*—who was your own father's sister—Ana is the youngest and thus at this moment the last direct descendant of Lord James Ramsay, the Earl of Dúndragon, who stole that accursed emerald to begin with! Now, Christine has told me that there have long been rumors in the village that lies beyond Castle Dúndragon that the Foscarellis have no legitimate claim to the place, and although I would be the first to admit that I don't know whether that's true or not, what if 'tis? What if there actually *were* something highly irregular about Lord Dúndragon's—I'm speaking now of Lord Iain Ramsay, and not Lord James—having gambled away the property to Lord Bruno, Count Foscarelli? What if the estate had been entailed or something, so that Lord Dúndragon wasn't free to have wagered it? The Foscarellis must surely be cognizant of the local gossip. Perhaps they even know it to be true. We don't know. But in either case, why, then, what better way to secure their own hold upon Castle Dúndragon than by Lord Ugo's marrying Ana and ensuring that you and I, the only other direct legal heirs, are dead?" Mr. Ravener suggested softly and, to Malcolm, chillingly.

After pausing to allow this to sink in, he then went on.

"I am going to wed Christine—not only because I have fallen deeply in love with her, but also because I want to keep her safe. Because she was but a child at the time of her parents' deaths and has kept silent until now, the Foscarellis had no reason to suspect that she even knew anything at all about the Heart of Kheperi or that 'twas they—and not real highwaymen—who forced her parents' carriage off the road that night in the Highlands, killing and then robbing them. But now, because of her association with us and also, indirectly, with Madame Polgár, the

Foscarellis may begin to fear what Christine does, in fact, know and remember. They cannot be certain that she cannot in reality identify them as her parents' murderers, and on that basis alone, they may try to do her some harm. That, I do not intend to permit." Mr. Ravener's dark handsome face was grim with determination. "Christine's uncle and aunt are due home just shortly, at which time I shall ask them for her hand in marriage. Further, I am going to obtain a special license to wed her, so that we need not wait for the banns to be read—which, in and of itself, might prove dangerous to Christine, alerting the Foscarellis to the fact that she will soon have a young, strong, capable husband, instead of just an elderly uncle and aunt, to protect her. In such an event, the Foscarellis might be driven to act prior to our marriage, and that is a risk I will not take."

Mr. Ravener again fell silent for a minute. Then he continued.

"Think hard on all I have said, Malcolm. We could make it a double ceremony—and I, for one, would be as honored and glad to call you 'brother,' as I am to call you 'cousin,' and to see my sister settled not only safely, but also happily. Even as a child, she was always stubborn and willful, so I know that having fallen in love with you, she will have no other man. Now I shall bid both you and her good-night."

Carrying the book he had taken from the library's bookshelves, Mr. Ravener then departed from the chamber, leaving Malcolm and Ariana alone together, in the silence broken only by the crackling and sparking of the fire that burnt in the hearth and the thrumming of the rain against the windows.

"So much about Madame Polgár's predictions to me about my future that night she read the tarot cards for me in the pavilion at Maman's masquerade ball is now so startlingly clear to me." Ariana spoke quietly at last. "Until tonight, I did fear that however much he might attempt to conceal it, perhaps Nicky *did* resent me bitterly for having so much growing up, whilst he was left with so very little—when he ought to have had the county of Jourdain. And whilst I realize that in some ways he is a hard, daring man who takes his opportunities as he finds them, there is still a great deal of kindness and good in him, I think. Truly, he is the King of Wands whom Madame Polgár foresaw in my future and who would protect me even unto death. How he must love me—his little sister! 'Tis extremely grievous and shameful to me that I should have forgotten him, that I should not even have recognized him when first I met him!"

"You must not blame yourself for that, Ana—for he is much changed now from the boy I recall. During the past thirteen years he has grown to manhood, and even though Aunt Hélène is right, and Nicolas *does* greatly resemble Uncle Charles, even I, who was sixteen when I knew your real father, did not make the connection until 'twas pointed out to me. I think that perhaps the terrible image of poor Uncle Charles's face when he was so suddenly and violently stabbed to death by Lord Vittore, Count Foscarelli—for I inadvertently witnessed the murder, you know—was so hideously and indelibly ingrained upon my memory that I could see him in no other light, and that was why I did not at first associate Nicolas with him. And I know from all he said to us that Nicolas himself does not blame you for not recognizing or remembering him, Ana. He would not care so very much for you and your happiness if he did."

Pausing, Malcolm gave a low, wry laugh tinged with bitterness and self-recrimination.

"'Tis *I* who ought to be ashamed!" he asserted, angry at himself. "For I have thought only of myself and my own pride in this affair! No wonder Madame Polgár told you that she did not know whether I—the King of Swords—would prove your friend or foe! She must somehow have discerned the inner conflict and indecision I would experience where you are concerned, and not been able to foresee whether I would become your husband and protector—or whether, because of my own damnable pride, I would unwittingly place you in peril, in the wholly untenable position of becoming prey for Lord Ugo. For he is, of course, unquestionably the sinister King of Pentacles, about whom Madame Polgár warned you, Ana!"

"But, Collie, until Nicky spoke of them to you tonight, you were, I believe, totally unaware of the rumors that have long circulated in the village that lies beyond Castle Dúndragon," Ariana pointed out gently. "So you did not know of this possible threat to my safety and well-being."

"No—but I *did* know that the Foscarellis would stop at naught to achieve their evil ends, that their family has for far more than a century now been obsessed with finding the missing emerald and that they have allowed nothing and no one to stand in their way. The present Count Foscarelli brutally and remorselessly murdered my own father and yours, and he and his son, Lord Ugo, also killed Lady Christine's parents and, aye, even poor Madame Polgár, as surely as though they drove a knife straight through her heart! Can you ever forgive me for being such a proud fool, Ana?"

"Oh, Collie, of course I can."

"'Tis the greatest humiliation to me that I have so little to offer you beyond my own self and my protection."

"But it should not be—for 'tis through no fault of your own, and I myself care about nothing, so long as we are together!"

"But you deserve so much more than what I can give you, Ana!"

"Oh, Collie, don't you know that 'tis only you I want? I have loved you ever since I was a child, I think."

"And I love you, Ana, with all my heart—for whatever that may be worth."

"'Tis worth everything to me, Collie!"

"Then…will you take me as I am—foolish pride and all—and marry me, Ana? Shall we indeed have a double ceremony with Nicolas and Lady Christine, as he suggested?"

"*Oui*—and again, *oui*. Nothing would make me happier!"

At that, Malcolm once more took Ariana in his arms and kissed her—tenderly this time and with all the love he felt inside for her, his heart filled to overflowing with gladness, and his mind deliberately shutting out all his previous misgivings. He would find the lost emerald and restore his family's fortunes, he vowed silently, not for the first time. Then Ariana would never regret becoming his wife, and he would be well able to take care of her. But even as the thought occurred to him, beyond the library windows, dark with mist and rain, a nebulous, shadowy cloud suddenly passed again across the unfathomable face of the moon, sending an ominous chill of premonition and dread through him.

Chapter Seventeen

Knaves and Graves

This is the excellent foppery of the world,
that, when we are sick in fortune—often the surfeit
of our own behavior—we make guilty of our disasters
the sun, the moon, and the stars; as if we were villains
by necessity, fools by heavenly compulsion, knaves,
thieves, and teachers by spherical predominance,
drunkards, liars, and adulterers by an enforced obedience
of planetary influence.

—William Shakespeare
King Lear [1605-1606]

We have seen the best of our time:
machinations, hollowness, treachery, and all ruinous
disorders, follow us disquietly to our graves.

—William Shakespeare
King Lear [1605-1606]

I lingered round them, under that benign sky:
watched the moths fluttering among the heath and
harebells; listened to the soft wind breathing through
the grass; and wondered how anyone could ever imagine
unquiet slumbers for the sleepers in that quiet earth.

—Emily Brontë
Wuthering Heights [1847]. Last words

1848
*The General Cemetery of All Souls at Kensal Green,
London, England*

Because of fears for their safety, and Madame Polgár's death, as well, Malcolm and Mrs. Blackfriars had, at Madame Valcoeur's request, continued to lodge at the Lévesques' town house in Portman Square, to assist however they could. "For truly, even though I was often a little afraid of Madame Polgár, she was still my friend, and I am greatly distraught at her death, for which I feel a good deal to blame," the comtesse had declared sadly. "So 'twould be such a kindness, *ma chère* Elizabeth, if you and Malcolm would consent to stay on. Besides which, after all that has happened this dreadful night, I truly do worry about you returning home to Hawthorn Cottage—for who knows what those madmen, the Foscarellis, may be planning next?" At that, Mrs. Blackfriars had been only too happy to agree to remain, for she herself had been no less distressed by the evening's turn of events, and also by the thought of her and her son being set upon at Hawthorn Cottage by the Foscarellis. She wished fervently that she had never told Malcolm anything at all about his heritage and the Heart of Kheperi, for she feared horribly that they would prove the death of him, just as they had his father and uncle Charles.

From the undertaker, Madame Polgár was to have the finest of winding-sheets and coffins, the former of full-worked glazed cambric, and the latter consisting of a sturdy inner shell of elm wood fitted with a tufted mattress and a pillow, and lined with ruffled superfine cambric, a strong middle shell of lead, soldered all around to form a weather-tight seal and bearing an inscription plate; and, finally, a half-inch-thick oak outer shell, covered with red velvet, the lid hammered into place with the most expensive brass nails, set in three rows all around, with a further matching brass inscription plate, four pairs of ornately engraved brass handles and grips on the sides, and intricate brass ornaments on the lid. On all of this, the morning after her death, Dukker adamantly insisted, saying that Madame Polgár had, shortly before her demise, given him detailed instructions with regard to her funeral arrangements, as well as set aside in a small bank account, to which he had access, the necessary money to pay for same.

"The evening that I came here to Portman Square for help, after Madame Polgár had been put into Bedlam by the Foscarellis, I did not come straightaway," the dwarf now explained to all those in the household who were gathered at the breakfast table in the Lévesques' dining room. "I went first to *madame's* own town house, in Henrietta Street. 'Twas as I had feared. During our absence, the Foscarellis had ransacked the place, in search of a very valuable crucifix, which belonged to *madame*. Besides me, she had only a few other servants, and as they slept in the attic rooms, they had heard nothing. But the town house was all sixes and sevens, so I knew that the Foscarellis had been there."

"But they did not get what they had come for, did they?" Malcolm observed shrewdly. "Because if they had, they would not have needed to keep Madame Polgár alive."

"*Non,* that is true, *monsieur.*" Now, carrying the small gilded box he had not parted with since entering the Lévesques' town house, Dukker rose from the chair he occupied in one corner and went to stand beside Ariana, where she sat at the dining table. "Madame Polgár charged me most sternly, *mademoiselle,* that if anything untoward befell her, you were to have this." Gravely placing the box on the table, the dwarf slowly opened its lid. "As you see, she kept her tarot cards inside. The Foscarellis had opened the box, of course, and scattered the cards all over the floor, but I picked them all up and replaced them."

"Madame Polgár wanted me to have her tarot cards?" Ariana inquired, curious. "But…why? I wonder."

"*Non, mademoiselle.* Not the cards—they but served as a ruse to deceive any who might try to investigate the box. 'Tis the box itself and what it contains that *madame* wished you to have," the dwarf elucidated mysteriously, confusing her. "For unbeknown to the Foscarellis, fortunately, 'tis a puzzle box, with a second lid, which you open like this."

Much to Ariana's surprise, although the box appeared to be

a single whole, it was actually composed of a number of small wooden pieces that slid this way and that, and by turning the box over and pushing them out in their proper sequence, as Dukker did now, the second lid, which had initially seemed to be the bottom of the box, opened—to reveal the cross that lay within. Carefully the dwarf lifted it from its resting place and handed it to Ariana, who was now wholly stunned and incredulous.

"Madame Polgár said that if you did not yet know the purpose of the crucifix, Messieurs Blackfriars and Ravener would—for she informed me that, in reality, they are your cousin, Monsieur Ramsay, and your brother, Monsieur de Ramezay, le Comte de Jourdain. Is that true?"

"I—I am not…certain how to…how to answer that, Dukker," Ariana stated honestly, gazing in helpless inquiry at her fiancé and her brother.

"'Tis indeed true," Malcolm said slowly at last, not sure whether they could trust the dwarf, but deciding that since he already appeared to know so much, it seemed pointless to attempt to deceive him. "But how did Madame Polgár know?"

"For many years she had searched for the descendants of an order called the Sons of Isis, who once possessed and worshiped the priceless missing emerald known as the Heart of Kheperi, which had, Monsieur Blackfriars, been stolen by a common ancestor of yours, Monsieur Jourdain's and Mademoiselle Ariana's, from the tomb of an Egyptian high priest, and about which stone, if you will remember, that strange Egyptian gentleman Mr. al-Walid spoke at one of Madame Valcoeur's conversation parties one evening. Madame Polgár's own grandmother, who had come from Scotland and married into *madame's* family, was herself a descendant of one of the original brothers of the Sons of Isis, and, after telling her the tale of the lost emerald, had bequeathed to her the cross, which is supposed to be a key to the stone's location. Madame Polgár believed that other descendants must have other crucifixes, because if you will examine hers closely, Mademoiselle Ariana, you will see that it bears the number eight."

"I—I need a magnifying glass." Ariana now peered closely at the cross she held gingerly, still disbelievingly, but she could not discern its number.

"I'll get one." Rising, Mr. Ravener made his way from the dining room, returning shortly thereafter with the magnifying glass and Madame Valcoeur's Bible.

"You—you look, Nicky." Ariana handed him the crucifix.

"Yes, this is definitely number eight," he announced, after a long moment of scrutiny through the magnifying glass. "And on the back 'tis inscribed 'Nahum 2:8.'" Handing the cross and magnifying glass to Ariana, he leafed through the Bible. "'And Nineveh has become like a pool of water, like the waters around her, which are ebbing away. "Stop! Stop!" they cry; but none turns back.'"

"Do you understand to what the passage alludes, Monsieur Jourdain?" the dwarf asked.

"No, not exactly." Mr. Ravener shook his head. "And for the time being, you must call me 'Mr. Ravener,' not 'Monsieur Jourdain.' For I would conceal my real identity from our enemies, the Foscarellis, as long as I can. Naturally, the chapter and verse must somehow be a clue to the location of the missing emerald, but unfortunately, the words are as cryptic as those on the other crosses we now possess."

"So…Madame Polgár was right! There *are* other crucifixes, and you *do* have them!" Dukker cried, with sudden excitement.

"Some—but not all of them." It was Malcolm who spoke— cautiously.

"How many?"

"Four—counting the one you have just now given to Mademoiselle Ariana."

"Only four?" The dwarf's expression was now crestfallen. "Madame Polgár hoped you would have many more, that you and she might become allies against the Foscarellis!"

"Oh, if only she had told us all that from the very beginning of our acquaintance!" Madame Valcoeur's face evidenced her distress. "We might have protected her and saved her from the Foscarellis!"

"Madame Polgár was extremely prudent, *madame*," Dukker declared soberly. "She trusted no one, except for me. She knew I would have given up even my very life for her, for she saved it many years ago, and ever since that time, I have been her devoted and faithful servant. And now, if you will have me, *mademoiselle*—" he turned to address Ariana again "—such I will be to you. On my honor, this I swear!"

"I'm—I'm…truly flattered and—and deeply touched, Dukker," she said, much startled by the dwarf's offer. "But quite frankly, I'm also curious. Why should you want to serve me?"

"I wish to make amends." Dukker's visage was now filled with shame and sorrow. "For 'twas I who pushed you into Oxford Street that day you were nearly trampled by the runaway horse and hansom cab. Truly, I meant only to knock you down, so I could snatch from your neck any cross you might be wearing. But although I am a dwarf and so not very tall, I am still inordinately strong, and sometimes even I don't know my own strength. So I shoved you far too hard. Madame Polgár was most angry and upset with me afterward, horrified that I might have killed you—and so I might, had it not been for Monsieur Blackfriars. I'm so sorry, *mademoiselle,* for I never intended you any harm."

"*Non,* I feel certain you did not, and so I forgive you, Dukker—and I thank you, as well, for 'twas that incident that brought Monsieur Blackfriars back into my life." Ariana blushed faintly, for she and Malcolm had not yet announced their engagement. Before that, he must first speak to her father, and there had been no opportunity as yet this morning for him to do so.

But immediately following breakfast, Malcolm joined Monsieur Valcoeur in his study, and at once gained his consent to marry his daughter.

"Malcolm, I assure you that nothing would please me and your aunt Hélène more than to see Ariana safely and happily wed to you!" The comte beamed with delight. "These are glad tidings, indeed—and will go a long way toward helping take Hélène's mind off the death of poor Madame Polgár."

"You must know, Uncle Jean-Paul, that I have come to love Ariana deeply. Yet my status in life is such that I have hesitated to ask for her hand in marriage until now. For I would not be thought a fortune hunter! But nor, on the other hand, after all Nicolas said to me last night, can I in all good conscience continue to permit my pride to stand between Ariana and me, knowing that it could well expose her to some danger at the hands of the Foscarellis. And I promise you that, as her husband, I will not only do everything within my power to ensure her safety and well-being, but also to recover the Heart of Kheperi and restore my family's fortune, so she will never want for aught in this life, if I can prevent it!" Malcolm vowed earnestly.

"I feel sure that you will, Malcolm, for over these past several months, even before Hélène and I began to suspect your true identity, I had come to recognize that you were a genuinely brave, decent, honorable and capable man—exactly the sort I should like to have for my son-in-law, even were you not a Ramsay of Dúndragon and thus already related to me by both blood and marriage. More important, I know that you will make Ariana happy, and although, as you are now aware, she is our goddaughter, still, Hélène and I could not love her more if she were our own flesh-and-blood child. So I trust that you will take good care of her, Malcolm."

"I will, *monsieur,* I swear it!"

"Good. Then let us go and announce this happy news at once! For 'twill brighten the spirits of both Hélène and your own dear mother immeasurably, I know, and there can be no objection to the timing, since Madame Polgár was not a relative, so we need not observe any official mourning for her."

The comte was correct in his supposition. The effect of the announcement of Malcolm and Ariana's engagement, followed instantly by Mr. Ravener's own declaration of his intention to marry Lady Christine and to speak to her uncle and aunt upon their return on the morrow, was to cheer both the comtesse and Mrs. Blackfriars exceedingly. Congratulations and best wishes were offered all around, after which Monsieur Valcoeur vanished again into his study, along with Malcolm and Mr. Ravener, to smoke celebratory cigars, while the four ladies gathered in the morning room to start making plans for the small, private double ceremony, which, it was agreed, would take place just as soon as possible.

"What a great pity that there must be all this secrecy, so that we cannot place the proper announcements in all the newspapers and have a large ceremony, to which everyone who is anyone could be invited." The comtesse sighed wistfully. "But there, given this dreadful affair of that accursed emerald and the perils posed by the Foscarellis, I suppose that Malcolm and Nicolas are right and that a quiet ceremony by way of special licenses is for the best. Oh, *ma chère* Ariana and *ma chère* Christine—for such you have become to us—I am so happy for you both! Once, despite how I longed for them, I had no children at all. But then Ariana was sent to us, and now Nicolas has been found and restored to us, and you, Christine, are to be as a second daughter to me, and Malcolm as a second son. Truly, *le bon Dieu* has blessed me greatly!"

"And me," Mrs. Blackfriars said, smiling gently, although a trifle sadly, even so. "I only wish that my dear friend and sister-in-law, Katherine, were still alive to share the joy of this day with us. For she would be so proud of you, Ariana—and of you, Hélène, for standing in her stead and being the kind of loving mother that Katherine herself was and would have been, had she lived. You have done so well by Ariana, Hélène. Katherine's trust and faith in you were more than deserved!"

"What…what was she like, Aunt Elizabeth?" Ariana queried softly. "I know that that day when first you saw me grown, you thought I was she. Am I so very like her, then?"

"In truth, yes, Ariana! Whenever I look at you, I see Katherine, also—for she had the same beautiful raven hair and amethyst eyes as you, and the same touching mixture of courage and vulnerability that I sense in you, as well. No wonder Malcolm fell in love with you! Even when you were a child, he always called you a 'brave, bonnie wee lass.'"

"I'm not so wee anymore!" Ariana laughed.

"No, perhaps not—but still brave and bonnie!" Mrs. Black-friars insisted, smiling again, more brightly now. "And like both Katherine and Hélène, I shall be very glad to have you for a daughter."

"And I shall count myself most fortunate, indeed, to have gained another wonderful mother. Truly, 'tis *I* whom *le bon Dieu* has greatly blessed!"

"I feel exactly as you do, Ariana," Christine averred. "I am so lucky to have met Nicolas! And now, to be welcomed so warmly and lovingly by his family, too…well, 'tis far more than I ever hoped for or dreamt of. 'Tis difficult to believe that in the midst of so much grief and danger we should have found such happiness."

"*Oui,* that is so. 'Tis like a ray of light shining into the darkness—a wholly unexpected gift, like that of the crucifix from Madame Polgár. Perhaps 'tis even in some way a message from her—an omen of what is to come, she would no doubt tell us. Let us hope that is indeed the case!"

But before the planned double ceremony of marriage could take place, there was the fortune-teller's funeral to attend to. She had, it was soon discovered, engaged a solicitor to deal with her affairs and appointed him and his partners as the executors of her estate. So once her last will and testament was probated, there remained only the closing up of her town house in Henrietta Street and the dispersal of all her worldly goods to take care of. Having apparently had little or no family left, she had bequeathed most of her wealth to various orders, some religious and the rest of a more esoteric nature, and also bestowed appropriate monetary legacies upon Dukker and her other few servants for their service to her. There was, as well, a letter to Dukker, in which she had set out instructions for all her funeral arrangements.

At a cost of thirty-nine pounds, two shillings and sixpence, she was to be interred in a brick vault at Kensal Green, which was why a lead coffin had been necessary, as these were required for burial in either vaults or catacombs in all the city's cemeteries. A visit to the Kensal Green offices, located at 95 Great Russell Street, settled all the requisite details, and Madame Polgár's funeral was scheduled to take place on Friday at 3:00 p.m., which was the usual time for burials at Kensal Green. Funeral notices, printed in black-letter type, on black-edged mourning paper obtained from a stationer, and sealed with black wax, were dispatched to all her friends, for whom mourning carriages were hired to collect them and convey them to and from the solemn rite.

The afternoon of Madame Polgár's funeral, all those mourners attending assembled at the Lévesques' town house in Portman Square, rather than at the fortune-teller's own in Henrietta Street, which, given her dearth of family, was now shut up tight, its blinds drawn and a black wreath adorning the front door. It was a cold, dreary winter's day, gray with billowing mist from the sea and the River Thames, and with a leaden sky from which drizzle spattered, so that the tall black ostrich plumes affixed to the heads of the multitude of horses were bedraggled, and the velvet that draped the hearse and all the mourning coaches was sodden. Accompanied by two mutes with gowns, silk hatbands and gloves, as well as fourteen men who served as pages, feathermen and coachmen, all bearing truncheons and wands, the funeral procession wound its way in somber parade west from Portman Square to Kensal Green, at last passing beneath the towering, imposing arch over the huge gates that guarded the entrance to the cemetery.

Situated just west of Paddington, on Harrow Road and at the top of Ladbroke Grove, on the southern bank of the Grand Junction Canal, the General Cemetery of All Souls, at Kensal Green, as it was officially called, was an expansive graveyard for the interment of persons of all religions. The first public and joint-stock necropolis to be established in the region of the city, it had been founded in 1832 by a barrister, George Frederick Carden, in the wake of the burial reform that had resulted from London's rapid population growth during the 1820s. Three miles from Oxford Street and lying upon a large rise that had once been a part of the Fillingham estate, Kensal Green Cemetery, as it was popularly referred to, comprised more than seventy acres of land, bounded on three sides by a massive stone curtain wall and on the fourth by an ornate wrought-iron fence.

It was an attractive, peaceful place, which had been carefully laid out in a style similar to that of Le Cimetière du Père-Lachaise, in Paris, and beautifully landscaped. The open gates through which the hearse and mourning carriages now rumbled gave way to wide avenues lined with ashes, chestnuts, elms, limes, oaks, poplars and silver beeches, which paths cleaved the otherwise natural meadowland overgrown with blackberry bushes, bracken, heather, lavender and prickly nettles. At the east end of the graveyard was a butterfly and bee garden, where the wardens had planted bergamot, buddleia, hyssop, rosemary and sage to attract bees and butterflies. Bats and owls lurked in the trees, and foxes prowled the copses and glades. At the heart of the consecrated grounds stood the Anglican Chapel, and in one corner of the unconsecrated grounds rose the Dissenters' Chapel, both constructed in the Greek-revival style and beneath which were the catacombs for burial of the very rich. Additional catacombs reposed along an elegant Georgian colonnade. Everywhere, small Greek temples—as well as stone obelisks, sarcophagi, tombs, urns and vaults—abounded, and in the long cold shadows cast by great family mausoleums in the feeble wintry daylight, spongy late mushrooms sprouted and decayed in the wet loam.

This was the first time that Ariana had ever seen the cemetery, and as, assisted by Malcolm, she descended from the mourning coach in which they had traveled, she thought that Madame Polgár had chosen a fitting final resting place.

"'Tis a most lovely cemetery," she observed quietly to him, beneath the umbrella held over them by the footmen.

"Aye." He nodded, taking her arm in his. "Although when my own time comes I would prefer to be buried in the Highlands, if it must be London, then, having seen the place now, I would not object to Kensal Green."

"Oh, do not speak to me of your dying, Collie!" Ariana entreated earnestly as they began to walk toward the brick vault where the fortune-teller was to be interred. "For I could not bear to lose you—especially now that we are to be wed." Anxiously she bit her lower lip. "And I *do* fear for you, for who knows what the Foscarellis may next attempt?"

"Please don't worry, Ana. We are on our guard against them."

"I know—but still, as Dukker said, so was Madame Polgár, and now she is dead. Yet even now, when we are come to the cemetery to bury her, I—I still can't quite believe it. She always seemed so…incredibly ancient to me somehow, almost as though she were ageless…immortal, even. As she did Maman, she frightened me, and I know she would have stolen my crucifix had Papa not locked it away for safekeeping. But still, strangely enough, I shall miss her."

"So will I—for I believe she had learnt a great deal more about the Sons of Isis than we have, and as she herself observed, she and we might eventually have become allies and then been able to pool our knowledge and resources to locate the Heart of Kheperi. But now 'tis too late for that, and all she knew, she will carry to her grave."

"Such a bizarre death she had, Collie—dying during the séance the way she did that night! I confess I have—I have wondered ever since if that accursed emerald was ultimately somehow to blame. Oh, Collie, perhaps you should abandon your search for it, lest it be the death of you, too!"

Resolutely, grimly Malcolm shook his head.

"No, that I cannot and will not do, Ana—not even for you. For otherwise, the curse the emerald has laid upon the Clan Ramsay of Dúndragon will only continue. 'Twould devolve upon our children, Ana! And Viscount Ugo's offspring would unquestionably become the enemies of our own, and the entire vicious cycle would go on and on— perhaps even endlessly. Your father and mine gave their very lives to attempt to prevent that from happening to us. Even if I, too, should fail, can I do any less to try to protect our own children?"

"*Non…non,* of course not." Ariana blushed deeply at the mention of offspring—and the implications of all that entailed. "I—I did not think about that…until just now. I suppose that with all that's happened, I—I hadn't really thought about the future at all."

But now, of a sudden, she wished fervently that she were clairvoyant, as Madame Polgár had been, and that she could see clearly what lay ahead for them, what the future held in store. But as she gazed out over the graveyard, there was only the fog and the rain, and a short distance away, as the veils of the former drifted and parted, the sight of the brick vault that was to receive the fortune-teller's remains. As she spied its dark, forbidding, gaping maw, Ariana unwittingly shivered, feeling abruptly, horribly, as though it somehow awaited her instead.

High above Lord Lucrezio Foscarelli, Viscount Ugo, the heavily carved stone angel soared, blowing its trumpet soundlessly—an ominous last trump whose muted warning note could not be heard by the mere mortals gathered at the Kensal Green Cemetery. But *he* discerned it, and as he did so, a supercilious smile curved his lips. Unlike those he spied upon, he was one of the immortals—or would be, once he and his father, Lord Vittore, Count Foscarelli, discovered the location of the Heart of Kheperi. For a century now, ever since they had learnt of the legendary emerald's existence, possession of the amulet had eluded his family. But he, Lord Ugo, did not mean to be defeated in his quest, as his predecessors had been. Instead, he would prove successful, and then he would harness the stone's great power and live forever. Ever since he had been a child, this goal had been inculcated in him by his father, and his father before him, and he had been taught how to deal ruthlessly with all those who attempted to thwart it—as Madame Polgár had.

He and his father had invested a great deal of time and effort in tracking her down, eventually tracing her through her Scottish grandmother, the Lady Sibyl Macbeth, whom they had known to be descended from one of the original brothers of the Sons of Isis. They had finally unexpectedly discovered that some months ago, the fortune-teller had immigrated to England, to London, and they had plotted to abduct her. But even threats and abuse had failed to elicit from the old witch the whereabouts of the crucifix Lord Ugo felt certain she had secreted away somewhere and that he had sought to obtain from her for himself and his own purposes. So he had locked her away in a cell in Bedlam, where he had intended her to remain until she had given him the information he desired. But the dwarf...the dwarf who had served her had got away from Lord Ugo's hirelings and thereby foiled his scheme, causing her to be rescued.

Now, as, from where he crouched behind a massive stone sepulchre crowned by the trumpeting angel, Lord Ugo stared through his binoculars at those assembled at Madame Polgár's brick vault, and at Dukker in particular, his venomous black eyes narrowed and his mouth tightened with anger. The dwarf would pay for his interference, he vowed silently, especially since the fortune-teller had died without revealing to him where she had hidden her cross. If not for that, Lord Ugo would have been glad that the old witch was dead, for despite himself, her piercing golden hawk's eyes and her strange, fatalistic predictions had unnerved him, sending an icy grue up his spine. His father had only laughed at Madame Polgár's divinations, insisting that she was nothing more than an actress and a charlatan, an old fraud. But Lord Ugo was not so certain, and if he were honest with himself, he must admit that, however his plans for her had gone awry, he was still slightly relieved that she had died.

This piece of news he had learnt from the Marchioness of Mayfield when he had called on her earlier this week.

"Madame Polgár's death was quite unexpected...heart failure, I understand," the marchioness had imparted as she rattled on about the latest gossip, which she always seemed to know and which was why he so carefully cultivated her friendship. "She's to be buried at Kensal Green, I hear. I shouldn't care to be interred there myself, in a public cemetery, even if His Royal Highness the Prince Augustus Frederick, the Duke of Sussex, and his sister Her Royal Highness the Princess Sophia *did* choose it as their own final resting places. They were only King George the Third's *sixth* son and *fifth* daughter, after all. I myself shall be buried at Mayfield, of course. One wonders why Madame Polgár's body wasn't returned to her homeland. She originally emigrated from one of those Romanian principalities, I believe… Wallachia? Moldavia? Transylvania? Who can keep them all straight? But since they've all always got some kind of political turmoil going on, no doubt she had no estate left to be returned to, but had been dispossessed."

"When is the funeral to be held?" Lord Ugo had inquired, pretending only a casual interest in the subject.

"This coming Friday afternoon, at three o'clock. But since she had not been in London even a year and so had relatively few friends here, I believe 'tis to be only a rather smallish, somewhat private affair. I met her through Lord and Lady Alvaston myself. However, since I didn't know her at all well, naturally I shall not be attending the funeral."

After that it had remained only for Lord Ugo to confirm all these details with the Kensal Green offices in Great Russell Street, then to ensure that he himself arrived at the graveyard prior to the funeral procession, so that he could learn whom Madame Polgár had counted among her friends in London. So as to more easily escape detection, he had dressed in mourning clothes to blend in with the rest of those who would be present at the cemetery, for the fortune-teller's funeral was unlikely to be the only one solemnized that afternoon. The public, joint-stock necropolises had been established to turn a profit for their shareholders, and adhered to a rigid schedule. At Kensal Green, to be interred at other than the usual appointed hour cost seven shillings and sixpence extra. Leaving his own carriage and coachmen waiting in Harrow Road, Lord Ugo had made his way on foot to the graveyard, carrying a wintry bouquet of evergreens, so that he would appear to be paying his respects to a deceased relative or friend. Once through the gates, he had surveyed the cemetery carefully and selected a hiding place well up the sloping meadow, from which vantage point he could, through his binoculars, see most of the cemetery.

Now, as his gaze swept the little band of mourners gathered at Madame Polgár's brick vault, he abruptly paused, completely taken aback and incredulous. With a hand that trembled slightly with sudden excitement, he withdrew a fine linen handkerchief from his pocket and, with it, cleaned the mist and mizzle from his binoculars, then adjusted the lenses to be certain they were in focus. Then he peered even harder through the eyepieces, now sure that the lenses had not deceived him.

There stood the Lady Christine Fraser, with whom he had been acquainted for quite some time, and beside her Mademoiselle Ariana Lévesque, who, that evening at the Marchioness of Mayfield's masquerade ball, had attracted his interest because she had reminded him of someone else, whom he had felt, and still felt, strongly that he ought to recall, but could not. On Christine's opposite side stood a tall dark man whom he did not recognize, and on Ariana's opposite side was the man who held him riveted to the scene, for Lord Ugo would have known him anywhere. It was his nemesis, Malcolm Ramsay! He was certain of it! Years ago in the Highlands he had spent countless solitary days upon the parapets of Castle Dúndragon, watching the equally solitary boy who had fished upon Loch Ness far below. Sometimes he had imagined that he and the lad could become friends, but Lord Ugo's father had sternly forbidden him to play with any of the other children in the surrounding villages or countryside, declaring that they were not proper companions for the only son of Count Foscarelli. And then, one morning following a fire at Whitrose Grange, the tenant farm on the eastern shore of the lake, where the boy had lived, Lord Ugo's father had further informed him that the lad they had believed to be Malcolm MacLeod was, in reality, Malcolm Ramsay—and therefore their enemy!

"The Ramsays have been here, spying on us all along, Lucrezio!" his father had announced, enraged. "For they mean to try somehow to reclaim Castle Dúndragon—and thus also to steal the priceless emerald, the Heart of Kheperi, from us before we can find it! Fortunately, I discovered all this before 'twas too late, and I have killed them, as they would have killed us had I not been so alert and diligent in my inquiries."

"They are all dead, then—even the boy?" Lord Ugo had asked, slightly stunned.

"*Sì, sì,* did I not just say as much?" His father's voice had been impatient. "For last night I went to Whitrose Grange and there confronted the father, Alexander Ramsay, and also the man I believe was his de Ramezay cousin, Charles, in the study, whilst the rest of the household slept. We argued and fought, during which struggle I slew them both, and the farmhouse itself was set ablaze by the lamp that burnt on Ramsay's desk. The place was an inferno when I left it. No one could have escaped, I tell you! The others will have died in their beds."

"Did Mr. Ramsay…was he wearing a crucifix?"

"No—so either he did not inherit one, or else he secreted it somewhere in Whitrose Grange."

After breakfast, once the blanket of Scotch mist had started to lift a little, Lord Ugo's father had gone with some men across the loch to investigate the farmhouse, but they had found nothing amid the still-steaming blackened ruin. The place had been devoid of life, and there had been no sign of a cross hidden anywhere.

"What if the Ramsay crucifix has now been lost forever?" Lord Ugo had queried upon his father's return. "How will we ever find the Heart of Kheperi, then?"

"I do not know," his father had answered, frowning. "Perhaps Ramsay did not possess one of the crosses, after all, or perhaps 'tis somewhere other than at Whitrose Grange. We must not give up, but continue to search."

"Father, we must face the fact that, aside from the one handed down through the generations from our ancestor Lord Bruno, Count Foscarelli, our family has recovered only two other crucifixes in the past century!"

"That is because we did not know where to look. But each generation has carried on the family's quest, and as a result, each has learnt a little more than what was known to that before. One day, we shall prevail—just as we have now triumphed over our adversaries! For the Ramsay boy and his two young de Ramezay cousins were the last of their lines. There is an end to them now!"

Or so his father had believed. But now Lord Ugo knew otherwise. For somehow Malcolm and his mother—for surely, it *was* she beside him—had escaped from the fire at Whitrose Grange! Recognizing that fact triggered a flood of hitherto hazy, long-forgotten memories, and as he again trained his binoculars on the tall dark man and Ariana, who flanked Christine, Lord Ugo suddenly realized of whom Ariana reminded him—the woman at the farmhouse whom his father had identified as Malcolm's aunt, Katherine de Ramezay! And the tall dark man…surely he resembled her dead husband, Charles de Ramczay, as well. They, then, must be Malcolm's two de Ramezay cousins! Lord Ugo could scarcely credit it. For more than a decade now, he had thought his family's foes utterly vanquished, burnt to death in the flames that had consumed Whitrose Grange. Now, to learn that, instead, they still lived and breathed—and had no doubt plotted against him with Madame Polgár!—delivered him a stunning blow, leaving him feeling as though the wind had been abruptly and violently knocked from him by some unseen opponent, who had taken him unawares.

For a long moment, his breath coming in hard rasps, he leaned against the mausoleum behind which he had earlier concealed himself, the wheels of his mind churning furiously. Then at last, deliberately forcing himself to collect his wits, he once more focused his binoculars on the mourners assembled at the fortune-teller's brick vault in the distance.

During the French Revolution vast numbers of the French clergy and nobility alike had fled the country to immigrate to England, a great many settling in London, so that by the turn of the century, the city had boasted five Catholic archbishops, twenty-seven bishops and five thousand priests, together with their congregations. As a result of this huge influx of French Catholics, it had become necessary to establish places of worship for them, and eight chapels had been constructed in London for their use. By 1814, when the majority of the exiles had been repatriated, all but one of the chapels—the Chapel of St. Louis, in Little George Street—had closed. This chapel, however, founded in 1799 and later renamed the Chapel Royal of France, had continued to remain open and to be served by French priests. It was one of these—Père Gérard St. Clair—who officiated at Madame Polgár's funeral. Upon her arrival in London, having learnt that Père Gérard was related not only to the St. Clairs of France, but also to the Sinclairs of Scotland, she had, Dukker had informed Ariana, taken a particular interest in the elderly priest and had especially requested that he perform the solemn rite he now conducted.

Initially, much to her guilt and shame, lost in her own reverie, Ariana had hardly paid Père Gérard any notice. But after a while, as she stood with her head bowed to conceal her thoughts and with her arm tucked securely beneath Malcolm's own, she became aware of the fact that his body was stiff with tension and that his gaze was riveted on the old priest. In light of Malcolm's concentration on Père Gérard and the service, she flushed with mortification at the idea that she had allowed her own mind to wander, and she forced herself to turn her attention to the priest and the funeral. It was only then that, for the first time, she grasped what had captured Malcolm's rapt interest, and she gasped, as stunned as though she had suddenly been dealt a ringing slap.

At her sharp inhalation of breath, Malcolm tightened his arm around hers, both steadying and warning her. But even so, it was all Ariana could do to keep still, for much to her astonishment, around his neck Père Gérard wore a large, ornate silver crucifix that she felt certain was a duplicate of the four now locked away in the secret compartment of the desk in her father's study. She started to speak, but Malcolm shook his head imperceptibly but meaningfully, so that she actually bit her tongue to keep silent. But still, she could not resist glancing up at him and then at everybody else present, to see if anyone else had observed the cross that lay boldly upon the priest's chest, glinting dully in the pale gray winter light that seeped beneath the canopy of black umbrellas held by all the footmen to shield the mourners from the rain. Nicolas and Christine, she was sure, had spied the crucifix, for her brother's dark visage was grim with determination and calculation, and Christine's eyes were round and startled, her face wan. Ariana suspected that her father, too, had seen the cross, but she could not be certain, for he and her aunt Elizabeth were comforting her mother, who wept copiously, as she always did at funerals, and who murmured, "*La pauvre* Madame Polgár," time and again.

Her heart pounding with nervous excitement and apprehension, Ariana stood beneath the canopy of umbrellas, her tumultuous thoughts now even more unfocused and chaotic than they had been before. She wondered what Malcolm and Nicolas would do. They could scarcely attack Père Gérard and tear the crucifix from his neck right here at the fortune-teller's graveside! she reflected. So it was that she was taken completely by surprise by what happened next. As, at last, the eight strong coffin bearers removed the black silk-velvet pall from Madame Polgár's weighty casket and carefully folded it up—for the heavy drape was always only lent by undertakers—then lifted the ponderous coffin itself to maneuver it into the brick vault, Dukker suddenly gave a loud, anguished cry and flung himself hysterically upon the priest.

"*Non, non!* You cannot bury *madame!* You cannot! She's not dead! She just can't be! She lives! She lives! You must open the coffin at once! She will suffocate in there!"

Amid the horrified stares of the onlookers, who stood frozen to the ground, Malcolm and Nicolas alone sprang forward to haul the dwarf from Père Gérard, to whom he clung tenaciously, babbling and bawling pitifully. Stating that Dukker was plainly overcome with shock and grief, and apologizing for him, the two men forcibly dragged him away from the graveside, disappearing into the billowing mist—and with a jolt that left her weak in the knees and clutching Christine for support, Ariana saw that the priest's cross had vanished with them.

Chapter Eighteen

Wedding and Other Plans

Zeus does not bring all men's plans to fulfillment.

—Homer
The Illiad

We for a certainty are not the first
    Have sat in taverns while the tempest hurled
Their hopeful plans to emptiness, and cursed
    Whatever brute and blackguard made the world.

—A. E. Housman
Last Poems [1922]

Hail wedded love, mysterious law, true source
Of human offspring, sole propriety,
In Paradise of all things common else.

—John Milton
Paradise Lost [1667]

1848
Portman and Berkley Squares, London, England

"How did Madame Polgár know about Père Gérard and his crucifix?" It was Mr. Quimby who asked the question uppermost in everyone's minds.

The fortune-teller's funeral had finally ended, and now, although the mourning coaches had returned most of those assembled at her graveside to their own homes, a close-knit select few—who consisted of Messieurs Quimby, Rosenkranz and

Cavendish—had instead been delivered to the Lévesques' town house in Portman Square. There they had gathered in the small drawing room to discuss the afternoon's events and to partake of the high tea that Madame Valcoeur had, upon their arrival, directed be served straightaway, even though it had still been a trifle early for same. All had been most anxious to learn what had become of Malcolm, Mr. Ravener and Dukker, for after disappearing into the mist at Kensal Green, they had not been seen again at the cemetery, so that Ariana and Christine, and their respective abigails, Sophie and Miss Innes, had been compelled to travel home in the mourning carriage without the three of them. Upon reaching the Lévesques' town house, however, everyone present had quickly discovered that after leaving the graveyard, the two men and the dwarf had hired a hackney coach in Harrow Road to convey them hither and that they had arrived home without further incident.

Now, as he habitually did, Dukker sat unobtrusively in one corner. But as, at Mr. Quimby's query, all eyes turned expectantly to him for some explanation, the dwarf at last spoke.

"Madame Polgár was very fortunate, I think, in that she had several pieces of information about the Order of the Sons of Isis and the mystery of the Heart of Kheperi available to her, which I believe that others, just like Messieurs Blackfriars and Ravener, have initially lacked—which is only to be expected, however, given the passage of time, during which 'tis reasonable to assume that much knowledge that was once clear subsequently grew obscured or even lost.

"But as I told you before, an ancestor of Madame Polgár's Scottish grandmother, the Lady Sibyl Macbeth, was one of the original brothers of the Order of the Sons of Isis, and this particular piece of information had been preserved through the generations of the Clan Macbeth, many of whom have had the 'second sight,' as they call it, the ability to foresee the future, which *madame* herself inherited. The gift of clairvoyance had entered the Clan Macbeth during the Middle Ages, when one of their number, Lord Hunter Macbeth, Earl of Bailekair and the son of a Macbeth laird and a Romany Gypsy wench, had married the Lady Mary Carmichael, whom many had thought a witch, for she had possessed the second sight. So from that time, the Clan Macbeth had always understood powers that are beyond the ken of most. From her grandmother, Madame Polgár had also learnt that both Lord Bailekair and his wife, who was his distant cousin, had had remarkably striking eyes—the color of amethysts."

Here the dwarf paused, as, gasping as one, all in the small drawing room suddenly turned to stare at Ariana wonderingly, their faces rapt, curious and speculative. After a moment, Dukker continued.

"*Oui*…you see, the reason that Mademoiselle Ariana's own eyes are that exact same color is because—as Madame Polgár knew, too, from her grandmother—Lord Robert Roy Ramsay, that Earl of Dúndragon who had founded the Order of the Sons of Isis, had been married to a Macbeth lady—the sister, in fact, of that same Macbeth laird who had been one of the original brothers of the order. That was why, when *madame* discovered that Monsieur Valcoeur was the cousin of Monsieur Charles de Ramezay, le Comte de Jourdain, and also learnt from the old nurse at Valcoeur that Madame Valcoeur herself could bear no children of her own, she knew that Mademoiselle Ariana must, in truth, be the missing de Ramezay daughter—a direct descendant of Lord Dúndragon and his Macbeth wife. But what does all this have to do with Père Gérard St. Clair? I know that you are all wondering. Only be patient, and you shall hear!

"Now, as you all know, having left her homeland and following the death of her husband, Madame Polgár decided to travel, and after journeying through many countries, she finally settled in France. By then, she had spent much time studying arcana and esoterica, and she had learnt a great deal about orders like the Knights Templar and the Knights Hospitalier, so she knew that when the Knights Templar had been compelled to disband in France, many of the order had fled to Scotland, where they had long had ties with various Scottish clans—among them the Sinclairs, one of whom, Sir William St. Clair, had built a strange, highly esoteric chapel not far from his holding, Rosslyn Castle. So it occurred to *madame* that if one had lived in Scotland during the seventeenth and eighteenth centuries and had wanted to found a new order, to attempt to harness the power of the Heart of Kheperi, then one would most likely have asked a Sinclair to become one of the brothers, since, like the Macbeths, the Sinclairs had long been steeped in the knowledge of arcana and esoterica.

"Further, *madame* was also aware that like the Ramsays, who had originated with the Norman de Ramezays in France, the Sinclairs had originated with the Norman de Sancto Claros or St. Clairs, also in France, and that just like the Ramsays and de Ramezays, the Sinclairs and St. Clairs had maintained ties of both blood and marriage across the English Channel. So now perhaps things begin to become a little clearer to you, *non?* Whilst in France, *madame* undertook to trace those Sinclairs and St. Clairs who had gone back and forth across the Channel, and eventually her search led her to Père Gérard St. Clair. Whether he is aware of the significance of the crucifix he had, I do not know— although *madame* herself thought not. Still, when she told him that she collected crosses and offered to buy his own, he would not part with it, saying that 'twas very old and had sentimental value to him. I myself would have stolen it from him before today, but he has worn it always, and since he is so elderly and hardly ever leaves the Chapel Royal of France, there has been little or no good opportunity to take the crucifix from him. But this afternoon I saw how I could do it—and although he may be suspicious of me, he cannot actually *prove* I took it!" the dwarf crowed triumphantly, obviously very pleased with himself. "In fact, if he *is* truly ignorant of the cross's import, he will no doubt believe he simply lost it somewhere en route to *madame's* funeral and not even suspect me! What do you think about that, Mademoiselle Ariana?"

"I think that 'twas a very dangerous thing to have done, Dukker!" she responded, frowning. "If you had been caught—and before so many witnesses, besides—then Père Gérard might have insisted on summoning the police and pressing charges against you! You would have wound up in gaol!"

"But I didn't—and Madame Polgár would be most proud of me for my cleverness! 'Twas what she would have wished me to do, I know, for that was why she especially requested that Père Gérard officiate at her funeral, so she could lure him away from the Chapel Royal of France, thereby giving me the chance to obtain the crucifix." The dwarf, previously beaming, now looked crestfallen and upset.

"My sister is only worried about what would have happened to you, Dukker, had you been caught in the act of theft," Mr. Ravener said soothingly, to smooth any ruffled feathers. "You have proved a most welcome addition to our little coterie, and we don't want to lose you. Still, 'twas indeed most clever and also very courageous of you to get the cross as you did." He paused for a moment, his fingers playing idly with the stolen crucifix, which he held. Then he went on, speaking now to all those present in the small drawing room, "This is crucifix number five, by the way, and 'tis inscribed on the back 'Second Chronicles 3:17,' which Bible chapter and verse run thusly—'He erected the two pillars in front of the temple, one on the right and one on the left; the one on the right he named Jachin and the one on the left Boaz.'"

"Well, that certainly seems straightforward enough!" Mr. Cavendish declared heartily, gesturing with his pipe to emphasize his words, heedless of the ash he spilled upon himself. "'Twould appear that the Heart of Kheperi must be located in or near a temple of some kind…perhaps an old Celtic or Roman ruin."

"I don't know how you can be so certain of that, Bonny," Mr. Rosenkranz rejoined irritably, as he set his teacup down in its saucer. "For none of the biblical chapters and verses on the other crosses we now possess would seem to indicate anything of the sort!"

"No? Then what about that one that refers to a pool, Jakob? Pools are quite often to be found at temples, you know."

"Yes, Bonny," Mr. Quimby agreed affably, "but what Jakob means is that the chapters and verses on the other crucifixes refer to…well, intangibles, for lack of a better word. They provide information—'I am Alpha and Omega'—and so forth, but don't really say anything concrete that would seem to point to any actual location as a place where the emerald is concealed."

"But alpha and omega are Greek letters—which could be carved into a temple!" Mr. Cavendish persisted enthusiastically, unabashed.

"Perhaps Mr. Cavendish *does* have a point," Madame Valcoeur remarked hesitantly. "Oh, I don't know. These clues all seem so terribly strange and vague that I can't make heads or tails of them myself. *Alors!* If you ask me, 'tis all just a muddle!"

"I'm afraid I'm inclined to agree with you, *ma chère.*" Sighing heavily, Monsieur Valcoeur rose from his chair. "I am going to get the other crosses. Maybe if we see them all together, something will occur to us." Exiting the small drawing room, he sought out his study, where he unlocked the secret compartment in his desk and removed the other four crucifixes. Then he returned to the small drawing room, laying all the crosses out upon a card table that sat to one side. "Now, I suggest that everyone gather around, and let us put our heads together and see what we can come up with."

For well over an hour Malcolm and Ariana, Mr. Ravener and Lady Christine, Monsieur and Madame Valcoeur, Mrs. Blackfriars, Messieurs Quimby, Rosenkranz and Cavendish, and the dwarf, Dukker, all studied the crucifixes intently, time and again reading aloud from the Bible the chapters and verses referred to by the various inscriptions on the backs of the five crosses, and making notes of all the sundry ideas that were put forth with regard to same, however far-fetched. But at the end of their scrutiny, those assembled in the small drawing room were reluctantly forced to admit that they were still no closer to solving the puzzle than they had been at the beginning.

Departing from the Kensal Green Cemetery, Viscount Ugo hurried home as fast as he could to the imposing town house he shared with his father, Lord Vittore, Count Foscarelli, in Berkeley Square. Once there, scarcely waiting for the steps to be lowered by the footmen, he sprang from the black carriage in which he had traveled to the graveyard, then raced inside the town house, shouting for his father, whom he presently located in the study.

"We have been outwitted, Padre! And not just by that old witch Madame Polgár, either!" Lord Ugo cried to his father, running one hand wildly through his jet-black hair and pacing the room, like a caged tiger.

"Whatever do you mean, Lucrezio?" From where he sat at his desk, bent over a number of documents, a pen in hand, Count Foscarelli glanced up, frowning at his plainly agitated son and the unexpected interruption to his business. "Madame Polgár is dead—so she has hardly outwitted us."

"*Sì*, that's what you said about Malcolm Ramsay and his cousins, Nicolas and Ariana—that they were dead, too…burnt to death in the fire that night at Whitrose Grange! But they're alive, as is Malcolm's mother, Mrs. Elizabeth Ramsay—for I saw them all today with my own eyes, at Madame Polgár's funeral at Kensal Green! So God only knows whether that old witch is really dead or not, also, Padre! The whole thing could be nothing more than a ruse to deceive us, whilst the five of them plot against us—as they have no doubt done for the past thirteen years now! How could you have been so unutterably stupid? You ought to have made certain that Malcolm and his cousins were dead! You ought to have killed Madame Polgár—instead of shutting her up in Bedlam, from where she could be rescued by her allies! *Dio buono!* Have you heard a single word I've said, Padre?"

"*Sì…sì*, Lucrezio," Count Foscarelli muttered, now sitting back numbly in his chair, looking incredibly old and haggard of a sudden, Lord Ugo thought, and deeply shocked by his son's report. "Alive, you say? Malcolm Ramsay, his mother and both his cousins alive? But I don't understand how that can be. Whitrose Grange was an inferno that night when I left it, I tell you! And except for Alexander and Charles, whom I killed myself, the rest were all abed. There is no way they could have escaped from the flames in time!"

"Well, somehow they did," Lord Ugo insisted grimly. "Perhaps one or more of them were not actually asleep and roused the others. Who knows? What matters now is the present. What is to be done, Padre? 'Tis clear that the Ramsays and their de Ramezay cousins are not only alive and arrayed against us, but Lady Christine Fraser was there with them at the funeral, as well. So she has plainly joined their ranks—and who knows what she may remember about her parents' deaths, or how many other allies the Ramsays and de Ramezays may now have? Are the rumors in the village that lies beyond Castle Dúndragon true? *Was* there something illegal about the manner in which our ancestor Lord Bruno, Count Foscarelli, obtained the holding, Padre? *Is* there any way in which Malcolm can get Castle Dúndragon back and dispossess us, leaving him free to search for the Heart of Kheperi at his leisure?"

"No…no, I don't believe there is." By now, Count Foscarelli had collected his wits, and his brain was working furiously; his black eyes were narrowed shrewdly and thoughtfully. "I've heard that same idle gossip for years now—ever since I was a child, in fact!—and I myself do not think 'tis anything more than malicious tittle-tattle put about by a handful of villagers, disgruntled about having Italians instead of Highlanders in possession of Castle Dúndragon. You know how those Scottish clans are—how they stick together against all outsiders, particularly foreigners! It wouldn't matter if we had been there a thousand years instead of only a hundred, Lucrezio! We would still be outlanders to those clannish barbarians! *Dio buono!* Even in this day and age, the Highlanders are a lot of backward savages—whilst we Italians have been civilized since the days of Rome's glory! No, depend upon it—if there were any truth at all to those rumors in the village, the Ramsays would surely long ago have found that out. No, the Ramsays cannot prove that our ancestor Lord Bruno, Count Foscarelli, cheated Lord Dúndragon at cards, and nothing has ever been discovered to provide any evidence whatsoever that Lord Dúndragon was not free to wager the Ramsay estates during that game of piquet, either. So my main concern at the moment is how much the Ramsays and the de Ramezays know about the Heart of Kheperi—and how many crucifixes they may now have in their possession. We ourselves have three. I think 'tis safe to assume that they have at least two—that Alexander Ramsay and Charles de Ramezay each had one, and that neither of those was lost in the fire in Whitrose Grange. For if Malcolm, his mother and his two cousins escaped from the blaze, as it now appears that they did, then they would have saved the crosses, too, if they could."

"And no doubt Madame Polgár—if the old witch really *is* dead—left them her own crucifix, as well, Padre…just to spite *us,* if for no other reason than that!" Lord Ugo spat. "In addition, much to my incredulity, the old priest who officiated at the fortune-teller's funeral was wearing a large, ornate silver cross—and although I could not, even with my binoculars, make out its details, I did observe the dwarf, Dukker, steal it, which made me believe that 'twas one of the crucifixes of the Order of the Sons of Isis, and that Madame Polgár must, before her death, have discovered its whereabouts and been cultivating the old priest herself in order to take it!"

"Then that makes four, and the Ramsays and de Ramezays may have still more—after all, they've had thirteen long years to search undisturbed!—and if they do, then they have the edge. So…we must find something to take that away, Lucrezio—and, hopefully, to acquire their own crosses in the bargain!"

"*Sì,* Padre." Lord Ugo nodded thoughtfully, his own mind racing. "And I think that perhaps I know a way…."

The necessary special licenses for the double wedding ceremony having been obtained by Malcolm and Mr. Ravener, the two marriages that had previously been arranged were now scheduled to go forth privately at Holy Trinity Church in Marylebone. In this way, both the calling of the banns and the public notice required for all such civil ceremonies were avoided, so that there need be no announcement of the weddings until after they had taken place.

The morning of the marriages, Ariana was so nervous that she could eat none of the breakfast that Fanny brought upstairs for her on a silver tray, and she wondered if Christine, now back with her uncle and aunt, Lord and Lady Eaton, at Hanover Square, was equally as excited and wrought up.

Deciding that it would only worry Lord and Lady Eaton, Mr. Ravener and Christine had kept from them the story of the Heart of Kheperi, instead stating as their reason for desiring a secret wedding the fact that Mr. Ravener, for purposes of his own, was traveling incognito and did not wish for his true identity as Monsieur Nicolas de Ramezay, le Comte de Jourdain, to become widely known just yet in England. Although slightly mystified, Lord and Lady Eaton had nevertheless been reassured by Monsieur and Madame Valcoeur's veiled references to their "nephew Mr. Ravener acting privately on important family business," and, persuaded that Christine was indeed making a highly advantageous match to an appropriately titled and moneyed lord, they had given their consent and blessing to the marriage.

It had been arranged that the three families would travel in separate carriages from their respective residences, meeting at the church, and that aside from Dukker and the ladies' abigails, the only other guests would be Messieurs Quimby, Rosenkranz and Cavendish.

Now, pushing aside her unwanted breakfast tray, Ariana sprang to her feet and ran to the windows of her bedchamber, which overlooked Portman Square and the park below.

"Oh, Sophie, I do hope 'tisn't going to pour down rain!" she said fervently as she gazed through the panes cloudy with mist and mizzle.

"Maybe 'twill hold off until after the weddings. You should try to eat something, however little, *mademoiselle,* so you will not grow hungry and light-headed—and perhaps even faint!—during the ceremony."

"*Non,* I'm far too excited to eat—and shall only be sick now if

I do! I have to pinch myself to be certain I am not dreaming, that I really *am* going to marry Malcolm this morning. Oh, Sophie! Even now I can scarcely believe it! I keep thinking that at any moment I shall awaken and discover that the past several months have indeed been only a dream—and I could not bear it if that were so! I shall worry all the way to the church that Malcolm will not show up, that something dreadful will happen to prevent us from ever being wed, and I will not be free of fear until the priest declares that we are man and wife, and I know that 'tis truly so!"

But despite all of Ariana's anxiety and apprehension, much to her vast relief nothing untoward occurred during the journey to the towering stone church, and although the morning seemed to pass with excruciating slowness, in reality, it was not long at all before she stood garbed in her elaborate wedding finery before the priest, with Malcolm at her side. Next to them stood Mr. Ravener and Christine, and in the pews behind them were gathered their family and the few friends they had invited to share this special day with them.

Eventually each of the two couples exchanged their vows. Then the ceremony was over, and at long last, Ariana was Malcolm's wife. But still, it hardly seemed possible to her, not even when they returned to the Lévesques' town house in Portman Square for the reception. There, during their absence, the dining room had been brightly bedecked with winter flowers and evergreens, and in addition to the luncheon that was to be served, a towering wedding cake and bottles of champagne were arrayed upon the sideboard, ready and waiting for the celebration. So although the wedding party was small, it was nevertheless merry as the footmen and housemaids filled plates and glasses, and one after another the gentlemen rose to toast the two happy couples. Even Mr. Rosenkranz bestirred himself to join in the joviality, raising his champagne glass and saying *"Mazel tov!"* which he told them meant "Good fortune!"

Malcolm hoped that would indeed prove the case, but still, because of the presence of Lord and Lady Eaton, who remained in ignorance about the Heart of Kheperi, he said nothing about the lost emerald or the dangers he, Ariana, Mr. Ravener and Lady Christine faced. Even had the latter's uncle and aunt not been in attendance, Malcolm would still have held his tongue, for he wanted nothing to spoil his wedding day to Ariana.

Even now he could scarcely believe she was actually his wife, that the beautiful, desirable woman who sat at his side was the same brave, bonnie wee lass with whom he had gone fishing in his small boat, the *Sea Witch*, on the dark peaty waters of Loch Ness thirteen years ago. How very far the two of them had come since that autumn afternoon! Yet…how much farther still they had to go if they were ever to be free from the curse of the Heart of Kheperi. Almost, Malcolm could laugh at the irony of the Foscarellis going to such lengths to obtain the emerald, so that they could live forever, while he, Malcolm, wished to get hold of it only to be rid of it! Never once had he thought of trying to harness its alleged powers, so that he could become immortal. For one thing, he believed that to live for an eternity while all whom he loved died could not be anything other than a curse itself, and the thought of losing Ariana, especially when he had only just claimed her as his bride, was even more unbearable to him. Malcolm wished they had neither of them ever even heard of the Heart of Kheperi, need not continue their perilous quest for it. But still, he knew in his heart that the only true way to ensure Ariana's ultimate safety and well-being was to locate the emerald and dispose of it.

"A penny for them, Collie." Ariana spoke quietly, gently nudging him from his reverie. "You look so serious that I cannot help but wonder what thoughts are in your mind."

"Only thoughts of you, my darling Ana," he responded lightly, forcing himself to smile, "and how best to secure your future."

"Oh, let us not speak or even think of such things at the moment, Collie! Just for today, let us not permit that accursed emerald to cast its dark, wicked shadow upon us, but pretend that it does not exist for us, that it still lies hidden away in the tomb of the Egyptian high priest from whom our ancestor Lord Dúndragon stole it. It may possess great power—I do not deny that.

But surely we have an even greater magic of our own, Collie—the power of love!" Ariana declared earnestly.

"Aye, you're right, Ana—and we must hold fast to that, come what may!"

They spoke no further then. For the excellent luncheon having been eaten, the wedding cake having been cut and consumed and the champagne drunk, Madame Valcoeur now conducted them all into the small drawing room. This chamber, too, had been gaily adorned with wintry flowers and evergreens; tables had been set up for cards; and space had been cleared for dancing. Monsieur Valcoeur had hired a small group of musicians to play, and now, clapping his hands together to garner everyone's attention, he insisted that the two newlywed couples take the floor for the first dance. This they did, and the festivities continued, both Ariana and Christine unable to restrain their joy and laughter as their husbands whirled them around the small drawing room. After that, because there were not enough ladies to go around, all the others took turns joining in, and Malcolm thought he had not seen his mother so happy in years as she was now, flushed and smiling with pleasure as she cut a caper with first Mr. Quimby and then Mr. Cavendish. Even Mr. Rosenkranz eventually danced, his usually dour face alight with unaccustomed merriment.

Thus the afternoon seemed to fly by, hastening into the twilight, which came so early during winter, and with the descending of the evening darkness, all the guests began one by one, however reluctantly, to take their leave of the Lévesques' town house. Finally only the immediate family remained. After supper, highly nervous and filled with anticipation, both Ariana and Christine slipped away to the new apartments that Madame Valcoeur had arranged for them at the town house. "For 'tis best that you both start off your marriages in suites that did not belong to either of you beforehand," she had explained wisely, "so that your husbands are not made to feel like interlopers in young maidens' rooms."

But now, as she stood alone in the new apartment that had been assigned to her and Malcolm, Ariana almost wished she *were* installed in her old bedchamber, where all was familiar to her, and she wondered if Christine, lodged across the hall, felt the same, if she longed to be back in her own room in her uncle and aunt's town house in Hanover Square. Of a sudden, then, it dawned on Ariana that this was the real end of her childhood and the true beginning of her womanhood, that she stood poised on a momentous threshold from which there would be no going back after this night was done. The thought at once scared and thrilled her. For the first time, she realized that in many ways, even though he was her cousin and she had known him since her youth, Malcolm was still a stranger to her, eleven years older than she, wiser and far more experienced in the ways of the world. Besides working at the map shop, how had he spent the past thirteen years of their separation? she wondered now. Not wanting to pry, she had asked so little about that before. But now she wondered if he had lain with other women, as he would lie with her tonight, if he had held them in his arms, kissed them and made love to them. As these questions rose, unbidden, in her mind, she felt a fierce sense of jealousy mingled with uncertainty sweep through her, and she bit her lower lip anxiously. While she had a rudimentary knowledge of what was expected of a woman on her wedding night, she was still innocent and ignorant of much, and as a result, she was beset by all the age-old maidenly curiosities, as well as equally discomposing qualms that in some fashion, she would be compared to her predecessors and found lacking.

Without warning, a knock came at the door, interrupting Ariana's musings and causing her heart to leap. Then the portal opened to admit Sophie, rather than Malcolm.

"I've come to help you with your toilet, *madame*," the abigail announced.

"Oh, Sophie, it sounds so strange to be addressed as *madame!*"

"But such you are now, so such I must call you. And I am so glad, *madame,* that in the end, you were able to marry Monsieur Blackfriars after all, that you did not have your heart broken! I hope the two of you will be very happy together!"

"*Merci,* Sophie. I know we will be."

After Ariana had finished bathing in the adjoining bath, she returned to the bedchamber, where Sophie assisted her into her nightgown and wrapper, then unbound and brushed her long black hair. Then, all too soon, it seemed to Ariana, she was alone in the room again, her pulse racing and butterflies fluttering in her stomach as she sat before her vanity, where Sophie had left her. But presently there came another soft rap upon the door, and this time when the portal opened, it *was* Malcolm who entered. As he stepped inside, Ariana sprang to her feet, accidentally knocking over her vanity bench as she did so.

"Oh, *mon Dieu!*" she cried, and with trembling fingers hastily righted the seat.

After a moment, she became aware that Malcolm was at her side, helping her to set the bench back in its proper place. Then he caught one of her shaking hands in his own steady grip and held it gently.

"You don't have to be afraid, Ana. I'm not going to hurt you," he said.

"I know." She nodded slowly. "'Tis just that I…I feel so young and—and naive. I don't want to—to be a disappointment to you, Collie."

"Oh, Ana." He smiled at her tenderly. "Don't you know that nothing about you could ever prove a disappointment to me? You're everything I ever dreamt of—and more…."

He embraced her then, and as his strong arms enfolded her, pressing her close, she had never before felt so secure and loved, as though he had woven of himself a cocoon around her, to shelter her from the world. Outside, the wild winter wind blew, its breath cloudy with mist that drifted ghostily through the gardens at the rear of the town house, and damp with mizzle that tapped against the mullioned windows. The naked deciduous trees shivered in the cold and wet, and brittle brown leaves flew from their branches to dance and whorl with each brumous gust, rasping and rattling like old bones, before finally joining their sodden brothers to decay in the rich fetid earth. But inside, all was still and hushed, save for the crackling and sparking of the fire in the hearth, and the thudding of Ariana's heart against Malcolm's own. As though she were a child, he continued to hold her, stroking her long, unbound hair and speaking to her softly.

But Ariana was not a child. She was a woman grown—and one who, despite all her maidenly fears, wanted her husband, and to know the full measure of her own womanhood. She glanced up at him then, and perhaps her expressive amethyst eyes revealed her innermost thoughts and desires to him, for no man had ever before gazed at her as Malcolm did then, as though he knew with certainty that within minutes he would possess her intimately, utterly, and that afterward she would belong to him solely and irrevocably for as long as she lived. At her own recognition of that fact, Ariana felt her breath catch in her throat, and an exquisite, slow-burning heat such as she had seldom ever before experienced ignited deep at the very core of her being to spread like a fever through her entire body, making her shudder with mingled fright and anticipation. For despite Malcolm's earlier reassurances, she was still unsure what to expect from him. The pulse at the delicate hollow of her graceful, swanlike throat fluttered erratically. Her mouth went dry…her lips parted; her tongue darted forth to moisten her lips. A soft, incoherent whimper emanated from her throat as slowly, tremulously, her body swayed against his, drawn irresistibly to him by the nameless, atavistic thing that had seized her so suddenly and fiercely, and that now inexorably sucked her down into its dark primeval flames.

Of their own volition, her hands crept up around his neck. Trembling uncontrollably, she lifted her face to his, and he kissed her then, his mouth closing over hers firmly, swallowing not only her breath, but also her little low cries of mingled incertitude and entreaty. Then, after a moment, as quick and light as a butterfly's wings, his lips fluttered over her mouth, her eyelids, her temples and the strands of her hair…touching, tasting, teasing. His fingers burrowed themselves in her mass of gleaming black hair, slid across her shoulders to slip from her body the silky wrapper she wore, so that, with the barest of whispers, it rippled to the floor to pool like quicksilver at her feet. And Ariana felt as though she were quicksilver, too, boneless and molten, and she was slightly surprised to find herself still standing, that she had not herself melted into a puddle on the floor. Even as, in some dim recess of her mind, the thought occurred to her, she felt Malcolm cup her breasts, and felt, too, her own eager, un-witting response—the tightening and hardening of her nipples, so that they strained against her bodice and against his palms, which glided across them lightly, brushing the silky fabric of her nightgown tauntingly against the highly sensitive peaks. From their centers, circles of delight radiated through her whole body, and her breasts swelled and ached with passion, in a way they never had before.

Sweet, sensual lips and sure, supple hands Malcolm had, to weave his magic spell upon her, and willingly was Ariana ensor-celled, her mouth opening like a dewy, unfurling rosebud to his, her fingers tensed and splayed as they clung to his lithe, whip-cord body, so different from her own, and felt the powerful mus-cles that bunched and quivered beneath his flesh as he clasped her to him. He was so tall and strong that she felt small and frag-ile in his embrace, as though she were a flower he could bend or break at will; and nebulously she wondered if, when the time came, he would pluck her maidenhead just as easily. She shud-dered slightly with trepidation at the unbidden thought, and he, guessing her sudden, renewed fears, tightened his hold on her, as though otherwise, like some startled creature, she would take to her heels, denying him what he so desired.

Sweeping her up in his arms, Malcolm bore Ariana to the can-opy bed at the heart of the apartment and laid her down upon it. Somehow their clothing was cast away, and his naked flesh pressed against hers; his weight bore her down into the feather mattress. Time passed—Ariana scarcely knew how much—and still Malcolm caressed and kissed her, his mouth growing ever more demanding, his hands ever bolder. His tongue that stabbed her everywhere with its heat, his fingers that roamed over her so skillfully, aroused in her both excitement and yearning, exquisite emotions and sensations she had not known existed, had never dreamt of in her wildest imaginings, so little had she known, in truth, of how a man could pleasure a woman. And she, in turn, reveled in the masculine fragrance and feel and taste of him. He smelled of sandalwood and vetiver, of tobacco and musk. The dark hair that matted his chest was as fine as down beneath her palms and against the sensitive tips of her breasts; his broad back was as smooth as satin; his corded thighs were like iron. He tasted of the champagne they had earlier drunk, and she was as intoxicated by him as though the sweet, bubbly wine had gone to her head. Eagerly she discovered him, explored him, mapped each line and every plane of him, and staked her claim upon his body, as he did hers.

And then, at last, he poised himself above her, and she felt the sharp, sweet pain that makes of maid a woman, and of a man a conqueror. She gasped, then cried out softly at the shock of it, for despite all she had been told, nothing had really prepared her for it—for his absolute invasion and her equally complete surrender in the joining that made them one. Together, then, they lay—breast to breast, thigh to thigh, no space between, no room for another, nor would there ever be. Malcolm's hands were beneath her, arching her hips to meet his own until, suddenly, the world spun away into nothingness, and he and Ariana tumbled headlong into the dark, blinding void, clinging tightly to each other as they soared and fell.

Chapter Nineteen

The Heart of Kheperi

The human heart has hidden treasures,
In secret kept, in silence sealed.

—Charlotte Brontë
Evening Solace [1846]

His heart is as firm as a stone;
Yea, as hard as a piece of the nether millstone.
—*The Holy Bible*
The Book of Job

So it is more useful to watch a man in
time of peril, and in adversity to discern what
kind of man he is; for then, at last, words of
truth are drawn from the depths of his heart,
and the mask is torn off; reality remains.
—Lucretius [Titus Lucretius Carus]
De Rerum Natura (On the Nature of Things)

1848
London, England, and the Highlands, Scotland

A few days after the two weddings had taken place, Jakob Rosenkranz and Boniface Cavendish arrived quite unexpectedly during the luncheon hour at Quimby & Company (Cartographers & Map Sellers), both of them clearly bursting with excitement. Spying Malcolm seated with Harry, Jem and Tuck around the hearth, eating their midday meal, the two men greeted him and the others warmly, then demanded to be taken to Mr. Quimby straightaway.

"I'm afraid he's not here," Malcolm explained. "He returns home every day at noon to have luncheon there and a short nap afterward."

"There, Bonny! What did I tell you?" The jeweler glanced, annoyed, at the bookseller. "I said we should go to Baker Street. But no, you insisted we come here to Oxford Street instead!"

"Well, how was I to know that Septimus had kept up his long habit of going home for luncheon?" Mr. Cavendish asked, shaking his head with astonishment. "Why, he's getting on in years, by heaven! So imagine him continuing to hobble all that way every day!"

"He's exactly the same age as we are, Bonny—and hardly decrepit," Mr. Rosenkranz insisted irritably. "'Tis only that he is troubled now and again by gout."

"Too much wine and rich food. Coffee and sandwiches from a coffee stall—now, there's the ticket to keep a man fit!" The bookseller's voice boomed heartily as he grinned and patted his solid stomach. "Well, Mr. Blackfriars—" he turned to address Malcolm once more "—there's nothing for it, then, but for you to accompany Jakob and me to Septimus's town house, for we've news of great import to impart to you both about matters that concern you most intimately!"

"Will this have anything to do with the personal problems you've been having, Malcolm?" Harry inquired as he rose from his stool before the fireplace.

"Aye." Malcolm nodded slowly. "Messieurs Rosenkranz and Cavendish have been so kind as to have undertaken to assist me with some extremely vital research."

"Then you go on with them to Mr. Quimby's town house. I'll take your turn at manning the counter and watching the shop during your absence, and if you're needed, I'll send Tuck to fetch you."

"Thank you, Harry. I really appreciate that!" Malcolm said,

grabbing his coat, hat, gloves and umbrella from the pegs and shelves at the rear of the premises.

Presently, after a brisk walk in the wintry air, he and Messieurs Rosenkranz and Cavendish arrived at Mr. Quimby's town house and, having wakened him from his doze, were installed in his library. A lap robe drawn across him against the chill of the dreary day, his feet propped up on a gout stool, Mr. Quimby sat in a wing chair by the hearth, the nightcap he had put upon his head before lying down for his nap still perched upon his head, although badly askew.

"Well, good Lord, what has happened? Something of import, obviously, or you three would not be here!" he now exclaimed, righting his nightcap.

"You will never guess, Septimus, so we'll tell you!" Bonny announced. Then he crowed, "Jakob has managed to learn who made the crucifixes belonging to the Sons of Isis, and I myself have discovered the names of the original brothers—and traced one of their descendants right here to London!"

"Oh, excellent! Well done, indeed! I knew I could count on the two of you!" With a great show of enthusiasm Mr. Quimby clapped his hands together proudly, beaming.

"I'm eternally grateful to you both…to all three of you," Malcolm declared. "I don't know how I shall ever repay you."

"You may consider all of our assistance and information as a trifle-belated wedding present," Mr. Cavendish insisted, "for I think I speak for all of us when I say that we have not taken part in your hazardous adventure for any monetary reward or anything else of that nature, but, rather, to try to help put right a very great wrong. That is more than enough for the three of us!"

"Hear, hear!" Mr. Quimby and Mr. Rosenkranz agreed, as one.

"Thank you. Thank you all so much!" Malcolm was so deeply touched with emotion and gratitude that his words were choked. "Now, Jakob, tell us who made the crosses," Mr. Quimby urged after a moment, "for as you may imagine, I am most eager to hear all before Malcolm and I must return to my establishment—

for Harry cannot draw maps or engrave plates if he's manning the counter and watching the shop! Oh, how I wish Jem were just a little bit older and more experienced!"

"Yes, very well, then." The jeweler was equally mindful of what might be happening at his own premises during his absence. "The crucifixes were fashioned by one Mordecai Weisel, who was apparently a most exacting man, for he kept exceedingly meticulous records—and his equally efficient descendant Isaac Weisel was still in possession of them when I finally located him in Bonn. I received his response to my inquiries only this morning. There are indeed, as we surmised, nine crosses. At the time that they were made, four of them were dispatched to Scotland, three to France, one to Italy and one to England...to London, in fact—which is where Bonny comes in."

"Indeed, I do, Jakob!" The bookseller grinned hugely. "For after much diligent searching, I have found the owner of what, I believe, must be the original London crucifix! His name is Colonel Hilliard Pemberton. He's retired from the dragoons, and he resides in Wimpole Street. Of course, I don't yet know if he is aware of the significance of his cross or not, but I don't think we can take the chance that he is. Rather, I believe we must figure out a way in which we can obtain it from him—whether by hook or by crook!"

"Bonny! Do you mean *steal* it—the way that Dukker stole Père Gérard St. Clair's crucifix at Madame Polgár's funeral?" Mr. Rosenkranz's face was filled with shock and disapproval at the very idea.

"Of course, Jakob." Mr. Cavendish's own visage expressed his amazement at what he clearly perceived as the jeweler's simplemindedness. "For heaven's sake, you don't suppose that if he knows its true value, Colonel Pemberton is just going to calmly hand his own cross over to us, do you? Besides, 'tisn't theft. All of the crucifixes—regardless of who owns them—are merely the means to locate the missing emerald, the Heart of Kheperi, and that belonged solely to young Mr. Blackfriars's ancestor, Lord Rob Roy Ramsay, the ninth Earl of Dúndragon, even if the Order of the Sons of Isis he founded *did* worship it. So now 'tis rightfully Mr. Blackfriars's."

"'Tis rightfully the Egyptian government's, Bonny," the jeweler stated firmly. "And young Mr. Blackfriars—" he turned to address Malcolm "—should you be so fortunate as to locate it, I most sincerely hope that you return it and that you receive a very handsome reward for doing so!"

"Christine! Oh, Christine! We must leave immediately!" Ariana cried as, a few days after Malcolm had been visited by Messieurs Rosenkranz and Cavendish at Quimby & Company (Cartographers & Map Sellers), she ran into the morning room of the Lévesques' town house at Portman Square. "There's— there's been a terrible accident…at the Red House tavern in Battersea Fields…and—and Collie and Nicky have been badly injured!"

"No, oh, no!" Her face blanching, Christine rose from her chair, the fine linen handkerchief she had been embroidering for her husband for Christmas tumbling from her lap. "How have you received this horrible news, Ariana?"

"A—a note has just this moment arrived. Butterworth gave it to me. 'Tis from the proprietor of the Red House! He—he begs us to come at once, before 'tis too late!"

"Oh, my God!"

"Non, mesdames," Dukker protested stoutly, having laid aside his harp, which he had been playing to entertain them while they sewed. "I cannot let you go anywhere—for this may be only a trick by our enemies!"

"Non, Dukker. That I cannot believe," Ariana insisted, frantic. "For the Red House tavern is indeed where Collie and Nicky were headed this morning, for their usual Saturday shooting session. I have called for Papa's second carriage to be made ready to convey Christine and me there as soon as possible."

*"Madame…*please listen to reason! Please allow me to go in your stead, to discover whether this is a genuine message. The Foscarellis were spying upon *la pauvre* Madame Polgár. For that

reason, they may now be spying upon those with whom she associated, including us! If so, by now, the Foscarellis may have learnt your and Monsieur Blackfriars's and Mr. Ravener's true identities. They may know our habits, our comings and goings. This may be but a clever ruse to lure you and Madame Ravener from the town house of Monsieur le Comte and Madame la Comtesse, in order to do you some harm!"

"That's the chance we'll just have to take, Dukker." Ariana's beautiful countenance was grimly determined. "For if the missive is indeed real, and Collie and Nicky truly *are* badly hurt, I should never forgive myself for not going to their sides at once!"

"Oh, how I wish Monsieur le Comte, Madame la Comtesse and Madame Blackfriars were here to put a stop to your leaving!" the dwarf declared, shaking his head with dismay. "For you know, *mesdames,* that both Messieurs Blackfriars and Ravener said you were not to step foot from the town house—not even to go Christmas shopping!"

"They did not know they were going to be involved in a serious accident, did they?" Ariana's voice caught on a ragged-edged sob, and one trembling hand flew to her tremulous mouth. Then she abruptly turned and fled from the morning room, demanding to know where the coach was, with Christine hard on her heels.

In the end, because of Dukker's fears, it was arranged that he would, on horseback, follow the carriage to the Red House tavern and Battersea Fields, so that if aught went amiss, he could at least sound an alarm. In addition, he insisted that the footmen who were to accompany the vehicle be armed with pistols, and even in their upset, both Ariana and Christine could see the wisdom of that. After that, apprising Butterworth of their intentions, they set out posthaste for their destination. Inside the equipage, Ariana and Christine clung desperately to each other for solace, fearing the worst, while behind them, mounted on Ariana's white mare, Gossamer, Dukker, too, feared the worst, although his own ideas of impending disaster were exceedingly different from those of the two women.

* * *

Ariana had never been so terrified in her life. One minute, she and Christine had been en route to the Red House tavern in Battersea Fields, and the next, not long after her father's coach had crossed Vauxhall Bridge into the unsavory district of Lambeth and swung on to Nine Elms Lane, they had been set upon by what had at first appeared to be highwaymen.

"Oh, my God, Ariana," Christine now moaned, clutching her sister-in-law's arm tightly, her lovely face draining of color. "This is exactly what happened that night my parents were killed! This is just how it started!"

In moments, their driver shouting and laying his whip to the backs of the horses harnessed to the vehicle, their carriage began to travel at such a high rate of speed that neither Ariana nor Christine could retain their holds on the leather safety straps inside and so were flung violently to the floor of the equipage, unable to see out, ignorant of most of what was happening—except that they knew shots were being exchanged, for they could hear the loud reports of the discharging pistols. As she crouched down between the coach seats, Ariana felt her heart pounding so hard and erratically with terror that she feared it would burst in her breast at any minute, and in some dark crevasse of her mind she thought that this must be an even worse nightmare for Christine, who had lived through all this once before, the night of her parents' deaths. Finally, after what seemed an eternity to the two women, but was in reality only minutes, their vehicle was forced off the road, and its door was ripped open wide. Then, before they even had time to grasp what was happening, to observe their driver and footmen lying bloody and motionless on the ground, the two women, despite their valiant struggles, were snatched from the carriage by their assailants and bundled into a nearby plain black equipage, which then sped down Nine Elms, traveling so rapidly that the few passersby on the relatively isolated stretch of road shrieked and scrambled from the coach's path, certain it was a runaway. Ariana and Christine screamed, too, and fumbled desperately at the handle of the door, hoping to leap from the vehicle. But the door refused to budge.

"It must be bolted from the outside!" Ariana gasped out, horrified.

By then the unknown carriage was moving at such a high rate of speed, she thought that even if she and Christine had managed to get the door open and to jump from the equipage, they would surely have been killed, anyway.

"Then we are lost." Christine groaned, burying her face in her hands and beginning to weep. "Oh, God. What is going to become of us now, Ariana? For we have surely been abducted by the Foscarellis—just like poor Madame Polgár!"

"Unfortunately, I fear that you are right, Christine. Oh, I should have listened to Dukker and heeded his warnings to me! Now he is probably dead because of me! But if he has survived, if the Foscarellis' hirelings did not notice him following us, then there is a chance that we will be rescued. For if he is alive, Dukker will ride like the wind to the Red House tavern, to tell Collie and Nicky what has befallen us. We must hope for that, Christine, and try not to worry."

But this was far easier said than done, especially when it became clear to the two women that they were leaving London and its surrounding suburbs behind, the coach in which they were trapped presently hurtling along what Christine told Ariana was the Great North Road, which ran from London to York and Edinburgh.

"The Foscarellis' henchmen must be taking us to Scotland— to the Highlands and Castle Dúndragon," Christine speculated dully. "Somehow they must indeed have learnt your and Nicky's and Malcolm's true identities, as poor Dukker feared, and be bent on holding us prisoner in exchange for the crucifixes we've managed to collect!"

This soon proved to be a devastatingly accurate assessment of the situation in which the two women found themselves, for eventually, after traveling ceaselessly for some time, the vehicle in which they were incarcerated stopped at a desolate wayside inn, and there the notorious Foscarellis themselves appeared, having journeyed in a separate carriage to the place.

"Good afternoon, my ladies," Lord Ugo greeted them after unlocking the door of their equipage, which had indeed, as Ariana had surmised, been bolted from the outside. His smile and pleasantry were such that the two women might have been experiencing a chance meeting with him on a London street. "I trust that you were not too uncomfortable on the way here. Mademoiselle Ariana, I don't believe you've met my father. Please allow me to present him to you. Count Foscarelli, Mademoiselle Ariana Lévesque—oh, no, my mistake! 'Tis Madame Ariana Ramsay now, is it not? And of course, Papa, I think you already know Lady Christine Fraser, who is now Lady Christine de Ramezay, however."

"Messieurs Foscarelli and Ugo, I demand that you release us at once!" Ariana spoke coldly, with a courage she did not feel, for it was now clear to her that the Foscarellis had not only learnt her and Malcolm's and Nicolas's true identities, but had also been spying on them all for several days—perhaps even weeks.

"But of course we will release you," Lord Ugo said, his teeth flashing whitely in his swarthy visage as he grinned at her in a manner that made her skin crawl. "In exchange for all of the crosses that are the clues to the location of the Heart of Kheperi."

"I don't know what you're talking about," Ariana insisted, trembling.

"And neither do I," Christine declared bravely.

"Then you had better hope that Ramsay and Jourdain do— or else you are both going to have a very long, unpleasant stay at Castle Dúndragon!"

Then, after warning the two women that things would go very ill for them if they made any trouble, they were escorted through a side door into a private room at the isolated tavern, where they were fed and then permitted a few minutes alone in the privy. After that, they were forced into a different coach from the one in which they had arrived, and this time Count Foscarelli and Lord Ugo climbed into the vehicle with them. Their journey continued at a breakneck pace, with seldom a moment's rest, except to change drivers and horses. Ariana could not, in fact, believe how quickly they traveled so far, and two days later, as she stared silently out the windows of the carriage at Castle Dúndragon in the distance, her heart leapt to her throat, and her spirits sank even lower, for she did not know how she and Christine would ever escape from the terrible place.

On the north shore of Loch Ness, from a large rocky promontory that jutted out roughly into the lake and whose black, crumbling cliffs on three sides fell away steeply from the knoll, Castle Dúndragon perched like the titanic fabled sea monster of the loch itself, sunning itself on the crag. Over seven hundred feet deep and surrounded by Highland hills that rose equally as high as the lake was deep, Loch Ness carved a huge divide into the Glen Mor or Great Glen, an enormous, gaping fissure that cut the Highlands in half, and at its very heart, Castle Dúndragon was set. The place where it stood had been occupied by one people or another for millennia, but the fortress itself had been built during the twelve hundreds, of native red sandstone that had over the centuries turned the color of a pale bloodstain and that had the peculiar, unnerving trick, in certain lights, of gleaming as white as old bones. Towered and turreted, battlemented and embrasured, its narrow Gothic windows like eyes behind the slits of a mask, the stronghold had, because of its seeming ability to change hues like a chameleon, gained the reputation of being a haunted place, and it never looked more so than on a hazily mooned night, with the fog floating eerily about its forbidding fortifications.

The journey to Castle Dúndragon had been long and arduous, but ever since learning of the kidnapping of their brides, Malcolm and Mr. Ravener had been frantic with fear. Following the abduction, Dukker, who had fortuitously gone unnoticed by the Foscarellis' hirelings, had ridden posthaste to the Red House tavern in Battersea Fields, there to inform Malcolm and Mr. Ravener about what had taken place. As a result, instructing the dwarf to return to the Lévesques' town house to apprise Monsieur Valcoeur of what had occurred and what steps to take, the two men had set out immediately on horseback after their wives, pausing during their urgent journey only to rest briefly, acquire supplies, change horses and make inquiries about Ariana, Christine and the Foscarellis. From what they had discovered from various innkeepers en route, Malcolm and Mr. Ravener had grown more and more certain that their brides were being transported to Castle Dúndragon, and the two men had realized that because of Dukker's foresight and proximity to the Red House tavern in Battersea Fields at the time of the kidnapping, they themselves could not be more than an hour or so behind their wives and the Foscarellis. They had, in fact, initially hoped to overtake them, but had been slowed down by being compelled to ensure that the Foscarellis had never doubled back and taken another route to a different destination.

Along the way, Malcolm and Mr. Ravener had discussed and discarded various plans for the rescue of their brides, finally hitting upon a scheme that they hoped would work. Having at last arrived in the Highlands, they had made camp at the ruins of Whitrose Grange, from where, with a pair of binoculars they had purchased, they had spied intently on Castle Dúndragon across Loch Ness, discovering by peering through the fortress's narrow windows that their wives had been imprisoned on the top floor of one of the stronghold's towers. Now, as night crept slowly toward dawn, they slipped from the ruins of Whitrose Grange, down to the shingled beach bounding Loch Ness. There they had earlier concealed a small fishing boat that Malcolm had borrowed in the nearby village, from one of his father's old farmhands. Rowing across Loch Ness, they beached the boat, then with difficulty climbed the promontory—slick with mist and mizzle—upon which Castle Dúndragon perched like a bloodthirsty vulture clinging to a carcass.

The small, seldom-used postern gate of the castle was chained, padlocked and rusted shut. But Malcolm and Mr. Ravener had come prepared with tools for that, and after a time, the heavy iron chain and padlock dropped away from the gate. A liberal amount of oil was applied to the latter's rusty hinges, but even so, it creaked and groaned ominously in the silence as the two men inexorably forced it open, letting themselves into the fortress, their hearts pounding. Using the long shadows and fog for cover, they moved stealthily across the stronghold's bailey, taking care to avoid being seen by the henchmen the Foscarellis had set to watch the walls. Fortunately, the night was cold, so that the hirelings walked briskly along the parapets, swinging and slapping their arms in an attempt to keep warm, and grousing audibly to one another about the miserable duty they had been assigned. So it was clear that they resented the Foscarellis and were not highly vigilant at their posts, and might, in fact, even desert them, given enough provocation.

Although Malcolm and Mr. Ravener knew in which tower their wives were being held captive, they did not know how to reach it from the ground. So once they had actually managed to enter the castle itself, it was necessary for them to slip covertly through its long dark corridors, searching each of its rooms for access to the proper tower. As they did so, they were much surprised to discover that almost all of the chambers they explored appeared to be long shut up and unused, layered with dust and draped with cobwebs. It seemed that either the Foscarellis were skinflints or else they had dissipated much of the wealth that had once been generated by the estate. Either way, it appeared obvious that they had closed off more than half the fortress in order to conserve funds. Much to Malcolm and Mr. Ravener's relief, there were also few servants to be seen, so that they were able to conduct their investigation relatively free from worry that they would be discovered and an alarm raised.

"Shhh." Mr. Ravener suddenly paused, pressing one hand against Malcolm's chest to hold him still. "What is that noise?" he asked in a whisper, his head cocked, listening intently.

"Snoring!" Malcolm shot back quietly, after a moment in which he analyzed and correctly identified the sound. "There's someone asleep in the room beyond!"

"Then it must be either Count Foscarelli or Lord Ugo, for the chambers in this wing would appear to be the original family apartments and no doubt are still used for that purpose."

"I think you're right. What do you want to do, Nicolas? Keep moving?"

"If we can surprise one of the bastards and get him to talk, we will find our brides that much quicker, Malcolm—and gain a most useful hostage in the process," Mr. Ravener reasoned grimly.

"Aye, let us enter the room, then."

Furtively the two men eased open the door, which proved to be unlocked, and sneaked into the bedchamber. By the dim, hazy moonlight that filtered in through the windows, and the glow of the fire that crackled in the huge stone hearth, they could see that at the heart of the room rose a large canopy bed, whose curtains were drawn shut against the chill of the wintry night. Creeping forward, Malcolm on one side of the bed and Mr. Ravener on the other, the two men softly slid open the bed hangings to reveal Viscount Ugo and—unexpectedly—a dark-haired woman tangled in his embrace, both of them naked and reeking of wine. For a moment, Malcolm's heart leapt to his throat and his stomach heaved, for in the indistinct light he had initially thought the woman was Ariana, and his worst fears had been realized. But then, finally, much to his vast relief, he recognized that he did not know Lord Ugo's companion. But still, the thought that it *could* so very easily have been Ariana lying in her abductor's arms, forced into sharing his bed, enraged Malcolm, and his eyes were hard and narrowed as he clapped one hand over Lord Ugo's mouth and jammed the muzzle of his pistol to the viscount's head, while simultaneously Mr. Ravener dragged the naked woman from beneath the bedclothes, his own hand smothering her lips to keep her silent, and ordered her tersely to get dressed.

"Then sit over there in that corner, and don't stir from it or attempt to call for help," Mr. Ravener warned the woman, "or you'll be sorry."

Clearly, she was only a frightened serving maid of some sort, because she made no protest against him, but did exactly what he had told her, her eyes scared and her face pale. Lord Ugo himself, however, was a different matter entirely, and neither Malcolm nor Mr. Ravener deceived himself into believing that the viscount would quietly obey orders and make no attempt to escape, given the chance. Keeping their pistols trained on him, the two men instructed him to get his garments on.

"Then you will lead us to the tower in which you have imprisoned our brides," Malcolm insisted grimly, "after which you will accompany us to the nearest police station, there to make a full report of your crimes."

"You know, somehow I don't think so," Lord Ugo said.

Then, taking the two men by surprise, despite how they had prepared themselves for him to strike out against them, the viscount suddenly snatched one of a pair of rapiers down from the wall and attacked Mr. Ravener, who was nearest to him. At that, the serving woman grabbed up her skirts and fled, and Malcolm, terrified that she would sound an alarm and rouse the entire castle, was torn between trying to aid his friend and chasing after the wench.

"For God's sake, get the woman, Malcolm!" Mr. Ravener cried as, with relish, he jerked down the other blade and vehemently engaged his foe.

Knowing that Mr. Ravener was far more experienced with a rapier than he and that time was precious, Malcolm ran from the room. But he was too late. The serving maid was racing along the hall beyond, screaming a warning, and now Malcolm could see Count Foscarelli himself, who, having been wakened by all the noise, was scuttling like a spider from his room. He had obviously hastily dressed and had armed himself with a pistol, with which, spying Malcolm, he fired off a quick, wild shot. Flattening himself against the corridor wall, Malcolm returned fire, and after shooting off another round, the count disappeared down a flight of stone steps. His heart pounding with fear at the thought that at any moment the Foscarellis' henchmen would burst upon the scene, and he and Mr. Ravener would be grossly outnumbered, Malcolm chased after Count Foscarelli, arriving at the top of the stairs in time to witness him vanishing through an interior doorway. Deeply afraid that the count was intent on summoning assistance, Malcolm hurried after him.

"Christine! Christine, wake up!" Ariana shook her sister-in-law insistently once more. "There's something happening at the castle!"

"What? What's…going on?" Christine asked as, rubbing her eyes, she at last sat up wearily and disoriented in the bed they had shared fitfully all evening in the tower in which they had been held captive ever since their arrival at the fortress.

"I—I don't know." Ariana's face was ashen with fear and cold, and she shivered violently, despite the woolen blanket she had wrapped around her for warmth. "But I've heard what—what sounded like shots from somewhere below! I think—I hope!—that perhaps Collie and Nicky have come to rescue us!"

"Oh, Ariana, how I devoutly pray that is so—and not just wishful thinking on your own part! Because I tell you, Nicky is right, and the Foscarellis are unquestionably insane! For only men who have run mad would have kidnapped us in the first place—to say nothing of locking us up in this desolate tower, without even a fire for warmth!" Christine's teeth chattered uncontrollably as she huddled beneath her own blanket.

"Shhh. Listen!" Ariana cocked her head a trifle, straining to hear through the thick stone walls of the stronghold. "There's that noise again! Oh, I'm sure 'tis gunshots! For it sounds like the firing I heard in the streets of Paris when the revolutionaries and the radicals incited the people against *le pauvre* King Louis-Philippe!" Rising from where she sat upon the bed, Ariana ran to the tower window and, opening the shutters, peered out into the bailey far below in a futile attempt to try to determine what was happening at the castle. But the Foscarellis' hirelings posted on the parapets either had not discerned the gunshots or else were ignoring them, for they continued to walk the walls, rather than hurrying inside the fortress.

"What's that smell?" Christine sniffed the air tentatively. "Smoke! There's smoke filtering up here!"

"From the fires burning in the Foscarellis' hearths, no doubt!" Ariana said angrily. "Whilst they leave us up here to freeze to death!"

"No…no, I don't think so." Standing, Christine ran to the door of the tower room and knelt upon the floor to press her face to the gap between it and the portal. "Oh, God, Ariana, there's smoke coming up the stairs! The castle must be on fire somewhere below!"

Even as Christine relayed this horrifying information, Ariana observed the henchmen on the parapets begin to leave their posts, running toward the various towers that studded the stronghold's walls.

"You must be right! The Foscarellis' hirelings are deserting their posts!"

"There's someone coming!"

Abruptly scrambling from the floor, Christine moved away from the door, she and Ariana now clutching each other tightly as they heard the key grating in the stout lock. Then the portal swung open wide to reveal a tall dark man standing without in the shadows, and for one hideous instant the two women believed that it was Lord Ugo, come to kill them. But then the man stepped into the tower, and by the candlelight within they saw that it was Nicolas.

"Nicky!" they cried as one, with overwhelming relief, running to his side.

"Come. There is no time to lose," he told them. "The castle is ablaze, and we must get out of here at once!"

"Where's Collie?" Ariana asked him, worried sick about her husband.

"I don't know." Mr. Ravener shook his head grimly. "We became separated. I only know that Lord Ugo is dead—I killed him myself—and that the fortress is on fire. We must make good our escape before the flames spread and we are burnt alive!"

"But we can't leave without Malcolm! He could be lying hurt or even dead somewhere! I won't go without him! I won't! I must find him!"

"Ariana! Ariana, come back!" Nicolas shouted after his sister as, suddenly bolting from the tower chamber, she raced down the stone steps that led to the floors below.

But she paid him no heed, sprinting through the corridors, desperately calling Malcolm's name. As she probed deeper into the stronghold, the smoke grew thicker, blacker and more acrid, blinding and suffocating her, and the tongues of flame leapt high, so that she was afraid that the heat alone would drive her back. Flying embers from the crackling wooden beams that had already caught fire stung her skin and charred holes in her gown and the blanket she had unwittingly taken from the tower room as, coughing and choking, she struggled on, despairing of locating her husband, uncertain whether he remained in the castle or had even now made good his escape. The fortress was so large that she would never find him, she thought, frantic. But then, above the roar of the spreading fire, the reverberation of shots reached her ears again, and turning in that direction, she picked up her skirts and raced toward the sound, shouting Malcolm's name. Here the blaze was hottest of all, so it seemed that it must be the source of the growing conflagration, and clouds of virtually impenetrable smoke billowed down the passages she traversed.

"Collie! Collie!" The blanket raised to shield her from the flames, Ariana pressed forward, peering through the smoke.

To her utter horror, as she stared into the castle's fiery study, she spied her husband and Count Foscarelli locked in mortal combat, struggling desperately for control of a single pistol. All around them the chamber itself was an inferno, its draperies and furniture aflame, its wooden beams burning furiously, snapping and breaking, plunging from the ceiling, along with great chunks of plaster. Ariana did not know how the two men could still be alive, and she knew that if they did not escape, and swiftly, their lives would be forfeit. Even as she watched, petrified, her heart in her throat, the pistol over which the two men battled discharged again, and of a sudden, as though in slow motion, Count Foscarelli staggered back, crimson blossoming on his fine white linen shirt. At the same time he stumbled back, clutching his chest, a huge beam directly above him abruptly gave way. At the sound of the explosive cracking of the beam, Count Foscarelli glanced up, crying out with fearful comprehension, but there was nothing he could do as the heavy beam plummeted downward, crushing him to death.

"Collie!" Ariana screamed.

Hearing her calling his name, her husband turned toward her. Then, pausing only to grab up a silver strongbox that sat upon the desk, he ran to her side.

"Nicolas and Christine?" he asked.

"Already safe, I hope."

"Here." Malcolm thrust the strongbox into her hands. "Hold tight to that." Then, gathering her into his arms, he lifted her up and began to fight his way down the corridors through the flames and swirling smoke.

Presently he and she were safely outside, where, much to their mutual relief, they saw that not only had Nicolas and Christine made good their escape, but also that Monsieur Valcoeur had arrived with Dukker and the authorities. The latter had gained access to the castle by climbing over the crumbling curtain wall that fronted the only side of the fortress that was not bounded by Loch Ness, but faced the sprawling meadowland and woods that lay to the west. Already the authorities had taken several of the Foscarellis' hirelings into custody and were now rounding up the rest, while the firemen who had been summoned from the nearby village did their best to extinguish the blaze, although it appeared that they were fighting a losing battle.

"Count Foscarelli?" Nicolas inquired, with great relief, at seeing Malcolm stagger from the stronghold, carrying Ariana.

"Dead. And Lord Ugo?"

"The same."

"That's it, then," Nicolas said soberly. "That's the end of the Foscarellis—and of the threat they have long posed to us and ours. Thank God they are no more! Now all that remains is to try and locate the Heart of Kheperi, if we can."

* * *

Despite everything, it seemed that the missing emerald would never be found. Having followed Count Foscarelli to the castle study and interrupted him in the act of attempting to abscond with the silver strongbox, Malcolm had saved it from the flames, believing that it contained the crucifixes that the Foscarellis had located over the years. In the early-morning hours after the Foscarellis had been killed, and Ariana and Christine had been rescued, he and Nicolas broke in to the strongbox and discovered that it did indeed harbor three crosses, numbered three, four and nine, and reading the inscription on the back of the ninth, Malcolm suddenly understood the key to the puzzle.

"Good God." He swore softly. "No wonder the emerald has never been located!"

"Why? What do you mean?" Nicolas queried equally quietly, so as not to waken their wives, who slept in the next room of the apartments they had taken at an inn in the local village.

"Crucifix number nine...on the back 'tis engraved 'Here be dragons.' That's not a biblical chapter and verse, Nicolas! 'Tis a motto employed by cartographers! On ancient maps, when they did not know what lay beyond lands and seas already explored, cartographers wrote 'Here be dragons.' So now I think...I think that the biblical chapters and verses on the backs of the other crosses are virtually meaningless—employed to deceive those who would try to find the emerald, but were not a brother of the Sons of Isis. Nahum, Exodus, Second Chronicles, Wisdom and so forth...don't you see? All of the biblical books from which the various quotations come start with either *N, E, S,* or *W—compass points!* And the numbers of the chapters and verses are, I believe, the paces to be counted out in each direction! Further, I think the crucifixes are to be followed backward—for cross number one which, like cross number nine, doesn't fit the pattern of the rest, says, 'I am the first and the last....' Remember? And 'Here be dragons' *must* be a reference to Castle Dúndragon itself, the starting point! But without crucifix number six, which is now the only one we lack, we can still never locate the Heart of Kheperi, for we'll be missing that cross's direction and requisite number of paces."

"We'll get it, Malcolm," Nicolas insisted, "just as we had planned to before Christine and Ariana were abducted."

"*Oui,* Malcolm," Monsieur Valcoeur chimed in stoutly as he puffed on a cigar. "Once the authorities have completed their investigation and inquest in connection with the Foscarellis and the events that occurred at Castle Dúndragon—about none of which I expect any difficulties, by the way, since the filthy *bâtards did* abduct my daughter and Lady Christine—then we will be able to return to London and get this Colonel Pemberton's crucifix, whatever it takes!"

"Indeed! I shall knock *le colonel* in the head and steal his cross myself, if necessary!" Dukker declared boldly.

But then, strangely, Fate again thrust her hand into the affair, and within the week, Madame Valcoeur, Mrs. Blackfriars and Messieurs Quimby, Rosenkranz and Cavendish quite unexpectedly arrived at the inn, bringing with them not only the five crucifixes that had been secreted in Monsieur Valcoeur's desk, but also the last cross, which had belonged to Colonel Pemberton.

"But…however did you acquire crucifix number six?" Malcolm asked, amazed, as in the apartments he and Nicolas had taken at the inn, he laid all the crosses out in order upon a table, still unable to believe that all nine had at long last been collected.

"Oh, that." Much to his surprise, his mother blushed like a schoolgirl. "Well, after you, Nicolas and Jean-Paul had set out after the Foscarellis, I went myself to Quimby and Company, to inform Mr. Quimby about what had happened and that I did not know when you would be able to return to work. During our conversation, he inadvertently let slip me to that Mr. Cavendish had traced one of the crucifixes to a Colonel Pemberton and that you and Nicolas had been planning to…acquire it that weekend, but that now, naturally, that would have to be put off. Of course, you may imagine my astonishment at hearing all that, Son, and I said to Mr. Quimby, 'Why, do you mean Colonel Hilliard Pemberton?' and upon learning that this was indeed the case, I told him that during my youth, Pemby—as his friends always called him—had been one of my most ardent beaux! So, being quite out of my mind with worry about you, Ariana, Nicolas and Christine, I took it upon myself to call on Pemby and tell him the entire story and beg his assistance! And, oh, Malcolm, he was as honorable and gentlemanly as I remembered, and after that, he would hear nothing except that I must accept his cross as a gift, for old times' sake, that the emerald did not belong to him, and that if he could help put right a great wrong that had been done to me and mine, then that was all the reward he needed—except that he would consider it an honor and a privilege if I would have dinner with him one evening, and let him know the outcome of our adventure!" Mrs. Blackfriars ended, flushing even more furiously as she related this last.

"I hope that you do, Mother," Malcolm insisted gently. "For much as we may wish otherwise, Father has been dead these many long years past now, and I know he would not have wanted you to grieve forever. Now, shall we discover whether I'm right and this…ninefold key is, in reality, a map to the hiding place of the Heart of Kheperi?"

This scheme being at once agreed to, and armed with shovels and other tools to assist them, the entire party then set out to follow the map formed by the ninefold key that would unlock the mystery of the Heart of Kheperi's location. After much searching, they found the spot at last and began to dig. Eventually, still incredulous and hardly daring to hope, they uncovered a small stone crypt, which they lifted gingerly from the hole they had dug in the ground. Removing the heavy lid from the crypt, they found yet another box inside—an iron strongbox padlocked and rusted by time. With hammers, Malcolm and Nicolas broke the padlock from the strongbox, then they forced open the lid to reveal a leather pouch inside, no longer supple, but hardened with age. With some difficulty Malcolm opened the bag, then turned it upside down to shake forth its contents.

And then the Heart of Kheperi lay in his grasp, the huge,

priceless emerald sparkling and glowing strangely in the pale wintry light, Power seeming to radiate from its very core.

"My God," he murmured. "Even now I can hardly believe that it really exists, much less that we actually succeeded in finding it, that I'm actually holding it in my hands!"

"But not for long! I'll take that, Mapper!"

As everyone glanced up, shocked, at the unexpected sound of the voice, Tobias Snitch strode triumphantly into the forest glade where they were gathered around the stone crypt that they had unearthed, a pistol held purposefully in one hand.

"You thought you kilt me, didn't you, Mapper? Lucky fer me that there was a lighter plyin' t' River Thames that night you shoved me in, or else I'd o' surely drowned. But t' lightermen spied me an' hauled me onto their vessel, an' I been watchin' you an' followin' you ever since! Now, gimme that emerald! There's no use in you tryin' to hide it, 'coz I know all about it from some o' t' Italians' henchmen who been spyin' on you. I wondered why they was takin' such an interest in you an' your friends, so I cotched one o' 'em an' learnt all about t' legend o' t' lost stone an' how t' Italians hoped to find it. Now, hand it over—an' then I'm goin' to shoot you, Mapper, fer how you kilt poor Badger that night." Raising his pistol threateningly, he pointed it straight at Malcolm's head.

But before Malcolm and the rest could act or even speak, a shot rang out, and Toby crumpled slowly to the ground, dead. Then, from the long cold shadows cast by the towering evergreen trees, Mr. al-Walid appeared, a smoking gun in one hand and his manservant, Hosni, along with another man, a stranger, hard on his heels.

"I could not permit that thief—that *interloper!*—to murder you, Monsieur Ramsay, and steal the Heart of Kheperi," Mr. al-Walid stated calmly to Malcolm. "For it rightfully belongs to the Egyptian government, whose representative I am—and, as I feel quite sure you must, in fact, have suspected, not a herpetologist at all, you see. Like Monsieur Snitch there—oh, *oui,* I know who he was, as I know many other things about you, as well, Monsieur Ramsay, including your and your mother's and cousins' true identities—I have long spied upon you and yours, although, unlike the Foscarellis and Monsieur Snitch, my own reasons for having done so were rather more benign. So I hope that you will acquit me of any evil motives. Now, please permit me to present to you Colonel Hilliard Pemberton." He introduced the stranger who accompanied him. "We became aware of him after Hosni had followed Madame Blackfriars to his town house and, through its windows, observed him bestowing his crucifix upon her. However, not content with this unselfish act alone, Colonel Pemberton, it seems—having been apprised by Madame Blackfriars that she intended to travel posthaste to Castle Dúndragon—decided to follow her here, in order to ensure her safety and well-being. As, by this time, Hosni and I, having discovered that Mesdames Ramsay and Jourdain had been kidnapped by the Foscarellis, had resolved to set out at once for Castle Dúndragon, too, we journeyed on the same public coach as Colonel Pemberton and resolved to pool our resources and efforts on your behalf."

"I see," Malcolm said at last, a muscle twitching in his jaw and still clutching the emerald, which, eerily, seemed almost alive, throbbing in his hands. "'Tis a great pleasure to meet you, sir." He addressed the Colonel. "I only wish it had been under wholly different circumstances."

"Yes, so I do. However, I'm glad if I have been of any assistance to you and your dear mother."

"You have indeed, sir. Thank you."

"I knew that if I but watched and waited, you would eventually find the emerald, Monsieur Ramsay," Mr. al-Walid declared. "For you alone of all those who ever searched for it over the years were motivated by love, I think, and not greed. Egypt would like the emerald returned to her. However, unlike either the Foscarellis or Monsieur Snitch, we are prepared to strike a bargain with you for it. You see, Monsieur Ramsay, many decades ago one of our agents intercepted a letter written by Lord Iain Ramsay, that Earl of Dúndragon who wagered away all your family's estates to Lord Bruno, Count Foscarelli. The missive was intended for Lord Dúndragon's younger brother, Lord Neill, Viscount Strathmór. In the letter, Lord Dúndragon explained that he had not been free to gamble away his family's property. His father, Lord Somerled Ramsay, the old Earl of Dúndragon, knowing his eldest son's profligate nature, had before his death composed a new last will and testament, which he had signed and had duly witnessed by two servants whilst on his deathbed. In this last will and testament, the Ramsay estates were bound by a strict settlement, so that they must pass intact from each heir to the next and could not be sold or otherwise disposed of. Because it would have been the ruin of him, preventing him from selling any of the family lands to pay his gambling debts, Lord Dúndragon had, after his father's death, wrongly suppressed this new last will and testament. Fortunately, however, for his younger brother's sake he had not destroyed the document but buried it. Unfortunately, however, he did not have time to finish his missive to his brother, but broke off abruptly after writing that he had buried it with— what? Where? For a long time we did not know. But then finally we realized that he must have meant he had buried the new last will and testament with his father, in his father's tomb. And there, yes, we did find the document." Reaching into one pocket of his long, flowing robes, Mr. al-Walid now produced Lord Dúndragon's father's long-concealed last will and testament. "Here 'tis. 'Tis yours for the emerald. A fair trade, is it not, Monsieur Ramsay?"

But Malcolm, utterly stunned by this news, was rendered speechless, and so did not answer.

Epilogue

The Inheritors

How seldom, friend! a good great man inherits
Honor or wealth, with all his worth and pains!
It sounds like stories from the land of spirits
If any man obtain that which he merits,
Or any merit that which he obtains.

—Samuel Taylor Coleridge
The Good Great Man [1802]

We owe it to our ancestors to preserve
entire those rights, which they have delivered
to our care: we owe it to our posterity, not to
suffer their dearest inheritance to be destroyed.

—Anonymous
The Letters of Junius [1769], No. 20

He that troubleth his own house shall inherit
the wind.

—*The Holy Bible*
The Proverbs

Heart and Soul

Yes, as my swift days near their goal,
'Tis all that I implore:
In life and death a chainless soul,
With courage to endure.

—Emily Brontë
The Old Stoic [1846]

Darest thou now O soul,
Walk out with me toward the unknown region
Where neither ground is for the feet nor any
path to follow?

—Walt Whitman
Leaves of Grass [1855-1892], Darest Thou Now O Soul

How good is man's life, the mere living! how
fit to employ
All the heart and the soul and the senses forever
in joy!

—Robert Browning
Saul [1855]

Lord Malcolm Ramsay, the rightful Earl of Dúndragon—as had been incontrovertibly proved by the last will and testament laid before the courts by his mother's solicitor, Mr. Nigel Gilchrist—stood quietly, embracing his wife, Lady Ariana, in the new town house they had purchased in Portman Square, right down the block from that of Monsieur and Madame Valcoeur, and right next door to that of le Comte and la Comtesse de Jourdain. After much persuading, Elizabeth Ramsay, the Dowager Countess of Dúndragon, had finally consented to let Hawthorn Cottage in St. John's Wood, and to take up residence with her son and his bride—although they thought that she would perhaps not be with them long, if Colonel Pemberton, who had begun seriously courting her, had his way. Mr. Rosenkranz's jewelry designs—shown to great advantage at all the fashionable parties, routs and balls by no less than the four countesses themselves—had recently become all the rage, so that he could scarcely keep up with all the orders placed by his newfound clientele; and for like reasons, Mr. Cavendish's bookshop was now *the* establishment in which to acquire literature for discussion at all the best conversation parties. Mr. Quimby's map shop continued to flourish, as well, although Malcolm was no longer employed there. He suspected that Harry Devenish, who would no doubt take over running the premises upon his employer's retirement, was slightly relieved about that. Mr. al-Walid and Hosni had returned to Egypt, bearing the invaluable emerald—and its age-old curse, Malcolm knew—away with them. Like Whitrose Grange, Castle Dúndragon stood in blackened ruins, although Malcolm thought that perhaps, someday, when the place no longer haunted him and Ariana, he would rebuild his family's imposing ancestral home on the shores of Loch Ness.

"You know, Ana, my dearest love—" Malcolm spoke now to his bride, drawing her even nearer "—as strange as it may seem to you, my only regret after everything that's happened is that I never permitted Madame Polgár to read my fortune. I wonder what she would have told me, what destiny she would have fore-seen in the cards for me had she ever looked into my future."

"I know, Collie, *mon coeur,* what fortune she would have predicted for you." Ariana gazed up happily at her greatly beloved husband. "'Twould have been exactly what she told me—that I would embark upon a dangerous quest for the Heart of Kheperi—but that what I would find would be my own true heart's desire."

"Aye, *that* I *did* find, in truth.", Malcolm kissed her deeply, passionately. Then after a long moment he said, "The ancient Egyptians were very learnt and wise. Now, holding you, Ana, I think that perhaps they were not wrong, after all, to believe that *'tis* the heart wherein one's soul abides."